A Mother Forever

Elaine Everest was born and brought up in north-west Kent, where her books are set, and has written widely for women's magazines – both short stories and features – as well as fiction and non-fiction books for the past twenty-four years. Successful in writing competitions, she was shortlisted for the Harry Bowling Prize and was BBC Radio Kent's short-story writer of the year in 2003.

A qualified tutor, she runs The Write Place creative writing school in Hextable, Kent. Elaine lives with her husband, Michael, and their Polish Lowland Sheepdog, Henry, in Swanley, Kent.

You can say hello to Elaine on
Twitter: @ElaineEverest
Facebook: Elaine Everest Author
Instagram: @elaine.everest
Website and blog: www.elaineeverest.com

Praise for Elaine Everest

'A warm tale of friendship and romance'
My Weekly

'Captures the spirit of wartime'
Woman's Weekly

'One of the most iconic stores comes back to life
in this heartwarming tale'
Woman's Own

'Elaine brings the heyday of the iconic high-street
giant to life in her charming novel'
S Magazine

Also by Elaine Everest

The Woolworths Girls
Carols at Woolworths (ebook novella)
Christmas at Woolworths
Wartime at Woolworths
A Gift from Woolworths
Wedding Bells for Woolworths

The Butlins Girls

The Teashop Girls
Christmas with the Teashop Girls

Elaine Everest

A Mother Forever

PAN BOOKS

ISBN 978-1-5290-1596-6

Copyright © Elaine Everest 2021

The right of Elaine Everest to be identified as the
author of this work has been asserted by her in accordance
with the Copyright, Designs and Patents Act 1988.

1 3 5 7 9 8 6 4 2

A CIP catalogue record for this book is available from the British Library.

Typeset by Palimpsest Book Production Ltd, Falkirk, Stirlingshire
Printed and bound by CPI Group (UK) Ltd, Croydon, CR0 4YY

FSC
www.fsc.org

MIX
Paper from
responsible sources
FSC® C116313

Visit **www.panmacmillan.com** to read more about all our books
and to buy them. You will also find features, author interviews and
news of any author events, and you can sign up for e-newsletters
so that you're always first to hear about our new releases.

Dedicated to the memory of the twelve women
and their foreman who died in the explosion at
the W. V. Gilbert munition works, on the banks
of the Thames between Erith and Slades
Green, on 18th February 1924.

Edna Allen, aged seventeen, of Alexandra Road.
Alice Craddock, aged eighteen, of Arthur Street.
Elizabeth Dalton, aged twenty-four, of Lewis Road, Welling.
Alice Harvey, aged forty, of Arthur Street.
Gladys Herbert, aged twenty-three, of Bexley Road.
Stella Huntley, aged twenty, of Corinthian Road.
Edith Lamb, aged twenty-three, of Upper Road, Belvedere.
Ethel Pullen, aged eighteen, of Bexley Road.
Polly Smith, aged eighteen, of Powell Street.
Doris Sturtevant, aged eighteen, of Manor Road.
Alice Sweeney, aged seventeen, of St Francis Road.
Irene Turtle, aged twenty-two, of Maxim Road.
Mr T. Jones, from East Dulwich.

1

Erith, Kent
August 1905

'You've got ideas above your station, my girl. If your father was alive now, he'd want nothing to do with you. The Tomkins family have always known their place in life; he wouldn't want us rubbing shoulders with those who think they're better than us,' Milly Tomkins said to her daughter.

Ruby Caselton gave a big sigh and continued to pull a heavy rug from the back of the drayman's cart, while he held the horse's head steady. 'It's just a street of houses with hard-working people living in them. Could you take the other end of this please, Mum?'

'What, with my bad ticker? You'll see me into my grave, young lady. But then, perhaps that's what you want – then there'll be no one left to remind you of where you come from,' Milly sniffed, folding her arms over her ample chest and turning away to look at the house the family were about to move into. 'Those windows need a clean and the doorstep a good scrub.'

'I can help you, Mum,' George said, reaching up to help Ruby pull at the rug. It came tumbling off the cart, almost flattening him as he staggered back under its weight.

Ruby couldn't help but laugh as she watched her five-year-old son disappearing under the rug. 'Lord love you, George. Thank you for helping all the same. Why don't you carry that basket of groceries into the kitchen? Then I can get some food on the table as soon as we have this load inside. Your dad may be home by then, and he'll be shouting for his dinner.' She didn't add that he never turned up until her work was done and he had no need to roll up his sleeves and help her.

'He's running true to form, I see,' Milly snorted as she pulled her knitted shawl tighter around her shoulders. 'That Eddie Caselton has a gift for sniffing out hard work and disappearing in the opposite direction. Now, your dad . . .'

Ruby knew her mum was about to lead off about her dad being an angel amongst all men, and she just didn't have the time or the inclination to listen. The drizzling rain had started again, and there was a definite nip in the air coming off the nearby River Thames. Added to that, the child she was carrying in her swollen belly would be entering the world within weeks. 'Mum, leave it to another time, will you? I never knew Dad, and I have other things on my mind at the moment. I could kill a cuppa, so why don't you go in and see to the kitchen, eh? You'll find a meat and potato pie in that basket our George carried in. We can eat once this load is off the cart.' She knew her mum was partial to a pie and noticed her eyes light up at once.

'I'll get cracking,' Milly replied, licking her lips as she headed up the short path to the front door, her hands empty. 'It's no place for me out in this rain – not at my time of life, anyroad.'

'You've got yer hands full there, love,' a friendly voice called out from over the road.

Ruby looked up from where she was examining the rug lying in a heap in the dust. She wasn't sure if the woman watching from her gate was referring to her mum, or the furniture waiting to be unloaded and taken into the house. She stood up straight, wincing as a pain shot across the lower part of her back. As much as she'd been warned to take things easy, she'd gone against advice and insisted she could move the family into their new home without paying for hired help. It was their first proper home, as up to now they'd lived in rooms in a house shared with three other families near the river in Woolwich. There wasn't a lot of money spare to pay for such things as moving men.

Smiling at the ruddy-faced neighbour, she replied, 'You could say that,' and then grimaced as another pain consumed her. She reached out to hang on to the side of the cart to help her stay upright.

'My Lord, you shouldn't be up on your feet in your condition. When are you due?' the woman asked as she hurried to Ruby's side and supported her. 'You're coming with me,' she added, not waiting for an answer as she guided Ruby towards her own open front door.

'Not for another month – but my furniture . . .' Ruby gasped, unable to say much more.

'Don't worry your head about that. It looks to me as though there's a baby wanting to be born. Sometimes they just can't wait,' her new neighbour advised. She paused to take in Ruby, who was so thin that she looked no more than a child herself. Her face was far too pale, and her blue eyes were circled in black shadows. She didn't look well enough to deliver a healthy baby. 'My oldest two are home from work for their dinner soon and they'll have that lot shifted,' she continued, in a voice Ruby knew she wasn't meant to argue with. At that moment she didn't even have the power to speak as yet another pain, like she'd never known when having her George, swept over her. She leant against the woman for support.

After being almost dragged up a steep flight of stairs, Ruby was gently helped onto a large brass bed. 'I'm just going to put some newspaper and old sheets down and then we can make you comfortable. Will you be all right on your own, just for a couple of minutes?'

Still unable to speak, Ruby nodded as she took deep breaths until her body stopped complaining.

'By the way, I'm Stella,' the woman said. 'Stella Green. And although I say it myself, you're in good hands now – so don't you worry, hear me?'

She stepped out into the hallway – which was no more than a small space at the top of the stairs, with another door opposite the bedroom they were in – and bellowed: 'Donald, get your nose out of that book and down to Mrs Leighton's. Tell her there's a baby wanting to be born. After that, get down to the corner and look out for your brothers. Tell them I want 'em home now, and they aren't to dawdle. Do you hear me?'

'Yes, Mum,' a young voice shouted back, followed by the front door slamming shut.

Stella bustled back into the room, her arms full of linen.

'Now, I'm going to have you stand up for a minute while I put these sheets over the mattress. Do you think you can start removing your clothes? I have a nightgown for you to wear.' She shook out a white, high-necked voluminous gown and laid it over a nearby chest of drawers. 'Once we've settled you, I'll get the fire lit.' She nodded towards a blackleaded iron grate.

'I can't thank you enough,' Ruby whispered as she unbuttoned her shabby brown coat. She wished she wasn't wearing her oldest clothes underneath, although her best clothes were not much better.

'That's it, lovey, get every stitch off. We women don't have any secrets from each other,' Stella smiled, trying not to looked shocked at the threadbare undergarments Ruby passed to her. 'Now, let's get you settled, and I'll make us a nice cup of tea. There's no knowing how long this'll take, although I'd lay money on the child being with us today rather than tomorrow. I'll just pop down to the kitchen and put the kettle on the hob, then I'll be back. Will you be all right?'

Ruby nodded her head. 'I can't thank you enough. I was fine not half an hour ago and now . . .'

'And now you're about to be a mother.'

'I am already,' Ruby winced. 'George is over the road with my mum. He's five,' she added with a sharp intake of breath. 'Can you let them know where I am, please?'

'I'll take care of everything. You just rest,' Stella said, hurrying from the room.

Ruby closed her eyes, trying to take stock of her situation between waves of excruciating pain and a heat shooting through her body that made her feel faint.

*

5

When Eddie had come home the week before and thrown a set of keys onto the kitchen table, she hadn't known what to think. 'What are these for?'

'You wanted your own home, didn't you?'

'It has been my dream ever since we married,' she'd answered, unsure of what he was getting at. She knew not to antagonize her husband when he'd had a drink, and by the smell on his breath, he'd visited the pub on his way home. He'd changed so much in recent times.

'I've been doing a bit of debt collecting for Cedric Mulligan and someone who owed him money settled his debt with the deeds to his house, along with the contents. The only problem is, it's down in Erith. What's for dinner?' he asked, as Ruby started to feel giddy with delight. Eddie didn't seem to understand that her dream was to get away from the slum area where they lived and to bring their son up in a better neighbourhood. With their baby due in September, she wanted nothing more than to have a lovely home with a bit of a garden and nice neighbours. Here in the part of Woolwich where they lived, she was frightened to step outside their door, and on more than one occasion she'd come home to find it open and someone ransacking their rooms. Her mother, Milly – who lived with them, much to Eddie's consternation – had taken to barricading herself in her room each evening in case of unwanted visitors. They lived close to the Thames, where at low tide the stench from the river reached every nook and cranny of the place they called home.

'Where in Erith is it?' she asked as she pulled a mutton pie from the oven and put it in front of him. 'I've eaten,' she added, in case he asked why she wasn't sitting down to join him. He never did ask. Of late she'd gone off her food, and anyway, there was little to put on the table from the meagre money Eddie gave her to keep the family. Before they'd moved to these rooms, she'd taken in washing and cleaned at a local pub; but when Eddie got behind with the rent on their last place and they had to do a moonlight flit, she'd given up doing the laundry work. There wasn't any space for such things in their new rooms.

'Alexandra Road. Not far from the river and the town. The houses have only been built a short while.'

A new home, she thought to herself. Was her dream coming true already? But there was usually a catch with anything Eddie was involved with. 'So why is the person giving up his home?' she asked. She knew that if she had a proper house, rather than renting a few rooms in a building, she'd hang on to it until her dying breath. A house of her own, and one that was so new, was beyond her wildest dreams. Once she'd moved in there'd be no getting her out of there, that was for sure.

'He had no choice,' Eddie said as he put down his knife and fork, not speaking until he'd swallowed what was in his mouth. For all his shortcomings, Ruby did admire his manners when eating his food. The decent side of Eddie was still there and surfaced sometimes. 'The bloke is a builder, and he owned six houses in the road. This one was handed over to settle his gambling debts. Cedric wants to hang on to it and knowing we've got a second nipper on the way, he asked if I'd be interested. Mind you, you'll have to clean yourself up a bit when we live down there. It's not quite as posh as the Avenue where the nobs live, but it's up in the world a bit from this doss-hole.'

7

Ruby bristled. 'I've been out doing my cleaning job. I'll not wear my best bib and tucker to get on my hands and knees to scrub the floors of the Red Lion,' she threw back at him. 'So how much rent do we have to pay to Cedric?' She was wary of the amount being outside of their earnings, and with her not being able to work as much while the baby was dependent on her, she didn't want to get into debt with Cedric Mulligan and be out on their ears with nowhere to live.

'He wants more than we pay for this place, but I thought your mother could have the small bedroom and chip in a bit. She could also look after the kids while you worked.'

'That's bloody good of you,' Ruby sniffed as she turned her back on her husband and started scrubbing the saucepan she'd left to soak in the chipped china sink. There again, if it meant moving up in the world she could put up with her mother's ways for a bit longer and perhaps, once things were better and they could live without Milly Tomkins' contribution, she could have one of her sisters take on the responsibility. It was time Fanny and Janie did more to help their mother. Older than Ruby, both women worked for their husbands, who were in the wholesale business, doing well for themselves up in Bexleyheath. Yes, she thought, nodding her head to confirm her decision, that was a plan and she'd stick to it. 'I think we should consider taking the house, Eddie. Once I've finished here I'll get myself tidied up and go down there and give the place the once over. There might be time to pick up a few bits and bobs down the market to make it more homely,' she said, thinking of the money she'd hidden away under a loose floorboard inside a battered tobacco tin.

'There's nothing to look at. I've given notice here and we move on Saturday,' he said, before tucking back in to the remains of his pie.

Ruby winced as the baby kicked in protest, as if complaining at Eddie Caselton's announcement. 'I know just how you feel,' she whispered as she gently rubbed her swelling stomach, protected beneath a voluminous apron. In the past, she'd questioned Eddie's grand ideas if she'd thought they were not right for their family. However, on this occasion she was in agreement, although it would have been nice to have a little more time to plan ahead.

'Now doesn't that feel better?' Stella said as she tucked clean bed linen around Ruby's exhausted body and brushed a few stray hairs from her pale face. 'I know it must have been a strain to be carried across the road by my Frank, but at least now you're in your own home and can sleep in your own bed. We'll soon have you as right as rain. Now, I'm going to leave you to sleep, and I'll be back in a few hours with some broth I have simmering on the stove.'

Ruby licked her dry lips. In the few days since she'd lost her baby, she'd hardly been able to face a morsel of food. The delirium following the shock of the birth had her new neighbour, along with her mother, fearing the worst. At the height of her illness as she tossed and turned, her body wracked with fever, she recalled hearing her mother say: 'If she dies, I won't look after the boy. He's too much of a handful, and what with my dodgy ticker it's best he goes into a home.' Ruby had tried to call out to tell them she wanted George by her side and needed to know about her baby, but as hard as she tried, no one took any notice. Something deep inside told her to fight whatever was keeping her away from her beloved son. By the following morning the fever had started to subside, but then grief took over when Stella explained her baby had not survived the traumatic birth and had been taken away. As much as Ruby begged to see the baby, her constant requests were ignored. Her mother told her it was for the best, and that Eddie had agreed. Of her husband there was no sign. Stella informed her, between pursed lips, that men grieved in different ways.

Alone at last, Ruby tried not to dwell on the past days, instead forcing herself to concentrate on her new home and the future. She was glad that her mother had thought to put new sheets on her bed rather than the much-boiled patched ones that she kept for daily use. She could smell a faint perfume of lavender, which reminded her of the dainty lace lavender bags she'd purchased on a whim when she spotted a young girl selling them in Woolwich market. An extravagance she could barely afford, but that week had been a good one, with Eddie not frittering away his pay packet on horses and beer. The sheets had been a gift from her sisters on her wedding day, and in those early happy months, she'd prepared her marriage bed with love. Later, as Eddie distanced himself from family life and acted more as if he was a single man, drinking to all hours and coming home when he pleased, she'd packed away her few good pieces of bedding and used the everyday sheets that had been purchased second-hand – not that they weren't clean, she reminded herself. Wriggling to make herself comfortable, she gazed around the large room and gasped in delight. Eddie had informed her the previous tenant had left behind a few sticks of furniture in his haste to depart, but what she could see was more than the kind of old, knocked-about items she was used to. She was lying in a large brass double bed that faced two tall windows, between which was a dressing table with three shining mirrors. To her left was a chimney breast where a coal fire was burning brightly. Although still August, it had been a miserable, cold month. At each side of the blackleaded grate, a row of painted green and yellow tiles framed the fireplace and matched the darker green tiles in the hearth. She could see that someone had placed her two treasured photographs on the black iron mantelpiece.

On the opposite wall stood a large wardrobe, and beside that a chest of drawers. Every piece matched and, twisting her head sideways, she spotted bedside tables – and all in what she assumed was walnut. Hadn't she often stood gazing into the windows of the posh furniture shops, promising herself that one day she too would be able to afford such luxurious items? 'Perhaps it is all a dream,' she murmured as she fell asleep, with the worry lines around her lips starting to disappear for the first time in weeks.

'Mummy!' a voice shouted, as her bed bounced and Ruby jolted awake with a start. 'Mummy, I have my own bedroom and so does Grandma,' her son exclaimed excitedly. 'Do you want to come and see our beds?'

Ruby held out her hand to ruffle his light brown curls, but it felt like lead and flopped back down onto the covers. 'My darling boy, have you been good for your nan?'

'As good as a child of that age can be,' Milly Tomkins huffed as she sat on a hardwood chair set by the fireside. 'I saw the baby,' she said quietly, noticing George was out of earshot, having climbed down from the bed and wandered over to the window.

Ruby gazed beseechingly at her mother. 'I know I'm to blame for killing her.'

'Kill? What are you talking about, girl? The child wasn't killed.'

Ruby glanced over to where George was still looking out of one of the tall windows and waving to passing neighbours. Lowering her voice, she said, 'It must have been something I did, as our George didn't come along early, and look at him now. As fit as a fiddle. I must have overdone things, what with scrubbing floors to bring in money and then humping our belongings on and off the drayman's cart.'

Milly put her hands on her hips and huffed again. 'The child would not have survived if you'd taken to your bed for the past six months and never lifted a finger. It wasn't meant for this world. It's best you forget all about it. There will be more babies, just as night follows day; you mark my words.'

Ruby wiped her eyes on the edge of the bed sheet. 'What do you mean by "never meant for this world?" What was wrong with her?'

Milly pursed her lips. 'It's best you don't know. As I said before, forget about her.'

Ruby shuddered as she fought to hold back sobs of frustration. 'She's my daughter, how can I forget her? Besides, there's the funeral to think about,' she added, wondering if the few shillings she still had put by for things for the new house would be enough to bury her daughter. It didn't feel right to be thinking about burying her own child, but sadly it happened. Why, there was a woman she'd known who'd worked down the market who'd died birthing her child, and the baby had gone to the grave with her. Ruby had been told that the woman had lost as many as had lived – and there'd been five young kiddies who'd ended up in the orphanage after their father dumped them and ran off, rather than face his responsibilities.

'It's been taken care of, so don't you go worrying yourself.'

'What do you mean? Don't I get a say on where my daughter is to be buried? I want her name on the marker until I can have a headstone made. I can do that, can't I?'

Milly gave a deep sigh and turned to her grandson. 'Georgie boy, why don't you pop downstairs and put some more butter on Mr Tibbs' paws for me? We don't want him wandering off and getting himself lost, now, do we?'

'Yes, Nana,' the child said as he ran to the stairs.

'And mind you hold on to the banister rail. If you fall and break your neck, don't come running to me in tears,' she called after him as she perched herself on the side of her bed and took Ruby's hand in her own. 'Now, I don't want you fretting yourself over this. It's just something women have to put up with. You need to harden your heart and get yourself back on your feet. I'll allow you this one day in bed, but there are things needing doing in this house, so pull yourself together and stop wallowing. It's time you thought about others, and weren't so selfish,'

13

she concluded, before hauling herself to her feet and heading downstairs, muttering as she went.

Ruby lay staring at the ceiling. Was her mum right? She didn't feel as though she was wallowing in grief. All she knew was, one day she was carrying a child and the next day she wasn't – and there was nothing to show for it apart from a pain so raw she wanted to scream out loud, even though no one would listen to her. Where was her baby – what had they done with it? Didn't the poor scrap of life deserve a grave – somewhere its mother could go to mourn? Someone must know, and she was determined to find out what had happened to her daughter.

Ruby must have slept again for a while, as she came to with a start when she heard heavy footsteps on the stairs. 'Is that you, Mum?' she called out. She would press Milly to tell her more of what had happened.

'No, it's me, your husband,' Eddie Caselton said loudly as he entered the room and stared down at his wife.

'I wondered when I'd see you,' she said, looking for just a spark of sorrow in his face at the loss of his child. 'It was a baby girl,' she whispered.

'So your mother told me, although it doesn't matter what it was. There'll be others,' he added, looking towards his side of the bed.

Ruby couldn't believe what he was insinuating. 'Perhaps you can bunk down with our George for a few days? Being poorly, I don't want to disturb you, and you'll need your sleep if you're to get to work on time.'

Eddie shrugged his shoulders and turned to look out of the window. 'They didn't want me after all. I'll have to go back to doing odd jobs for Cedric.'

Ruby sighed as she fought a lump forming in her throat. 'Oh, Eddie. I thought this move would be a fresh start for us – a lovely new home, a new baby, and you with a decent job. Now we've just got the home, and no way to pay the rent. What are we going to do?'

There was a short silence before he replied. 'You'll be back on your feet soon and can pick up some work cleaning, or perhaps even working in one of the shops in the town. After all, they're only round the corner. You could be back to get me dinner, and your mother can do her bit around the house and look after the kid.'

Ruby digested his words. It was as if nothing was going to change. She could see her dreams fading before her eyes. 'I'm going to call her Sarah, after my nan. I always liked the name.'

'What are you talking about, woman? There's nothing to name.'

An ache deep inside told Ruby otherwise. She'd not argue with her husband. What was the point? For him, it was over and done with. Stella was right: men just didn't understand, or the few who did grieved differently. For all they knew, having a baby simply meant a wife disappeared into the bedroom while the husband was ushered from the house. Hours later, there was a baby, and he was treated to drinks, a slap on the back and a good evening down the pub, she thought bitterly.

When she'd met Eddie Caselton, Ruby had thought herself the luckiest woman in the world. He was a good ten years older than her and considered a lucky catch. Her mother, Milly, had not been so impressed. 'The only reason he's married you is because of what you're carrying in your belly. How could you be so stupid, girl? He wanted you for one thing only. I should wash my hands of you. Your two sisters made good marriages and I expected more of you,' she'd sniffed.

Ruby had been adamant that Eddie loved her. Hadn't he treated her like a lady and courted her in the manner expected? It had only been the once that their kisses had gone too far and she'd consented and enjoyed his love-making. When she'd cried afterwards, thinking of what had occurred, he'd apologized and promised to care for her if there were any consequences. He'd been as good as his word and married her, declaring to the world it was time he settled down. Sadly, not long after George had been born, Ruby had begun to see that her husband had a different side to him. He preferred doing the odd bit of work for Cedric over holding down a proper job; not that the money he earned often reached home. If not for the few coppers she earned cleaning down the pub, she had no idea how they would have coped. On occasion, when Eddie stumbled home the worse for wear after celebrating a lucky win on the horses, she'd gone through his pockets, taking several coins and hiding them away while he slept off the drink. Was that what she had to look forward to for the rest of her life? Granted, he doted on his son, and no one could say he was a bad father.

Perhaps it was her fault that he behaved the way he did. After she'd given birth to a healthy boy, further preg-nancies had failed within weeks of her knowing she was expecting. Sarah was the only one who had almost gone full term. As the weeks turned to months and Ruby's stomach expanded, she had clung on to the hope that she

16

could give her husband a second child. There must be something wrong with her, to fail her husband like this. There again, her sisters had not provided their husbands with any offspring. She'd once mentioned this to Milly, suggesting there must be something wrong in the family, what with all three sisters having only the one child between them. Milly had scoffed at the suggestion, pointing out that she herself had birthed three healthy girls and Ruby should stop with her fanciful thoughts.

Ruby reached for her bag, which had been placed by the side of the bed. Pulling out her purse, she took a couple of coins and held them out to her husband. 'Why don't you go and get yourself a jug of beer? I reckon Mum would like to share a glass with you.'

Eddie took the money and gently stroked her cheek. 'Look after yourself. I don't know what I'd do if anything happened to you,' he said as he left her alone.

She lay back down, pulling the covers up over her shoulders. The fire in the bedroom was burning well and, with the rain again rattling against the windows, she took a little comfort in its warmth. Who'd have thought it was August? She shivered as she thought again of her daughter, who should have been a September baby. 'I'm going to do my best to find you, Sarah,' she whispered. 'You deserve to have a decent resting place – and I deserve to be able to pay my respects. As soon as I'm on my feet, I'll find you . . .'

2

'I'm not sure you should be out and about so soon. You still look very pale,' Stella Green said as she accompanied Ruby on her walk into town. 'It hasn't been three weeks since . . .'

'Since my daughter died,' Ruby finished, giving the older woman a sympathetic look. 'Please don't feel you can't mention it. It's bad enough indoors, with Mum refusing to talk about it. Her last comment was "it's done and dusted", as if I could ever forget about losing Sarah. I'm glad to be out of the house for a while, and away from her advice. I'm all right, honestly I am.'

'If you say so,' Stella said, giving her a hard stare. 'Sarah?'

Ruby's face looked a little flushed as she tried to explain. 'I've named her Sarah. My baby deserved a name, at the very least. I may never have seen her, but somehow she feels more real if I can think of her as Sarah.' She looked sideways at the older woman. 'Do you think I'm daft?'

Stella stopped walking and turned to face her young neighbour. 'You must do as you feel fit. I wish I'd given my oldest a name. I love my three sons dearly, but my firstborn is a ghost of a person . . . a ghost I reach out to,

18

but can never quite touch,' she said with a note of sadness to her voice. 'Giving him a name might well have helped me grieve his death. I was told by my mother that as he hadn't cried or taken a breath, he was never a person and must be forgotten. When I lost a second child – he was born after my Donald – it was different. I named him and I could grieve; I know him as my little Stanley.'

Ruby slipped her arm through Stella's and gave it a squeeze. 'I'm sorry for your loss. It must have been so hard, being your first.'

'First, second, third. Is it ever any different? I've known women never have another child because they couldn't bear another loss.'

Ruby frowned. 'But how . . . ?'

'They either had understanding husbands, or they were strong characters and banished their man to another bed.'

Ruby thought of how Eddie had begged and sulked until she had relented and allowed him back into their marital bed, even though she had no interest in what went on between them. In the past few days she had simply gone through the motions of being a wife and mother, her mind firmly on the daughter she'd lost. Eddie and her mum acted as though the pregnancy and Sarah's death had not occurred. 'I can understand why they did it,' she answered, with a haunted look in her eyes.

'You and me have got a lot in common, Ruby Caselton. There may be nearly thirty years between us, but we've both shared a suffering that we hold deep inside us. I'll always be here for you, if you need to talk about this. Now, let's get our shopping done, and then I'll treat us to a cup of tea in the cafe. I reckon we deserve it, don't you?'

Ruby gave her new friend a weak smile. 'I'd like that, thank you. There is something else I'd like to speak to you about, but it doesn't seem right here in the street.'

'Then leave it until we're in the cafe. Hopefully we can find a quiet table. Speaking of being quiet, where is your George today?'

'Mum's got him. I had to beg her to keep an eye on him, as shopping with a lively child is something I couldn't cope with today. Give it a while and I'll be as right as rain and back to normal. Well, if I ever feel really normal again.'

Stella patted her hand, and they continued walking. For Ruby, this outing was her first look around the thriving riverside town. Shiny new trams followed tracks in the road while linked to overhead cables that seemed to be alive. She could hear a distinct hum from the carriages and spotted sparks, which she found unnerving. Businesses and shops filled the two main roads, with horses and carts delivering all kinds of wares to the traders. She even spotted a motor vehicle parked by the cottage hospital. 'George will love seeing all this,' she declared, as the uniformed chauffeur nodded good morning to the two women. 'It's much posher than where we lived before.'

'You're not from Erith, then?' Stella asked as they stopped by a butcher's shop and she peered at a display of skinned rabbits in the window. 'You know, there was a time my husband brought them home for me to skin . . .'

Ruby wrinkled her nose at the thought of skinning an animal. She was partial to a bit of rabbit for her dinner, but didn't want one in her kitchen wearing its fur coat. 'I suppose needs must if you're hungry enough, but I've not got the stomach for doing the skinning,' she said, turning away from the window. 'And no, I'm not from round here, but I'm pleased we made the move from Woolwich. I didn't much like it there. Well, not where we lived, anyroad. This is a lovely town, and I've only seen a bit of one street. Is there much work to be had?' she asked, thinking that Eddie could do well if he put his mind to it and settled into one job.

'There's plenty, even if a man doesn't have a trade.'

'My Eddie would be looking for labouring work. He had a job, but wants to work down this way now we have the house,' she explained. 'He's a grafter and doesn't mind getting his hands dirty.' She didn't add that of late, hardly any of the money reached home on payday – and although it was true Eddie was a hard worker, he'd had many jobs. 'I'll be looking for something for myself as well, once I'm on my feet. Mum will be caring for George – he'd not be left on his own,' she added, with a spark of defiance in her eyes.

Stella gave a thoughtful nod as she handed coins over to the butcher for the scrag end she'd chosen, placing the wrapped packet in her basket. Ruby Caselton wasn't telling all, but it was early days, and who was she to question a young woman she'd only known for a few weeks? She liked Ruby a lot, but thought of her more as a young girl than a woman of twenty-five with a small son. In age she sat neatly between her oldest son, Frank, and middle son, Derek. Stella would have loved a daughter of her own. Well, perhaps Ruby Caselton would fill her need for a daughter, even though the waspish Milly Tomkins could claim the position of mother, being the real blood relative. She'd mentioned this very fact to her husband just the evening before. Wilf had laughed, warning her not to interfere in a stranger's life. He'd mentioned that he thought Eddie Caselton was one of life's wasters, and as much as he too was taken with Ruby, his opinion was that getting involved in their lives could bring trouble to their own family.

Whatever her husband said, though, Stella knew she would look out for the girl and be a good neighbour to her.

'There are boards up outside the Vickers factory most days, along with others, calling for people with a trade as well as labourers. Then there's the docks, the coalyards as well as the brickfields. Why, my Derek is doing well working down the brickfield, and the money is regular during the summer months. Making bricks is a good honest trade if you don't mind outside work.'

Ruby looked thoughtful as she listened to Stella. 'Does your Frank work there too?'

'No, he works down at the coalyard. He's a clerk in the office,' she said proudly. 'My Wilf wanted Frank to join him on the river, but Frank's not so keen. It's a shame, as being a lighterman runs in the family. Unless a family member puts you forward for a job, you can't get in. Wilf is the master of his own tug, the *Merry England*, and he has rowed in the annual Doggett's cup race on the river.'

'That sounds really important,' Ruby replied, although she didn't really understand half of what her neighbour had said. She liked Stella's husband and sons, who had sat with her when she was poorly. Frank had read to her while she was weak and lent her a well-thumbed copy of *Great Expectations* to take back to number thirteen. Wilfred Green had sat smoking his pipe, pointing out items of interest from his newspaper. They were polite to Eddie the few times he'd popped over the road and they'd entertained George, too, pulling out old wooden toys that had belonged to the three brothers when they'd been younger.

'Wilf says Frank is a thinker, not someone to work with his hands on the river. Even Derek would rather work with his mates making bricks. Perhaps Frank will reconsider when he's older. It would be good to keep the tug boat in our family.'

Once Stella's doctor declared Ruby strong enough to be moved, her eldest son had carried her with ease across the road and up to her bed, Stella hurrying behind all the time telling him to be careful and watching out for the nosy neighbours who peered from behind their lace curtains. Ruby had still been very weak, and she had little memory of it now apart from Frank's strong arms and twinkling blue eyes. This wasn't Eddie, the man who had stolen her heart when she was a mere slip of a girl, and who her mother had hassled to marry her when she was expecting her George. Any man was better than being an unmarried mother. A moment of madness when she fell for Eddie's charms had resulted in her mother marching them both down the aisle long before anyone outside the family was aware there was a child on the way – which was surprising, considering her slim outline at that time.

At the age of twenty, Ruby had been pleased to be with child. Many girls her age had already been married a while. She'd almost thought herself on the shelf, destined to be a spinster living with her mother for the rest of her days. Granted, she had a real fondness for Eddie – otherwise, she had no idea what she would have done. Her two sisters had backed their mother. Both of them had found themselves good husbands, and in their eyes a younger sister having a child out of wedlock would blacken the family name. Only weeks after the wedding, though, Ruby had realized that Eddie's promises were not to be believed. What was that saying about promises and piecrusts, she thought to herself? Long before their son arrived, they were living in one room in a building that should have been pulled down years earlier, instead of in a little house with a garden where she could grow roses, as he'd promised. Ruby had no idea about gardening, but on a Sunday school trip into the country she'd spotted such a house and had mentioned it to Eddie in the days leading up to their wedding. She'd kept holding on to her dream as they had moved from one awful home to another. Along the way, Milly had joined them; she hardly had the means to support herself and her meagre earnings diverted to Eddie's pocket to pay for her keep.

'Watch it!' Stella shouted, grabbing Ruby's arm and pulling her back onto the pavement and away from an approaching tram. 'Blimey, love, we didn't get you over your illness just to have you perish under one of these new-fangled tramcars. You was in another world there for a while.'

Ruby was shaking from the shock, but stopped to look at Stella. 'I wasn't ill. I was grieving for my Sarah,' she said, before bursting into tears.

'Oh my, you are in a state. I'm sorry if my words

24

offended you. Look, there's a cafe just here. Much better than those posh tearooms in Pier Road. Let me get you sat down with a hot drink and we can have a chat,' Stella said, steering her into the busy establishment, where they found an empty table.

Ruby wiped her eyes on the cuff of her faded wool coat and tried to pull herself together. 'Sorry. I don't know what came over me,' she said as she sat down on a small wooden chair in the corner of the room. Stella removed a used white plate and mug from the table and placed them onto the high counter.

'Two teas and a couple of those, when you're ready, Marge,' she said, indicating a pile of small meat pies stacked under a glass dome.

Marge, a generously built woman swathed in a clean cotton apron, nodded in acknowledgement while frantically buttering bread.

'I'll be with you in two ticks, love. I'm run off me feet today, what with being on me own. My Sid's got another of his chests.'

Stella made a sympathetic noise and turned away from the counter to sit down with Ruby, who had done her best to compose herself. She reached out and covered Ruby's hand with her own. 'You know, it is all right to be angry. I know we've not known each other long but because of what happened I feel we're already close friends. Why, I look on you as the daughter I never had . . .' She stopped speaking mid-sentence as a stricken look crossed Ruby's pale face. 'I'm sorry – I must be more careful what I say,' she added, as Ruby reached into her pocket for a square of rag on which to wipe her eyes.

'No – I've got to learn not to get so upset. You are the only one I can talk to about . . . about Sarah. Please, you mustn't ever think you have upset me. I'll do my best not to get so tearful. I just wish I knew what they'd done with her. Does that sound wrong?'

'No, my love. You have a right to know. When you took poorly and we could see this baby wasn't coming as it should have done, we sent for Doctor Hind, and he came along with Nurse Rose. I was sent from the room, and your mum stayed with you for a while – until it got too much for her, and she left in a hurry. She mumbled that it was all over, so I went back into the room to be with you.'

Ruby searched Stella's face and could only see sympathy and concern. 'Did you see her . . . ? It's just that Mum said it wasn't pleasant, and she wouldn't have had a good life if she'd survived. I can't get that thought out of my mind.' She bit her lip, fighting the tears that threatened to return.

Stella shook her head in disgust. Why would a mother say such things to a daughter who had just lost a child? 'I did see her, and she had the most beautiful hair, just like your George's. Very fine, but you could see there would be curls.'

Ruby sighed. 'I'm so pleased. Mum must have been wrong, then?'

Stella paused for a moment. She didn't want to base their new friendship on lies, but all the same, would never say what she'd really witnessed. 'Let's just say Milly was probably distraught at losing a grandchild. It was hard for everyone present. Why, even Doctor Hind had a tear in his eye.'

Ruby felt a weight of relief flood over her. 'I imagined they bundled her away with no respect for what might have been . . . Where is she, Stella? I really thought I could have had a funeral for her.'

They stopped speaking as Marge put two mugs of tea on the table. Both mugs were held in one of her chubby hands, while in the other were two pies on a plate. 'Pay me when you're ready to leave,' she said, seeing that the younger woman with Stella seemed upset. 'I don't think we've met before, love. I'm Marge Dobkins. Me and the old fella run this place. Are you visiting the town?'

'This is Mrs Caselton. She's not long moved in across the road from me, Marge,' Stella said, smiling at the larger woman.

'How do you do, Mrs Caselton?' Marge wiped her hands on her apron before offering one to Ruby.

Ruby took her hand and winced as it was pumped up and down in a vice-like grip. 'Please, you must call me Ruby. You have a very nice place here, Marge.'

'It keeps me busy and the old man out of trouble,' Marge said, puffing herself up with pride. 'If I do say so myself, my meat puddings and mutton pies are the best in all the town. People leave here satisfied and without cause for complaint. I just wish I had some more help around the place. I get home every night exhausted. Oh well, mustn't complain,' she said as someone called to her to be served. 'Enjoy your tea, and welcome to Erith.'

'She seems very nice,' Ruby said as she sipped the scalding hot amber liquid from the large mug.

'Salt of the earth,' Stella said, noting what lovely manners Ruby had. 'Now, where were we?'

'I wondered what they'd done with my daughter,' Ruby said, staring into her mug. 'Once I know, I'll feel at peace. I've had such dreams about her. She's been calling for me and crying out. I woke up once and thought I could hear her.'

Stella thought it was more likely to be Mrs Henderson from number seventeen's old moggy out on the tiles, but did not say so. 'Grief can do strange things to us,' she said, not wanting to tell any more of what she knew.

Ruby became frustrated, clenching her hands together until her knuckles turned white, but dared not scream and shout at Stella even though she wanted nothing more than to demand to know what had happened to her baby. 'Please, Stella, I really do want to know where she is, even if it is not pleasant,' she implored.

'Pleasant? Goodness me, as if I'd let anything awful happen to an innocent baby. They just take them away, Ruby. The ones that never wake up are simply taken away.'

'Is that what happened to your baby boy?' Ruby asked softly, now she had started to get somewhere.

'No, my Stanley has a grave up at Saint Paulinus church-yard. You see, he took a breath and he cried. He was so poorly and passed away before the day was out. However, I'll never forget my first baby . . .'

It was Ruby's turn to reach across the marble-topped table and take Stella's hand. 'I'm sorry to have asked. It wasn't my intention to hurt you.'

Stella waved away the apology. 'I've had long enough to accept what happened. I have my faith,' she said, reaching for a small silver cross that hung on a chain at her throat. 'I'll meet him again one day.'

28

Ruby nodded in agreement. Although she wasn't one for religion, she knew it was of help to some people. 'It must be a comfort to you. But what about my Sarah, where is she?'

Stella sighed. She knew that Ruby would never let up asking her. She'd be the same if it were her little one that hadn't survived. 'I know the nurse who was attending with Doctor Hind took her away. She told me it's what they do,' she said, as she saw a distressed look cross Ruby's face. 'Perhaps we could pay the doctor a visit and ask him? Would that help?'

'Oh please, it would help so much. When can we go and ask him?'

'Let's finish up here, then we can pop in and see him. He is no doubt working in the cottage hospital – he's a big supporter of our hospital,' she added proudly, noticing Ruby's quizzical look.

'Is that the large house we walked past just now – the one with the trees and wooden fence? I spotted a nurse at the door.'

'That's the place. Now, come on, tuck in to that pie. We need to get some meat back on your bones. There's hardly anything of you.'

Ruby could have screamed: after standing for ages in the reception room of the cottage hospital, they were told the doctor was with a poorly patient and it would be best for them to return another time.

'I'm so sorry,' the nurse said, seeing Ruby's disappointment. 'Are you ill? I may be able to help.'

'We just wanted to ask him something,' Stella said, taking Ruby's arm to lead her towards the door.

Ruby pulled away, not wishing to leave the building that might hold the secret of what had happened to her daughter. 'Please, I just want to know what Doctor Hind did with my baby after she was stillborn. Can someone help me?' she begged, as her tears started to fall unchecked.

The nurse felt a surge of sympathy as she looked at the distraught young woman in front of her. There was nothing of her, and she looked younger than her own daughter, who had not long given birth to a bouncing baby boy. 'Were you admitted to this hospital?'

Ruby shook her head, unable to speak. Was it possible the nurse would help her? There again, she wouldn't know anything about Sarah, as she had been born at Stella's house. As she took a shuddering breath and opened her mouth to speak, Stella stepped forward.

'Mrs Caselton's baby daughter was born in my front bedroom just around the corner in Alexandra Road. Doctor Hind was in attendance, due to her being so poorly. The child did not survive and was taken away. We just wondered . . .'

All three women fell silent, Ruby and Stella hoping against hope that the nurse would be able to give them some information.

The nurse wondered whether she would get into trouble if she imparted what she knew. She glanced over her shoulder towards the double doors leading into the small hospital, aware that at any time a colleague or superior might come through them and catch her saying something she shouldn't. She drew them to one side, where there was a wooden bench. 'Would you like to sit down?'

'No, thank you,' Ruby answered, keen to know why the woman had not led them straight to the front door. Stella tugged Ruby's sleeve to make her do as requested, and they both sat down.

'Do you know something?' Stella urged, noticing for the first time the stray grey hairs escaping from beneath the elaborate white starched cap, as well as the rising colour of the nurse's cheeks and trembling hands. 'We don't want you to get into trouble. Perhaps it would be best if we just left?'

Ruby wanted to scream again. She closed her eyes and quickly prayed that the nurse, if she knew something, would not change her mind about sharing what she had to say.

'I'll have to be quick,' the woman said, as two nurses entered through the front door and hurried into the hospital through the double doors. The three women jumped as the doors swung open, with Stella putting her hand to her chest to still her beating heart. It felt as though it was hammering nineteen to the dozen.

'In cases where the child fails to waken . . . I know that Doctor Hind arranges for the body to be laid to rest.'

'My daughter has a grave?' Ruby asked, as emotion stirred deep inside. 'I feared the worst,' she added as the other two women hushed her high-pitched tone in case it alerted the almoner, whose office door was close to a wide staircase next to the double doors.

'Sshh,' the nurse hissed. 'You must remain quiet or I'll have to ask you to leave.'

Both women apologized and Stella took Ruby's hand, ready to give it a hard squeeze if her young neighbour became over-excited again. 'Where does he send the children?' she asked. 'I assume they go to an undertaker?'

'Yes. I only know this as I have a cousin who works for the undertaker. Both Doctor Hind and the under-taker are benefactors of this hospital and wish to do what they can for the people of Erith. However, it may be that your child does not have a marked grave. I know little more than that,' she said, as Ruby gave a quizzical look.

'May we speak to your cousin?'

The nurse looked alarmed. 'No, I dare not give you his name, as then he would know I'd broken his confidence.'

'Then please, can you at least tell us which funeral director would have laid Sarah to rest?' Stella begged.

'I named my child Sarah,' Ruby explained.

'Why, that's my name also,' the nurse said, as if it had helped her make up her mind. 'All I will tell you is that the business where you may find all you wish to know is in the high street,' she added, before wishing them luck and scurrying away just as the almoner came from her office, her black gown rustling as she moved.

'May I help you, ladies?' she enquired, her dark, hooded eyes peering at Stella and Ruby.

Stella pulled Ruby to her feet and gave a polite nod. 'We came to see Doctor Hind, but he is busy. Thank you for your interest,' she said, as the pair hurried away.

'We are no closer to knowing where Sarah was taken,' Ruby sighed.

'But we are. There are only two undertakers in the

town, and just one in the high street. Follow me,' Stella said, weaving her way through the busy shoppers.

Ruby found it hard to catch up. For one thing, she wasn't feeling very fit: it was the first time she'd left home since being so poorly. Secondly, her ill-fitting shoes were giving her grief. She'd packed the insoles with newspaper due to them leaking in wet weather, and she could feel her toes becoming sore from the chafing. She was relieved when Stella halted in front of a sombre-looking establishment, the window draped in black crepe sashes with the sign above in gold lettering declaring the business to be Michael Hind, Funeral Director.

'He has the same name as the doctor,' Stella remarked, trying to read the letters while jumping aside to avoid a woman pushing a perambulator. She opened the door and walked in. Ruby followed close behind, a little unsure of what to expect, as she'd never been in such a place before. She looked around warily. A man in a sombre black suit and a wing-collared shirt rose to his feet from behind a highly polished desk. Nodding respectfully while placing his hands together, which Ruby thought made him look rather pious, he gave a thin-lipped smile.

'How can I help you?' he said, giving Ruby a look that suggested she was unworthy of stepping over the threshold of his establishment.

'We've come to make an enquiry about a baby that may have been buried by your company in the past three weeks. It was taken from my house in Alexandra Road by Doctor Hind. My name is Mrs Stella Green.'

The man flinched at the mention of Doctor Hind's name. 'You would need to speak to my employer. I'm afraid I'm not at liberty to give out confidential information,' he said as he sat down, dismissing Stella's question.

'Please,' Ruby begged, 'can't you at least tell us if you help the stillborn babies find a final resting place? Is there a special grave for them?'

The man coughed and ran a finger round his stiff collar. 'If my employer is party to such charitable concerns, it is none of my business. I suggest you speak to him.'

Ruby felt a frisson of excitement course through her veins. The man hadn't dismissed her question, so there was hope that indeed they had come to the right place.

'When will Mr Hind return to his office?' Stella asked.

'He is away on business for the rest of this week. I suggest you put any questions you might have in writing. He will deal with it upon his return. Now, if you will excuse me.' He opened a leather-bound ledger on his desk and picked up his fountain pen.

Stella nudged Ruby's arm, and they stepped out onto the street.

'I'm not one for writing letters. Surely if that man knew about Sarah, he could tell us?'

Stella shook her head. 'He's doing his job, and no doubt has been given his orders. But there was something in the way he acted when we explained why we were there . . . It was as if he knew what had happened to Sarah, but didn't wish to say – or did not approve. There must be another way to find out.' She looked at an alleyway that ran alongside the shop. 'Follow me,' she said over her shoulder as she stepped briskly towards it.

Ruby shivered as she followed closely behind her new friend. 'Where are we going?' She did her best to hold up the skirt of her coat and dress so they wouldn't drag on the muddy ground beneath her feet. With August being so unseasonably wet, and the close walls of the buildings each side of them blocking out what sun there was, the alleyway gave off an atmosphere of wintry gloom.

Stella ignored Ruby's question and ploughed ahead until the narrow alley opened out into a yard where several men went about their business. They were hitching horses wearing black plumes to a fine-looking carriage, inside of which was a polished ebony coffin. Ruby shivered and crossed herself, as she'd seen others do when a funeral cortege passed by.

Stella approached a man who was leaning against a wall smoking a cigarette. 'Excuse me . . .'

'What can I do for you, love?'

'This may seem a little strange, but I need to find something out that would help my friend here get over her grief. We did ask in the office, but the man was not very helpful.'

Ruby thought it best to let Stella do the talking and simply nodded her head.

'Albert Brownlow wouldn't give someone help if they was gasping their last breath,' the man sneered as another worker nearby called out in agreement. 'Perhaps we can help you?'

'Could you?' Ruby begged, forgetting that she had decided to keep quiet.

The man gave her a grin. 'I definitely can, if it means putting another smile on that sad face of yours. Has it got something to do with personal effects going missing? We've had two complaints in the past week, and we reckon old Brownlow has something to do with it. We all plan to 'ave a word with Mr Hind when he returns, before anyone pokes the finger of blame at us.'

'No, it's nothing like that. We wanted to know if Mr Hind ever helps women who lose babies during child-birth?'

'Does he give them a funeral?' Ruby chipped in, thinking Stella was too slow with her questions.

The man stubbed out his cigarette and rubbed the whiskers on his chin slowly as he thought. 'Er, Ernie, I think you could help these ladies,' he called to an older man who was rubbing a rag over the carriage.

Ernie tucked the rag in his pocket and joined them, taking his cap off as he did so. 'It's all right, Jim, I heard what the lady said. I'll take it from here.'

The two women held their breath, both worrying that they were about to be dismissed from the premises. Ruby thought it time they explained themselves. It was surely their last chance to ask for help. 'My baby never woke after she was born. I want to know what happened to her. I need to know where I can lay flowers and remember the child I carried,' she pleaded, placing her hand on her stomach as she spoke.

'I'm sorry for your loss,' the older man said. Ruby believed him, as she saw his eyes water. 'Yes, Mr Hind is a charitable man – he does much for the cottage hospital and the good people of Erith. It was when his own daughter lost a son that he wondered what happened to babies that did not survive childbirth. His brother is a doctor, and a cousin of theirs is a minister of the Baptist church. Together they make sure all those babies receive a burial, even though in the eyes of the law they are not registered.'

'You mean Ruby's daughter has been buried in consecrated ground thanks to these charitable gentlemen?' Stella asked. 'I suppose they do not inform the families in case a fuss is made. Imagine if all and sundry started turning up at the graves to pay their respects.'

'That's about it,' Ernie said, giving them a gentle smile. 'I hope in some way it helps with your grief?'

'It does,' Ruby said as she took his hand and shook it in gratitude. 'Is it possible to find out where my Sarah is laid to rest?'

'Now you're asking something,' he said, scratching his head. 'You'd be surprised how many young souls are helped. We don't have a special grave for them, you see.'

'Whatever do you mean?' Stella sounded confused.

Ernie turned and pointed to the carriage about to leave the yard for a funeral service. 'Do you see below the carriage there is a compartment? What do you think it is for?'

'Food for the horses?' Ruby said.

'Spades for the grave to be dug?' Stella suggested.

'In a way you're both right, as they have many uses. However, Mr Hind had them included when each carriage was commissioned. They can hold three, maybe four small coffins for the unregistered deceased babies, but it would depend on the size of the grave. I've never known us bury more than two together.'

'You mean Mr Hind goes to all this trouble for babies like my Sarah?' Ruby shook her head in disbelief. 'If only my daughter had breathed for a little while, I could have said goodbye properly. He deserves to be knighted for such charitable works.'

Stella nodded in agreement. 'Can you tell us where Ruby's Sarah is buried – and how would they bury her, if there is no special grave for these babies?'

'If you can tell me the date she was born, I can most likely say where she is,' he said, looking between the two women.

'It was the fifth of August and Doctor Hind, along with his nurse, left my house at just after four o'clock. They had the child with them. I will never forget that day,' Stella said as she put her arm around Ruby's shoulders and pulled the now-crying young woman to her.

'I'll get her a cup of water.' Ernie blew his nose on a handkerchief pulled from his pocket before going to the pump in the corner of the yard and filling a tin cup with clear water. 'Get that down you, girl, you've had a lot to put up with by the sounds of things,' he said as he made sure she was holding the cup securely. 'I'm going to check my logbook to see what work we had on the fifth of August. If anyone should come out of the office and question why you're here, you can tell them Ernie Grafton asked you to drop off a fresh supply of shrouds. We often get deliveries from the seamstresses so no one will be any the wiser.'

Stella felt a shudder run through her body at the thought of making such items, but with Ruby still upset, it quickly went from her mind. 'Here, love, finish the water, it will make you feel a lot better.'

'Thanks, but I've had enough.' Ruby refused the mug. 'Why don't you have some? You must be as shaken and thirsty as I was.'

Stella thankfully finished what was left. 'That went down well. I don't know about you, but I could manage another cup of tea from the cafe.'

'And another of Marge's meat pies,' Ruby said, licking her lips.

'Why don't we go back there again after we say goodbye to Ernie? I do need to pick up some black bootlaces, but apart from that I've got a while before I need to be home sorting out dinner for my hungry lot.'

'It's a deal,' Ruby said, 'but please let me treat you. I couldn't have done this without your help. In fact, God knows what would've happened to me that day if you haven't come out into the street when I collapsed.'

'Don't be so daft. That's what neighbours are for. I expect you'd do the same for me if I was in the same circumstances. Not that I'm likely to catch at my age,' she added.

Ruby could only give her a sympathetic smile. Stella was a tonic, and even though she was grieving for Sarah, she couldn't help but feel joyous that she had found a good friend.

'That's put the colour back in your cheeks,' Ernie said, returning with a small cloth-covered ledger. 'The fifth of August, you say,' he added, thumbing through the pages.

'Yes, and it was late afternoon.' Stella peered over his shoulder. She couldn't make out any of the words as the handwriting was too small and neat.

'Here it is,' he said triumphantly, tapping the page with his finger. 'I thought it was so, but wanted to check before I said anything to you. We buried a Miss Allinson on the sixth along with a small unmarked coffin containing a female child. That'll be the one.'

'Are you sure?' Stella asked. 'Could it have been another baby?'

Ernie flicked through the pages. 'There was a boy two days later, so the girl buried with Miss Allinson is definitely your baby.'

Ruby shook her head in disbelief. 'I don't understand why a family would allow an unknown baby to be buried with their loved one. It doesn't make sense.'

Ernie gave Ruby a hard stare. 'The family know nothing about it. We slip the child into the fresh grave and cover it with earth. Then, after the service in the chapel, the deceased is laid to rest and the family are none the wiser.'

Stella thought it an ideal situation, in the circumstances, but didn't like to say so in case of upsetting Ruby. 'So now you know, girl. Do you feel any happier?'

Ruby kept her gaze on Ernie. 'So where is this grave?'

Ernie looked uncomfortable. 'I shouldn't really say, but as you already know the name of the deceased, it wouldn't take much ferreting about for you to find it. It's up at Brook Street cemetery.'

Ruby looked to Stella. 'Do you know this cemetery? Is it far away?'

'You're not thinking of going up there, are you?' Stella asked. 'You're still recovering, my girl. You don't need any more excitement today.'

'Of course I am. I've not found the information only to go home without paying my respects to my daughter. I'll not tell a soul,' she assured a worried-looking Ernie.

'Thank you for all you've done. I'm happy to go alone, if one of you would point the way.'

Ernie thought for a moment. 'The quickest way would be to get on one of those new trams and go as far as Northumberland Heath, then walk down Brook Street. You can't miss the cemetery, although it's a fair walk,' he said, thinking she'd find the walk taxing.

'My George would like to go on the trams. He has spoken of nothing else since his nan walked him around the road to watch them. Perhaps I should wait until tomorrow before I go to this cemetery. I can take George as a special treat. He'd like that. Yes, that's what I'll do,' she said, before thanking Ernie for his help and following Stella back through the alleyway and out into the busy high street.

3

Ruby burst through the front door of number thirteen. Even a sudden downpour of rain couldn't dampen her spirits.

'What's taken you so long?' Milly grumbled from the kitchen. 'I can't be expected to take care of your kid as well as your husband, not with my dodgy ticker.'

Ignoring her mother's words, Ruby smiled softly. 'I found her, Mum. I found where they laid Sarah to rest.'

'Have you gone barmy or something? What the hell are you talking about?'

Ruby froze. She'd not told her mother the name she'd given to her daughter. 'The baby, Mum, I found where they buried her. I'm going to take George to see the grave tomorrow. Do you want to come with us so we can lay some flowers and pay our respects?'

Milly threw down the cloth she was using to wipe dust from the black iron mantelpiece in the front room and glared at her daughter. As yet there was very little furniture in the room, apart from two armchairs left by the previous tenant. Ruby had plans for the room but until there was money coming in it was all she could do to pay the rent and put food in their bellies. 'What do you mean lay flowers on a grave and pay our respects? You can only pay your respects to the living what died. That thing you gave birth to never lived.'

Ruby felt as though her mother had slapped her round the face. She put her hand to her mouth and stepped back in horror. 'Why would you say such a thing? Sarah was beautiful. Stella saw her and she said my baby . . . my baby was beautiful . . .'

Milly laughed out loud. It was a harsh laugh devoid of warmth. 'There was no beauty in what I saw. It makes me wonder how a child of mine could give birth to such an ugly thing.'

George ran into the room to see his mother, but then hid behind her skirts when he became frightened of the way his grandmother was shouting.

'Mum, please, you're frightening the boy,' Ruby said, reaching down to hug her son. 'Don't be frightened, George, Nanny and I are just having a few words. It means nothing. Why not go fetch your slate and I will write some numbers and letters for you to copy. Then I'll put away my shopping and see to your dad – that's if he's home from work.'

Ruby tousled the boy's hair and kissed his cheek, closing the door behind him as he left the room. Turning on her mother, she wagged her finger at her. 'How dare you talk about a child I gave birth to like that? If, and I don't believe it, there was anything ugly about my daughter it came from you – her grandmother. You are the one with an ugly soul, and I don't want it in my home for a minute more. You can pack your bag and go live with Fanny or Janie. I've had enough of you. I came home with joyous news, something that made my heart sing when I felt it had turned to ice and would never thaw, and you have done nothing but create a bad atmosphere.'

Milly opened her mouth to speak, her face full of indignation, but Ruby was having none of it and placed her hands on her hips, ready to lay into her mum once again if needed.

'What's all this racket?' Eddie said as he pushed open the door, knocking Ruby sideways. 'Can't a man have a nap without you two going at it like fishwives?' he shouted.

Ruby, who had grabbed the back of an armchair to stop herself falling, wrinkled her nose in disgust at the smell. 'Have you been drinking?' she asked as beer fumes overcame her, making her gag. 'How come you've had time to go to the boozer when you can't have left your work more than half an hour ago?'

'They let him go,' Milly jeered, still hell-bent on arguing.

'Is this true, Eddie?' Ruby asked, fearful of his reply. Without her earning any money in recent weeks, and with Eddie's wages at the best of times erratic, things had been tight. She thought of her savings, hidden in a tobacco tin at the back of the pantry. The money was dwindling fast, and she wasn't sure if the rent had been paid. He slumped into the armchair not saying a word. 'Eddie – have you lost your job?' Ruby all but screamed as her mum continued to cackle gleefully. 'Shut up, Mum. Eddie, speak to me,' she demanded, pulling at his hands until they fell from his face. 'What the hell happened? You've only been in that job a couple of weeks. I thought you liked it?'

He gazed up at her, looking doleful. 'I got caught

fighting – but it wasn't my fault,' he added quickly. 'I was defending myself.'

'You always are, Eddie, you always are,' she sighed, as any happiness she'd arrived home with seeped away. 'I thought moving here would be a new start for us all. A nice house, a new baby, and you in a proper job for once. I was that delighted when you stopped working for Cedric Mulligan and settled into a job that gave you a pay packet every week rather than bits of money here and there from Cedric when it suited him, or when he wanted you to use your fists. Don't think I hadn't heard you'd started hanging around him again,' she said as he gave her a surprised look. 'There's always someone who wants to make sure I knew what you've been up to,' she said, glancing towards Milly, who had become quiet but was still relishing the scene unfolding in front of her. 'I thought with us paying our rent to a collector we'd not have any contact with Cedric again. This is the second job you've lost since we moved here!'

'We will get by, girl.' He reached for her hand. 'We always do, even if it means moving from here and finding something cheaper to rent.'

'Oh no, not this time Eddie Caselton. I happen to like this house and this town, and I want to make a go of living here. So, will you work with me to make a decent future for all of us, or do I have to show you the door?' she demanded, wondering what had happened to the man she married. At times a spark of the old Eddie appeared, but then the drinking and gambling took over. Add Cedric to the pot, offering him easy money to do his dirty work, and her dream for a happy family life flew out of the window.

45

'Aw, Ruby,' he said, looking to his mother-in-law for support and being ignored. 'This street is too posh for the likes of us. I'm not the kind of bloke to earn the kind of money for us to stay here. Every other bloke living in this street has some high and mighty job on the river or running a shop in the town. I'm not like them. Tell her, Milly.'

'Don't get me involved in your quarrels. It's bad enough I have nowhere to live at my time of life, what with your wife showing me the door. I know you don't want me here.'

Ruby gave a big sigh. As much as she'd prefer her mum to move out, she knew it wasn't possible. Why was life always so difficult for her? 'Now, there's no need to go on so. Between the pair of you I don't know whether I'm coming or going. I think we need to all sit down and talk things through. I do have other news, but it can keep for the time being. Mum, put the kettle on and warm up the bowl of faggots I brought home for our tea. We can eat and talk at the same time,' she said, giving her husband a warning look, as she knew he'd creep off out rather than face her to talk about their money problems. While he was hungry and eager to eat, she held him captive.

Ruby waited until the family were tucking into their meal of hot faggots, with a pile of fresh bread in front of them to wipe up the hot succulent gravy, to make her announcement. 'I've found myself a job,' she said before popping a piece of crusty bread into her mouth.

'That's my girl,' Eddie replied. 'If you want us to stay here, we need more money coming in. I still think it's not the road for us to live on,' he added, not wanting Ruby to know she had fully won the argument. He nodded at

Milly. 'You could do us all a favour and think about bringing a few bob in too, like Ruby here. Cleaning, are you, or is it bar work?' he asked her, without looking up from his plate.

'I'm going to be working in a cafe in the high street. It's steady work and regular hours,' she said, thinking back to when, along with Stella, she'd returned to the cafe for a cup of tea to settle their nerves after visiting the funeral establishment. They'd walked in just as Marge had sworn loudly after dropping a tray of dirty crockery. Bending down to sort out the mess, she'd cut her finger on a smashed plate. While Stella sat her down and cleaned her wound, Ruby had set to clearing up the mess. She'd found a mop and bucket in a back room and given the floor a quick wipe over, warning customers to mind the wet floor before getting behind the counter and serving the queue of people, who were starting to grumble.

'You don't want a job, do you?' Marge had asked as she'd joined Ruby, once her finger had stopped bleeding and had been dressed by Stella with a clean strip of rag.

'She's not been well,' Stella said, giving Ruby a stern look in case she accepted the offer.

'I can see she's all skin and bones.' Marge gave Ruby a look up and down. 'I'd not run you into the ground like an old workhorse,' she smiled. 'You can tell me if you aren't feeling good and I'd not expect you to be on your feet all day. It's just that with my old man not around as much these days – he runs our other place in Bexleyheath – I could do with a bit of help serving and washing up, and perhaps making a few pies when we get short. You could sit down to do that,' she added hopefully, watching

Ruby to see how she was taking her offer. 'If there's anything left over at the end of the day, you can take it home with you . . .'

Ruby was interested. It could be the answer to something that had been worrying her. In the few weeks she'd lived at number thirteen, she had come to love the solidly built house. She had a friend in Stella from across the road, and already other neighbours had stopped to enquire after her health and leave a few eggs, or vegetables from their back gardens. Although this was her first trip into the town, she knew Erith was the place for her and she didn't want to leave if she could help it. However, there was the worry of keeping up with the rent – one of the reasons they'd had to move frequently when living in rooms in Woolwich and the surrounding area.

'I have a little boy to care for and it depends on the pay, but don't get me wrong, I need to find work . . .' she said, trying to keep her excitement hidden. It always helped to barter a little, and Marge might be paying a pittance. She couldn't work for nothing. Taking home stale bread and cake would not be so enticing if she was still short of money come payday.

Marge cocked her head to one side. 'I take it your lad goes to school?'

Ruby beamed. 'Yes, come September he starts at the school in Slades Green. Stella had a word with them for me while I was ill.'

'It was the least I could do,' Stella said. 'My lads all enjoyed their time there. Even though there's a school closer, young George will be hard pressed to get a better education this side of Kent.'

'He's already learnt some of his numbers and letters,' Ruby said proudly. 'Granted he's my own flesh and blood, but I know he's a bright kid, and with luck George will have a good future.'

'I'll second that,' Stella agreed. 'My youngest told me the lad's as bright as a button picking up things. George follows him everywhere – like his little shadow, he is.'

'That's nice, ducks. Have you only got the one?'

Stella watched Ruby's face and noticed a shadow pass fleetingly over. Would she say anything about her recent loss?

Ruby thought for a second. She knew it was best not to have secrets from someone she could be working with and who might soon be paying her wages. However, would Marge still employ her if she knew why she'd been so poorly only weeks before, and was just venturing out? In for a penny, she thought to herself. 'My daughter was born only weeks ago but never took a breath. I've been ill since the birth. Stella here has been a diamond, considering I had never met her until I collapsed in front of her the day I was moving into my house down Alexandra Road.'

Marge put down the teapot she was holding and hurried to envelop Ruby in her chubby arms. 'My love, we could be sisters,' she said, forgetting that she was twice the size of Ruby and much older. 'You've been luckier than me, as not one of mine gasped a breath. It's my one regret that I never gave my husband a child. Come on, let's all sit down and have a cuppa while we work out how you can come here and work for me without your son suffering. I like you, Ruby Caselton. From the little I've seen, I know you've got pluck and will fit in just fine.'

*

Eddie gave his wife a broad smile. 'Well done, love, and with your mother doing her bit we will be living in clover, as they say.'

'Only if you stay in work and don't expect the pair of us to keep you in beer,' Milly sneered. 'At my age, I shouldn't have to go to work. My other daughters may have something to say about this.'

'You are welcome to go live with Fanny or Janie, Mum, but we will miss you. However, if you do intend to stay with us, it would be a great help if you could earn a few shillings to contribute to the coffers.'

Milly was silent for a little while as she pondered what her daughter had said. 'Who is going to look after the boy if we're all out grafting? There again, Eddie's sat there as quiet as the grave and not saying where he's going to work next . . .' she added, nodding to where Eddie was mopping up the last of the faggot gravy with a crust of bread. 'Are you going to find a job, or will you be lazing about here and down the pub?' When she didn't get a reply, she kicked him under the table. 'Oi, answer me. An elderly woman and a sickly wife should not be supporting you,' she said.

'Ouch – there was no need for that,' he moaned, rubbing his shin. 'I'll go and find something tomorrow. Is that good enough for you?'

'Make sure you do,' Milly said, reaching for the brown earthenware teapot to top up her cup. She turned her attention to Ruby. 'Tell me, who's going to be looking after the lad with us all out of the house? Once he goes to school we'll have to traipse back and forwards to Slades Green to get him there. I'm not sure it's something I can do at my age.'

Ruby laughed to herself. If she'd been a gambler she'd have laid good money on her mum saying that. However, one gambler in the house was enough. The few times she'd been to a pub with Eddie, she'd seen seedy-looking men sneakily collecting bets from the drinkers and taking them back to their bosses. It was a mug's game and she'd not be part of it. Now they were settled here in Erith, she would do her hardest to make sure Eddie never lost another penny on a bet. 'Stella told me that they're taking men on down the coalyard, and Fraser's have a board hung on the gate of the factory with a list of jobs that need filling. It seems the town is the good place to find work – that's if someone is looking,' she said, giving her husband a hard stare.

'I said I'd look for some work and I mean it,' he growled. 'I'm going out the back to see what needs doing in the garden, and to get away from nagging women.' He left the table. Ruby flinched as she heard the door slam so hard it almost bounced off its hinges.

He'll need to do more than look, she thought to herself. 'As for George here,' she said to Milly, 'he can come with me when I start at the cafe the day after tomorrow; the owner said he can sit in the back room. She likes kids. She even said I can work me hours around dropping him off and collecting him. Once he knows the way down the cinder path he can walk to school on his own. However, tomorrow we're going to ride on a tram to Northumberland Heath. You'd like that, wouldn't you, Georgie boy?'

The lad's eyes lit up. 'Can we go on the upstairs part?'

'If you want,' she smiled, although she wasn't looking forward to climbing to the top, not when the tram moved and electricity was involved – she wasn't sure about these things at all. The thought of the tram made her feel wobbly, but she'd face her fear for the sake of her son – and also to make the journey to see the grave where her daughter lay at rest.

'Come with us, Mum,' she said, wanting more than anything for Milly to approve of what she planned to do.

'If I'm to find myself a job, I'll have to get cracking before I'm turned out with nowhere to live,' Milly sniffed, giving Ruby her best hurt expression.

Ruby took a deep breath as she stood beside George, looking at the imposing gate of Brook Street cemetery. They'd watched as an impressive funeral cortege had entered through the gates. Ruby recognized the horses wearing their black plumes and pulling the carriage she'd seen at the undertakers the previous day. In front she could see Ernie leading the procession at a respectful pace. The carriage was followed by many mourners, all dressed in black. Women were weeping openly in the second carriage that followed the one carrying the coffin. Ruby and George waited until they saw the mourners enter a small chapel in the grounds before taking slow steps in the same direction, passing row upon row of headstones. Ruby had never thought to ask where Miss Allinson, with whom her Sarah shared a grave, would be. Wherever should she start looking? 'We will have to ask somebody for help,' she said to a now pale-faced George. The excitement of travelling on a tram followed by the long walk down Brook Street past children playing in front of two-up, two-down houses had passed. He now looked unsure of his surroundings as he gripped her hand tightly.

'Perhaps we should ask the man with the big stick,' he suggested, pointing to where Ernie stood, having just exited the small chapel. From inside, mourners could be heard singing 'Abide with Me' as the service began.

Ruby smiled at her son's suggestion. 'That is a walking cane,' she explained, pointing to the ornate silver-tipped cane. 'He uses it to guide the mourners from his place at the head of the possession. However, that is a good idea. I recognize the gentleman as someone I spoke to yesterday. Shall we go and speak to him, and perhaps you could look more closely at the horses?'

Ernie, dressed in the formal attire of an undertaker, nodded formally to Ruby before removing his shiny black top hat. 'Fancy seeing you here,' he said politely. 'You are a little late for the service, but I'm sure we can seat you at the back of the chapel if we are quiet.'

Ruby shook her head, looking worried. The last thing she wanted was to have to sit through the funeral service of somebody she didn't even know; she wasn't sure George would like it either, never having attended such a ceremony before. She knew he was already unsettled by being in the cemetery. 'No, thank you, I'm here to pay my respects to my daughter. You may recall you gave me some information yesterday?' While she spoke, George was happily being lifted up by one of Ernie's colleagues so that he could stroke the head of one of the magnificent black horses. 'The problem is, I have no idea where to find the grave. Do you know if there's someone who can help me?'

Ernie scratched his head thoughtfully. 'I have a feeling the stonemason is laying the headstone today, so if you walk down that footpath you will see someone at work. That'll be where you'll find your baby's resting place.'

Ruby thanked the man and took George by the hand, urging him to go with her when he wanted nothing more than to stay and stroke the horses. 'Look, George, there's the river,' she said, bending down beside him, pointing to where the Thames glistened in the sunshine.

'Is that where our house is?' he asked.

'I would think it's further over to the right, behind those big factory buildings. I didn't realize we were so high up here. It's a magnificent view.' And a lovely place to lay loved ones to rest, she thought, as they resumed their slow walk along the narrow pathway that wound between the graves. Around the cemetery there was an expanse of grass that would no doubt one day be filled with line upon line of similar gravestones to the ones they walked past. Occasionally a larger monument was seen. There must be important people interred there, she thought, not wishing to voice her words aloud in case it worried George. Perhaps it had not been very wise to bring him with her, but then, he had asked about the baby, and it was only right for him to understand the truth. She was not a believer in keeping things from a child. 'That looks like the stonemason,' she said, pointing to where a man in a brown apron was instructing two young helpers. A woman stood watching.

Ruby ran a hand across her hot brow. The weather had warmed up a little after the wet days earlier in the month. She hadn't expected to have to walk as far as they had, and her legs felt wobbly and just about able to hold her upright. She leant against a nearby gravestone and took a deep breath.

'I say, are you unwell?' A woman wearing a smart black velvet hat and matching coat, with a fox fur draped elegantly around her shoulders, stopped and took Ruby's arm. 'Are you here for a funeral?' she asked, looking back to where the carriages stood in front of the chapel.

'I just need to catch my breath for a few minutes,' Ruby said as George gave her a worried look.

'We've come to see my baby sister Sarah's grave,' he said solemnly.

The woman looked genuinely sorrowful. 'Oh, my poor dears. Come, let me help you. Where is the grave?'

Ruby took a deep gulp of air. 'George, why not run on ahead?' she said, not wishing him to hear too much of what she was about to say. As he did as he was told, she turned to the woman. 'Thank you for your concern. I'm not sure I should be saying this, but my daughter doesn't have her own grave. I came here to look for her.'

'I don't understand . . .'

'When Sarah was born, she never took a breath. It meant she was taken away from me while I was ill with a fever. Through the kindness of friends . . . I discovered she was buried with another recently deceased person . . .' Her voice faltered.

'My dear, there is no need to say any more. I do understand the situation. I have heard of this happening. You say you have been advised of where she has been interred?'

'Yes, I was told the stonemason is at the grave and about to lay the headstone for a Miss Allinson. I was heading in that direction when I felt a little weak.'

'The deceased Miss Allinson was my younger sister; I am Mrs Grant . . .'

If Ruby had the strength in her legs to turn and run at that point she would have done so. Would she get anyone into trouble by saying what she knew?

'I can see you wish to tell me something. Please don't be afraid,' Mrs Grant said. 'I believe I have already guessed it.'

Ruby took a deep breath and explained about Sarah's death and what she had discovered. She didn't name Ernie, who had been such a comfort to her. 'I just wanted to know where she was resting,' she said. 'I had no wish to bother Miss Allinson's family.'

Mrs Grant took Ruby's elbow and led her to where George was watching the stonemason at work. 'My sister was a keen gardener. She took much comfort from sitting in her rose garden during her final illness. It was my wish that she had roses engraved on her marker. Although the stone is now in place, I required several more engraved upon it. That is why Mr Daniels is working in situ,' she explained.

'It is a fine memorial,' Ruby said, noting that Miss Allinson had only been in her forties when she passed.

'She was never able to enjoy good health,' her sister said, and bowed her head in silent prayer. Ruby followed, lowering her head and thinking of her daughter, who would never enjoy the sun on her face or the perfume of roses. 'If you will excuse me for a moment,' Mrs Grant said, as she left Ruby to go to speak with the stonemason.

Although Ruby could not hear what was being said, she knew that Mrs Grant was giving instructions with a firm hand. The man scratched his head, before nodding and kneeling down close to the stone to continue his work. Mrs Grant returned to her side.

'Have you travelled far?'

'We recently moved to the town. Sarah was born a month early on the day we moved in. I was told Sarah was a pretty baby,' she smiled, thinking fondly of what might have been.

'You never saw her?' Mrs Grant took a dainty white linen handkerchief from her pocket and dabbed at her eyes.

'No, I had a fever and was poorly for several weeks. By the time I was in a fit state to know what had happened, and to think clearly again, it was as if the world had moved on and I was expected to forget about her – I couldn't,' she added, with a tremor in her voice.

'I admire you for looking for your daughter, and for having such a handsome son,' Mrs Grant said, as they looked to where George had wandered away from watching the stonemason. He was now reading the words from a nearby marble memorial, his lips moving to form words as a quizzical look crossed his face. Running back to Ruby's side, he looked shyly at Mrs Grant before speaking to his mother.

'What does "in God's care" mean?' he asked. 'I have read it in three different places.'

Ruby started to speak but faltered. How did you explain death to a child? she wondered.

'It means that God is looking after us, and we can rest happy in the knowledge he is looking over us,' Mrs Grant smiled. 'You can read words very well. Would you like to read something to me?'

George nodded his head as she held out her hand and took him closer to the headstone. The stonemason stood back from his work as he wiped his hands on a cloth, allowing George to kneel down close to the bottom corner of the headstone. 'There's a little flower,' he said.

'It is a rosebud,' Mrs Grant said. 'When a rosebud grows it opens into a rose,' she explained, running her fingers over the intricate roses freshly chiselled into the top of the stone. 'Sometimes a bud never develops into a full-grown rose, but it is just as special. Can you read the words?'

George ran his little fingers over the five letters, copying how Mrs Grant had touched the stone. 'Sarah, it says Sarah,' he grinned as he recognized the word. 'That is my sister's name.'

'Clever boy,' she smiled, patting him on the head.

Ruby couldn't speak. The kindness of this woman she'd just met astounded her. 'I don't know how to thank you,' she said, fighting hard not to cry as she didn't wish to alarm George. 'You must let me contribute to the cost of this work,' she added, wondering if her meagre savings would cover the work of the skilled tradesman.

'Nonsense,' Mrs Grant said, waving away Ruby's offer. 'I know my sister would have been delighted to know she shared her eternal resting place with a baby. When she had better health, she would visit the village school and talk to the children about flowers and their names. She never married, but would have made a wonderful mother. What might have been?' she sighed, and they all stood looking at the grave in silence for a few moments. 'Now, I wish you to take my card, as I would like to hear about how this young man progresses with his lessons. I take it you attend classes?'

'He starts school the week after next. We have been fortunate to place him into a school that comes highly recommended by my neighbours. I have worked with him on his numbers and letters and, as you can see, he is able to form words,' Ruby said proudly.

'Most commendable.' Mrs Grant opened a small bag that hung from her arm, and pulled out a white card. 'Here is my address. My husband is one of the managers at the Vickers works.' She pointed towards one of the factories close to the river. 'Now, you may have other plans for the boy, but when he is of an age to be thinking of work, I would like him to meet my husband and consider an apprenticeship. Smart lads are always required, and he would have a bright future with the company.'

Ruby took the card and looked at the address. Avenue Road: she thought she recognized the name. Stella would be able to tell her where it was. 'I don't know what to say; we only met a little while ago. Why would you make such a generous offer?'

Mrs Grant nodded towards the grave. 'You could say we are almost family,' she smiled. 'Now, I must be on my way. I can see my chauffeur at the gates, and he seems to be agitated. No doubt he is wanting his meal.' With a word to the stonemason to send on his bill, she bid them good day and left Ruby wondering about the generosity and kindness of strangers.

'May I follow Mrs Grant and look at her motorcar?' George asked, hopping up and down on one foot in excitement.

'I don't see why not – but be careful not to go near the vehicle if it is moving, or to step into the road. I couldn't bear to bury another child,' she said to thin air, as her son was already racing to catch up with Mrs Grant.

Ruby went to the graveside, nodding goodbye to the mason as he loaded his equipment and headed off. She knelt down, reaching out to touch the delicately carved rosebud and the word Sarah. 'This is the first time I've been alone with you, my darling. I want to say how much I love you. You may not be here in body, but your spirit will remain in my heart as long as I live. If only God had been more lenient and let you live. Though I've never been a big believer. Why would there be so much heartbreak in the world if there was truly a God who could make things better? I did ask a man of the cloth why God could be so wicked; it was after I'd been sent to church by your nanny to pray for my dad. I could only have been as old as your brother, George, and I couldn't understand why I'd never had a daddy like my friends. The vicar seemed angry that I needed to ask, telling me it was man who caused problems, not God. I knew not to argue with him, even at that age; instead I made excuses not to go to Sunday school. However, if there is a God, I hope that one day he grants my wish to see you once more. Until then, you have Miss Allinson to keep you company, and I will visit as often as I can,' she whispered, kissing the fingers of her left hand and placing them onto her daughter's name.

'I promise to come with you as well,' a little voice chirped up close behind her, causing Ruby to jump.

'Why, George! I thought you'd gone to see the motorcar?'

'It was already driving away as I reached the gates, but Mrs Grant and the driver both waved to me. She's a nice lady, isn't she, Mum?'

'Very nice indeed. I'm sure we'll meet her again one day. I intend to write a letter to thank her for her kindness.'

'May I do the same?' George asked. 'If you write down the words for me to copy, that is. I don't want her to think I don't know all my letters.'

Ruby pulled her son close and gave him the biggest hug, wishing she had two children in her arms. 'I think that's an admirable idea. We can do that as soon as we get home. There may even be time to walk up to her house and place it through the letter box.'

As she got to her feet, taking George's hand in hers and giving it a squeeze, they both turned to look back at the grave. 'Mummy, do you think you'll have any more babies? Mrs Green has three, but they are all grown up.'

'We shall have to wait and see what happens,' she smiled. George had such an enquiring mind.

'If you have a baby girl, we can call it Sarah again,' he said.

Ruby froze. She knew it was common practice for parents to use the same name if they lost a child; but for her, Sarah was a special name, and she didn't feel she could ever use it again. 'I'm not so sure about that, George. I'd quite like to choose another name if it were to happen,' she told him gently.

'Then when I'm grown up and marry, I shall call my baby Sarah,' he said.

Ruby chuckled. 'Don't wish your life away, George,

61

whatever you do. Life is too short for that. First you need to enjoy being a little boy who lives in a nice house and will go to a very nice school. You have a mummy and daddy, and a nanny, who love you very much.'

'And a sister,' George said, looking back over his shoulder as they walked away from the grave.

4

'My, I never thought when I took you on that you'd be such a hard worker,' Marge Dobkins said, as she gazed at the stack of clean plates and the mugs that hung from hooks at the back of the serving counter. 'Of course, I could tell you were a grafter, but it's only been two weeks and you've transformed the place. Not that it was ever dirty, but . . . Oh, you know what I mean,' she laughed, slapping Ruby on the back so hard she stumbled forward and put her hands out to stop herself crashing into the counter.

'It's a pleasure. I love my job. I've met more locals here than I ever would staying at home or taking on a cleaning job.' She didn't add that she liked to be seen to be working when there weren't many customers in the cafe, just in case Marge decided to cut her hours. Ruby had watched the jovial woman closely, and it seemed she didn't miss a trick when it came to cutting corners and saving a few bob.

'Well, my regulars have taken to you and no mistake. I always say having a welcoming smile costs nothing and warms the cockles of the heart on a miserable day.'

Ruby laughed. 'In the days I've been working here the weather's been good, so perhaps that's what has cheered them up.'

'With a bit of luck it will rain tomorrow and we'll be busy most of the day. I dare you to keep up with the washing-up then,' Marge said, roaring with laughter again at the look on Ruby's face.

'Why would you wish for rain? Haven't we had enough these past few months? I've never known such a miserable summer.'

Marge tapped the side of her nose as if imparting some important secret. 'You watch them come rushing in to get out of the rain. I sell more tea and buns, as well as cups of Bovril, to people who come in to shelter from the weather than I do some dinnertimes.'

'In that case, we must pray for rain,' Ruby chuckled. 'As long as it isn't on wash day.'

'Ah, about Monday. Is there any chance your mother could help you out with the washing? It's just that my old man has had another of his queer turns, and he's been told by the doctor to stay in bed for the next week. I'm going to have to look after the other place – which means you'll be on your own here, and I need you to work on Monday as well. Is that a problem? Anyroad, I'll leave you to crack on and you can tell me before we lock up later. All right?'

Ruby nodded and returned to drying the last of the crockery, stacking it as she went. Of course, she could do with the money, if only to tuck it away in her savings tin hidden at the back of the pantry, ready for a rainy day. She'd not had to dip into the tin once to pay the rent since working here because, as good as his word, Eddie had picked up a few shifts down at the coalyard, with the promise of more once the colder months crept in. Milly too had found herself a few hours cleaning each day in the Prince of Wales Hotel, only a five-minute walk from their home. With luck, they'd soon have enough put by for more furniture and some home comforts. They had use of the pieces left by the previous tenant, but Ruby had a fancy to have her own bits and pieces around her so she felt more settled – not that she had any thoughts of moving away from Alexandra Road. If she had her way, she'd one day purchase the house from Cedric and have, for the first time in her life, a security she'd never known before. If she envied her two older sisters anything, it was that their husbands had invested wisely and now owned their homes. While living in rented rooms in Woolwich she had dreamt of being like her sisters – a property owner. At the time, she'd scoffed at her own dreams, but held them close to her heart in the hope that one day . . . If she shared her dream with her husband, she knew Eddie would say she was barmy. He probably wasn't even interested in owning their own home. But just perhaps, with three adults working, it could be done. Stella had told her how some of the sixty-plus terraced homes that ran each side of Alexandra Road were already sold to families, while others remained in the ownership of the family of builders who'd created the rows of bay-fronted homes. It was one of these builders who had passed a house to Cedric to clear his gambling debts. Ruby had never been so thankful to be able to rent number thirteen.

When the time came to lock up the cafe and head for

home, Ruby turned to Marge. 'I'd like to work on Monday. I'll do the laundry on Sunday.'

Marge enveloped Ruby in her chubby arms and thanked her. 'Mind you, I'd think twice about doing your washing on the Lord's day. You could be bringing trouble down on your head.'

'I'll be in more trouble if my husband doesn't have any clean undergarments,' she grinned. 'The Lord I can deal with, but Eddie's another kettle of fish.'

'Be off with you,' Marge guffawed, nudging Ruby in the ribs. 'It would take a braver woman than me to hang out my washing on a Sunday. What are your neighbours like – would they approve?'

Ruby shrugged her shoulders. 'I can't say I've met them. I know there's an old lady on one side; she seems to live on her own. I've only seen her when she twitched her net curtains to watch our George kick a ball about in the road. I waved in a friendly way, but she straightened her curtains and disappeared. Whether she approved of that or not, I don't know. On the other side there are a couple with two older children. I would think they are past the age of fourteen, so must work somewhere. They seemed friendly enough when I saw them at their gate one morning leaving for work, although they were a little aloof. I'll get up extra early tomorrow and have the washing on the line, then I'll disappear indoors. If my neighbours can't see me to speak to, they can't complain.' Ruby grinned, kissing Marge on the cheek and heading for home. She nodded to customers she recognized as she headed down the high street and into Manor Road.

The pay packet Marge had handed to her weighed

heavy in her pocket. Hopefully the extra hours she'd worked this week would show in the envelope and it wasn't just full of farthings and halfpennies taken from the jar left on the counter for tips. She might just have enough to pay off the splendid sideboard she'd placed a deposit on while browsing last week in Mitchell's second-hand furniture emporium. To her eyes it looked almost new, and it would fit perfectly in the front room, with its four cupboard doors and a mirrored back. She'd soon have the splendid mahogany cabinet shining in the sun that came through the bay window.

With a smile on her face, she entered the front door of number thirteen – then froze on the spot as she heard the hullabaloo coming from her kitchen.

'Drunk at this time of the day. You should be ashamed of yourself!'

'Shut up, old woman! I'm head of this household and I can drink whenever I wish,' Eddie bawled back, as suddenly furniture went crashing to the ground. Her husband swore loudly.

'Mummy?' George cried softly from the top of the staircase, which was situated between the front room and living room. 'Make them stop,' he cried, holding his hands to his ears.

Ruby held her arms out, and he ran down the steep stairs and into her embrace. 'Sshh, my love; I'm sure this is nothing to worry about,' she said, although she knew that wasn't true. When Eddie and her mum started to row like this, nine times out of ten it would end in tears. 'I tell you what,' she said, delving into her shopping bag, which had been dropped on the floor when she spotted

George so distressed. 'Why don't you take these pies over the road to Stella? Tell her Mummy brought them home from work, and would she warm one for your tea?' She wiped his eyes with the hem of the apron she still wore under her unbuttoned coat, and kissed his cheek. 'You are not to worry, do you hear me?'

'Can I tell Aunty Stella why I've been crying?' he hiccupped.

'If she asks, but try to put a happy smile on your face and enjoy your tea,' she said, hoping that Stella and her boys didn't come rushing over the road to get involved. If there had been time she'd have penned a few words on a scrap of paper, but she wanted George out of the house before the row started up again. She trusted Stella would cotton on to what had happened, as she was aware from chatting to Ruby that both Eddie and Milly had volatile tempers. She watched as George crossed the road and was let into her friend's house.

Closing the front door, Ruby took a deep breath before turning and marching through into the living room. Placing her hands on her hips, she glared at her husband, who was slumped in a wooden chair, and her mum, who she could see through the open door into the kitchen. Milly was banging about as she wiped a large pan and slammed it onto the wooden draining board. She seemed to be brewing for another argument, and had just opened her mouth to call out when she saw Ruby standing there. 'Oh, you're home then? You might want to sort out this useless lump of lard you call your husband,' she glared at Eddie, who pointed an angry finger in her direction.

'Tell her to mind her own business! If she don't like

what I do, she can sling her bloody hook,' he said, reaching to the floor and picking up a small bottle of beer, then throwing it back down when he noticed it was empty.

Ruby glared at Eddie. 'Pray tell me what you've done that has caused this row? I've had to send your son over the road as he was so upset. You should think about him once in a while, Eddie.'

'Yes, he should,' Milly butted in. 'I've told him as much . . .'

'And you're just as bad, so please don't give us your views,' Ruby spat back. 'Neither of you gave him a thought when you started fighting like cat and dog. Now, are you going to tell me what this is all about?' She turned again to a belligerent Eddie.

'He's lost his job, that's what he's done,' Milly said, giving Eddie a smirk that said "I told you I'd tell on you".

'Oh, Eddie.' Ruby all but fell into another of the old wooden seats, set around a scrubbed wooden table they used to prepare and eat their meals. 'Whatever have you done now?' she asked, placing her head into her hands. 'I thought for once we were set up, with us all bringing a bit of money into the house. With you doing shifts down the coalyard, and being promised more as winter came in, I thought we'd be all right this time,' she said, her words catching in her throat as she did her best not to cry. Nothing ever came of tears, and she needed to keep her wits about her.

'It wasn't my fault,' he shrugged. 'I was defending myself.'

'He was caught thieving,' Milly gloated.

'They can't prove it. I was set up.' He sneered at Milly.

'You can't accuse me of something you were told in the Prince of Wales.'

Milly shrugged her shoulders. 'I wasn't told about it. I overheard two foremen going on. Seems you've been caught out pinching coal and flogging it off cheap. There was also something about you fiddling the tally book you carried with you when they sent you off on a delivery round.'

'That's a lie,' Eddie slurred, raising his fist at Milly as he started to get up out of his seat.

'Did you see that?' Milly shrieked as she backed away.

'For heaven's sake, will the pair of you calm down?' Ruby demanded, grabbing Eddie's sleeve and pulling him back into his seat. 'You're not going anywhere until I've heard everything there is to know,' she scolded him. 'And if you are going to stand there like that, Mum, you can at least put the kettle on. Some of us have been working today and have mouths as dry as the bottom of a budgie's cage. So, this happened today, did it?'

Eddie stayed quiet.

'Last Saturday,' Milly called, from where she was carefully measuring tea leaves into the pot. 'I only found out today, otherwise I'd have tackled him sooner, the lazy so and so.'

'Mum,' Ruby warned, before all hell kicked off again. 'Have you found another job yet, Eddie?'

'Not unless it's in the bottom of a pint pot,' Milly called.

'I'll swing for her in a minute if she doesn't shut her trap,' Eddie growled.

'You can stop talking about my mother liked that as well, Eddie Caselton,' Ruby said, looking stern. 'Have you found another job yet?' she repeated.

'I'm not likely to, what with people like her spreading rumours,' he huffed.

'Oh, come off it. Erith is a large town. I wouldn't think you getting the sack is known by every person who lives here, let alone every business owner. You need to pick yourself up, get out there and find yourself something else.'

'I doubt anyone else would have me, around here. It's time to pack up our bags and leave,' he answered, without meeting her eyes. He knew his wife's views on staying put in Erith.

'Oh, for heaven's sake. I'm tired, my feet ache and I'm hungry. I don't expect to come home after a hard day's graft and have to put up with a drunk husband, an argumentative mother, and no food on the table. Sort yourselves out. I'm going over the road to have a cup of tea with Stella and collect our son. I'll be back in an hour and by then I want you to have a smile on your face, Mother – and you to have sobered up, and have a few positive thoughts in your head about finding another job, Eddie. We are not moving, have I made that clear? If you want to leave Erith, you can pack your bag and leave right now. But you will be on your own,' Ruby said angrily, before walking out of number thirteen and slamming the door behind her.

Stella topped up Ruby's empty cup with hot tea while giving her a sympathetic smile. The younger woman had poured her heart out as Stella had sat and listened without speaking.

71

'Blimey, you don't half have to put up with a lot. I'd have kicked him up the backside by now and shown him the door. But then, when you love someone it's a bit different, I suppose.'

Ruby sniffed. 'Love – what's that when it's at home? The Eddie I married has long disappeared.'

'I'm sorry to hear that. Me and my old man, well, I'm as happy as the day we met. I suppose not many can say that. You'll just have to find your happiness elsewhere,' Stella commiserated.

Ruby was shocked. 'You mean, carry on with another man? I couldn't do that. I took my vows seriously, even if Eddie didn't.'

Stella slapped a hand to her mouth. 'Gawd, love, I didn't mean carry on with another bloke. I meant . . . well, find interests outside the home. You could go to church. I hear they have many interests for women.'

Ruby snorted with laughter. 'I'm not one for church-going, but I agree I have to get myself out the house and away from Eddie and my miserable mother. I suppose me and George could take some trips on the tram. Visit new places and get some sun on our faces. Speaking of my lad, where is he?'

'He's out the back with my boys. They're teaching him how to play cricket. I need to call them in as their grub's ready. I've warmed up that pie you sent George over with, and he can have it with some mashed potato I prepared for their tea. They're having leftover rabbit stew from yesterday.'

'Cheers, Stella, he loves being with your boys. I'd best get back home and see what's happening over there.'

'Don't you worry about George, he's always welcome

over here. He adores my sons and having a little lad about the house makes me feel quite broody, even at my age. I'll have one of them bring him over later.'

'What would I do without you, Stella? You're a real diamond. I'm hoping Eddie has put some thoughts to finding another job. Either that or he's packed his bag and sodded off. I don't much care. Since losing my Sarah, I just want peace and quiet and a decent roof over my head. I was just about feeling at peace since finding her grave, and now all this with my Eddie . . . It feels as though someone up there's got it in for me.'

Stella, who knew all about Ruby's trip to the cemetery, nodded in agreement. 'It might feel like it at the moment, but stay strong and things can only get better. I'll ask the boys if they've heard of any jobs going begging. You never know – he could be back in work by Monday. Look, why don't you make him wait a little longer. Stay and have some grub with us, eh?'

'No, ta, it's enough that you can look after George for me. I don't want to put upon you any more than I have already.'

'Anytime at all. You don't have to thank me. That's what friends are for. And I hope Eddie has had time to think about what you've said to him.'

'I hope so, too.' Ruby gave her friend a quick peck on the cheek and prepared herself to face whatever was going on over the road.

Letting herself back into number thirteen, she found Milly sitting alone in the front room. 'I've tidied up out there. I got rid of the empty bottle, so there's no need to check,' her mother said in a tight voice.

Ruby slumped down in the other armchair. 'Where is Eddie?' she asked, wondering whether he had indeed packed his bags and gone. The thought made her feel sad. Perhaps deep down she still loved him, but that was of no use when he treated her so badly and seemed uninterested in being a father to George or a provider for the family.

'He's out the back, digging over the garden. After you left, he muttered something about putting in some vegetables and disappeared out the back door.'

Ruby looked at her mother and they both burst out laughing. 'Why, Eddie wouldn't know one end of a potato from the other,' she said, as tears of laughter ran down her cheeks.

'I have an idea he just wanted to get out of my way, and he knew that if he went out the front door, I'd think he was off to the boozer and go after him. The back door was the only way of escape for him.'

Despite her tiredness and anger, Ruby had to laugh at the thought of Eddie messing with the garden. The previous owner had made a job of laying out rows for a vegetable garden and another for flowers, but from what she could tell it hadn't had much attention for a while. She'd thought it would be good to have a go herself, but hadn't yet found the time. A shed at the end of the long, thin garden still housed a few garden tools that had been left behind in the man's haste to leave the property. 'I'd best go down and see what he's up to,' she said with a sigh. 'Had you done anything for our tea yet?'

'I'd started some liver and onions before he kicked off. It won't take long to finish. Do you want a cup of tea first?'

'No, ta, I'm swimming in the stuff. I had a couple of cups over at Stella's house. I'll go and see him first.' Ruby heaved herself out of the chair, wishing she could just settle back and have a snooze.

'Hello, love. I thought it was about time I made a start out here,' Eddie said, not making eye contact with Ruby.

'A bit pointless if you want us to move away, isn't it?' She sat down on an upturned wooden box and made a show of straightening the skirts of her shabby navy-blue work dress. The hem was frayed from dragging on the ground; it had been too long when she picked it up cheap on the second-hand stall up Woolwich market before they moved away. There'd never been time to take it up and then, as her tummy grew, there'd been no real need. Perhaps she could use some of her savings to pick up another dress. She'd seen a shop that sold cast-offs; a dress from there would do her for work, once she'd given it a wash.

'Perhaps I was a bit hasty,' Eddie said.

Ruby noticed how his hands shook as he bent over the spade and guided it into the hard earth with his foot. 'Maybe you were, but think how I felt when I saw you the worse for drink. You still look rough now. It's not good for you, Eddie. We've not long buried our daughter. I don't want to be standing over your grave in my widow's weeds. We could have a good life here, if you just knuckled down and thought of us rather than where the next drink's coming from.'

'I still say it wasn't my fault I lost the job,' he muttered.

'I was miserable and wanted to drown my sorrows. What else could I do?'

'You could have come home and talked it over with me. Am I that bad a wife, that you can't speak to me and share your problems?'

Eddie lifted his head and looked at Ruby. He could see her eyes brimming with tears, just as he felt his were. 'I'm just a silly old bugger. I don't know why you put up with me,' he said, lowering his head.

'Less of the old,' Ruby smiled, attempting to lighten the atmosphere. 'Just remember, I'm your wife – we should be able to face anything together. I know me mum can be a pain in the backside, but if we'd chatted through this the day you lost your job . . . why, we could have done something without her finding out and having her two penn'orth.'

'I don't deserve you, Ruby Caselton,' Eddie said. 'What you said to me about leaving you really hit home. I knew you meant what you said, and I could so easily have lost me family. Not only will I get looking for a job first thing on Monday, but I promise to dig over this garden tomorrow and have it ready to grow you some beautiful flowers.'

Ruby reached out and took his hand. There must be something behind the way he drank, and it worried her so. He needed to knock it on the head, and she was determined to help him do just that. 'If you don't mind, I need to hang the washing out tomorrow, as I'm going in to work on Monday. I don't want dirt flying over the sheets.'

Eddie slung his arm over her shoulders and they started to walk to the back door when the head of their elderly neighbour popped up from the other side of the fence.

'Tomorrow is a day of rest, when we read our bible and attend church. No decent woman hangs out her washing on the Sabbath,' she said in a stern voice. 'You, young woman, have a lot to learn if you wish to live in a respectable road like this.'

Ruby sighed and muttered under her breath before smiling to her neighbour. 'Good evening, Miss Hunter. We didn't see you there. Do you often eavesdrop on private conversations?'

'I was merely in my garden, Mrs Caselton. If you and your drunken husband must insist on discussing your lives so loudly, then you must expect others to comment.'

Ruby shrugged off Eddie's arm and nodded to him to go indoors. He didn't need a second bidding. Two women falling out was of no interest to him. 'Miss Hunter, making oneself known is more neighbourly than hiding and listening to a husband and wife's conversation.'

The older woman sniffed her disapproval. 'The man who lived in this house before you was a true gentleman. He never had children who played like ragamuffins in the street, he never argued and fell about drunk, or dragged sacks of coal down the back pathway and left behind a mess. As for wishing to hang out washing on a Sunday, I fear the Reverend Grayson will have something to say about this when he is informed.'

Ruby walked to the side of her garden, where a short wooden fence and bushes separated number thirteen from number fifteen. She'd yet to be formally introduced to her neighbour, and had given up trying after being rebuked by the woman. This time, she intended to try to be friendly, although it was proving difficult. 'I have no idea who the

Reverend Grayson is, but if he wishes to speak to me about my laundry, he is more than welcome. Where will I find him?' she smiled graciously, while counting to ten under her breath.

Miss Hunter gave Ruby a steely look. 'Why, in church, of course. You do know where our churches are in Erith?'

Ruby bit her lip. 'I'm new to the area. I have a home to sort out, a child, and a job to do each day. I've also been poorly as I lost my baby. I have yet to find time for pursuits outside of my family. If you had heard all of my private discussion with my husband you would know that I am not able to do my washing on Monday as I need to be working.' Even more so now Eddie doesn't have a job, she thought to herself.

'Could your mother not do your washing, so you do not offend the Lord?'

'My mother is a busy woman. She works in the Prince of Wales Hotel. I'm surprised you don't know this,' Ruby explained, wishing she could add, *you nosy old witch.*

'I have never entered a public house,' Miss Hunter sniffed, before adding: 'You will keep your child under control?'

'My son is a good boy. I wish you would keep your views to yourself. Why is it I feel as though you've been watching my family?' Ruby asked as she started to shake with anger. 'For a God-fearing church-goer you certainly seem to like saying horrid things about people you hardly know.'

'It is my Christian duty to speak as I see things. You'd do well to sort out that husband of yours. I had to walk the length of the back pathway collecting the coal he dropped and had not cleared up.'

Ruby was confused. What was the woman talking about? 'Where is this coal you collected?'

'I placed it in my coal shed.'

Ruby laughed out loud. 'Was that your Christian duty, too? I promise you, I will speak to my husband. However, I will do it in the privacy of my home, and if he is upset by what you have told me I'm sure he will be knocking on your front door very soon.'

Miss Hunter gasped, reaching for the cross she was wearing on a chain at her throat, before hurrying into her house.

Ruby knew she'd gone too far, but if that's what it took to stop the prying old witch, then so be it. She had enough problems already without adding a difficult neighbour to the list.

Shaking her head as she walked towards the house, Ruby stopped at the door that opened into the coal shed, next to the outside lavatory. Both were built into the back of the house, which had fascinated Ruby when they first moved in. She was astonished to see such pristine facilities, having always shared an outside lav with others in the building where they'd had rooms. To Ruby, this was luxury. Also, having their own coal hole, as Milly called it, meant no one would pinch what coal they could afford to buy. Ruby knew before too long she'd have to dip into her savings to stock up on fuel for the winter. After pulling open the door to look inside, she stepped back in shock. The coal shed was full to the brim. So that old bat had been speaking the truth about Eddie dragging bags of coal down the back pathway.

Ruby's spirits dropped as she realized that Eddie must

have pinched it from the coalyard before he was given the sack. She was married to a liar and a thief. Slamming the door shut, she stormed indoors. If it took every penny of the money she had hidden away at the back of the stone pantry, she would pay back the coalyard owner and beg for his forgiveness. She'd not have anyone label her family as thieves, although in her heart of hearts she knew Eddie had indeed been stealing.

Storming into the house, Ruby shoved past her mother and opened the door of the pantry. Pushing aside packets and a few cans, she grabbed the small battered tin where she kept her secret savings. Pulling off the tight lid, she cried out in shock. There were only a few coins left.

'Ruby, love . . .' Milly started to say, as she saw her daughter's distressed face, 'don't get too upset.'

'What do you mean, don't get upset? Where's the bloody money?'

'It's not what it seems, love.' Milly tried to hold on to her daughter. 'I took most of it . . .'

Ruby froze to the spot. There she was thinking Eddie had pinched her money, and all along it was her mother. 'I don't understand – why would you take the savings? I thought I was the only one that knew there was money here. Why, Mum, why did you steal it all?'

Milly shook her head, her eyes full of sadness. 'I'm upset that you think I'd do such a thing, when all along I've been doing what's best for this family.'

'I think you'd better explain,' Ruby said. 'Only hours ago I was telling Eddie to leave the house, but maybe I should have told you to pack your bags and go. Stealing from your own family – is there anything worse?' she said bitterly.

'I want you to come and sit down and listen to me,' Milly said. 'If after what you hear you still want me to leave home, then I will. No doubt one of your sisters will put me up.'

'I doubt it, when they know what's happened,' Ruby snarled; but she did follow Milly into the living room and sat at the table opposite her mum, placing the empty tin between them. 'Now, tell me what happened – and it'd better be good.'

'It was a couple of weeks ago. I got in a bit early and found Eddie snooping about. He was the worse for drink and digging about in the pantry. I thought he was looking for some grub and told him I'd cook something, as it was nearly teatime and you'd all soon be home and hungry. He didn't expect to hear me, and almost jumped out of his skin and dropped the tin. He stuffed a couple of notes in his pocket and chucked the tin back into the pantry. I guessed he was up to no good – and when I took a look at the tin, I recognized it as being your dad's tobacco tin I gave you when you was a kiddie. You always used it to keep your precious bits and pieces; a button, a shiny piece of glass, even the odd coin. I guessed you'd been using it to hide away your savings. I tackled Eddie, but he denied taking anything that wasn't his. I didn't know what to do. I didn't want to tell you, as you'd brightened up such a lot since being poorly. Instead I put what money I had in the tin and hoped it was enough. To be on the safe side, I did a couple of cleaning shifts in the pub while you was at work. I pawned the ring your dad gave me and put some of the money in there. I kept checking the tin, and until today, the money had stayed in the tin. God knows why he tried to pinch it now, while I was in the house and you was out in the garden. Any one of us could've caught him – and I did just now. So I've taken the money and hidden it.'

'I'll bloody kill him!' Ruby cried as she ran to the bottom of the stairs. 'Eddie, if you're up there, come down right now. We need to have a word!' She heard him shuffling about in the bedroom and yelled again. 'I said, get down here – now!' Returning to the table she sat down and buried her head in her hands. Too angry to weep, she heaved a big sigh. 'I'm sorry, Mum, I shouldn't have blamed you.'

'You wasn't to know, love,' Milly said as Eddie came downstairs, placing a bundle of clothes on the floor in the hall. 'I assume you're taking the coward's way out,' she snarled at her son-in-law.

Eddie slunk into the room and sat down in the chair Ruby had pulled out from the table. 'Were you really going to leave without saying goodbye to me or your son? I assume your sudden change of heart is because of what you heard our neighbour say? Why did you have to steal? You had a decent job, and they might even have taken you on full-time. Not only have you brought shame on this family, but you've also blackened your name for any future employment in the town.'

'I was doing it for the family,' he mumbled. 'At least you'll all keep warm during the winter.'

'But why, Eddie? You were earning and could have paid for it yourself. I take it all your wages have gone on beer and gambling, so you took to stealing instead?'

Eddie had the shame to nod his head. 'You're better off

without me. I'll tell Cedric that you won't be able to afford the rent on your own and will be out of the house by next week. That will give you time to look for somewhere else to live. It won't be as fancy as this place, as all you'll need is a room for you, your mother, and the nipper,' he said, getting to his feet.

'Oh no you don't, Eddie Caselton,' Ruby said, barring his way. 'You don't drop your family in all this mess and then walk away. I have enough money to pay the rent from what I brought home in my pay packet . . .'

'And I've got the rest of the money I hid so you didn't get your filthy hands on it,' Milly spat at him.

Eddie looked down at his feet.

'Oh no, Eddie, you haven't . . .' Ruby cried, rushing to where she had left her bag on the floor. Pulling out her purse, she discovered the pay packet missing. 'How could you?' she sobbed.

'I've got my own debts to pay, you've got no idea . . .' he said, looking sad.

'Don't take any notice of him,' Milly shouted.

'And as the head of this household, I say what happens to the money,' he snapped, digging deep for some bravery, although he still could not meet Ruby's eyes or tell her the truth. He couldn't do that to her.

Milly swore loudly and picked up the brown earthen-ware teapot, which was sitting in the middle of the table among dirty cups and saucers. 'I used to think you was a decent sort, but now I know I was wrong. No one does this to a daughter of mine,' she shouted before swinging the teapot high and bringing it down on the side of his head. With a grunt, Eddie slumped into the chair before rolling onto the floor, his head covered in cold tea stained with blood. Around him, chunks of broken teapot were scattered on Ruby's best rag rug.

'Oh, God – I think I've killed him!' Milly cried, before falling into a dead faint beside her son-in-law.

5

Ruby froze, staring down at her mother and husband lying on the floor, struggling to absorb what had just happened. 'Mum? Eddie?' she whispered, putting her hands to her face to hide the scene in front of her. She would have to do something – but what? Before she could take a step towards them there was a loud banging on the front door, followed by George shouting through the letter box for his mum to let him in.

Closing the door to the living room, she hurried along the hall and pulled open the front door. George was excitedly jumping up and down. Standing behind him were two of Stella's sons.

Frank looked at Ruby's stricken face as she glanced back over her shoulder. 'Donald, why don't you take George into the front room for a little while?' he said, giving him a wink. 'I think Mrs Caselton needs my help.'

Donald looked between his brother and Ruby, and could see at once that something was amiss. 'Come on, Georgie boy, let's do some more drawing,' he said, holding out the paper and pencils he'd brought with him.

'Can I, Mummy?'

'Of course, love. You run along while I speak to Frank.'

'What's wrong, Ruby? You look as though you've seen a ghost,' Frank said, reaching for her elbow and moving her away from the front room while the two boys settled themselves on the floor, laying out sheets of paper between them. 'They'll be fine. Dad brought home a pile of paper he was given down at the dock. A packing case had split open on its way to the printer's and Dad knew the kids would like it for drawing paper. There's a lot more over at home, if Georgie wants it. Mum said to check with you first . . .' He watched Ruby closely. She looked a million miles away as she gazed into the distance. 'Ruby?'

'Oh, yes, that's very kind. I'll thank her when I next see her,' she replied, again glancing over her shoulder.

'What's going on, Ruby? Has something happened?'

Ruby nodded her head as she started to cry silently. 'I think my mum's killed Eddie, then she dropped down dead.'

Frank started to laugh, then realized Ruby wasn't joking. 'You're not kidding me – are you?'

'No,' she replied, pushing open the living room door. 'It had only just happened when you knocked. Please, can you help them?'

Frank rushed to where Milly lay and bent down beside her. 'Mrs Tomkins? Can you hear me?' he asked as he put his hand to her chest. 'Does she have a bad heart? I recall her mentioning it to Mum.'

'She has flutters sometimes, but the doctor told her it was nothing serious. Can you feel a heartbeat?' Ruby chewed her fingernail anxiously. 'There's so much blood;

they must both be dead. She gave Eddie such a belter with the teapot.'

'Her heartbeat is nice and strong. I think she's just fainted from the shock, but at her age we need to make sure she's all right. Can you get me a cup of water?' He moved over to Eddie, who had started to groan. 'And at least he's not dead, so your mum won't be done for murder.'

'Thank God for that.' Ruby rushed back to kneel beside Milly and place the cup to her lips. 'Here, Mum, take a sip,' she said before Frank pushed her hand away.

'No, not while she's out cold. She could choke. Splash her face – it may help bring her round quicker.'

Ruby nodded and started to pat the cold water around Milly's cheeks. 'Come on, Mum. Let's be having you. There's no point in lying on the hard floor, now, is there?' she chided. 'Wake yourself up and we can have a nice cuppa. I brought some pies and buns home from the cafe. I bet you'd like some of them, wouldn't you?'

Milly fluttered her eyelids and gave Ruby a puzzled look. 'Why am I laying on the floor?'

'You had a bit of a funny turn, Mum. We'll have you on your feet in a tick. Just tell me when you're ready for us to help you up.' She stroked Milly's grey hair back from her face, where it had escaped from a tortoiseshell clip.

'Give me a minute,' Milly muttered, wincing a little. 'My ankle feels funny,' she said. 'Do you think it's broken?'

In spite of the situation, Ruby smiled. She was so relieved her mum wasn't dead, but all the same, she knew how much Milly enjoyed bad health. 'Perhaps we can have the doctor check you over later, if you can't walk on it.'

She carried on chatting to her mum while Frank was seeing to Eddie, who was groaning and starting to swear loudly.

'What the bloody hell happened? Who thumped me?' he asked as he put his hand to his head, looking startled when he saw the blood.

'You're not badly injured, Eddie.' Frank helped him to his feet and back onto the chair he'd vacated suddenly when his mother-in-law walloped him with the teapot.

'What's she doing down there? And why is there all this bloody mess?' Eddie gestured around the chaotic room as Frank took a closer look at the gash on the side of his head.

'Mum fell into a faint, and you tried to catch her but hit your head on the teapot she was holding,' Ruby explained. 'You are a little unsteady on your feet due to the drink. I'm not sure how I'm going to be able to make a brew until I can afford another one,' she added for effect. She knew Eddie wouldn't be interested in what she made the tea in, as long as there was a hot drink on the table with his meals.

Frank looked at her and grinned. He was surprised at Ruby's words, but understood she was defending her mother and putting the blame back on Eddie. From the smell on Eddie's breath and his unsteady movements, he could tell the man had a belly full of booze. What Frank didn't understand was why a decent woman like Ruby Caselton stayed with a bloke like Eddie. He'd spent a good few hours sitting by her bed as she regained her strength after losing the baby, at first reading to her when she was still weak, and then chatting about this and that. He'd found her keen to ask questions when he mentioned his work and his interests. He knew that if he was ever to give in to his mum's insistent nudging and find himself a wife, it would be someone like Ruby Caselton – but that was unlikely to happen. Women like her didn't come around too often. He knew he'd be lucky to find such a person. Until he did find his way in life, he'd be the best friend he could to the woman. She'd not had a good time of late, from what his mum had said, and had been through a lot considering she was a year younger than him. Yes, he'd do his best to make her smile and make her life better. Ruby looked so pretty when she smiled; her eyes lit up, and there was a sparkle about her, he thought to himself.

'Frank?'

He jumped at his name and saw that Ruby was holding out a damp cloth. 'Thanks,' he said as he took the cloth and held it to Eddie's head. 'I was miles away for a minute there.'

'Probably dreaming about your girl,' Ruby said, as she started to clear up the broken crockery.

'You could be right,' he grinned, wishing life were that simple.

'You're up bright and early,' Stella said as Ruby opened the door to her. 'I was going to leave this on the doorstep and pop a note through the letter box to let you know it was here.' She held out a teapot that almost matched the one that had been smashed the night before. 'It's got a small crack in the lid, but you're welcome to have it. I have another and it's no good to anyone sitting in the back of my cupboard. I don't want it back,' she said quickly, knowing that Ruby didn't like charity.

'Come in and I'll put it to good use right now,' Ruby said, as she removed the white apron that all but covered her dress. 'Everyone's still in bed so I had a bit of peace and quiet and I got the washing done early before that nosy old bat from next door stuck her oar in and told me off for hanging washing out on the Sabbath. If she lived my life, she'd really have something to complain about,' she sighed as they went through to the kitchen.

'You have been busy,' Stella said, looking out of the back door to where a line of washing was flapping in the warm breeze. 'How did you manage to do your sheets while the family are still in their beds?'

Ruby chuckled as she put the kettle onto the hob. 'I wondered how I would do it, but last night while mum and Eddie were down here, I shot upstairs and changed the bed sheets. I didn't want them holding up my wash day.' Ruby didn't add that she was glad she had her decent sheets on the line for Stella to see. The ones on their beds had worn that thin she'd cut them down the middle and stitched the sides together, making them last a little longer. It was a trick her mum had taught her years ago when, as she often said, they didn't have a pot to piss in. Ruby grew up knowing how to make the best of something, and that included her few possessions as well as what life had thrown at her. It had only been recently, after losing Sarah, that she'd felt weak and nigh on unable to cope. 'Now, if that miserable old woman next door starts on her moaning again, I'll not care as in another couple of hours everything will be dry and on the clothes airer waiting for me to give it a good iron. Tell me, why is an old woman living in one of these houses on her own?' she asked as she sat opposite Stella at the table.

'Ah, when she moved here it was with her father. Yes, it's hard to believe someone her age still had a living parent three years ago. He was heavily involved with the local Baptist church and Miss Hunter seems to have carried the baton.'

'Blimey,' Ruby laughed. 'Her life must be full of fun. I take it she never married?'

'From what I was told by someone who lives further up the road and went to school with her, she had plenty of admirers as a youngster. At some point she went away to live with an elderly aunt as her companion. She came back to the area to help her father, then they moved into number fifteen when the houses were built. I vaguely recall people going into the house for Bible meetings, and there was many a Sunday evening we could hear hymns being sung to the accompaniment of Miss Hunter playing the piano. These days no one visits the house since he passed away, and Miss Hunter instead visits the Baptist church. I would think she's well into her seventies, so her father must have been close to one hundred years of age when he passed.'

'They sound a barrel of laughs, but each to their own. Goodness knows what they'd have thought of my Eddie rolling home from the pub at all hours the worse for wear. One disapproving neighbour I can handle. Her father as well would have had me turning to the gin.'

'Me and my brood were invited to their prayer meetings, but they soon gave up when I told them we're Roman Catholic.'

'Are you really?'

'No, but a little lie never hurt anyone. I did start receiving flowery cards with verses from the Bible etched on them. I posted them back through their letter box. You'd be best to be civil to the woman rather than make an enemy of her. The people that go to that church can be rather pious and may just make your life uncomfortable.'

'Does she have any friends? It must be awful to get to that age and not be surrounded by people who care.'

Stella shrugged her shoulders. 'She's not one for a cup of tea and a natter, if that's what you mean. Then again, she may be happy doing her Christian duty. As you say, each to their own. Speaking of which, my Frank told me what happened over here last night. I wanted to ask if there's anything I can help with?'

'The loan of your teapot is more than enough. I'm very grateful,' Ruby said, turning away so that Stella didn't see the sadness in her eyes.

'You know you can talk to me and it will go no further. I can tell your Eddie is at the bottom of this.'

Ruby gave a bitter laugh. 'Isn't he always?'

'I'm a patient listener,' Stella said. 'Why don't we fill that teapot and have a good chat?'

Ruby left Stella with her tea and popped out into the back garden to check the washing on the line. It was strung from the back of the house to a pole at the end of the garden. A wooden prop she'd found lying in the grass was ideal for holding up the line halfway down, where it tended to sag under the weight of the washing. She unpegged a couple of items that were already dry and threw them over her shoulder as she checked the rest. Ruby kept the hanging sheets between her and the garden next door, just in case Miss Hunter was already up and about. She didn't feel like a barney this early in the morning. Hurrying back inside, she put the few dry items over a wooden clothes horse she'd found in the cupboard under the stairs. She blessed the day she'd moved to this house, as she'd never in her life had so many pieces of furniture along with bits and bobs for the kitchen. Ruby loved this little house in Erith and could gladly live out her days here. She smiled to herself as she sat back down at the table.

'That's a lovely smile, what put that on your face?'

'I was thinking how I could live out my days here in Alexandra Road. I'll hang on to this house until my dying breath, Eddie or no Eddie.'

'That's fighting talk if ever I heard it,' Stella said as she topped up her cup.

Ruby picked up a teaspoon and stirred the tea thoughtfully. 'At the moment I feel as though I don't know the man I married. Eddie is a bit older than me, and he knew a lot more about life when we got hitched. I was expecting our George when we walked down the aisle. I was forced into marrying him in that sense, but I truly loved him. He courted me, gave me little trinkets and spoke of his dreams for the future. Six years ago, he was a man who other women fluttered their eyelashes at. I was considered a lucky girl. My heart skipped a beat every time he said my name. But the more he worked for Cedric Mulligan, the more he changed.'

Stella, who had been listening without interrupting Ruby, frowned. 'I know that name from somewhere.'

'Eddie fell in with him while we lived in the Woolwich area. He would do odd jobs for the man, and I honestly thought it was all innocent. I had no reason to question my husband at that time. Gradually his drinking became worse, and he didn't always bring money home at the end of the week. From the nice rooms we first rented that I'd tried to make into a lovely home, to others where we had to move at the dead of night before the landlord came knocking. Four times this happened and each time the rooms became fewer and smaller, and we moved closer to the unpleasant side of town. I feared going out on my own with a young child. My mother moved in with us, but for me it was an added burden. By then I knew that not everything Eddie did was above board. He would collect debts that were owed to Cedric. He also got to know the runners in the pubs who took bets on horse races. A few pennies bet on a nag became shillings, and the more money he lost the blacker his moods became. The Eddie you know – it's not the man I first knew. And after last night, I'm at a crossroads in my life.'

Stella could have cried for the young woman opposite her. In the little time she'd known Ruby Caselton, she had found her to be a responsible and intelligent person. Since moving to Alexandra Road, Stella hadn't found a neighbour she felt she could talk to. So when Ruby collapsed at her feet that day, it was as if someone up there had handed her a friend. There was an age difference, so in some ways Ruby was the daughter she'd never had. Add to that, her gorgeous little boy George was almost like a grandson. With three sons, Stella felt at times that she lacked female company. By now she'd hoped her eldest son, Frank, would have been courting, but so far he'd not had a serious lady friend. However, she had noticed the way he watched Ruby and how much time he'd had for her when she was ill. In an ideal world, she could see her Frank and Ruby setting up home at number thirteen. There would be no drunken husband or interfering mother, just Frank, Ruby, a new baby, and young George.

She shook her head to clear her preposterous thoughts. Daydreaming could be dangerous. Instead she would be the best friend she could to Ruby, and at the moment that was clearly what Ruby needed the most. She sipped her tea, then cleared her throat, as what she was about to say made her nervous. 'Ruby, do you think perhaps it would be best if Eddie was no longer in your life?'

Ruby nodded her head in agreement. 'I do. It sounds bad of me to say so, but to be truthful, me, Mum and George could bump along quite happily here on our own. As long as Mum could bring in a bit of money and Marge was able to keep giving me a week's work, we'd be able to keep our heads above water. However, I made my vows in church to love, honour and obey my husband. I may not believe in all that church nonsense, but I do believe there is someone good looking over us, and to break such a promise is a sin.'

'I do agree with you on that,' Stella said, reaching for the teapot to check if she could squeeze out another cup for them both. But Ruby put her hand over her cup, as she was full up. 'I do wonder, though, if it is a sin to move on from a bad marriage, rather than being miserable for the rest of your life? Perhaps you should ask yourself how many days of the week you are truly happy living with Eddie, putting up with his failures and his drunkenness as you do?'

Ruby thought for a moment. 'I'd never really thought about it. Two, possibly three days . . . There again, other weeks, if he's flush with money he'll come home merry, if not drunk.'

'Are you happy to live that way? Can you see a future where you put up with what he has become every single day?'

Ruby looked at her friend with tears in her eyes. 'You've certainly given me food for thought. In a way, I've just got on with things moving here. Apart from losing Sarah, I focused on the house, George's happiness and my job. Eddie has not been a priority. Do you know, in my heart of hearts I've blanked what he has become – but something's got to change, hasn't it?' She ran her fingers through her dark brown hair in frustration.

'Your married life only has to change if you think it should. If you are happy with the way things are, then let sleeping dogs lie. Many women turn a blind eye to what their husbands get up to – that's if they've picked the wrong one.'

A fleeting smile crossed Ruby's face as she thought of the man she'd married. 'Eddie certainly isn't the same as he was six years ago, but you could just as easily say I'm not the same woman. We all change, don't we?'

'I like to think that overall people change for the good, not the bad. Speaking of which, I can hear movement upstairs. Do you want me to stay or go?'

Ruby listened for a moment. 'That's Mum coming down.

I told her to stay in bed to rest after her experience yesterday. She was quite shaken up with what happened.'

Stella greeted Milly as she hobbled into the room. 'Hello, Mrs Tomkins, how are you feeling today? I heard you had a bit of a fall?'

'Bad news travels fast,' Milly grumbled as she checked the teapot, not even noticing it was a replacement for the one broken yesterday. 'If you must know, I'm not feeling so good. I can hardly walk on this leg, and it will probably never be the same again.'

'Oh dear,' Stella said, avoiding looking at Ruby, as she knew she would smile at the woman's dramatic words. 'I'll make a fresh pot, then I'll help you bring in the laundry, Ruby. It's a good drying day.'

'It's unlucky to hang out washing on the Sabbath,' Milly pointed out. 'Something bad will happen, you mark my words.'

'Oh, Mum. It's just one of those old wives' tales. Monday is not convenient for me to do the laundry as I'm working, as well you know. You are getting as bad as her next door, telling me I'll upset God by hanging out my smalls on the Lord's day,' Ruby laughed.

Milly sniffed. 'As you know, the Tomkins don't hold with church and all that, so I can't say what God likes and what he doesn't. All I'm saying is it's unlucky.'

'Didn't you say you married in church, Ruby?' Stella asked, as she returned from putting the kettle on the hob.

'I insisted on it,' Milly butted in, crossing her arms over her chest. 'It is good to have a wedding people can remember, and we had a wonderful do after Ruby and Eddie's nuptials. People still talk about that party.'

'I think Stella meant the church part, Mum.'

'You've got to get married somewhere,' Milly huffed at her daughter. 'What's this got to do with you hanging out your washing on a Sunday? All I said was it shouldn't be done as it's unlucky.'

The two women laughed at Milly's confused look. 'You could always do the washing yourself,' Ruby suggested. 'It would help me a lot if you did. There's a fair amount with four people living in the house.'

'I'd like nothing more than to help out, but with my dodgy ticker and now my bad leg I'm not even sure if I'm up to going back to my bit of a job at the Prince of Wales.'

Ruby felt her heart drop into her boots. 'Please don't say that, Mum. What with Eddie . . .'

'Gone, has he?' Milly's bird-like eyes glistened with joy. 'I thought he might once I'd given him what for.'

'You're jumping the gun, Mum. Eddie is still upstairs in bed, no doubt sleeping off yesterday's booze, along with the crack on the head you gave him with our teapot. I'll be having words with him when he comes down, so would be grateful if you could take George out with you for a little while. I don't want him knowing what his dad's been up to. The lad needs to grow up respecting his elders, rather than seeing their weaknesses. Perhaps a walk down to the riverside to watch the barges? I take it you can manage a short stroll?' Ruby could see Milly thinking about her request. No doubt she'd prefer to stay at home and make her contribution to whatever was said between husband and wife. 'Or, if a walk is too much, you could always start on the garden with a bit of weeding? George could help you.'

Milly could see there was no chance of her staying indoors and blacking her nose. 'If I take it slow, I can reach the river without making myself bad. But if I feel poorly, we will have to turn back.'

'Thank you, Mum. As long as you stay out for an hour, it will give me time to talk to Eddie. Now, do you want a bite to eat for your breakfast?'

Milly nodded. 'Ta, love, then I'll get myself ready and wake the boy at the same time. Are you staying here all day?' she asked Stella, with a disapproving look. Clearly Milly felt that if she could not stay to listen to the conversation Ruby would have with Eddie, then why should a neighbour?

'I'm going to bring in the washing while Ruby gets your breakfast, then I'll be off over home to sort out my lot. Old Miss Hunter won't say anything to me if she sees me taking in the dry sheets. It'll save Ruby getting any grief. In my book she seems to have enough of that at the moment,' Stella said, with a smile that defied Milly to answer back.

Milly huffed as she got to her feet. 'What did I say about doing your laundry on a Sunday? It will bring bad luck, you mark my words.'

Ruby took a deep breath and did her best not to be distracted by Eddie's puppy-dog expression. How many times had she seen that look? This time she would harden her heart, otherwise their lives would continue like this into old age. She didn't want to look back and regret her life, or that of her son. 'Eddie, I can't listen to your excuses any more. Why, only yesterday afternoon you were promising things would be different. I don't know what to believe. I know you are the head of this family and in the eyes of the law I have to take your lead. But I'm not going to, as I want more for my life and that of my – our son. I do want to respect you, Eddie, but it's getting harder and harder. Each time you come home with some cock-and-bull story about having been given the sack from your job, or when you lose what you earned on a horse.'

Eddie had enough shame to look down at the table where they sat. Milly and George had already been gone nearly an hour by the time he finally woke up, and Ruby kept glancing at the clock on the mantelpiece. A wedding present from her two sisters, it was a prized possession and one she'd not taken to pawn when times had been harder than they were at present. She hoped Milly wouldn't rush George back too soon from their walk. Tapping her fingers on the table, she waited for Eddie to speak.

He rubbed his hands over his careworn face and licked his lips, wishing he had a drink in front of him – and he didn't mean tea. He was awash with the stuff, as Ruby kept filling his cup. 'I'm just one of those unlucky chaps who makes mistakes. I don't think I'm made out to do a job where I clock on every day and pick up a pay packet at the end of the week. I like to move about and do bits and pieces for different people.'

'That was all well and good while you didn't have responsibilities. Now you have a wife and a son, and dare I say a mother-in-law too.'

'And don't I know it?' Eddie all but snarled. 'How come

she ended up living with us, when your Janie and Fanny have homes of their own and are doing well for themselves?'

Ruby had often thought the same, but in truth she knew that it was probably because her sisters had married well and moved up in the world. They now both spoke with plums in their mouths; to have Milly Tomkins under either roof would risk exposing their lowly roots. 'I know it doesn't always seem as though she is, but Mum's happy with us. She loves our George and fits in,' she tried to explain, although she had to agree there were times when she'd have gladly shown Milly the door. 'You have to remember that I never knew my dad. Him dying as he did before I was born, I have only ever known my mum. Fanny and Janie being older than me, they can remember him. It's important to me to have Mum about. She's my only contact with my past.'

Eddie shook his head. 'I have no idea why these things are important to a woman. I left home as soon as I was able to make my way in the world and I've never looked back.'

'I'd like to have known your family,' Ruby said.

'There's not much to know,' he said, shrugging off her words. He'd never opened up about his family, even though she'd asked him many times. 'A man makes his own way in life. He doesn't need family hanging on his coat-tails,' was all he'd ever said on the subject. In fact, at their wedding he'd had just a few friends, along with Cedric Mulligan, sitting on his side of the church. He didn't seem to have any roots, and perhaps this was the reason he wandered so easily from job to job and home to home.

'Oh well, that's not what I want to discuss with you at the moment. Eddie, I know you think I keep going on about it, but I want you to understand that I like living here. We have the kind of home I've always dreamt of and I don't want to move on. Our George needs to have a stable home and go to school and learn as much as he can in order to have a decent job and a good future.' She'd never mentioned meeting Mrs Grant in the cemetery, or her offer of a job for George when he was old enough to be taken on as an apprentice. That might be nine years away, but it would be nine years of studying and learning as much as he could in order to be considered good enough for a decent job. They couldn't do that if the lad was moved from home to home and school to school. 'We need to stick it out here and plan for the future. You never know, there may be another child that comes along one day and he or she will need to come into a family with a decent future.'

Eddie's eyes twinkled as he reached out and took her hand. 'You've started to think of another child,' he said, kissing her fingers.

Ruby snatched her hand back, even though she had felt a thrill run through her body at Eddie's tender touch. 'Oh no you don't, Eddie Caselton. You're not getting round me with your sweet talk. I want some promises that you will pull your finger out and think about this family. No more stealing, especially from me, and no doing odd and dangerous jobs for Cedric. You've got to realize that he owns this house, and come the day we can't pay the rent he'll soon have one of his heavies banging on the door and kicking us out onto the pavement. He's no friend of yours. You need to find a job and toe the line. Do you hear me?'

Eddie squirmed in his seat. 'I know what you're saying, love, but who will take me on? Word's already out about me getting the boot from the coalyard and helping myself to what wasn't mine.'

'You mean stealing. Start using the right words, and it might just get into that bloody head of yours why it's so wrong. I'll ask people while I'm working at the cafe. We have all sorts come in, and someone is bound to know someone who will take you on without asking too many questions about your past. In the meantime, why don't you get stuck into the garden and make it somewhere nice for us to sit out in? Later I'll heat the water in the copper, and you can have a soak in the tin bath.'

Eddie got to his feet and pulled her close. 'You're a good'n, Ruby Caselton. I don't know what I've done to deserve such a good wife. Will you scrub my back?' he asked, knowing he could not tell Ruby why he'd stooped to taking what wasn't his in order to save his own bacon and protect his family. He vowed there and then to make it up to her one day. When that day would be, he wasn't sure.

She slapped his arm. 'Be off with you. It takes more than a promise to have me forgive you, Eddie.' It was only as she watched him laugh out loud before heading out the back door that she realized he hadn't made any promises. Shaking her head, she cleared the table and started to think about their dinner. Spotting Eddie's canvas bag he'd left on the floor last night, she opened it to check if there was anything that needed washing. A cold chill swept over her as she pulled out the pay packet he had stolen from her the day before, along with the only two pieces of jewellery she had to her name. It was a reminder that Eddie was far from changing his ways. She clasped the jewellery to her breast and sighed. If only there was a way to bring back the man Eddie had once been. Oh yes, she was angry with him, and would continue to be angry – but she would see things through to the bitter end in order to keep her family together. Without saying a word, she dropped her possessions into her pocket and emptied the bag, chucking it into the cupboard under the stairs. If he mentioned it, she would crown him, and it would be with something heavier than a teapot.

Heavy of heart once again, Ruby returned to her housework, glancing at the clock every now and then as the minutes ticked by. It was long past the time she'd expected George and her mum to be home. There again, it was a lovely day, so why shouldn't they stay out and enjoy the sunshine?

Having swept the floors in every room of the house and wiped down surfaces with a damp rag, she took the few rugs she owned outside and gave them a good beating. Deciding to have a short rest before tackling the bay window at the front of the house, she poured herself a glass of cold water and sat down at the table to take a look at a newspaper that had been left in the cafe the day before. She dreamt of having time to herself in order to read more. Not only would it set a good example to her son, but she also wanted to finish reading *The Hound of the Baskervilles*, which had been lent to her by Frank Green. He'd enquired how she was enjoying the book when he'd brought over a copy of *The Wonderful Wizard of Oz* for her to read to George. Stella had told her Frank had amassed many books that were lined up on shelves he'd built himself in his bedroom. Ruby couldn't think of anything better and would have loved to see the books herself, but felt it would have been an improper request. Fortunately, Frank knew Ruby liked to read from the time he'd sat at her bedside when she was still poorly, and was keen to share his books with her. He'd spoken of the excitement in the town as a Carnegie library was to be built, and hopefully up and running within the year. He was a member of W. H. Smith's circulating library and had suggested that Eddie join too, so Ruby and George would have the benefit of reading new books. The idea had worried Ruby. Apart from Eddie not being much of a reader, she was not sure about caring for a book – what happened if the book was damaged or lost? How much would it all cost? However, she remembered a second-hand shop in Woolwich that had rows upon rows of books that were lined up on the pavement in front of the shop window on fine days. She had planned to use a few coppers from her savings to start George's own collection. Her son needed to be well-read if he was to succeed in life. Fat chance of that now, with the lad's dad having pinched much of her savings.

Thinking of her husband now as he toiled in the garden, she did wonder if it was too late for him to change his ways. Ever an optimist, she would give him time to prove himself. She knew how women were looked down on by neighbours when their husbands left or were kicked out of the house for their wrongdoings. She knew she could hold her head high, but it wouldn't be fair for George, as kids could be cruel once they latched on to what was going on. Besides, Eddie was the only man she'd ever loved, and in her book that was something worth fighting for.

Deep in thought, it took a couple of moments for her to hear the banging at her front door. Surely Milly hadn't forgotten her key? No, this was more insistent, and in between the hammering with the brass door knocker she could hear a frantic pounding on the wood and a voice calling her name. It was George.

Hurrying to open the door, she was faced with her son, red-faced and sobbing loudly. He clung to her skirts and mumbled incoherently.

'Whatever is wrong, my love? Where's Nanny?' she asked, looking out into the street as she stood on the doorstep.

'She . . . she . . . she had a funny turn and fell in the middle of the road in front of the pub by the river. A couple of workmen came out to help her. They put her in a wheelbarrow . . .'

6

With her head still full of Eddie and his drunken ways, Ruby's first thought was that Milly too was drunk. Had her mum taken George into a public house – and on a Sunday? The pubs down by the river weren't as refined as the Prince of Wales and were no place for a child. Come to that, only a certain type of woman frequented those pubs. Kneeling down so she was face to face with George, she kissed his forehead and gave him a reassuring smile. 'What happened to Nanny? Where did the men take her?'

'They put her in a wheelbarrow. I followed them in case they were stealing her. They went into the hospital up the road,' he sniffed.

The cottage hospital, Ruby thought. Then her mum must be poorly. Feeling ashamed of her previous thoughts, she wiped George's face with a handkerchief. 'What did the men say, my darling?'

'The men said to tell you they thought she was a goner and she's going to pop her clogs. What's a goner?'

Ruby felt her heart plummet. Her mum could be a right moaner at times, but Ruby didn't want to lose her.

Ignoring his question, she stroked his cheek. 'Stay right there while I get my coat and call your dad,' she said as she hurried through the house and called loudly to Eddie to come indoors, and to hurry up about it. She just caught a glimpse of Miss Hunter tutting over the fence as she headed back inside to grab her bag, pull on her better coat and hat, then slip her feet into her best shoes. Goodness knows who she would be speaking to in the hospital and she didn't wish to let her mother down by appearing scruffy.

'What's all the fuss about?' Eddie asked, walking in without his shirt and scratching his chest.

'Mum's been taken into the cottage hospital. George came home on his own. The poor mite is so distressed. I've left him on the doorstep, so he doesn't hear me speak to you about it. Eddie, I have a horrid feeling in my bones that Mum's not long for this world,' she said, pressing her handkerchief to her mouth.

'Don't be daft. She only puts on all those complaints. She's got years in her yet.'

Ruby shook her head. 'That's neither here nor there. I want you to wipe a flannel over your face and pull on your best shirt – and hurry,' she snapped, as he stood in front of her looking puzzled.

'You don't mean I've got to come with you?'

'It may be the last time we see her alive, and I want her to go to her maker thinking we are a united family. She doesn't want to be fading away listening to what you've been up to. I don't want the nurses and doctors knowing, either. What happens at home should stay there.'

Eddie glared at Ruby. 'Then you stop your nagging. Even the old girl next door asked me about my job. She must have been listening to you, as I've not been talking to her.'

'She's just a lonely, nosy old woman,' Ruby said, shaking her head and pushing him towards the kitchen sink so he could wash. 'If she knows anything, it's because she's had her ear to the wall, or she's got it from elsewhere. If you didn't get up to no good, you'd not have cause for concern. Now, I'll be out the front with George. Hurry yourself or we'll be too late,' she hissed, leaving him to mutter to himself as he washed his face.

Entering the cottage hospital by the front door, Ruby was again impressed by the high ceilings and the quiet way she was approached by a woman in a severe black dress, who reminded her of a nun. However, she couldn't shake off the memory of visiting the hospital to enquire after Doctor Hind and where her baby's body would have been taken. She did her utmost to push the thought to the back of her mind. 'I'm here to enquire about my mother, Mrs Millicent Tomkins. She was brought in about an hour ago.'

'In a wheelbarrow,' George piped up, causing Eddie to laugh loudly, then shut up just as quickly when given a stern look by Ruby.

'She was taken poorly down by the river while out walking with my son,' Ruby explained, trying her best to mind how she spoke. She didn't want anyone thinking they were common. 'My mother lives with us, a few streets away in Alexandra Road,' she added, hoping it would impress the woman and she'd look on them favourably.

'If you would like to wait, I will see how your mother is,' the woman said, before disappearing through a side door.

'This place gives me the willies,' Eddie said, twisting his cap in his hands. 'I'll wait outside.'

'You will stay where you are,' Ruby murmured, placing her hand on George's shoulder and grabbing Eddie's sleeve with the other. 'We are here for my mother, so forget about how uncomfortable you feel and think of someone else for once.'

'I don't like hospitals,' he muttered back.

'Who does? But it's not for us to be selfish at times like this. How would you feel if you were unwell in hospital and no one visited you because they didn't like hospitals? You'd soon have something to gripe about then.'

Eddie opened his mouth to answer but stopped as a man appeared, followed by a nurse wearing the most elaborate starched cap Ruby had ever seen. The man held his hand out to Eddie. 'I'm Doctor Gregson. Your mother is extremely poorly, I'm afraid . . .'

Ruby stepped in front of Eddie. 'She's my mother. Is she going to die?' she asked, forgetting for a moment that George was with them. She was soon reminded when he burst into a fresh flood of tears.

'Nurse, would you take the young man to the children's ward, please? This is no place for him at the moment.'

George fought and screamed as the nurse tried to take his hand. 'Leave me alone. I want to stay here with my mum and see my nan pop her clogs,' he yelled.

The doctor bent down until he was face to face with George. 'Now, young man. Do you like trains?'

George stopped creating a fuss and looked at the man. 'What kind of trains?'

'Wooden trains that run on a track. We have a splendid one in the room next to the children's ward. A father of one of our patients donated it to say thank you for making his little girl better. Would you like to play with it?'

George thought for a moment. 'You make people better?'

The doctor looked bemused. 'But of course we do.'

'And they don't pop their clogs?'

The doctor laughed and ruffled George's hair. 'He's a bright lad, isn't he?' he said to Ruby as he stood up.

'We think so,' Ruby replied, thankful that George had calmed down. As much as she loved her son, she wanted to see her mum.

'Take him along to play with the train, Nurse,' he said as he held out his arm for Ruby to accompany him back through the door.

Ruby looked at Eddie and gave him a nod to follow her. She didn't trust him not to run off. With her heart beating faster than it had ever done before, she followed the doctor into the ward. Looking around her, she tried to identify her mum, but the women in the beds all looked the same, with the crisp white sheets pulled up to their chins as they rested. 'Where is she?' she whispered.

They were led to the end of the ward, where a green screen was pulled round the last bed. At this point the doctor stopped. 'I'm afraid your mother is very unwell. All we can do is make her comfortable. She has been calling for you.'

Ruby fought back tears as she hurried to Milly's bedside

111

and sat on a wooden bench close to the bed. Taking Milly's hand and squeezing it tight, she held it to her chest. 'I'm here now, Mum. Whatever have you been doing to yourself?'

Milly's eyelids fluttered as she heard her daughter's voice. Ruby had never seen her look so pale and old. Deep shadows around her eyes and a blue tinge to her lips showed how ill her mother was. A white bandage hid most of her grey hair. 'You got here, then?' she whispered. 'I thought I'd be gone before you arrived.'

'Don't talk like that, Mum. The doctor will soon have you up on your feet and fighting fit, just you wait and see,' Ruby said brightly, forcing a smile.

'You think what you want . . . if it makes you feel better . . . but I'll not see . . . dawn break tomorrow,' Milly said, taking weak breaths between her words. 'Now, I want you . . . to do a couple of things . . . for me.' She gripped Ruby's hand and swallowed hard.

'I'll do whatever you want,' Ruby promised as she held a cup of water to Milly's lips.

Milly turned her head away, refusing the liquid. 'There's a box under my bed at home . . . if you look inside . . . you'll see . . . some things I want you to have,' she said stopping to take a shuddering breath. She closed her eyes for a little while before continuing. 'In my old purse . . . you'll find the money I hid . . . from that bastard husband of yours. Make sure he doesn't get his hands on it . . . it's all yours, so don't go sharing it with your sisters.'

Ruby couldn't answer, as tears streamed down her face. 'I'll get the word to Fanny and Janie to come and see you,' she said, looking behind her and hoping Eddie had heard. 'Can you do that for me, Eddie?'

'No . . . get him out of here,' Milly gasped as she tried to sit up. 'Don't trust him further . . . than you can spit . . . I always thought . . . I always thought he was a good one . . . I was wrong.' She raised her hand and pointed towards him. 'Change your ways . . . Eddie Caselton . . . I swear I'll find you from my grave . . . and chase you to yours.' She gasped out the last of the words before collapsing back onto the pillow.

'It's best you take George home. I don't want Mum distressed more than she is already,' Ruby said without looking round.

Milly turned her face to Ruby. 'There's some more money in the box . . . it's not a lot . . . but it'll help you . . . give me a decent send-off . . . I've been putting . . . a copper or two by since . . . since I was told . . . about my dicky ticker . . . I didn't want . . . to be a burden to you.'

'Mum, you have never been a burden to me and shouldn't be worrying about such things at the moment. You need to rest.'

Milly gave a weak laugh. 'I'll be resting aplenty before too long . . . There's something else . . . you will find an envelope and my will . . . stitched into the lining of . . . my Sunday coat. There's more money there too . . . If that's not enough . . . you are to sell all me bits and pieces . . . to make up the difference. But what's left . . . if anything . . . is all yours . . . no need to tell your sisters. They are doing all right . . . without my help . . . You've been a proper daughter to me . . . not like those two with their posh houses up in Bexleyheath. Promise me?' she begged, still gripping Ruby's hand.

Ruby stroked Milly's cheek. 'I promise. Please don't

fret. Why don't you close your eyes and rest for a while? Fanny and Janie will be here before too long,' she murmured, hoping that Eddie had the sense to rush to let them know.

Milly closed her eyes, but continued to grip Ruby's hand tightly. 'They'd best hurry,' she said, before falling into a deep sleep.

Apart from a nurse who looked in occasionally to check on Milly, Ruby sat alone with her thoughts. She never let go of her mum's hand, giving a gentle squeeze now and then, whispering a few words to assure Milly she was still there by her side. Tea, left by a thoughtful ward orderly, went cold as she thought back to her childhood, which had been spent mainly alone with Milly after her sisters, who were much older, went out to work, then married and rarely visited. There was never much money without a husband and father to provide for them, but they got by.

'Thank you, Mum. I may not have said it very much, but thank you for caring for me and trying not to judge too much when I married Eddie after I fell with our George. I didn't mean to shame you ...' Ruby didn't know if Milly could hear her words. Perhaps not, as Milly never stirred.

As the sun dropped in the sky and nightfall gradually darkened the screened-off section of the ward a nurse appeared with a small oil lamp and set it down on the wide window ledge. 'Am I able to stay?' Ruby asked, thinking that she would be sent home for the night. She was surprised she'd not been dismissed before now, as the signs she'd spotted in the entrance hall had strict visiting times for family.

Milly's eyelids fluttered and opened. 'Where . . . am . . . I?' she murmured faintly.

'It's all right, Mum. You had a fall earlier and your ticker's been playing up. If you rest up you'll be home before too long,' Ruby reassured her, wondering if perhaps Milly had turned a corner and was getting better.

Milly took a shuddering breath. 'Nah . . . my Bert . . . he's waiting for me,' she said, looking past Ruby towards the window. 'Look . . . look there . . .'

Ruby felt fear grip her stomach. 'But, Mum. Dad – well, Dad died before I was born. Don't you remember?'

Milly continued to smile for a few seconds more. Her eyes twinkled just like they did when she'd had a bit of a knees-up and a tot too much of something down the pub. 'Bert . . .' she murmured, before sighing her last breath and sinking into the pillows.

'Mum – no, Mum!' Ruby sobbed, throwing herself onto the still body and hugging her mum for all she was worth. 'Don't leave me, Mum, please don't leave me . . . You've got to wait to see Fanny and Janie, and in the morning George will be coming to visit you. Mum . . .'

The gentle arms of a nurse took Ruby by the shoulders and pulled her away from her mother. A second nurse bent over to check Milly before closing her eyes and pulling the white bed sheet up under her chin. 'She had a peaceful death, Mrs Caselton,' she said, turning to give Ruby a hug. 'What a lucky lady she was to have such a devoted daughter.' She handed her a handkerchief.

Ruby took a few more deep shuddering sobs before doing her utmost to calm herself. The patients in their beds just the other side of the screens didn't need to be

115

wakened by her crying or be aware someone had passed away. 'My sisters need to know,' she finally managed to say.

'There is a lady waiting outside. She's been there some time, but insisted on waiting.'

'It must be one of my sisters. Why wasn't she allowed in? She's missed saying goodbye,' Ruby said, feeling suddenly angry.

'No, it is your neighbour – a Mrs Green. Unfortunately our usual rules don't permit people to enter the ward out of hours, but she insisted on staying. One of my colleagues gave her a hot drink,' the nurse explained, seeing that Ruby looked puzzled. 'It takes a good friend to wait so patiently and for so long.'

Ruby was thoughtful. 'Do you think she could come in and pay her respects to Mum?'

The two nurses looked at each other and, without speaking, one left Milly's bedside. She returned a few moments later with Stella.

'Oh, my poor love. You've had so much heartache,' Stella said as she sat beside Ruby and rocked her in her arms. The two nurses disappeared, leaving them alone with Milly.

Once Ruby had composed herself she turned to Stella. 'Mum looks very peaceful, doesn't she? This may sound daft, but . . . right at the end, she spoke to me.'

'They often do have a few lucid moments. Did it make sense, what she said?'

'She told me my dad was here. Do you think he came for her?'

Stella looked towards Milly and the smile that showed

on her lips. 'I've heard it said that can happen. How long has it been since your dad . . . ?'

'He was in the army and he died overseas a month before I was born. I never knew him, and my sisters don't talk about him. They must have been between ten and twelve years of age, so they would remember our dad. I've always thought they had a secret that they alone shared and chose to keep from me. I'd love to have known more about him.'

Stella shook her head in sympathy. 'There's nothing stranger than folk. You know, my Wilf has six brothers and not one of them sees us from one year to the next. It doesn't worry him one little bit, but I used to stay awake nights worrying about it. I thought family stuck together through thick and thin.'

'Does it really not bother him?' Ruby asked as she glanced at her mum lying peacefully in the bed. She half expected her to sit up and ask a few questions too, as she never missed a tasty morsel of gossip.

'He says it doesn't, but I know deep down he's hurt badly.'

Ruby felt she was truly her mother's daughter as she asked. 'But what happened for the family to ignore him – that's if you don't mind saying?' It was a shock to hear that the family living over the road from her had such turmoil in their life. The Greens seemed the perfect family, with three bright sons and a doting mother and father. Who would have thought that if you peeled back the layers, their life wasn't quite so rosy?

'Oh, it's a long story, but – being the eldest son, the family business passed to my Wilf. As much as he would have liked to, there was not enough business for him to take on all of his brothers. Also, since he alone had worked with his father on the tugboat, he refused to sell up and divide the money, as several of my sisters-in-law suggested. The whole thing left a bitter taste in my mouth and gradually it split the family. Wilf thought that when our lads were old enough, they'd like to join him in the business. As it is, none of them are interested. Perhaps we should've sold up after all,' she sighed. 'Family can be so strange.'

Ruby agreed. 'I'm sorry for your troubles. If there's anything I can do at any time, please let me know. In the short while I've known you, you've been a good friend to my family,' she said, glancing to her mother for a final time before bending down and kissing her cheek. After a moment, she added, 'I suppose I should get back home. Eddie will be starting to wonder where I am, and George is no doubt refusing to sleep until he hears how his nanny is. This news is going to break his heart.'

Stella kissed Milly's forehead and followed Ruby from the screened-off area. Walking quietly out of the ward, they stopped to thank the nurses. Ruby told them that she would be contacting the funeral director first thing in the morning.

As they stepped outside, Stella said: 'Your George is at our house, as it happens. Eddie dropped him over earlier and asked if I would keep an eye on the lad, as he had things to do. That's how I knew what had happened to Milly and came hurrying round to the cottage hospital to be with you. My boys promised to look after George, and to feed him. Frank said they would make up a bed for him in our front room if he became tired.'

'That's very good of them,' Ruby said gratefully as they linked arms and hurried back to Alexandra Road. It was now the early hours of the morning and there was hardly a soul about, which felt strange when they were so used to seeing Erith bustling with people. 'Eddie must have gone to tell my sisters. It seems strange they never arrived at the hospital, though. Perhaps with it being so late, they are sitting at my house waiting for news?'

They turned the corner of Alexandra Road and could see number thirteen. The house was in darkness. As they arrived at Ruby's gate, she stopped to rummage for the house key in her bag and to thank Stella for her support. Stella was just saying that she would accompany Ruby in the morning to give her support while she arranged her mother's funeral, when Frank came out of her front door and hurried over. Stella quickly explained that Milly had passed away.

'I'm sorry for your loss,' Frank said to Ruby. 'If there's anything I can do to help, please let me know. I came out to tell you that George is sound asleep. To begin with he was fretful; then sleep caught up with him in the end.'

Ruby thanked Frank. 'But why hasn't Eddie come over to collect him?' she wondered, looking at their house. 'Surely he's not gone to bed?'

'We'll come inside with you to check everything is all right,' Stella said, taking the keys from Ruby's hand and opening the front door.

Ruby could see at once that Eddie's coat was missing from the hooks on the wall. He never got on with her sisters, so it was unlikely that he was still at one of their houses. A sudden thought gripped her. 'Oh, please God, no,' she cried as she ran upstairs to her mother's bedroom. On the bed was the ornate box in which Milly had kept her few cherished possessions, normally stashed under the bed for safety. Ruby picked it up and checked to see if there was anything inside. It was empty. All that remained scattered on the bed was a broken brooch and a faded letter, sent long ago, informing her of Bert's death while on duty. Ruby sank to her knees and sobbed into the eiderdown bedspread.

'My goodness, whatever is it?' Stella asked as she hurried into the bedroom, closely followed by Frank. They both helped Ruby to her feet and sat her down on the bed.

'Mum told me only hours ago that in this box I would find some money to put towards burying her. She'd also hidden some savings she'd been keeping after Eddie took mine.' She felt ashamed to have to say to these two good people that her husband could not be trusted.

'Go downstairs and stick the kettle on the hob, love,' Stella instructed Frank. 'We will be down shortly, once Ruby is feeling better.'

Frank looked as though the last thing he wanted to do was leave Ruby while she was upset, but he gave her a sympathetic nod and did as he was told.

Before saying a word, Stella picked up the box, putting a few items inside and placing it on a nearby chest of drawers. Pulling the eiderdown up around Ruby's shoulders to comfort and keep her warm, she sat down next to her and placed an arm around her. 'I don't want to interfere in what goes on behind a husband and wife's front door, as that is their business. You could tell me to go home if you want? But I get the feeling your Eddie is a bit of a wrong'n and has taken your mum's money.'

Ruby could only nod before taking a deep breath to say: 'He's never been good with money. It's all my fault; I should've hidden our savings somewhere safer. Mum caught him poking about in the pantry and managed to take some of the money and hide it in her room, along with her own. I can only think that when he heard her tell me at the hospital where she'd put her money, he came home and took it.' She dissolved into tears once again. 'Whatever am I going to do? I haven't got a penny to bury Mum. He's taken it all, and to use one of Mum's favourite sayings, I haven't got a pot to piss in.'

7

'Don't be too angry, Frank,' Stella said as she placed his breakfast in front of him. 'No one knows what goes on in the privacy of someone's home.'

Frank thumped his fist on the table, making cutlery jump and cups rattle on their saucers. Stella grabbed the teapot as it wobbled. She'd given her spare one to Ruby so had to be careful, as she didn't trust her lot not to break this one. If they did she'd have to use her best teapot, which had been a wedding present.

'We did know about Eddie, though,' Frank said in frustration. 'Look at how many jobs he's had in the month or so since the Caseltons have lived in the road. Didn't I tell you only the other day he'd been given the boot from the coalyard for stealing and fiddling coal deliveries?'

Stella sank into the spare seat next to her eldest son. 'Knowing something about the man and having a say about it to Ruby are not the same thing. What if she knew what he was up to and wasn't bothered? I'm only saying,' she added quickly, as Frank glared at her. She knew her son was very fond of Ruby, but of course nothing could come of it – Ruby was a married woman with a child.

Even if her husband did walk out on her, she was still married. It would have been lovely to have a daughter-in-law like Ruby, Stella thought wistfully.

'I must do something for her.' Frank pushed his plate away, leaving food uneaten. 'I'm going to offer her some money. It won't go far, but it will help with the funeral costs. The last thing she needs is to see Mrs Tomkins going into a pauper's grave.'

'I can chip in a bit. I'm sure your dad won't mind. He's got a soft spot for Ruby and the lad. It's bad enough Ruby couldn't bury Sarah herself, let alone see her mum go into an unmarked grave.'

'Sarah?'

'Eat the rest of that while I tell you,' she said, pushing the plate back in front of him before starting to explain.

'Bloody hell, I had no idea. I'm ashamed to say that once she was over the birth, I gave no thought to what happened – you know, with the body. I'm sorry,' he said, not able to look at his mother.

'Don't apologize. It's the way of the world, and most of us wouldn't think twice about such a thing unless it affected us. It worked out well in the end, and that's what counts. I'm more concerned with what happens next in Ruby's life. She will need to be making arrangements for a funeral today as well as wondering about her future.'

'I'm going to go over there and see what I can do to help. Even if it's to take George off her hands for the day while she does what has to be done. Why don't you sit and talk to her while the kid's out of the way? You always give good advice, and she will need a shoulder to cry on, with that Eddie having done a bunk.' Even to speak Eddie's name gave Frank a bad taste in his mouth. Why would a man treat a woman in such a way? He knew that if Ruby was his wife, he'd treat her like a precious jewel. For him, Ruby was exactly the right name for the woman he admired. Worried his mother could read his thoughts, he got to his feet and announced: 'I'm going over there now. I'll get word to the depot manager that I'll not be in work today because of a bereavement.'

'You're a good lad, Frank. Let me put the plates in the sink and I'll be right behind you. The washing-up can wait for once. I'll leave George asleep and give Donald a shout to listen out for him.'

Together they walked across the road, aware they were being watched by Ruby's neighbour, Miss Hunter, who was wiping the wide ledge of her bay window with a cloth.

'Good morning, Miss Hunter. You've started your housework bright and early,' Stella said in a clipped tone.

'I have a lot to be getting on with after spending yesterday in prayer. It's a shame not everyone can do the same.' Miss Hunter glanced towards the door of number thirteen. 'I can't say the same for all in this street.'

'Now is not the time for such thoughts. Mrs Caselton's mother passed away in the early hours of this morning, so perhaps don't share your views with her today?' As Stella spoke, an ashen-faced Ruby opened the door.

'I will add Mrs Tomkins to my prayers,' the elderly spinster replied, without an ounce of compassion passing her thin face.

'Thank you, Miss Hunter, but we don't need your prayers,' Ruby said stiffly as she let Stella and Frank into the house and closed the door, not waiting to hear Miss Hunter's reply. Her mother wouldn't have thanked her for accepting prayers on her behalf. Milly Tomkins had fallen out with the Almighty after losing her husband at an early age. In her book, a church was just a place to marry or say goodbye to loved ones. There was no need for religion to be mentioned.

Stella gave Ruby a quick hug and placed her basket onto the table in the living room. 'I've put some bits and bobs in there to keep you and George going. I know you'll be too busy to get to the grocer.'

'Thank you, let me give you the money,' Ruby said, reaching for the purse she'd left on the mantelpiece.

'No! If I can't bring a few things over to help you out, what kind of neighbour am I? I know you'd do the same for me or mine if the boot was on the other foot.'

'I would, but I hope that day never comes. I'd hate to think of your family suffering like mine,' Ruby said, taking the basket into the kitchen to unpack. There was enough to see her and George through a few days until life got back to normal, if it ever would. Stella's generosity lifted her heart; whatever would she do without good friends? It was a huge comfort to her, but then she suddenly started to tremble so much that she had to grip the side of the sink to stop herself sinking to her knees.

'My goodness, Ruby! Frank, quick, help me get Ruby to a seat. The poor girl has had a bit of a turn,' Stella exclaimed as she caught Ruby before she sank to the floor completely.

Frank scooped Ruby up in his arms and carried her through to the front room, depositing her in one of the hard horsehair armchairs. Stella brought in a cup of water and held it to her lips. 'Here you go, love. With everything that's gone on, it's no wonder you've come over all queer. I bet you've not even eaten, have you?' she fussed. 'Frank, get some breakfast going while I fetch a blanket to tuck round this young lady. No arguing,' she added as Ruby started to protest. 'I know it's warm enough outside, but you need a bit of cosseting. When I think of what you've been through, why, I could cry. If putting some food in your belly and keeping you warm is what it takes to get you back on your feet, then you can shut up and let me take charge.'

Ruby mumbled her thanks, leant back in the armchair and closed her eyes. Apart from the cup of tea she'd let go cold while sitting at the hospital, nothing had touched her lips since early yesterday. Frank and Stella had tried to ply her with a hot drink when she'd arrived home in the early hours, but she couldn't stomach the thought of anything. No wonder she didn't feel quite the ticket at the moment. Lying awake for the few hours she was in bed, she couldn't sleep for thinking of the list of what had to be done today. Almost everything required money, and she hardly had a penny to her name. Rather than curse Eddie, as she knew it would get her nowhere, she wondered why he'd let her down at such a time. When she needed him by her side being strong, he'd instead left her to flounder alone. Was the lure of drinking and gambling so strong that he had left her alone with a young child? She fought a shuddering sob as it ripped through her. She would not be a victim at the hands of her husband.

'Here you go, lovey. Let's tuck this round you and once we've had a cup of tea, we will do what we can to help you,' Stella said as she sat in the other chair.

Ruby nodded in agreement. Grateful though she was, she had no idea how Stella could possibly help her. 'Thank you. I hope George hasn't been a bother? I dread to think how I'm going to tell him that not only has his nanny died, but his daddy will not be coming home.'

'Are you sure Eddie hasn't just gone off somewhere drinking and will roll home again before too long? I recall you mentioning that's happened before.'

'No, he's gone for good this time. Most of his clothes have disappeared from the chest of drawers, along with the shaving kit and the watch he only wore with his suit, and that's gone too.'

Stella shook her head. She was thankful that her Wilf was a good family man and would never do such a thing. Even in times of trouble, he would sit down with her and they would talk things through. What kind of man would act the way Eddie Caselton had? 'Oh dear, that does sound final, doesn't it?'

'I truly thought Eddie loved me and George, and had some respect for my mum. To go like that without saying anything when Mum was fading fast, and then to take her money, is unforgivable. I feel as though I've lost everything. My husband, my mother, the wherewithal to give her a decent send-off, and also this house. George's future looks bleak. What kind of mother am I, to not be able to provide for my son?' Ruby forced the words out slowly, not wanting to voice her fears.

Stella took her hand and held it tightly. 'You'll get

through this, my love, and you have friends here to help. Ah, here comes some breakfast – well done, Frank.'

Frank placed the tea tray on a battered-looking side table, the one piece of furniture in the room apart from the armchairs. 'I made you a bit of toast. Please eat it, as you need to keep up your strength. I'll just get a chair from the other room, then we can start to make a plan of action. I'll leave you to pour the tea, Mum, you know I always make a mess,' he grinned, trying to lighten the sadness that hung heavy in the room.

'He's a good lad,' Stella said as she stirred the hot tea in the teapot. 'He'll make someone a good husband one of these days.'

Ruby gave a weak smile. 'That's what I could have done with. I didn't choose so well, did I?'

'No one is to know what will happen in life,' Stella said as she passed the plate of toast over. 'Now eat that up before it goes cold,' she directed. 'You need all your strength to see you through today.'

Ruby did as she was told, although the first mouthful was hard to chew, but as the flavour of the melted butter hit her taste buds, she found herself salivating and very soon cleared the plate. 'That was delicious,' she told Frank as he returned, carrying a chair.

'I'll make some more in a while,' he said, taking a pencil and a well-worn notebook from the pocket of his jacket. 'I thought, if you don't mind, we could make a few notes – a plan of action, so to speak. Do you agree?'

'If you think it will help, then of course I agree,' she replied, although she held out little hope of her problems being solved with just a list.

'Mum, I know you had some thoughts, so would you like to voice them first?'

Stella passed a cup of tea to Ruby before sitting back down with her own drink, leaving Frank's on the table so he had his hands free to write. 'I hope you don't think I'm being nosy, but what provisions had been made for when she passed away? I know lots of old folk, and none of them want to be a burden on those they leave behind.'

'Of course you're not being nosy. I'm grateful for your interest. Mum only told me last night, while Eddie was at her bedside, about the box under her bed. From all accounts there were a few bits and bobs of jewellery, along with the money she'd rescued from the pantry where I'd hidden it. She'd noticed Eddie looking at it and whisked it away before he got his dirty hands on it. She also said there was some money in the box to give her a send-off. You both see what was left,' she added, looking embarrassed.

'Would you recognize the jewellery if you saw it again?' Frank asked. 'We could let the coppers know, and also pay a visit to a few pawnshops?'

Ruby was horrified. 'Please, no – I don't want to get the police involved! I'd be so ashamed for anyone to know my circumstances. The jewellery would not have been of much value to anyone. I don't think my father's medals would have brought much in either. It would have been nice for George to have had them, though. At the moment I'm more concerned about her funeral.'

Frank noted as he scribbled her words down, 'You mentioned before that you have two sisters. Is it likely your mother had left anything with them?'

Ruby gave a brittle laugh. 'It's highly unlikely. The pair of them had little to do with Mum. I'm dreading having to let them know Mum has died and there's no money to bury her. No doubt they will see it as their Christian duty to take over and will never let me forget how I chose a bad husband and couldn't provide for our mother. In fact, the one decision I have made is not to let the pair of them know that Mum has died until I have some sort of answer to how I will cope. They've not seen much of Mum over the years, since they moved up in the world. I need to have things straight before they try to help. It may be well meant, but I can't bear the thought of them knowing our circumstances.'

'I'm with you there,' Stella agreed. 'The less they know the better, for now. Did Milly say any more?'

'She mainly slept,' Ruby said, thinking back to the hours she'd spent at the hospital alone with her mum. 'She did say something about her coat – now what was it? My mind is in such a muddle.'

'Drink your tea – it'll come to you when you don't think too hard,' Stella assured her, as something caught her eye through the large bay window. 'It's our Donald and your George coming over the road. Frank, can you let them in and save us ladies getting up?' She grinned at Ruby as she raised her little finger and sipped her tea daintily.

Ruby snorted with half a laugh. Stella was a real tonic and Ruby was grateful the older woman was a friend, especially at a time like this. 'Hello, my love,' she said, giving George a hug as he ran into the room.

'Are you not well?' he asked, looking at his mum wrapped in a blanket.

'Mummy was just a little chilly,' Stella explained, saving Ruby from answering. 'Now, Donald, why the long face?'

'I thought our Frank was going to take me with him to work today to show me what happens in the clerk's office. I've got an essay to write for school about my family and the work they do.'

Frank slapped his hand to his forehead. 'Blast, I meant to send word in that I'm taking the day off to help with a problem in the family,' he said, giving Ruby a shy look. 'You are like family to us. Donald, would you take a note to the office for me? I'm sure Mr Porter will allow you to stay and watch for a while,' he added, bringing a smile to his younger brother's face.

'But first, you go over home and wash your face. Oh, and you can put on your best coat as well. I don't want anyone thinking my son dresses like a ragamuffin,' Stella admonished him, although she was smiling too. Donald was a bright lad, and she hoped he'd do well in life. For him to follow Frank into the office of the coal merchant would be a good move, although her husband still dearly wished for one of their lads to join him as a lighterman on the river.

'I'll come over with you and sort out the note,' Frank said, not adding that he wanted to use the nice paper he saved for letters, rather than tear a page from his notebook.

Ruby watched the interaction between mother and son, as something buzzed around inside her head.

Stella noticed the puzzled look on Ruby's face. 'Is there something bothering you, lovey?'

Ruby frowned and tried to clear her thoughts. 'It was something you've just said to Donald . . . Oh well,' she shrugged her shoulders. 'If it's important, it'll come to me.'

'What are you going to do about your job?' Stella asked. 'Marge will be expecting you by now. Would you like me to pop round to the cafe and let her know what's happened?' She nodded towards George, not wishing to mention his nan having died.

Ruby gasped. 'Oh my goodness, I'd completely forgotten what day it was. I must get round to the cafe right now,' she said, standing up suddenly and letting the blanket fall to the floor. Feeling dizzy, she gasped and clutched the nearby mantelpiece for support.

'Oh no, you don't,' Stella glared, forcing her back into the armchair. 'You are poorly, and you've had more than a shock after . . .'

'After what, Mummy?' George asked, his worried face looking between Ruby and Stella.

Stella took command. 'I'm going to the cafe and I will tell Marge you won't be in for a few days. I'm sure she'll understand. Frank, you get that note written then wash the crocks up, and Donald, you hurry along and wash your face, tidy yourself and get off to the coalyard. You sit that lad of yours down, lovey, and tell him what's been happening,' she finished, giving Ruby a sympathetic look.

Ruby thanked Stella and beckoned to George to snuggle up under the blanket with her. As her friends set about their tasks, she gave her son a gentle squeeze before she cleared her throat. It was bad enough having to tell the lad his nanny had died, but to say his dad had scarpered with all their money was not going to be pleasant.

'Has something happened?' he asked.

'You know how your nan was poorly with her dodgy ticker?'

'And the men took her to the cottage hospital on a barrow?' he said with a smile. 'Then I ran home to let you know . . .'

'Yes, you did very well. I'm proud of you for being so brave and not getting upset.'

'I did have a little cry when I was in bed last night at Stella's house. I am only five,' he pointed out solemnly.

For all the seriousness of their situation, Ruby felt herself smile. 'I know, my sweet, and you are allowed to cry. It isn't a crime.'

'Daddy told me he would be annoyed if he ever sees me cry,' he replied. 'I didn't want him tanning my backside like Freddie Martin down the road's dad does.'

'Your daddy would never strike you, and he won't be telling you off again,' she said, holding him closer still while surreptitiously wiping her eyes on the blanket. She had wanted to continue telling him about Milly's death, but perhaps George had given her an opportunity to explain about Eddie doing a vanishing act. She wouldn't have to let him know about the missing money and her problems. 'Daddy has gone away, and I doubt we will see him again,' she said, choosing her words with care.

'Did I do something to make him go away?' he asked with trembling lips.

'No, my love. Your daddy loves you very much. His leaving has nothing to do with you.'

George thought for a few seconds. 'Perhaps he ran away with a floozy?'

133

Ruby couldn't help but laugh. 'Whatever made you think that?'

'Nanny said he probably had a fancy woman, and when I asked what that was, she said it was the same as a floozy. She wouldn't tell me any more. She said I had small ears, and people with small ears shouldn't know such things.'

Ruby felt tears sting her eyes. She could imagine her mother parting with her pearls of wisdom about Eddie and his wrongdoings.

'I doubt your daddy had a floozy; Nanny would have been joking. She was probably pulling your leg.'

'I don't think she was, as she said a rude word after that. Shall I tell you what she said?'

'No, thank you. Georgie, about Nanny Milly. She was very ill, you know . . .'

'Is she brown bread? One of the men pushing her on the barrow said she'd probably be brown bread before the night was out. How can she be brown bread?'

'Well . . . the man meant he thought Nanny would be going to heaven before too long.' She hated herself for falling back on using the word, but 'dead' sounded so brutal – and so final for a little boy to hear.

George sighed. 'Do you mean she has died?'

Not for the first time, Ruby thought that her son was an old soul in a young body. 'Yes, my love. Nanny died early this morning. It was very peaceful, and I don't think she suffered. She did tell me to send you her love, and to say she would be watching over you to see no harm befell you.' The more she spoke, the more she thought she was digging a hole for herself. Her mother had not given a message for her grandson, or for anyone else for that matter. Had she committed a sin for telling fibs? 'It is just you and me on our own from now on,' she added, giving him another squeeze.

'Did Nanny remind you to give me Grandad's medals? She said I can have them when she pops her clogs.'

Ruby ignored the way George spoke; he was only repeating her mother's much-used words. 'I have no idea what she would have done with them. But if we come across them, then they will go to you as the only man in the family.'

George wriggled out from beneath the blanket and stood in front of Ruby with his hands on his hips. 'Didn't she tell you where she'd hidden them?'

Ruby thought of the empty box Eddie had emptied of any valuables while Milly lay on her deathbed only two roads away. She couldn't tell her son that his dad had pinched the medals. However badly her husband had behaved, she needed to keep his memory as positive as possible in her son's eyes. If Eddie ever did return home, she couldn't bear to see George upset by knowing what he'd done. He could make his own mind up when he was an adult; until then, she'd do her best not to sully her son's memories with her bitterness. Besides, she still loved Eddie, regardless of what he'd done. Love was something you couldn't turn on and off. 'Nanny never told me what had happened to the medals, George. But if we find them then they are yours.'

George looked thoughtful but accepted Ruby's words. 'I'm hungry. Can I have something to eat?'

Oh, to be young and so innocent that you could move from learning about the loss of a loved one to thinking about food, Ruby thought to herself. 'There's a fresh loaf of bread and some cheese in the kitchen. Shall I make you a sandwich?' she asked, getting to her feet cautiously in case she felt dizzy again. Holding out her hand, she took George's and they went out to the kitchen.

Ruby wiped the crumbs from her son's mouth. 'Why don't you go out into the back garden and play for a little while? It will do you good to get some sun on your face. I'll stay here, in case Stella or Frank knocks on the door,' she said before watching George skip quite happily out through the back door.

Rinsing the plates, she left them to dry on the wooden draining board before filling the kettle and putting it back on the hob, ready for when her friends returned. She looked round the small kitchen, remembering the plans she'd had for the house. Nothing grand, but a bit of distemper in the outside toilet, a piece of lace curtain at the windows; and, when she had time, she'd planned to make a couple of new rag rugs for their bedrooms. Milly had taught her how to make the rugs out of scraps of old fabric. There was no point now, as no doubt the landlord would be slinging them both out on their ears once he knew she didn't have a penny to her name. Deep in thought, she didn't at first hear the front door being knocked frantically. It was only after she heard her name called through the letter box, followed by more knocking, that she hurried to open the door.

'Oh my goodness,' Stella panted. 'I thought something had happened to you.'

'I was tidying the kitchen. Why are you out of breath?' Ruby asked as she led Stella into the living room and watched her sit at the table, breathing deeply and trying to compose herself.

'There's a right kerfuffle round at the cafe. Someone has been in there and helped themselves to what money was left under the counter, as well as bits and pieces of food. Marge is doing her nut and accusing you of all sorts to the policeman.'

'Oh God, I was supposed to have opened up this morning as Marge was wanted elsewhere. With everything that's gone on, it completely slipped my mind. I'd best go down there and see what I can do to help.'

Stella shook her head. 'No, don't go near the place unless you want to be arrested.'

'But why would anyone want to arrest me? I've not done anything wrong apart from not turning up from work,' Ruby said, looking confused.

'The thief got in through the front door. He had a set of keys . . .'

Ruby looked to where her bag was placed, where she always left it on the floor by the cupboard under the stairs. 'I have a set of keys. Marge gave them to me on Saturday so I could let myself into the premises.'

'You'd best check they're still there, as my gut is telling me that they will be gone, along with your Eddie,' Stella said angrily.

'Please, no, they must be there,' Ruby cried as she grabbed the bag and tipped the contents out onto the table. 'I know I put them there along with my wages on Saturday.'

'What happened to your wages?' Stella asked.

'He took them . . . I know he took them,' Ruby said as she sat opposite Stella and put her head in her arms and sobbed. 'Whatever can I do?'

'Crying like a baby is not going to help you, is it?' a little voice said from the back door.

Ruby looked up to where George was standing, his head cocked to one side and his hands on his hips. Her young son was perfectly mimicking the way her mum had always spoken to him when he cried. 'You are right, love,' she said, cuffing the tears from her eyes before starting to chuckle. Stella joined in with the laughter. George was so comical. More banging on the front door caused them to stop. 'Would you get that, please, Stella?'

Before Stella could move, George had raced past them and was at the door, reaching up to turn the latch. He returned much more subdued. 'There are policemen at the door, Mummy. Shall I ask them to come in?'

'It's all right, love, I'll get this,' Stella said, patting him on the head. 'Why don't you go back outside to play?'

George nodded his head. He knew something was up and he wasn't meant to listen.

Stella showed the two uniformed men into the front room and offered them seats. Ruby followed and looked up gratefully as she spotted Frank about to knock on the front door. She felt so much less afraid with her friends around her.

As he stepped over the threshold, slightly out of breath, Ruby held the door open. 'I take it there's news about Eddie?' he asked.

'Yes. And it gets much worse,' Ruby said quickly as

they both went into the room to see what the policemen had to say.

The senior policeman introduced himself as Sergeant Daniel Jackson. The younger constable looked no older than Ruby, and his red face and perfect uniform suggested he must be new to the job. 'This is Constable Robert Jackson, who is here to take notes,' the older man said before giving a slight cough, at which Constable Jackson jumped to and pulled a notebook and pencil from his pocket.

'Do all policemen in Erith share the same surname, or are you related?' Stella enquired politely.

'PC Jackson is my son. He joined the force two weeks ago. However, that is neither here nor there. Do you think you could sit down while I ask my questions?'

Frank quickly brought in three chairs from the other room whereupon they sat down waiting for the policeman to speak. 'I'm sure I know you from somewhere,' Frank said to the younger officer as he held out his hand to shake.

'Possibly the bowls club, or perhaps the police male voice choir. We do have a few members who don't belong to the force,' Robert said with a grin.

'It'd be the bowls club – I'm not much of a singer,' Frank smiled back. 'Do you live round here?'

'Cross Street, with my wife and young nipper,' he replied. 'You . . . ?'

Another cough from the sergeant brought their conversation to a halt. 'Mrs Caselton, I need to ask you a few questions about a theft at the cafe where you work. Are you happy for these people to remain in the room?'

'Please, I'd like them to stay. I have no secrets and Mrs Green has been with me since my mother passed away in the cottage hospital early this morning.'

'Please accept my condolences,' he said, looking a little uncomfortable. 'Would you be able to explain your movements since leaving the cafe on Saturday evening?'

Ruby took a deep breath and explained that she had been at home until Sunday afternoon, when she got word of Milly's collapse. Stella and Frank chipped in to confirm what they knew.

'Are these the keys that were left in your possession for you to open up the cafe this morning?' he asked, pulling the keys Ruby had been searching for from his pocket.

'Yes – I recognize the knots in the piece of string that keeps them together. I thought they were in my bag. I didn't get to the cafe to open up as my mind was elsewhere. Since coming back here early this morning, I've not left the house.'

'Can anyone confirm that? Your husband, perhaps?'

'I was here alone. My son slept over the road at Mrs Green's house,' Ruby said, giving Stella a worried look. She hoped he wouldn't ask about Eddie. Explaining what her husband had done would feel too much like washing her dirty linen in front of these policemen.

'About your husband, Mrs Caselton . . .'

Ruby froze. What could she say?

'May I speak, Sergeant?' Stella asked.

'If it is relevant to the break-in at the cafe,' the sergeant said, linking his fingers together on his lap.

'I feel it is,' she said, giving Ruby a questioning look. When Ruby nodded for her to continue, she went on to explain how Ruby had found her mother's money and possessions missing, along with Eddie's clothes. 'Eddie Caselton has abandoned his wife, taking valuables and their money with him,' she said, trying not to show any emotion in her voice in case the police officer thought she was biased in her opinion of Ruby's husband.

'This does throw a new light on the situation,' he said, looking to the constable to see if he'd written everything down. When the younger man looked up and nodded, the sergeant stood up. 'That will be all for now.'

Ruby was confused. 'I don't understand. Are you going to chase after my husband to get my money back? What about the things he took from the cafe? Will you be able to charge him for that? It's not as if I did anything wrong; I'm just the silly cow left in the lurch now he's sodded off. I can't even pay the rent on this place, so me and my son will be kicked out in the street come next weekend when the rent's due.'

Sergeant Jackson looked embarrassed. 'Mrs Caselton, you have nothing to blame yourself for. If we can prove Eddie Caselton used the keys to steal from the cafe then we can pull him in for questioning. As for your money – I'm sorry, but as the head of this household, your husband has done nothing wrong by taking the money for his own use.'

'What's mine is his, do you mean?' Ruby sniffed, fighting back tears.

Stella put her arm around Ruby. 'It's the way of the world, my love.'

'How about the man abandoning his wife and child?' Frank asked.

Sergeant Jackson shook his head. 'How long has he been gone?'

'Less than a day,' Ruby said, knowing as she spoke that it didn't sound significant. Many men were away from home far longer just by going to work. 'It's fruitless, isn't it?'

'I wouldn't say that, Madam,' he assured her as the two policemen stood to take their leave. 'I will talk to the owners of the cafe, so they know you are not to blame for the theft.'

Stella opened the door, ready to see them out on Ruby's behalf. 'I'd do it quickly if I was you,' she remarked as she looked out. 'There's Marge coming up the road now – and she looks pretty angry from where I'm standing.'

The policemen offered to stay, but Ruby refused their help. She had to face Marge alone. 'If you could just tell her how things stand,' she said as they quickly closed the door.

Frank went out back into the garden to keep George company, while Stella waited to open the door to Marge. She could see from the bay window that there was a heated discussion going on in front of the house – and she could also see curtains twitching at almost every window on the opposite side of the road. The residents would dine out on this scene for many a day. 'Are you sure you don't want me to stay? That Marge can be a force to be reckoned with at times. I've seen her in action before when people have tried it on with her in the cafe.'

'No, thanks all the same; this is one battle I have to face alone. It's my husband who's put me in this mess, and as he isn't here, it's down to me to sort it out.'

'Then I'll be in the other room. If I hear her leading off at you, I'll be in here waving your frying pan at her.'

Despite the circumstances, Ruby giggled at the thought. 'No, Stella, please. I can manage, no matter what she says.'

'Right, here she comes. I'll let her in and then keep out of the way. Chin up, love.' Stella patted Ruby's shoulder before going to the door.

When Ruby looked back afterwards, she couldn't believe she hadn't blown her top at Marge. It could only have been the shock of the past day and losing her mum so suddenly that made her sit and take a tongue-lashing from her employer. Marge rejected an offer of tea and refused to sit down, instead towering over Ruby while she bellowed and fumed.

When she stopped to draw breath, Ruby took the chance to speak. 'I'm sorry things have come to this, Marge. None of what happened in the cafe was my fault. The policemen must have told you just now that my husband took the set of keys from my bag without my knowing. And I'm sorry I wasn't at the cafe to open up as planned – but my mother has just passed away in the early hours of this morning, and it was a shock. You will also have been told, I'm sure, that Eddie left me while I was at the hospital overnight. I know this has nothing to do with you, but I want you to understand the situation. I have no idea what has been taken from your business, but I will try to pay it back bit by bit from my wages each week – that's if it can be proved my husband really was to blame.' She leant back in her chair, relieved to have got that off her chest. Hopefully Marge would not take too much each week, and she'd still have enough to get by.

Marge gave a harsh, brittle laugh. 'You sit there thinking I'll have you back working for me? You've got to be having a laugh.'

'But . . . I thought you liked me working for you? I've always been hard-working and turned up on time, until today. Why are you doing this to me when I really need to work now? I'm the only breadwinner in the house! I have nothing because of Eddie. I can't even afford to bury my mother. Please, Marge, don't do this to me!'

Marge looked at Ruby as she begged for her job, and just for a moment she seemed to falter before making her mind up. 'No. I can't risk you doing the same as your old man and fleecing me. I'll not chase you for the money that he pinched, as I know you don't have it. However, I'll spread the word, so you'll find it hard to work in this town ever again. I know many shop owners in the high street, and most are friends. They won't give you the time of day, so you might think about moving away. We don't want your husband or his kind in this town.' Waving her finger at Ruby, she turned and marched out of number thirteen, slamming the door behind her.

Ruby took a shuddering breath. What's done is done, she thought, taking a deep breath and letting it out slowly.

'What an old cow,' Stella said as she hurried into the room, ready to comfort Ruby. She was surprised to see her up and straightening the chairs, looking around the room and checking for dust.

'It's all said now, and I know where I stand,' Ruby said with a newfound confidence. 'God knows how I'll get by, but I swear I will, and I won't let go of this house until my dying breath.'

'That's more like it,' Stella said, although she did wonder how Ruby intended to live when there wasn't even enough money for next week's rent.

'Mummy,' George said as he came running into the room, followed by a red-faced Frank. 'Can we go and get the medals now?'

'He's run me ragged round that garden,' Frank puffed. 'You've got to listen to this. Tell your mum what you told me, George.'

'The medals. Nanny told me where she hid them for safekeeping. Come on and I'll show you,' he said as he rushed out into the hall and headed upstairs.

Ruby frowned at Stella and Frank. 'I have no idea what he's thinking, but let's go and see.'

They hurried up the steep staircase and found George in Milly's bedroom. He was rummaging through the few clothes hanging in a wardrobe that had been left by the previous tenant.

'He'll be out of luck. Eddie went through that wardrobe last night. I remember straightening her clothes and closing the door while we were all up here,' Stella said.

Ruby stopped dead. 'George is right. Mum did hide the medals. She told me to look in the lining of her Sunday coat. With all that happened, it slipped my mind. I only remembered the box under the bed.' Joining George in his search, she found a black woollen coat in the wardrobe, pulled it out and laid it on the bed. Running her fingers over a basket-shaped brooch, picked out with red and green beads, she smiled. 'I gave this to Mum one Christmas. I couldn't have been much older than George,' she said.

Slipping her hands into the pockets, she pulled out a

clean white handkerchief. 'She never went anywhere without one.'

George hopped up and down in excitement. 'Undo the buttons so we can see inside,' he begged her.

Ruby did just that, and ran her hands down the lining until her fingers touched a couple of bumps close to a side seam. 'I need some scissors,' she said.

'Here, use this.' Frank handed over a small penknife.

Flicking up the blade, she picked carefully at a hand-stitched part of the seam. She let George put his small hand inside, and with glee he pulled out two fabric bags. Whoops of joy came from his lips as three medals pinned to ribbons were shaken loose from one of the bags. The other, Ruby tentatively picked up and emptied onto the bed.

Milly had been true to her word: there was money enough here to give her a good send-off, and some over for Ruby to use as she wished. No doubt she had left a little money in her box to fool anyone who was after taking her possessions. Amongst the notes was a neatly folded piece of paper with Ruby's name on the outside.

'I'll read this later,' she said, tucking it into the pocket of her skirt. She wanted to be alone when she read her mum's final words. Pulling her son close, she said, 'God bless Nanny, eh, George?'

8

New Year's Eve 1905

Eddie Caselton stood in the shadows of the alleyway running between the terraced houses of Alexandra Road. From his vantage point across the road, he could see number thirteen. The curtains had yet to be drawn and as he stared at the bay window he caught a glimpse of his wife, Ruby. There was a smile on her face as she swayed from side to side. He could see she was singing, and kept looking down to where his son stood holding her hand. It wasn't the first time he'd come back to check all was well, although he never knocked on the door or spoke to his family. He didn't wish to be seen or to bring danger to their doorstep.

He hated what he'd done to them. If only they could understand his hand had been forced. If he hadn't fled that night as his mother-in-law lay dying, Ruby might well have had two funerals to organize. Eddie had watched from afar as Milly was laid to rest shortly afterwards, and had been puzzled to see Ruby and George visit a nearby grave to place a posy of flowers before rejoining her sisters in the waiting carriage.

Once he was alone in the cemetery, he'd paid his own respects to his mother-in-law. Bowing his head, he begged her forgiveness and did his best to explain. It did him good to get things off his chest, even though she couldn't hear or reply. Curiosity got the best of him, and he went over to read the headstone of the grave that Ruby and George had visited before they left. He scratched his head in puzzlement – the name of the woman meant nothing to him. He could see she had died around the time they'd moved to Erith, but still had no idea who she was.

As his eyes were drawn to the posy, he noticed a small engraving. Bending to move the flowers to one side, he saw the word 'Sarah'. A fleeting memory came to him of his wife saying that the child she had lost would be called Sarah. Was this his daughter's resting place? But why in this grave? Pondering, he stood up and looked out towards the River Thames. This town had prospects, and he hoped his wife and child would prosper. They were better off without him.

Deep in thought in the alleyway, Eddie was startled as doors suddenly began to open along Alexandra Road. Excited residents flowed into the street, some banging saucepans with wooden spoons while boats on the nearby river tooted their horns. Eddie pulled back further into the shadows, fearful of being spotted as the door to number thirteen opened. Amongst people flowing out of the door, he saw Ruby. She looked so pretty in the lamplight. Her dark hair was pulled high on her head, and she wore a dark purple dress befitting a woman in mourning. Despite her situation, she was smiling and laughing as residents clasped hands, forming a circle and starting to sing 'Auld

Lang Syne'. Eddie's stomach clenched as he spotted a man swing Ruby in his arms and plant a kiss on her lips. Anger surged through him; what man dared to kiss his wife? Why, he'd not been gone four months and she was allowing another man to kiss her. He watched for a while as people started to return to their homes and the vessels on the river fell silent. By then Ruby had been kissed by several men, young and old, and he'd calmed down, knowing it was the season rather than romance – although he could see that Frank Green didn't move far from his wife's side.

He reached into his pocket, pulling out a crumpled envelope. 'Here, lad,' he called to a child still racing up and down the road. 'Do us a favour and post this through the door of number thirteen, will you? Here's thruppence for you to keep your mouth shut about it.' He tossed a coin to the child and watched long enough to see the deed carried out, before picking up his backpack and heading away towards the town.

Since leaving Erith he'd headed to the hop fields of Kent and worked his back off in the fields until the season was done, then moved on to the coast, finding work where he could on fishing boats around Whitstable and down the coastline. It was a hankering to know how his family was that had brought him back here now. Saving every penny he could, he'd decided to leave it for Ruby without her knowing who it came from. He'd not left a note inside the envelope, as he couldn't risk being found. Neither could he make himself known to Ruby or George, in case they came into danger. He vowed there and then to make the trip to Erith and leave money for his family whenever he was able. It was a plan that would give him hope and keep him going in his new life. What had happened to him was his own fault and he only had himself to blame. Whether or not Ruby ever spoke to him again, he would do his best for her and the boy.

Even so, as he walked into the darkness, Eddie felt his heart break.

'Here, Ruby, this has just come through the letter box,' Frank called out as he passed the envelope to Ruby.

'How strange,' she said as she opened the envelope and pulled out the money, then gasped. 'Four pounds! But there's no note of who it is from.' She hurried to the door and looked out, but the street was empty.

'Who do you think could have left it?' Frank asked.

'I have no idea. There's only my name on the envelope.'

'Don't knock it, love,' Stella said as she peered over Ruby's shoulder. 'You can do with every penny right now.'

Ruby clutched the envelope to her breast and smiled to herself. When, back in September, she'd lost Milly and Eddie had done his vanishing act leaving them nigh on destitute, she'd thought her life couldn't get any worse. If it hadn't been for her mother leaving money for the funeral and wake, plus a little more on top, they would not have survived. Ruby had found herself out of work after Marge bad-mouthed her to every shop-owner in town, and her future had looked bleak. It was just four days before the funeral that her fortunes began to look brighter. Her two sisters had arrived out of the blue to speak with her, asking about their mother's will.

Ruby had laughed and told them there was no will, and she was doing her best to give their mum a decent send-off.

Knowing Ruby would be receiving visitors in the lead-up to Milly's funeral, Stella had lent her a tea set while her husband and sons had carried armchairs, a rug, a dark-green chenille tablecloth and two matching occasional tables to furnish the front room. When Ruby protested, Stella had dismissed her words, telling her they hardly used the front room; like many in the road, it was used for high days, holidays and laying out the deceased. Ruby had shuddered at her last word. With a child in the house, she'd decided not to bring Milly home the night before the funeral.

Leaving her sisters sipping tea from the matching cups and saucers, Ruby had gone to the kitchen to refresh the teapot and place dainty cakes onto a serving plate. She took her time, knowing Fanny and Janie would be discussing her remark about there not being a will. Returning to the front room carrying a laden tray, she was pleased to see George sitting between the women chatting politely.

'George has told us that Eddie no longer lives here,' Fanny said.

'That is correct,' Ruby said as she set down the tray and sat next to Janie. The look she gave urged them not to discuss the problem in front of George.

'All I'll say is, we didn't appreciate your circumstances,' Fanny said.

'Given what has happened, you have done very well for yourself. We considered purchasing one of these houses when they were built three years ago,' Janie said, nodding approvingly.

'At the moment I'm renting the house,' Ruby replied. Her dream of one day owning number thirteen had come to seem impossible with Eddie's disappearance. It was all she could do just to keep a roof over their heads – and if not for the landlord of the Prince of Wales Hotel offering her Milly's job and a few hours extra, she couldn't even have managed that. She had been honest and told the man what had happened at the cafe, but he shrugged off her explanation, saying he didn't listen to gossip – and that if she worked half as hard as Milly had done, then he'd be satisfied.

'We've decided we will contribute to mother's funeral,' Janie told her, brushing aside Ruby's explanation that there was money enough put aside by their mother. 'I know I can speak for both of us when I say that we are grateful you've looked after Mother these past years. Your life cannot have been easy. Just remember, we are here for you and George, so please don't be a stranger.'

Thinking back to that conversation now, Ruby felt tears prick her eyes.

'Ruby, are you all right?' Stella asked, bringing her back to the present with a start.

'I'm fine. I'm more than fine,' she smiled. 'Let's just think of this money as coming from a benefactor. It will be put to good use.'

9

May 1910

Ruby had never seen so many people gathered together in one place. When Stella had first mentioned going to London to pay their respects to the late king, she'd been unsure. She wasn't one for crowded trains and the like. But once Stella had explained that she doubted they'd ever experience such an occasion again – after all, look how long the king's mother had lived – she'd relented. It would be good for George to see the grandeur of London and the soldiers on guard around the coffin. It would be something to tell his children, she'd thought to herself. 'Mum went up to London to see the late queen's funeral procession. She talked of nothing else for weeks. She always loved a good send-off.'

Stella and Wilf had burst out laughing. 'My old mum was the same. She'd compare her neighbours' funerals against each other, then weeks later she checked the graves to see who had the best headstone,' Stella said.

'Don't forget to tell Ruby about the list she made so you'd give her a better send-off than her friends had. I can see them all now, up there comparing notes,' Wilf guffawed.

'Oh, my goodness!' Ruby said. 'I hope we don't get as bad as that when we grow old.'

'You have a way to go to catch us up,' Stella laughed. 'Seriously, I could pack up some food and once we've been to pay our respects, we could take the children to look at Buckingham Palace or sit by the river and relax.'

Ruby had relented and along with the Green family they'd set off to London.

Waiting at Erith station, they were jostled this way and that as it seemed most of the townspeople had decided to make the trip on the same day. 'George – don't get too close to the edge of the platform,' she called out nervously.

'It's all right, Ruby, I have hold of George as well as our Donald,' Derek called out to her as he held up George's hand and nodded to where he had hold of Donald's collar to reassure her.

'And I'll watch you,' Frank said as he stood alongside her.

Ruby smiled up at Frank. He'd been a good friend to her over the years. They shared the same love of reading, and would often meet just to chat about books. As a rule, it would be Frank recommending a book to Ruby, and usually she went along with his suggestions. Occasionally she would accompany him to a lending library, where they shared the thrill of poring over books they'd yet to read.

'I've not seen much of you lately, Frank. Have you been busy at work?' He was now in charge of a section of the accounting department of the coal merchant's office, but he didn't talk much about his work as he said it would not interest her.

'No, not really – but there is something I wish to talk to you about, Ruby. I have plans for the future and if you're interested . . . well, they could include you.'

Ruby took a deep breath. She'd feared that this might happen before much longer. Was it possible that what Frank was about to say had something to do with them becoming a couple? It was getting on for five years since Eddie had gone, and although she missed him sorely, Ruby did wonder whether it was unnatural not to consider finding another man with whom to share her life. Although she was close to Frank, she wasn't sure if she had the same depth of feeling for him that she'd had with Eddie. When she'd first met her husband she would tingle at his slightest touch and could happily stay in his arms forever. With Frank, it was different: they shared the same thoughts and interests, and at times it was as if they could read each other's minds. However, on the few occasions he'd kissed her it had felt more like the kiss a brother might bestow on his sister's cheek, with no hint of passion or romance. Ruby knew that Stella would like nothing more than for her to become the wife of her eldest son – but of course, until she knew what had happened to Eddie, she could not draw a line under their marriage and move forward with her life. As much as she would dearly love a brother or sister for George, it could not be.

Ruby was at a loss to know what to say to Frank. The last thing she wanted to do was encourage him, but to knock him back could cause a rift between the two families. 'I look forward to hearing all about it,' she murmured as the train pulled into the station, shrouding the family in steam.

They pushed through the crowd so that they could all be seated in the same carriage. Ruby sat down with a sigh of relief, as for the moment the subject was dropped.

Arriving in London, they paused outside Charing Cross station as Frank consulted his map. 'We jump on a tram at the Embankment and get off at Westminster. It's only a short walk from there.'

'Sounds good to me,' Wilf Green said.

'I'm not too sure about jumping onto a tram at my age, but I'd prefer that to walking,' Stella agreed, while George hopped up and down in excitement. Donald, now fifteen years of age, looked suitably keen.

'I'm just glad to be out of the station,' Ruby shivered, recalling a story in the newspaper about the roof of the station collapsing only a few years ago. There had been fatalities. Although repairs were evident and none of the travellers seemed worried, she just wanted to be away from the building and in the open air.

'Follow me,' Frank said as he set off at a brisk pace.

On the tram, Ruby sat on the lower deck with Wilf and Stella while the others rushed upstairs to the open deck. 'I'll pay,' Wilf called out to the boys.

'It's rather sad, isn't it?' Stella said as they pointed out flags on buildings hung at half-mast.

'Have you seen the black wreaths on the doors?' Ruby answered.

Wilf puffed on his pipe. 'There's a lot of important buildings around this way connected to the royal family as well as our government.'

Stella peered through the window. 'There's nothing like it in Erith, although we do have a few posh houses up the Avenue.'

'All the same, love, we live in an important street.'

Ruby was puzzled. 'Why do you say that, Wilf?'

'Alexandra Road is named after the late king's wife, because the houses were built around the time of Edward VII's coronation,' he explained.

'You learn something new every day. George will be fascinated with that fact,' Ruby said, wishing she'd thought to put a piece of paper and a pencil in her bag to write down any interesting snippets she came across. She and George had recently started keeping a scrapbook, cutting out newspaper articles about the death of their king and stories about the future king and coronation. While she was working in the Prince of Wales Hotel locals had been most helpful, giving her anything that would build towards George's collection.

'It's a bit chilly, isn't it?' Stella gave a small shiver. 'You'd not think it was the middle of May.'

'The weather is right for the situation. Bright sunshine wouldn't seem fitting while our king is lying dead not many yards from here,' Wilf said thoughtfully. 'At least it's not raining as well. Bound to have to queue before we can pay our respects.'

'Queue?' Stella asked.

'I did tell you that the lads down on the docks came up yesterday, and they said the queue runs right down to the river.' Wilf raised his eyebrows at his wife. 'You've put your best shoes on, haven't you?'

'I wanted to look smart for the royal family,' Stella huffed indignantly.

'Believe me, woman, when I say that if we do meet a member of the royal family, they will not be looking at your feet. You'll not be fit for anything come tomorrow when your feet are sore.'

Stella nudged Ruby. 'He's right – but I'll not give him the satisfaction of knowing it. I've put me slippers in my bag.'

Ruby tried not to laugh. Stella could be a tonic at times.

'Look lively,' Wilf said, getting to his feet a few minutes later. 'This is our stop.'

Waiting for the boys to join them, Ruby looked around her. What a grand place London was, she thought. She recognized Big Ben from the many pictures she'd seen, and wondered if she would hear the chimes when it struck the hour.

'Keep together, now,' Frank instructed them. 'We have to cross the road, so hang on to each other so no one gets lost. The trams move faster here than they do back home.'

Ruby clung on to George's hand as if his life depended on it, while Derek took hold of her other hand and also his younger brother's. 'Are you enjoying the trip so far?' he asked with a cheeky grin.

'I'd like to have visited under different circumstances,' she replied. 'I'm surprised you've not brought one of your young lady friends with you?' Derek was a popular lad these days.

'It's a family day today. Family and friends,' he corrected himself. 'Mum wouldn't have been happy if I'd brought along a stranger.'

'Your mother brought you up right,' she grinned at him as they reached the other side of the road and joined the back of a queue that seemed to go on forever.

'Do you think it would be rude if we had one of our sandwiches while we're stood here?' Stella wondered as she turned to check their party were still together. 'My stomach's rumbling like a good'n.'

'I don't see why not. There are others eating. Better out here on the street before we get any closer,' Ruby said as she looked down the queue and then behind them. 'Crikey – there must be another fifty people who have joined us already.'

Stella dished out the food, telling the younger lads to stand still while they ate and to mind their best clothes didn't get mucky.

For two hours the friends shuffled slowly forward until at last the doors of Westminster Hall appeared in front of them. Ruby checked George's face and wiped his cheeks with her handkerchief before running her fingers through his unruly hair. 'There you are. You look respectable enough to say goodbye to our king,' she said, stepping back to check him over before planting a kiss on the tip of his nose.

'Urgh, get off,' he said, scrubbing his nose. 'Someone might see. I'm not a kid any more. I'll be a working man when I'm fourteen. You won't be kissing me then, will you?'

'That's four years off, George, and I'll keep kissing you until my dying breath, so you'll just have to put up with it,' she laughed, pinching his cheek. 'I take it you aren't too old to hold your mum's hand, are you?'

'I'm only joking, Mum. You can kiss me as much as you like, and I'll keep kissing you until I'm an old man too,' he said, taking her hand as they entered the sombre building.

'What do you think you'll remember most about today?' Frank asked Ruby as he sat next to her on the train home, supporting a sleeping George who was slumped against him.

'I suppose you think I'm going to say the grandeur of the building and the solemnity of the occasion,' Ruby answered, a faraway look on her face. 'But I'm more inclined to picture the thousands of people who silently passed by the coffin, no doubt remembering this was the son of Queen Victoria.'

'I can understand how you feel. Did you travel to London to see the queen's funeral procession?'

'No. George was a baby, and I didn't want to leave him with Mum as I'd have worried too much. Eddie went, though, and told me all about it,' she said. 'Perhaps I'll take George to watch the coronation. He would enjoy seeing the parades and the posh carriages. It seems strange to think Queen Victoria has not been gone ten years and already we are talking of her grandson being king. Imagine if my mum had been queen – I couldn't even contemplate taking over her crown while still mourning her loss,' she said sadly.

'The royal family know no different. They were born into it,' Frank said as he shifted slightly to get more comfortable. 'George may only be ten years of age, but it's like propping up a sack of potatoes,' he grinned.

'Here, let me take him for a while,' Ruby said, holding out her arms to take her son. 'He can squeeze in here next to me.'

'No, I'm fine now I've stretched my arm. If you like, I'll give him a piggyback home?'

Ruby chuckled. 'Just like a sack of potatoes?'

'He's no trouble. You must be proud of him. I don't know a brighter kid. He knocks our Donald into a cocked hat.'

Ruby felt proud that Frank thought well of her son. She'd found him to be an intelligent man, so his words meant something to her. 'I do wish I'd been able to give him a brother or sister. It is good he has your Donald to talk with, but now Donald is that bit older I fear George will appear too childish to have hanging on his shirt tails.'

'There's still time. You've not reached old bones yet,' Frank said, lowering his voice so fellow travellers didn't hear.

Ruby rubbed the window with the cuff of her coat, trying to look out into the darkness to see where they were. 'I could say the same of you, Frank Green. I've not seen you go courting as much as other men your age,' she smiled as the train came to a halt. 'My goodness, this is our station,' she added as a whistle could be heard, with the stationmaster announcing they'd arrived in Erith.

The group of friends walked in companionable silence, apart from Frank. He'd noticed his mum was wearing her indoor slippers now, and joshed her playfully about not being able to take her anywhere posh. Stella was quick to answer that the person they'd gone to pay their respects to would be none the wiser.

Ruby fell behind to walk with Frank who, despite him saying otherwise, was struggling with the sleeping George on his back.

'Come here, you weakling, let me take him,' Derek said, taking George from his brother and sweeping him up in his arms with ease. 'If you did a man's job you'd have the muscles,' he grinned good-naturedly.

'And if you had the brains you'd not be working down in the brickfield,' Frank was quick to reply as they watched Derek move at speed ahead of them.

'It's a joy to see you brothers get on so well,' Ruby said as Frank offered his arm and relieved her of her heavy bag. Slipping her arm through his, she thought how lucky she was to have such good friends.

'There's something I wanted to ask you,' Frank said as they approached Alexandra Road. 'Can I come in and have a few words?'

Ruby felt her heart lurch. If he was going to swear his undying love to her, it wasn't the right time. She loved Frank as she would a brother, if she'd had one. To let him down could cause pain not only for him, but also Stella and Wilf, and that was the last thing she wanted – especially when they were all tired after the trip to London, and George needed his bed. 'For a few minutes,' she said as Frank took the yawning boy from Derek's arms and she made her thanks. Opening the front door, she ushered them inside and turned to look back at the street she'd come to know and love so well. With the row of houses bathed in the glow of the streetlamps, there was a certain magic in the air. Ruby prayed that nothing would change her life, but as she wondered about the future, a shiver ran through her body.

'Bless him, he didn't need any persuading to get to his bed. It was all I could do to get him undressed and run a flannel over his face,' Ruby said as she joined Frank in the front room. He'd lit the two gas lights on the wall either side of the chimney breast and had carried in a tea tray.

'You are lucky to have a gas stove. Mum went on for ages until Dad relented when the coal stove took too long to get going.'

Ruby sat down and took the teacup he handed to her. 'It wasn't my doing. You can thank the chap who owned the house before my landlord got hold of it. Surely you must have known the owner?'

'We never really crossed paths. Dad said he left pretty quickly.'

Ruby told Frank the story of how the house had been lost due to the man's addiction to gambling and Eddie being in the right place to take on the tenancy. 'It was one of the best things to happen in my life. Here we are as near as damn it five years later, with a lovely home.'

'But no husband,' he said, watching her closely to see how she would react.

'I'm happy as I am, Frank. I do miss Eddie – whatever you may think, there was a time when he was a good husband. In hindsight, I can see that he changed around the time we moved here. Perhaps I am to blame for what happened. I wanted a nice home and the perfect family. Even that went wrong when we lost Sarah. I must claim some responsibility for my marriage failing. I should have thought more about Eddie than about having a comfortable home.' In the time since Eddie had left, Ruby had thought long and hard about him straying from the straight and narrow, and her current thoughts were that she must have contributed to his decision to leave.

Frank placed his tea on a side table and knelt in front of her, taking her hands in his own. For a moment Ruby froze – was he going to propose? Please God he wasn't going to say anything rash. 'Ruby, you must never think you are to blame for what happened with Eddie. I only knew him after he moved here, but he must have once had some very good qualities for you to fall in love with him. You're no fool, Ruby Caselton. I just want you to know that I'll be your friend – the best friend I can. I love you, and I feel that in another life we would have been soulmates.'

Ruby looked down at his earnest expression and pulled her hands away from his. 'Please, Frank, please don't do this. Don't ruin our friendship . . .'

'Ruin it?' Frank cried out. Then he put his face in his hands and took several deep breaths. 'No, all I wanted you to know was that I would always be your friend, and . . .'

Ruby fell to her knees next to him and pulled his hands away so they could look eye to eye. 'Oh Frank, was that all you wanted to tell me? There was me thinking you were going to propose – not that I'm free to marry again,' she laughed, feeling embarrassed. 'However, you did prompt me to think about Eddie and realize I still love him, for all his faults. Come what may, I'm his until death us do part. We made our vows and I'll stick to them. Even though I'm no churchgoer, I do like to keep a promise.'

'That's as it should be. And if the time should ever come when Eddie is back in your life, I want to be able to look him square in the face and say I was a true friend and nothing more.' Frank took a deep breath and looked away. 'I've never told a living soul this before, but ... I'm different from most men. I have no interest in having a wife,' he said, looking back at Ruby to see if she understood.

'Oh ... I think I understand.' Ruby knew that men were breaking the law for having relationships with other men, and had to keep their feelings to themselves. She didn't wish to know what they did behind closed doors – the very thought of it shocked her. However, if a man loved another man in the way she'd felt love for her Eddie, she saw no wrong in it. Frank was a good and gentle man, and he deserved to experience love. She could see now that his love for her was that of a good friend – a brother. She nodded in agreement before looking a little puzzled. 'But didn't you walk out with that girl from the Co-op?'

'Only because Mum pushed us together. She soon got tired of me. She's engaged to someone on the cheese counter now.'

Ruby felt her cheeks start to twitch and when she spotted the twinkle in Frank's eyes, they both started to laugh. 'Blimey, Frank, I thought I had a problem with Eddie going missing. We're a right pair, aren't we?'

They got to their feet and hugged before sitting back in their armchairs and finishing their tea.

'Do you mean to tell me your parents really don't know about you being . . . different?'

'What, that I read more books than the rest of the family put together, you mean?'

Ruby laughed with him, but then a great sadness washed over her as she considered her friend's situation. 'You can't make jokes for the rest of your life. You can't live a lie.'

'That's what I wanted to talk to you about. I know you'll understand why I want to change my life and move away from Alexandra Road.'

Ruby frowned. 'But what will you do? Where will you go? I'll miss you, and our chats about books. Who will advise me on the best books to read?'

Frank looked exhilarated. 'Well, you could come with me – that's if you want to.'

'Come with you . . . but where? What about George and my house? My job in the pub? Frank, this is all such a shock. You have a good job at the coalyard. Why throw it all away because you are unhappy with your love life? Why not tell your family, so that you can stay here?'

Frank shook his head, laughing. 'Dear, sweet Ruby – I am happy with my life. I've simply come to a crossroads and made a decision to travel on the road that means gambling with my future. There is no one in my life at the moment, and possibly never will be. I just know I don't wish to court and marry a woman.'

'That's your choice and I respect it, but how does this plan include me? I have no money to speak of, and even less if I leave my job and come with you. And I have George to consider . . .'

Frank reached into his pocket and pulled out the

notebook he always carried with him. 'Let me explain. You know I love books and I came to think how good it would be to work with them all day long.'

Ruby became excited. 'You mean you're going to write books?'

'No – if only I had the talent, I'd have started doing that years ago. I prefer to read them. I want to run a second-hand bookshop, right here in Erith. What do you think?'

Ruby thought for a moment. 'I think that's a blooming good idea. You love books, and your customers will know that from your enthusiasm. Why, you'll be able to encourage people to read who have never bought a book before. But where would you find these second-hand books to stock your shop?'

Frank opened the back of his notebook and pulled out a clipping from the local newspaper, passing it over to her with a grin. 'A couple of weeks ago, I decided to test the water. I placed this advert in the *Erith Times*, asking for people to get in touch if they were interested in selling their books. I was worried Mum and Dad would wonder why I received so many letters and start to ask questions, and want to tell them about my plans in my own time – when I have premises secured, and not before. So I started to hang about by the front door before heading off to work, to intercept the post. It's always on time. I did have to take a chance Mum wouldn't ask what I was up to if anything arrived in the other two post deliveries of the day, but I managed to get away with it. Ruby, I had over fifty letters! Some people want to get rid of whole collections of books that have been owned by deceased members of their family; other people enquired about me taking ten or twenty books off their hands.'

'Have you bought any? Were any of them any good? How exciting!'

'Well, so far I have one hundred and fifty books,' he said.

'Where have you put them? It's not as if you can hide that many books in your bedroom. Stella would be extremely suspicious about your reading habits.'

Frank shook his head. 'I've rented part of a barn up the top of Crayford Road. It's clean and dry, so it will do for now. But I'll need plenty more books before I even open the shop, and more than that to loan them out. I must admit, the idea of a lending library appeals to me too.'

'Have you seen any shops you could rent? I assume that will be rather expensive,' Ruby said thoughtfully.

Frank chuckled. He could see the enthusiasm shining from Ruby's face and appreciated her questions. 'There is a shop at the top end of Pier Road. I've spoken to the landlord, and as it has stood empty for a while and needs a lick of paint and a thorough clean inside, he said I can have it for half the rent for the first six months. Of course, I need to build bookshelves and sort out the counter – and most importantly, I need someone to work with me.'

'Oh, Frank, it will be wonderful! I promise to be your first customer, and George will be your second. You will have reading material for children, won't you? I'll come and help clean the shop, and I'm a dab hand with a paint-brush these days.'

'I just knew you'd be as excited as I am. But there is a

question I need to ask in all of this. Will you come and work for me?'

Ruby was thoughtful for a short while. She enjoyed her job working in the Prince of Wales Hotel; she got on with the landlord and the customers, but couldn't envisage being a cleaner and doing the odd shift behind the bar for many more years to come. She'd already been there nigh on five years and was beginning to get itchy feet for a change. 'Oh, that would be a dream of a job – but can you afford to take on a shop assistant? All this will cost money, Frank.'

'I know it will. I've put quite a bit away over the years and I know I can make a go of it, especially with the offer of six months' cheap rent. I should know by the end of that time if I have the makings of being a bookshop owner or not. It is going to be such an adventure. I'm not so sure my parents will approve, but at my age, most men don't live with their parents any more and already have a wife and a family. I've been thinking I may move into the rooms over the shop.'

'You've certainly thought this over, haven't you? I am a little worried for you, though. What if after six months the business fails? What will you do with your life then?'

'If it fails, I reckon I can get another job as a bookkeeper at any one of the local coalyards, so don't worry about that.' Frank turned the pages of his notebook and showed Ruby his plans. She could see how much he'd saved, what he'd spent on books so far and how much he thought it would cost to have the shop ready to open. There was also a note of wages that would be paid to his assistant. 'I have enough money in my savings to tide the business over for three months. I'm hoping by then to have enough customers. What do you think, Ruby? Could you become a shopkeeper's assistant? Perhaps you'd like some time to think about it.'

'I don't need to think about it. It's a wonderful idea, but there is a problem,' she said, pointing to the row of figures showing how much Frank intended to pay his assistant each week.

Frank looked at it. 'I'm sorry, Ruby – that's the most I can afford to pay. I'd make it more if I could.'

'Oh, you idiot,' she laughed. 'My problem is that it's too much! I can live on a lot less, Frank.'

He took her hands in his and looked into her eyes. 'Are you sure? I don't want you and George going without just because I want to play at being a shopkeeper.'

'Then let's agree on a figure,' she said, taking his pencil and jotting down a sum that was just over half of the figure he'd noted. 'Will you be happy to pay me this?'

'On one condition,' he said. 'We will review the amount after three months. Is that a deal?'

'It's a deal,' she said, holding out her hand for him to shake.

Instead he placed his hands onto her shoulders and gave her a gentle kiss on the cheek.

'I hope that's purely platonic,' Ruby laughed.

'I can confirm that it is platonic,' he said.

'Thank goodness for that. Your mother would have something to say if you took me for your fancy woman, carrying on with you in the flat over the shop,' she chuckled. 'Now, would you like another cup of tea to celebrate the start of your business empire?'

'No, I'd best get going. I want to finish work a couple of hours early tomorrow to go and view the shop, so best not roll in late due to oversleeping. Would you like to come with me to view it?'

'I can think of nothing better. Oh, Frank, I'm so excited for you – this must be a dream come true.'

'It certainly is,' he said as he opened the front door to let himself out. Turning to face her at the gate, he gave her a kiss on the cheek. 'Thank you for believing in me, and for being a true friend, Ruby. If I can ever pay you back, I will,' he promised.

Ruby stood on tiptoe and returned his kiss. 'Thank you for inviting me to be part of the adventure. I'm so thrilled for you. Sleep tight, Frank,' she said as he waved goodbye, crossing the road and letting himself into number fourteen.

Stepping into the hallway, Ruby closed the door and leant against it, thinking of how bright her future now looked. She had not seen the bedroom curtains part as Stella watched her kiss Frank. Neither did she see the man standing in the shadows, watching thoughtfully.

Yawning widely, she decided to head to bed; the washing-up could wait for the morning. She hadn't taken one step away from the door when she heard a slight rattle of the letter box, and an envelope fell onto the doormat. She recognized the handwriting – the swirl of the 'y' and the short line struck below her name. Even though there was just the one word – *Ruby*, neatly written in the middle of the envelope – this was a chance to find out who had been sending her money over the past five years. Opening the door, she hurried down the short path, recognizing the outline of the person as he walked away.

'Eddie!' she called, catching up to him and grabbing the back of his jacket. He turned and silently looked at her, his eyes burning into hers.

She couldn't believe this was her husband. Somehow, she'd imagined him sinking into the depths of depravation as the drink and gambling took more of a hold on his body and mind. Instead he was clean-shaven, leaner, and just as handsome as she remembered from the days before the demons arrived and ruined their marriage.

She held out her hand. 'Please – come inside. We need to talk.'

'But George?'

'He's sound asleep. If we are quiet, he won't even know you're here – if that's what you want?'

He nodded. 'Your visitor . . . ?'

'It was Frank Green. We are friends, nothing more. Please, Eddie, come indoors,' she begged.

Eddie followed his wife, stepping over the threshold into what had been his home. Memories of past arguments, his unhappiness and his drinking were forgotten as he followed Ruby and closed the front door.

Ruby beckoned him to follow her into the front room and pulled the door to. 'George is unlikely to hear you from his room at the back of the house. If that's the way you want it? After the busy day he's had, he's in a deep sleep.'

Eddie nodded without saying a word.

'Eddie . . . why?' Ruby searched his face for an answer. 'I don't understand why you left as you did when Mum died. You must still have cared for us in some way to leave the money over the years. Please tell me what happened?' she begged.

172

Eddie didn't speak, he just looked hungrily at Ruby's face. He knew he should have walked away and not accepted her invitation to come into the house. His wife had grown more beautiful during the past years. 'God, Ruby, I've missed you,' he whispered, pulling her to him and holding her close.

'Oh, Eddie, this isn't a dream, is it? Have you come back for good?' she asked, not caring when he didn't answer her question.

'Shush,' he said before kissing her gently.

Ruby felt memories surface of the man she loved and thought she'd lost. Feelings she'd buried for so long came rushing back as their kisses became more intense. From the very first time Eddie had kissed her, she had known she was smitten. Nothing else mattered when she was in his arms; his gentle lovemaking stirred a longing in her that she'd never felt for any other man. Eddie wasn't solely to blame for the intensity of their love and her giving in to him so quickly when she fell with their George. She had wanted him as badly as he wanted her. If only life had not interfered, she knew she would have been with Eddie until the end of time.

Eddie felt for the buttons at the back of her dress and started to undo them slowly with one hand while holding her close with the other.

She thought she would burst with the intensity of her feelings as her dress fell from her shoulders. Pulling away from him, she fought to control her breathing. 'Not here, Eddie, not here,' she said, taking him by the hand and leading him slowly upstairs to their bedroom, stopping for a moment to listen for any sign that George was waking.

Pushing the door closed, they fell onto the large double bed, the past forgotten, thinking only of the moment.

Dawn broke, bringing fingers of light into the bedroom as Ruby stirred. She was still snuggled up to Eddie, her head on his bare chest. She ran her fingers delicately across his chest, marvelling at how his body had changed in five years. Now he had a torso rippling with muscles, his skin tanned and his face healthy. She felt herself blush as she thought of the night and their lovemaking. She would have been content to lie here forever, but thoughts of George came into her head. What would he think about seeing Eddie back in the home? She needed to prepare him for the surprise of his dad returning to live with them. Giving Eddie a gentle shake to wake him, she was rewarded with a bear hug and a kiss that melted her insides.

'Eddie, we need to have a talk about George and what to say to him when he comes down to breakfast. It is going to be a shock to see his daddy home once more.'

Eddie froze and pulled away from Ruby. 'My love, I can't stay. It's too dangerous for you to have me in the house. I promise you I will return when I can, but for now I need to go.'

'What do you mean? I thought you'd come home for good once you followed me into the house – what was last night about?'

'Darling Ruby – it shouldn't have happened. What we did was foolish, but I couldn't resist you. My heart has always been here with you in this house. You've got to believe me.'

Ruby sat up, pulling the sheet over her bare breasts. 'I don't understand. Why do you keep running away? We can't live like this. You've turned into a stranger, Eddie. You took Mum's money and then when I needed you most, you ran away. I should think of you as a thief and a coward, but I love you, Eddie,' she said, fighting the urge to shout at him. Instead she kept her voice to an intense whisper, afraid of waking George. 'I was angry for ages! The names I called you should never be repeated in public. I spent sleepless nights fuming, then worrying and being so angry with you. My head told me to forget you, but my heart wanted you back. Now you're here, and last night was like a dream come true – and now you tell me you're going away again? How long will it be this time? Tell me that, Eddie. How can I live without you?'

He climbed from the bed, and Ruby averted her eyes. She'd never looked directly at her husband without his clothes before; he had always covered himself out of respect for her shy disposition. When did that change – had there been another woman? She needed to know.

'Eddie, is there another woman?' He spun to look at her as he tightened the belt around his waist. There was hurt in his eyes.

'How can you even ask that question? There's never been anyone else. I swear to you, Ruby, on our son's life – you are the only woman for me.'

'Then why?'

'One day I'll be able to tell you, but for now, I have to go,' he said, buttoning up his shirt and reaching for his jacket, which had been thrown to the floor as they'd pulled at each other's clothes hours earlier. Kneeling on the side of the bed, he leant over to kiss her. She reached out to pull him closer, but he struggled and stepped away. 'No, Ruby, I'm going. I have to, because if I were to stay, it could put you and our son in danger. Please believe me – I'd tell you if I could, but for now, please just listen for George, so he doesn't hear me leave the house?'

Ruby now knew she couldn't keep him there. 'I'll remember this night for the rest of my life. Come back to me when you can, Eddie. There will never be another man for me. Whatever happens, remember I'm here, and I will be waiting for you as long as it takes.' She could see he was close to tears. 'You'd best go before you are spotted. There will soon be people out in the street heading to work, and curtains will start to twitch if they see you leave by the front door.'

'I'll go by the back door and along the alley to Britannia Bridge. If I can get a message to you, I will. I love you, Ruby,' were his parting words.

Ruby stepped into her dress and hurried through to the spare back bedroom. Pulling aside the curtain, she watched her husband disappear through the wooden gate at the end of the long garden. 'I love you, Eddie Caselton,' she whispered, kissing her fingers and waving as he disappeared from view.

10

~

August 1910

'You do look pale,' Frank said as he entered the bookshop from the back room, his arms full of books. 'Are you under the weather?'

Ruby brushed a stray hair from her hot face and fanned herself, using a sheet of paper picked up from the counter. 'It's nothing. We've had a rush on since you popped out. Your window display of adventure books certainly attracted shoppers. F. Green, Bookseller will be a resounding success, I can feel it in my water,' she smiled, trying hard to focus although her head was starting to spin. 'It is rather warm,' she faltered, as her knees started to buckle beneath her.

Frank dropped the books he was carrying and along with an elderly gentleman who was perusing books from the history shelves, he rushed to her side, just about catching her as she sunk to the floor. The man pulled up a wooden chair from the other side of the counter and helped Frank make her comfortable.

'Could you fetch some water, please?' Frank asked the

177

man. 'There's a tap just inside that door and you will find cups on the shelf.'

Ruby tried to push Frank away. 'I'm fine . . . I'm fine . . .' she mumbled.

'You're not fine at all,' Frank fussed. 'Sit there and take some deep breaths,' he told her sternly as she tried to get to her feet. 'I'd never forgive myself if you fell ill while working here. You do long hours in the shop, then rush off home to care for George and do your housework. The house is always as bright and clean as a new pin – then on top of that, I find you upstairs clearing out the spare rooms this morning. This can't go on, Ruby.'

'Here you are,' the customer said, handing a china cup full of cold water to Frank, who urged Ruby to take slow sips.

'Thank you – it's such a warm day, I was overcome for a little while. I'll be fine now.' She smiled at the man, who still looked worried. 'I'm sorry to have interrupted your browsing. Is there anything we can help you with?'

Frank laughed. 'Don't you ever rest? I'll serve the gentleman, Ruby. You sit there and take it easy for a few minutes, then I'm packing you off home. George will be back from school shortly, anyway.'

Ruby was grateful to be able to relax for a short while. Since the shop had opened the month before, they'd been run off their feet. Frank was often out collecting books from private addresses or attending auctions. Ruby would man the shop, waiting for him to return to the shop in Pier Road to see what gems he'd found. On Saturdays, George would help in the shop, and occasionally Donald would help out for a few hours.

Stella, however, never came near the premises at all; since the night Frank had told her about his plans, it was as if she had drifted away. No amount of explaining that it was his dream to run his own business could convince his mother that he was doing the right thing.

'I'm fine now – I feel a lot better. It must have been the heat that affected me; it's quite a close day. Do you think there's going to be a storm later?'

Frank looked at Ruby's flushed cheeks, noticing that her hands shook a little as she held the cup. He wasn't fooled by the smile on her face. Ruby hadn't been herself for a few weeks now. There was most certainly something wrong with her, which worried him. Under normal circumstances he would have turned to his mother for advice, but Stella's coolness towards him at the moment also extended to Ruby. He'd seen her turn away and rarely answer when Ruby was in the room. Was it because he'd given up a good job at the coalyard – a job with prospects – to set out on a venture that could fail? Perhaps it was because he'd asked Ruby for help with the shop, rather than his mum? Working long hours, he'd not yet got the upstairs rooms of the shop in Pier Road ready to move in to, so he was still living with his parents. However, the frosty reception he received whenever he was at home caused him to stay away as much as possible. Frank closed his ears to Stella advising him to go back to his secure job at the coalyard. The more he resisted her advice, the worse the atmosphere became.

The older gentleman accepted his purchases, now wrapped in brown paper and tied neatly with string, and pocketed his change. 'I hope your wife will be feeling better soon,' he said. 'She needs to keep her feet up more. My wife was the same when she was first expecting our nippers.'

Frank's chin almost hit the floor as he considered the man's words. Surely not? Making a note of the purchases, he bid the man a good afternoon. He returned to where Ruby was sitting, staring into space. She must have heard the exchange. She looked up at Frank as he placed a hand on her shoulder. 'He's right; I'm certain I'm expecting a baby.'

'Who . . . when . . . ?' Frank asked, looking puzzled. 'I had no idea you had a gentleman friend, let alone . . .'

Ruby's eyes shone with unshed tears. 'It's Eddie's.'

'But you've not seen him for years. I thought he'd vanished from your life?'

Ruby took her dear friend's hand and clasped it tightly. 'Five years. I've not seen him for five years, and then one night a few months ago, he turned up on my doorstep. He's changed, Frank – it seemed as if the good man I married had come back again.'

'If he's a good man, why did he love you and leave you?' he asked bitterly. 'That's not the behaviour of a decent husband.'

'I don't know. He wouldn't say – he mentioned putting me in danger if I knew. I'm sure he'll come back to me one day . . .'

'Meanwhile, he leaves you alone to carry a child while bringing up another one?'

'Please don't be angry. I need friends more than ever now. I would have told your mum about the baby, but she seems to have turned against me.'

'It's not just you,' Frank replied, squeezing her hand. 'I don't seem to be her favourite son at the moment,' he laughed harshly. Stella used to tell all three of her boys that they were her favourites; it had been the same for as long as he could remember. 'I'm worried about your reputation. A woman with one child, who was abandoned by her husband, can be judged harshly enough in some people's eyes, but an abandoned mother carrying a child could be seen as something different. I'm not one to worry about what people say. Let's face it, I'm a chap in my early thirties who has never married. We seem to have to fit into people's ideas of the correct way to live. In my case it's a wife and children, and in your case, you should be a dignified woman bringing up a child alone.'

Ruby agreed. 'People can be so judgemental. I put on a hard face, but inside . . . it hurts. I live next to someone who seems like the most bigoted woman in the world, but because she goes to church and lives a saintly life, she makes me look like the devil's child. I'm worried what people will think when it's seen I'm carrying a baby.'

Frank put his arm round Ruby. 'I'll always be here for you. I'm not sure how good I'll be with the baby, but I'll try to be the best uncle I can.'

'I'm worried for you too, Frank. This could affect *your* reputation.'

Frank was puzzled. 'What do you mean? It's not as if me and you . . .'

'But people might assume it is yours. We're always together, and some do consider it strange for a man and a woman to be good friends and nothing more.'

His face turned pale. 'I'd not considered such a thing.

I'm sorry if my friendship has put you in such a position. What a to-do!' He thought for a moment. 'Perhaps I should offer to marry you. We'd both be considered respectable then.'

Ruby's eyes welled up. 'That's the kindest offer anyone has ever made to me. As much as I'd be honoured to accept your kind gesture, there is one fly in the ointment – Eddie.' She smiled at Frank, assuming he was not serious.

Frank pulled a chair close to hers, checking there was no one about to enter the shop. 'I'm serious. Those who know you are aware Eddie deserted you five years ago. They can see we are close, and if they're putting two and two together anyway . . . why not let them see a solution to the problem, and assume we are a couple?'

'You'd do this for me?' Ruby asked, feeling humble that he was being so thoughtful.

'It's for both of us. People would stop whispering about me, and you would not be shunned or made the subject of gossip. If you thought it a good idea, I could move into your house and assume the role of your husband, even though we'd remain unmarried in case Eddie came back.'

'This could get very confusing,' Ruby said, shaking her head. 'I'd hate Eddie to think I'd been unfaithful to him, but your suggestion does make sense. And I do have a spare bedroom . . .'

'Is there no way you can get word to Eddie? If he knows about your condition, he might even return for good. What man wouldn't, if he knew he had another child on the way?'

'A man who is hiding from something – or someone,' Ruby pointed out. 'I have no idea where he is. He turned up just once, after five years, and that was out of the blue.

It could be another five years before I see him again! However, I can't manage on my own. I'm sure if he returns he will understand why you've moved in and are pretending to be my husband. But we can cross that bridge when we come to it.'

Frank dropped to his knees and took his friend's hand. 'Ruby Caselton, will you do me the honour of being my pretend wife, until death do us part?'

Ruby shuddered as a chill ran up her back. 'At least until Eddie returns,' she smiled, kissing his cheek. 'My dearest Frank, whatever would I do without you?'

28th February 1911

'Why, she's the spit of her daddy,' Stella said, leaning over the cradle where baby Pat slept. Only three days old, she was the most contented child imaginable and adored by her family.

Ruby held her breath. Was Stella referring to Eddie or Frank?

'Frank had the same colour of hair when he was born,' the doting grandmother beamed.

Ruby let out a silent sigh. Her relationship with Stella had returned to normal on the day they both visited Frank's parents to announce they were expecting a child, and Frank would be moving in to number thirteen. Stella had thrown herself into preparing for the baby's arrival, knitting and sewing until the unborn child had the largest layette possible. Meanwhile, Wilf had disappeared into his shed to work on a wooden cradle with intricate engravings of ships and the river. 'He's after the child being a lighterman,' Frank had joshed.

'I must say, I had a feeling this day would come,' Stella said with a glint in her eye.

'She had to pop out some day,' Ruby laughed from where she lay propped up in her bed. 'Although there was a time I thought I was carrying a baby elephant.'

'I meant you two. I spotted my Frank leaving your house late one night around nine months ago. I was looking from my bedroom window at the time. I had hoped there would be something going on between you, although nothing was mentioned, and I began to disapprove of your secrecy. At one point I thought you were just using my son because your husband had left you. Can you forgive me?'

Ruby felt her cheeks start to burn. That was the night Eddie had turned up – just after Frank had left, when they'd first discussed the bookshop. Thank goodness Stella had not continued to watch her house, or she'd have seen Eddie's arrival minutes later. 'There's nothing to forgive – and I hadn't noticed your disapproval,' she said, crossing her fingers under the bedcovers to atone for such a blatant lie.

'Thank you for naming her after my mother. I'd have done the same if one of the boys had been a girl. Instead they all bear the names of my father and his brothers.'

'Don't forget her second name is Stella, after you. It's to thank you for all your help, especially when my Sarah was born. I'd not have coped if you'd not been there.'

'I did what any friend would do,' Stella smiled. 'I am surprised that you didn't call this little lady by the same name.'

Ruby was horrified. 'No, I'll only ever have one daughter called Sarah. She's as real to me as this little one,' she said as Pat stirred in her cradle.

'When I have children, I'll call the first girl Sarah,' George said as he climbed onto her bed and snuggled up.

Ruby and Stella laughed at his words. 'First you have to find a job, and then a girl who is willing to marry you,' Ruby said as she tickled him until he was in fits of laughter.

'Someone will soon snap him up,' Stella smiled. 'He's such a handsome little chap. What do you think you will do when you leave school, George?'

'I'm going to work at Vickers and build things,' he answered seriously. 'Mrs Grant said her husband would give me a job.'

Stella gave Ruby a bemused look. 'Mrs Grant?'

'It's a bit of a long story, but in a way, you and Sarah played a part in our meeting the lady.' Ruby went on to explain their meeting with the woman in the cemetery, and her benevolence over the years as she took an interest in George. 'We still correspond regularly, although it's mainly George who writes these days. She has also become a very good customer at Frank's bookshop, recommending many of her friends to visit and make purchases.'

Frank joined them and sat on the edge of Ruby's bed. Knowing Ruby would be having visitors, he'd moved some of his clothes from his room to her wardrobe and laid out his grooming kit on top of a chest of drawers. To all intents and purposes, it looked as though they shared a room and a bed. 'It was Mrs Grant who suggested I should dedicate a section of the shop to antiquarian books. It brings in different customers.'

'Don't forget my idea,' George chirped.

'Do tell,' Stella smiled at the lad.

'Books that have been much read and well-thumbed that we put outside in baskets for people who are poor to rummage through,' he said seriously. 'We sell them for a farthing each.'

'I see you are listening to Frank and learning the right bookselling words,' Ruby said indulgently.

'The lad is an entrepreneur,' Stella declared.

'What's that?' he asked.

'Someone who will go far, and be very rich.' Ruby smiled at her clever boy.

'I like the sound of that,' he exclaimed.

Stella chuckled. 'You'll soon be changing the name of your shop to Frank Green and Son,' she said as she caught George's hands to help him from the bed. 'You have the starting of a dynasty, Frank.'

Ruby opened her mouth to correct Stella, but thought better of it. A sadness engulfed her as she thought of Eddie, and how quickly he seemed to have been forgotten by his own son.

22nd June 1911

Eddie marched down Manor Road with a spring in his step: it was the first time he'd done this in a long time. His life was about to turn a corner. After staying away from his wife and son for so long, he felt that soon he'd be able to return to his rightful place as head of the household of number thirteen. The thought that Ruby still loved him, as she'd assured him during his last visit, brought joy to his heart.

Cedric Mulligan was dead – killed in cold blood by someone who owed him a lot of money and could not pay. Many secrets had been buried along with him, but once Eddie had been to the police with his evidence, the harshness of his life would finally be put to bed. Wanting to live closer to his wife, in the spring of this year he'd become a lodger in Arthur Street in the neighbourhood known as Northend, on the other side of Erith. Although only a ten-minute walk away, it could have been the other side of the world as far as his wife was concerned; it was away from the town centre, and he knew she would never have cause to visit. Yes, it was a risk living there, but he'd taken many risks since the day he left Alexandra Road six years ago.

His work now was honest if tiring, but he felt fit and healthy and at peace with himself. In the course of the various jobs he had tried, he'd found he enjoyed working in the open air as much as possible. Since the warmer weather, he'd secured a good job working in one of the brickfields on the marshes close to the river. He was part of a team producing bricks that were either used locally or transported via the river to all parts of the country. The downside to this job was that come the colder weather, the work would cease until the following spring, as bricks could not be produced when the weather was damp or cold. But Eddie knew that now he'd be able to find more work close to home. People tended to have short memories, and after several years away he was sure his previous wrongdoings would have been forgotten.

With new businesses and shops springing up all over the town, Eddie's life and his future looked good. This was why he had risked venturing out to see Ruby during daylight hours, rather than skulking around late at night dropping the occasional envelope through her letter box.

Although he wasn't ready yet to move back into their home, he would do so once he'd imparted the information he knew to the police. Eddie would be able to lay his cards on the table, explaining to Ruby more about why he'd run away. He also wanted to get to know his son. He'd missed enough of watching George grow up as it was, and wished to repair any damage that had already been done.

Reaching the corner of Alexandra Road, he stopped by the side of a fence. There seemed to be a group of people leaving number thirteen and heading towards his end of the road. He frowned as he saw Ruby pushing a pram, with a man putting his hand on George's shoulder in a fatherly manner. Eddie recognized an older woman – Stella Green from across the road – and was that not Derek Green and his younger brother following behind? Eddie knew Derek as one of the team leaders at the brickfields. Although they did not work together, they had passed the time of day. Eddie had had a quiet word, asking Derek not to mention to Ruby that he'd seen or worked with him. He had explained that his life was complicated, and he was doing his best to repair any damage done. In return, Derek had told him he was not interested in Eddie's past or Ruby's business, so he would not be mentioning he'd seen him or carrying any messages. This had re-assured Eddie and since then the men had nodded amiably enough when passing, with Eddie feeling confident his presence in Erith would not be mentioned.

'Are you sure you don't want to go with Frank, George and the lads? I can look after Pat for the day,' Stella said as she tried to take hold of the pram. Ruby stood her ground, gripping the handle tightly.

'I know how busy it will be in the capital, and to be honest I'd rather stay here and care for my daughter. You go, Stella. You'll enjoy seeing the pageantry, the crowds, and all the overseas royalty in their carriages. I'm sure the men will find you a good place to view. It would be a shame to miss it. Who knows when the next king will be crowned?'

'And me not being a spring chicken, I may not see another,' Stella said good-naturedly. 'If you're sure, then I'll go with them, and I know I will enjoy myself. I suppose you can have a restful day while we take George with us?'

Ruby smiled at Stella's comment. She intended to open up the bookshop for the morning, and it would be business as usual. Pat would sleep soundly in her baby carriage, and she should be able to tidy the shop and sell some books. That would surprise Frank upon his return, as he'd placed a sign in the window to say they would be closed for the day due to the coronation. There was to be a street party in Alexandra Road later in the afternoon, so Ruby would return home, collect the cake she'd made for the children's tea party, and enjoy socializing with her neighbours. She had wondered if George would prefer to stay and join in with the other children, but such was his closeness to Frank these days, the lad had jumped at the chance to go with him to London. He'd spoken so often of when they went last year to pay their respects to King Edward, and of wanting to see the new king in all his robes and finery. Any books they had in the bookshop about royalty and past kings and queens fascinated him. He'd become most knowledgeable on the subject and come the autumn, when he moved up to the big school in Crayford, Ruby knew her son's interests would help with his learning. George soaked up knowledge so easily, she just knew he would enjoy his new school.

Ruby walked with them as far as the Wheatley Hotel, then waved goodbye as the group crossed the road, heading down to the station. She was a little puzzled to see that Derek seemed to keep looking back over his shoulder and wondered if there was a young lady involved in his life – perhaps she too was going up to London to watch the coronation? Ruby liked Derek; he kept himself to himself, and she knew he worked long hours. He'd make someone a good husband one day.

Turning the large pram around, she walked back down Pier Road, stopping in front of the bookshop. The two bay windows either side of the door gleamed in the early June sunshine, and displays of books enticed passers-by to step over the threshold and browse. Bumping the pram up the small step, she unlocked the door and breathed in the smell of old books and lavender wax. When she wasn't serving customers, Ruby like nothing more than to polish the wooden bookshelves and the counter until they shone. She loved her job working with her friend; the only problem was deceiving his family into thinking they were a proper couple and Pat was his daughter. Frank had understood completely when Pat's birth certificate showed Eddie as the father, though. Stella was already hinting at further grandchildren, which embarrassed him immensely. Ruby had heard him more than once tell his mother they were more than happy with George and Pat in their little family unit – and that they had a business to run, so could she please stop asking for more. But Stella only heard what she wanted to hear, and that was the word 'family'. In her mind, young couples had many children; why should it be any different for her son? She also mentioned the possibility of Ruby seeking a divorce, having been abandoned by Eddie. Ruby would not be drawn on the subject, while a sad look haunted Frank's eyes.

With not a rain cloud in the sky, Ruby carried out the baskets of cheap books and placed them on the wide pavement in front of the shop. Frank had decided any money that came from the sale of these books should be passed to George – after all, it had been his idea to sell books that were not quite perfect, although the words were intact. He'd pointed out that many people only wanted to read the story, so if it helped someone who couldn't normally afford even a second-hand book, young George counted that as a job well done. An old tobacco tin kept under the counter was where all the farthings were dropped. Any time Frank brought back a fresh stock of books after visiting clients, George would sit on the floor going through them one by one, pulling out any he considered unworthy of being placed on the shelves. These he would commandeer for his baskets. Ruby and Frank had taken to naming his section of the shop 'George's baskets'. In one of the bay-fronted windows was a selection of books for children, and when George wasn't at school he liked to oversee these books and could often be found explaining to parents and children what he enjoyed about the publications. Frank had placed a selection of non-fiction books nearby for younger readers still in school. Ruby, impressed by her son's interest in reading, encouraged him to write down a few words about the books he'd read, and why he enjoyed them. These stood in front of each book, and became quite popular. Recently, a reporter from the *Erith Times* had visited the shop. His purpose had been to interview Frank about the business, but seeing George in action, he had ended up interviewing the lad as well. Nowhere could be found a prouder mother than Ruby. On the day the interview appeared in the paper, Frank laughed when he saw that she'd purchased six copies. She told him that she wanted to be able to show George's children and grandchildren how young he was when he started out in business.

At the back of her mind, she remembered Mrs Grant's offer about George working at Vickers when he was old enough. She still corresponded with the lady often, as did George, and Ruby had visited her Women's Circle at Christ Church to chat about being a mother and the wife of a bookseller. Mrs Grant was aware of Ruby's circumstances, but chose to gloss over that part of her life. People wanted to speak about books. The well-to-do ladies in the group were able to offer old books they no longer required, although Ruby found it amusing that after her talk more than a few of the ladies came to make purchases. One lady bought a complete series of books bound in red leather because she said they would look nice in her drawing room. It sounded as if the books would not be read, but were simply required to fit into the decor. Ruby shrugged her shoulders: it was a sale, at the end of the day.

Straightening up from sorting out the baskets, she heard her name being called from across the street.

'Mrs Green, I'm surprised to see you open today. Why are you not in London watching the coronation parade?'

Ruby had become used to being called 'Mrs Green' and didn't bother to correct people any more. Instead she smiled at one of her regular customers. 'Hello, Mrs James. I decided to stay at home with Pat and open the shop for the morning. Will you be celebrating today?'

'Yes, we're having a street party.' Mrs James crossed the road to join Ruby. 'I'm about to start making sandwiches for the children, although I feel their eyes will be more drawn to the cakes. It will be a splendid do. A neighbour is pushing her piano into the front garden so that we can have a sing-song as well.'

'How jolly,' Ruby replied as she brushed the dust from her skirt. 'We too are having a street party, but I'm not so sure about a piano and a sing-song.' She fleetingly wondered if her own nosy neighbour would offer her piano; but then, it was only ever used for hymn singing, as far as she could tell from hearing the tunes through the adjoining wall. 'I would love a piano for our front room – not that I can play. I'd like George to learn. It seems such a sociable hobby, and there are so many times at family gatherings when it would be pleasant to stand around the piano and sing.'

The women continued to chat about this and that before Mrs James stepped into the shop to see Pat and make a purchase.

Eddie had stood for some time at the end of Alexandra Road, wondering what to do. One thing was for sure: Ruby had not only moved on with her life, but had a child with another man. He felt his hopes and dreams shatter around him. It looked as though he had lost George as well – but then, who was to blame? 'No one but me,' he muttered to himself.

Not knowing what to do next, he followed the little group of men, keeping as far back as possible in case he was spotted. Once, as they crossed the road, he worried that Derek had seen him, but the younger man never waved or called out, so perhaps he was wrong. He'd had to dash into an alley at the side of the shops when Ruby waved goodbye to the party and turned back. He wondered whether to speak to her, now she was alone . . . Distressed at what he'd seen and deep in thought, Eddie sat on the wall further down the road and watched as she entered a bookshop. He was surprised to see her leave the pram inside the shop and carry books and baskets out onto the pavement. It seemed a strange thing to do. Perhaps she worked there, in which case he would go and speak to her as long as there were no customers present. Plucking up courage, he approached the shop – only to duck back when a woman called out to her from across the road. Already feeling miserable, his life got even worse when he heard Ruby addressed as Mrs Green. Looking at the bookshop, he could see the sign across the window: Frank Green. Stella's eldest son.

Deep down, Eddie knew that everything that had gone wrong in their marriage was his own doing – but still he felt angry at Ruby for rushing into another marriage. It felt like deception, especially after all the promises she'd made to him on their last night together. He wasn't sure how she had legally been able to marry, but then, what did he know about divorce, not having come across it before? Nobody knew where Eddie lived now, so no one would have been able to contact him about such things.

He watched Ruby as she laughed and chatted with her customer before they went back into the bookshop together. Full of rage and self-pity, he turned his back on the woman he loved with all his heart and headed away through the town to his lodgings.

He would continue working in Erith; he could see no point in leaving the brickfields. His lodging house was clean and comfortable, so he'd remain, but he'd make no effort to contact Ruby or George ever again. They were lost to him forever.

11

August 1914

Ruby leant back in her armchair and tried to breathe slowly and deeply. The country had been on tenterhooks for the past few weeks ever since Archduke Franz Ferdinand had been killed alongside his wife. Rumours of war had been rife and the thought of what the future held was all anyone could talk about. However, it was not that which was playing her on her mind, but the fact that George didn't appear to be settling into his apprenticeship at Vickers.

Mrs Grant had been as good as her word, as the month approached when George was due to leave school. Thanks to her influence, he'd attended several interviews at the large, sprawling factory on the other side of Erith. She'd put in a good word with her husband, who was a senior manager and well thought of. Ruby, usually the brave one in the family, had been so nervous; this was her son's future at stake, everything she'd dreamt about since that day back in 1905 when she'd first met Mrs Grant at Brook Street cemetery. The woman's interest in George had never wavered, and over the years the two of them had formed a tight bond.

After the first interview, Ruby had felt unable to return to the offices connected to the busy factory, as her nerves got the better of her. The size and the number of people working there were daunting. Instead it had been Frank who went with George and sat waiting while he undertook test after test, checking his intelligence and his ability with numbers. Without good marks he could not be trained as an engineer. George enjoyed his first experience of visiting the company; he was polite and courteous to the managers he met and showed great interest, asking questions during the tour of the factory. It was no wonder that only a week later a letter arrived informing him that he was to be offered an apprenticeship. His working day would be long, and during his training he would progress from department to department learning all the skills required to make him a proficient engineer.

When the day came for him to start work he was up early, keen to walk to the factory. Ruby had made sandwiches, wrapping them in greaseproof paper before packing them into a tin box; she'd not see him go hungry during the long day. As George's wage would be very small, he had asked if he could still help out at the bookshop occasionally. Frank had agreed, although Ruby felt it would be too much hard work for the lad, who also had to study in order to learn his trade. She promised that the sales from the baskets of books would still be his. Every little would help.

George was keen to work hard. What Ruby hadn't accounted for was the fact that as the youngest lad he would be the butt of many of the men's jokes, and pranks were often dished out to new apprentices. He took it all with good grace, telling his mum about the pranks as well as his work. But yesterday he had come home with his bottom lip trembling as he explained how the latest trick had thrown him to begin with. He'd been given the important job of going to the stores department to collect some paint, and felt proud that the workmen trusted him. It was only when the storeman laughed loudly before kindly explaining that there was no such thing as 'tartan paint' that George understood he'd been duped. Fortunately, the storeman was kind and sent him back to the engineering workshop with the task of telling the main joker that his order for a glass hammer had just come in. Ruby smiled when George explained he'd played along with the trick, gaining some friends amongst the older workers. She could see that the transition from schoolboy to worker was proving hard for George. She hoped and prayed that today would be easier for her boy.

Looking at the clock on the mantelpiece, she went to collect her coat and her daughter who was playing in the garden. It was time to open up the bookshop. Frank was out attending a house sale, where he hoped to pick up a selection of titles for the antiquarian side of the business. At least, being Tuesday, it would be quiet in the town, she thought to herself.

Ruby had put out the book displays and settled Pat on the floor in the back room with her rag doll. She was just thinking about putting the kettle on when a breathless Stella burst into the shop.

'You'll never guess what those silly buggers have done?' she said, leaning against a bookshelf gasping for breath. 'After being up in London most of yesterday afternoon, wanting to be part of the crowds waiting for news about us possibly going to war, and celebrating like there's no tomorrow, they rolled up indoors asking for their breakfast. Now they reckon they're going up to Woolwich to sign up for king and country and fight the Hun!'

Ruby frowned as she pushed a seat forward for Stella to sit down. 'What do you mean – are Derek and Donald joining up? Why?'

Stella looked confused. 'You mean you've not heard? By all accounts it was announced at eleven o'clock last night. That's why the boys and their mates were outside Buckingham Palace waiting for news. I can understand Derek signing up – he's spoken of nothing else for weeks. He says that the lads down the brickyard are going to join up too, but my Donald is still a baby in my eyes. I don't want him being killed by those murdering Hun.' She looked round the shop. 'Where is Frank? Don't say he's gone with them?'

Ruby felt as though her head was spinning. She'd not had time to look at the early edition of the newspaper, which was still lying on the counter. Reaching out for the folded paper, she only needed to look at the headlines to see that Stella was right: the country was at war. She collapsed onto the other seat. Although she'd been expecting it to happen, the shock still hit her hard.

'Frank's gone to an auction – he left early. I'm expecting him back mid-morning, as the books he was interested in are some of the first lots. He'll cadge a lift back with some furniture buyers from Dartford he's got to know. Why have the boys gone to Woolwich to sign up?'

Stella shrugged her shoulders. 'It seems that's where it's all done. God knows why. I begged them not to go, but they were that excited and full of themselves when they raced off. I had such a feeling of foreboding wash over me as I watched them from the doorstep. I wanted to run after them and drag them back. I could see a group from the brickyard hanging about, waiting on the corner of the road. There was that much excitement, you'd have thought they was off for a booze-up down the coast on one of the pleasure steamers.'

Ruby was dismayed by what Stella told her. 'Oh, the silly idiots.' She took a deep breath, putting her hands to her face as if to block out the news. 'I can't profess to be an expert about all this war stuff, but I thought the government would call the men up if they wanted them to join the army?'

'No, there's some fellow called Kitchener telling them the country needs them to fight right now and winding them all up. If I get my hands on the bloody bloke, I'll give him what for, taking our lads away from us like this.'

'Don't upset yourself so,' Ruby said as Stella burst into tears. 'Let me get you a cup of tea and we will have a think about it all. It may not be as bad as you say. Perhaps when Derek and Donald get back we can have a serious word with them – get them to reconsider what they've done.'

'It will be far too late. Once they've taken the king's shilling, they can't change their minds.'

Ruby didn't know what to say; it seemed so final.

'Perhaps it won't last long and will just be a lot of politicians screaming and shouting at each other. Why, Polly down at the greengrocer's said the other day that if there is a war, it will be all over by Christmas.'

'I don't take any notice of her – what does she know? I've had a feeling in my water, ever since that Franz Ferdinand was murdered along with his wife, that there'd be trouble. You know what men are like. They can't leave these strange countries to fight it out amongst themselves, they've got to poke their bloody noses in. And now I'm going to lose my Donald and Derek,' she wailed, reaching out to grab Ruby's hand. 'Whatever you do, don't let Frank join up with his brothers.'

Ruby wasn't one for politics with other countries. 'But that was over in a place called Sarajevo. I only know that as George mentioned the name of the place. I don't understand how we've got involved.' She wished now she'd listened when Frank had tried to explain about countries sticking up for each other and the ultimatums and threats of war. She'd been busy knitting a cardigan for Pat at the time and it had gone in one ear and out the other. 'Let me get that tea,' was all she could think of to say. 'Pat, why don't you show Nanny Stella your drawings? I'm sure she'd like to see them,' she said before disappearing into the back room of the shop. She knew it would break her heart if her George went off to war, and so she could understand how Stella felt right now. Donald she still thought of as a youngster, but he was old enough to sign up. All the same, the lads should have thought about their parents before being so hot-headed and rushing off like that.

After drinking their tea in silence, with no sign of any customers appearing, Ruby decided to shut up shop and go home. After all, who would want to buy a book on the first day the country was at war? As they walked back down Pier Road, turning a corner into the high street, they could see that most shopkeepers had had the same idea. Ruby stopped to pick up another newspaper in case there was any more news. At the back of her mind, she thought it might be a good idea to put the paper away and save it. It wasn't often such important news was announced, and she had a mind to store it away for the future.

Frank had laughed at her when she'd put away a copy of the newspaper from the day of the coronation. Once she'd explained to him that this would one day be history, and the children might be interested in looking back to see what their life was like at that time, he had agreed and found a suitable box. Ruby had placed her souvenir inside, slipping it under her bed. She'd then thought of her mother, remembering how Milly had also kept precious things beneath her bed.

Now her mind turned to thoughts of Eddie. Where is he now? she thought before saying aloud, 'What would Mum have thought of today, I wonder?'

Stella gave a wry smile. 'Your mum would've had a lot to say about it, love – just like we have. Don't forget she lost her husband to war, and no doubt she will fear for other young men.'

'I pray that Polly down the greengrocer's is right and it is over by Christmas – then Derek and Donald will come back safe,' Ruby said. It seemed better not to mention her gratitude that George was still too young to join up. 'I wonder where the army will send the men, once they turn them into soldiers?'

They reached number thirteen and she ushered Pat inside. She and Stella followed the child in and closed the door behind them. There was an air of desolation in the road and they had no wish to stop to speak with the worried women clustered in a group several houses away.

By the time Frank arrived home, Ruby had made a bite to eat. She smiled as he entered the room. 'How did it go?' she asked as he kissed her cheek.

'I won all the bids and got them at a good price. There were less than half the usual number of people there. No doubt others had better things on their mind than buying books and knick-knacks. How are you, Mum?' he said, noticing Stella's pale face. 'Is Dad all right?'

'Your dad's as fine as he can be, love – nothing will stop him doing his job. It's like he says: all hell will let loose if there aren't enough tugboats to do the work. It's your brothers I'm more worried about. They've both gone up to Woolwich to sign up to join the army.'

'I had a feeling they might,' Frank said, unable to meet Stella's eyes. 'They mentioned as much the other day.'

Stella jumped to her feet, giving her son an angry look. 'Why the hell didn't you say something? Me or your dad could've stopped them.'

Frank looked shamefaced. 'It was just idle talk; I didn't think much of it. Derek had been telling us how the chaps in his team would be going to sign up. He was keen anyway, but if he was the only one left out of his team there was a likelihood of him being out of work anyway. I know Donald was keen too, but we did tell him you'd kill him if he signed up. I didn't expect him to go ahead and do it.' He shook his head sadly.

'I tried to reason with him, but he's nineteen now and knows his own mind. It was as if he didn't care what his old mum thought. Does that mean you're going to sign up as well? God knows what your dad'll have to say about that!'

Frank took Stella's arm and guided her to sit down again before he told her that Wilf had also known about the boys wanting to join up, and had said he'd do the same if he were younger.

Stella was livid. She shook Frank's arm away in distaste. 'It's as if you've all been conspiring against me. Don't tell me you knew, too,' she said, glaring at Ruby.

'No, they kept me in the dark as well.' Ruby's expression was no less angry. 'All I know is, Frank's always told me he's against war, so at least one of them won't be going. Unless you've changed your mind?' she challenged him.

'I can promise you both, I'll never be a soldier. Call me strange, but I don't believe that war is the answer.' He looked sad as he continued, 'Both my brothers think I'm soft in the head. Derek called me a nancy boy.' He looked sideways at Ruby, and she blushed. If the boys knew of their sleeping arrangements, Frank would be called more than that.

'It's just men talking – don't take any notice. Frank, you're a good man. If anyone asked me or your mum, we'd have said we wouldn't go to war either. There's nothing soft about it. It's called being sensible,' Ruby said, although she wasn't sure what she was saying was right. But she desperately wanted to support her dear friend.

'Perhaps,' Frank said, 'but it made me feel uncomfortable. I never would have thought my brother would talk to me like that. That's why I didn't get involved, Mum,' he said, looking apologetic.

Stella's expression softened. 'Don't worry, Frank. They are a pair of hotheads. I could bang their heads together when I get home, in fact – and your father's.'

'I'd like to see that, Mum. I think perhaps I might have my food and get back to the shop. Even if we don't have many customers, I can at least sort out what I brought back from the auction. I'd like to catalogue the books and get them onto the shelves. There are a few books for George's baskets.'

'And mine,' little Pat said, from where she'd been playing with her dolls.

'Oh God, I forgot about the little one sitting there. Whatever will she think of my angry words?'

'I didn't hear you, Nana,' Pat said, giving her a sweet smile.

'You are a little darling.' Stella reached into the pocket of her coat and pulled out a toffee for her granddaughter.

Ruby shook her head. Pat knew just how to twist her nana round her little finger.

'I'll take her over home with me for a few hours,' Stella offered. 'It'll keep my mind off what the lads are up to. No doubt by now they'll be filling their bellies

205

with ale and come rolling home as merry as anything. Life would've been so different if only I'd had daughters,' she sighed.

After Frank, Stella and Pat had gone, Ruby pottered around for a couple of hours, but she found it hard to concentrate. She'd even turned the newspaper over so as not to see the headlines that seemed to leap from the front page. Whatever was going to happen next?

Feeling restless, she decided to walk up to the bookshop and keep Frank company. There was always something to do there, and it would keep her mind away from thoughts of the future.

She'd just reached the high street when a group of men came in sight. They were in jovial spirits and joked with each other loudly as they waited on the pavement for a tram to pass before crossing the road to the Prince of Wales Hotel. In amongst the group she spotted Derek and young Donald Green, and hurried towards them. 'If you've got any thoughts of going in there for a drink, you'd best change your mind. Your mother is waiting at home and she's none too pleased with the pair of you,' she said, placing her hands on her hips as she gave the two young men a piece of her mind.

Without answering Ruby, the pair hung their heads in shame and hurried past her towards home with shouts from their mates echoing in their ears. The rest of the men carried on their journey towards the pub; only one remained. Ruby glanced at him, then caught her breath in shock. 'Eddie?'

'Ruby . . . can we talk?' he called, reaching out a hand as if to pull her back to him as she turned to hurry away.

She stopped and thought for a moment. Did she want to speak to the man who had yet again abandoned her and the children? She spun on her heel, walking back towards him, her anger showing no bounds. Slapping his hand away, she waved her fist in his face. 'How dare you ask to speak to me? It has been four years since . . . since the night we spent together,' she shouted in his face. 'Where have you been? Why have you not sent any money for the children? If it wasn't for what I bring in, the children would starve. You had your way with me and then you vanished. I've had no way of getting in touch with you. Why, Eddie, why?'

Eddie pushed her hand from his face and gripped her wrist tightly. 'I don't recall you complaining at the time,' he said, a smile flitting across his weather-worn face. 'You are looking well, though,' he said, pushing from his mind the memory of seeing her with Frank and a baby in a pram on the day of the king's coronation. 'How is our son?'

'Our son? You'd not recognize our son if you walked past him in the street.'

Eddie would like to have said that that was not the case, as he'd made a point of being by the boy's school on more than a few occasions, watching out for him just to satisfy himself that George was fit and well. In her angry mood, it was going to be difficult to speak to Ruby, and he'd so wanted to talk with her before he left town. It was fortuitous she'd appeared when she did, as he'd been wondering whether to knock on the door of number thirteen – to face Ruby and tell her the truth at last. While he still had the chance.

'Ruby, whatever's happened before . . . can you forget it for a moment, please? I really need to speak to you.'

'I don't think we have anything to say to each other, Eddie. I thought after that night four years ago you'd be returning to me, and you, me and George would have a life together. With our union that night, I'd foolishly thought we would be a family once more. You mentioned at the time that if you stayed it would bring trouble to our door. Did you have no thought of the trouble George and I could be in on our own? If it wasn't for Frank, I don't know what I'd have done,' she said, her face flushed as the angry words poured out of her.

'I had no idea you'd be that quick to have another man climb into my bed, take over my family, and give you a child. Perhaps if you hadn't been so brazen with your affections elsewhere, I would've returned rather than wait to speak to you until now,' Eddie retorted, thinking back to the day he'd seen the happy family leaving number thirteen. To say his heart had been broken was an understatement. Although he'd stayed close to the town and kept an eye out for his son, part of him had become frozen with the effort of trying not to imagine his wife with another man. 'For you to divorce me and marry Frank Green so quickly speaks volumes about your feelings for me,' he snarled.

'Oh, for heaven's sake, Eddie, what the hell are you talking about? Perhaps we do need to talk things over. And I do need to introduce you to your daughter.' Ruby shook her head at how confusing their conversation had become.

'My daughter? What the hell are you talking about, woman?'

Grabbing the sleeve of Eddie's jacket, she muttered, 'Follow me.' Not wishing to have any passers-by overhear the conversation, they walked in silence to a nearby cafe. It was Marge's old business, but she had long ago given it up, which meant Ruby could feel comfortable crossing the threshold. Telling Eddie to order two cups of tea, she sat at one of the scrubbed tables and waited, wringing her hands, worrying that he would make a scene as memories of his volatile character came flooding back to her.

When he returned, he sat opposite her. 'Well, come on, I'm listening,' he said, sliding the cups so forcefully across the table that much of the tea slopped in the saucers.

'Pat is your child. I have never slept with another man. Whatever outward appearances show, Frank and I are just good friends.'

Eddie gave a bitter laugh. 'You can't pull the wool over my eyes, Ruby Caselton. Or is it Ruby Green now?' he asked, feeling a tightness grip his heart. How many times had he listened to Derek Green go on and on about his older brother's bookshop he ran with Ruby, and how happy they were with their child living together across the road at number thirteen? Who was Ruby fooling? Because it certainly wasn't him.

Ruby looked around the cafe. At that time of the afternoon, there were few people sitting at tables and the staff were busy preparing to close. What she was about to tell Eddie wasn't something she wished overheard by anyone living in the town.

'Eddie, I know you must have had secrets, reasons even, for not living with us. I too have reasons for wanting people to believe that Frank and I are a couple – and reasons to let people believe Pat is his daughter. It's more for Frank than for me. Have you not thought about what people would have said if I suddenly announced Pat was yours? With you in hiding, and me being the only one who knew you used to come back to deliver money? How would I suddenly explain being with child? That nosy old battleaxe from next door would be on to it in a flash. As it is, she keeps herself to herself because she has nothing to gossip about; all she can say is that Frank's now my husband. And no, I haven't divorced you. I wouldn't even know how to do that. You've got to remember, there are three bedrooms in our house. I sleep in one, with Pat having a cradle bed in the corner of the room. George has his back bedroom, just as he did when you lived with us, and the third bedroom . . . well, if you walked into that room right now, you'd see Frank's bed, Frank's clothes hanging in the wardrobe, and all of Frank's possessions in the chest of drawers. Does that make it clear to you?'

Eddie thought for a moment. What kind of man would move into the home of a beautiful married woman and pretend to be the father of her child? At Frank's age, he should be out looking for his own wife and starting his own family. 'How can you expect me to believe such a thing?' he said as he thought of what he'd been told.

Ruby could have wept. 'Is it not clear to you why he does this? Yes, I work for him in the bookshop; I love the job and to be honest, the money I earn keeps our heads above water. Yes, Frank pays his way, but to all intents and purposes he is my lodger. He has no designs on me, or any woman. Has the penny dropped yet, Eddie?'

Eddie frowned. 'Do you mean to say . . . Frank Green is a . . . is a . . . ?' He roared with laughter.

'Yes, Frank is not interested in women,' she whispered pointedly, not losing eye contact with Eddie. 'I beg you to keep that to yourself. He's my dearest friend, and he's a good friend to this family. You must keep this between us. Are you listening to me, Eddie?' she hissed.

Eddie took a gulp of his now lukewarm tea as thoughts rushed through his head. If all this was true – and he'd never think of Ruby as a liar – how would it affect him? 'Does anyone know?'

'Nobody knows. Frank is a gentle, peace-loving man. He is happy with his life, the bookshop, and he adores our children. Your name is on Pat's birth certificate. I do not want it any other way. My feelings for you are more of bewilderment after our night together and you vanishing again. God, Eddie, I should really hate you for what you've put me through . . . but all the same . . .' She couldn't continue as her voice cracked.

Eddie looked at his wife across the table. Now in her mid-thirties, she was still a good-looking woman. There were just a few lines at the corners of her eyes and her hair still held the colour of shining chestnuts that had caught his eye when he'd first seen her – and fallen in love. She licked her lips nervously, waiting for him to speak, and he could see a worried look in her eyes. Thoughts of the last time they were together caused feelings to stir deep inside, feelings he usually fought hard to suppress.

211

'I believe you,' he said at last. 'God knows you've had a lot to put up with, and most of it is because of me,' he added apologetically.

'Tell me, at long last, what happened for you to run away. Why have you stayed in hiding? And why have you suddenly appeared with the Green brothers?'

'I'll get us another one of these first.' Eddie picked up the cups and saucers.

Ruby crossed her arms onto the table and laid her head down. What had happened today had been bad enough so far. The country was at war, and now Eddie had turned up. Could things get any worse?

Eddie placed the fresh cups of tea on the table. 'I thought you might fancy these?' he said, putting a plate with two rather dried-up buns in front of her.

'No, thank you,' she said, pushing the plate away as she straightened her back and looked him in the eye. 'I have a lot to get on with at home; my family need me, so say what you have to say, and we will go our different paths. I don't see any other way we can deal with what's been thrown at us. It's not fair to Frank or the children. My goodness, Eddie, the country is at war and that's more than enough for anyone to put up with,' she sighed, feeling suddenly weary. 'Didn't you mention that I could be in danger, when you came back and stayed that one night? I thought our life would be back on an even keel, but off you went and we never saw you again, Eddie. I'd rather have lived in danger for the rest of my life and had you at home with us than what you put me through. So, say your piece and we'll go our separate ways.'

Eddie took a deep breath. 'I've not lived a blameless

life, not by far. When we first married, I dreamt that I could give you your own home, and we wouldn't need to keep moving from place to place; but we did. Yes, part of it was because I enjoyed a drink and I gambled. God, I threw money away left, right and centre but never towards you and George, and I apologize for that. So, when you fell for the baby you eventually lost . . .'

'Sarah. Her name was Sarah,' Ruby interrupted.

'When you were carrying Sarah, and Cedric Mulligan rented us the house, not only did I want to do good by you, I also wanted to turn over a new leaf. Then Cedric asked me to do another job for him. It was dangerous.'

'Was it illegal?' Ruby's eyes flashed.

'Not for me – not in the eyes of the law. But if it had gone wrong, Cedric would never have forgiven me. He could be a vengeful man, and he knew where you and my child lived. Remember how I wanted to move us away? I tried to see if it could be done. I looked for another home as decent as number thirteen, but we couldn't afford the few I saw in other towns. In the end it was best for me to disappear, and the best way was to make it look like I was a bad'n. If I'd had the guts, I would have faked my own death, but I didn't want you to grieve for me, and I knew you would. I even left the coalyard under a shadow, hoping that when I disappeared it wouldn't make you look bad.'

'What about Mum's money?' she asked, trying to piece together what he was saying.

'I took it thinking if people felt sorry for you then you could keep your head held high. I was still doing odd jobs for Cedric, trying to show him I was loyal to him

213

until I had the money to get you and George away from his grip. I had to appear loyal even though I knew he'd arranged for a man to be roughed over just because he owed money he couldn't pay back.'

Ruby felt faint. 'You mean you had a hand in hurting someone?'

'No, I simply went along to help the person who was collecting the debt. Ruby, I was small fry. I might have collected money and been a bit heavy with my fists on occasion when working for Cedric. I didn't know the bloke would be killed, but this debt was for hundreds of pounds – so different to what I'd been involved with before. Cedric had another chap collect the dosh. I was just there to keep lookout, and to shout if the coppers appeared. It all went wrong and meant that Cedric had a hold on me. He could have put the blame on me, paid witnesses to say it was me who killed the man.'

'Oh, Eddie,' she said, not realizing she'd reached out and gripped his hand. 'Why couldn't you tell me? I'd have understood, and I could have helped you.'

'I didn't feel I could confide in you, not with your mother on my back all the time. She was always going on about supporting the family and doing better for you. I knew you loved that house, so if I'd told you what had happened, you'd have insisted on leaving. And I couldn't tear you away from the home you'd always dreamt of. You deserve that at least,' he said, stroking her hand. 'It was better I left and tried to sort out the mess before coming back to you. Then I could explain, and if you'd forgiven me perhaps there would have been a future for us.'

Ruby was trying hard to understand all Eddie had to say. 'What about the money you left for us? Did it come from that man?'

'No, I wouldn't do that to you. That money was honestly earned, and I put away as much as I could. I was determined not to let you know where I was and I hoped you would recognize my handwriting on the envelopes. That was the only hint I was prepared to give you. If you'd not caught me that night four years back, then things would've changed for the better,' he said, a despondent look crossing his face.

'But what could be better then you showing your love for me, and Pat being the outcome of our love? I don't understand, Eddie.'

'I knew that night that Cedric had died – I should say, was killed. His hold on me was over at that stage. I finally had hope in my heart, and when I dropped an envelope through the letter box, I knew that next time I returned to Alexandra Road it would be as a man free of Cedric's hold. I had information on Cedric and his business that I'd collected and I took it to the police the next day. I told them everything about the man and as I've never been guilty of anything criminal, they were happy to listen to me. I'd kept careful records on his illegal betting business along with robberies and fraud. It took some months before those who had worked with Cedric were rounded up and charged. During that time, I moved back to Erith but found a job and lodgings in Northend, knowing that as soon as it was safe to do so I would come back to you. I had to make sure I'd not be charged and bring trouble to your door.'

215

'Then why didn't you?' Ruby demanded. She hated to think of what Eddie must have gone through.

'I did. I got as far as the end of the road. It was the day of the coronation – a happy day, full of joy for the future with a new king for our country, and for me I hoped it would be the start of a new life.'

'But why didn't you come, why didn't you knock on the door? What happened, Eddie?' Ruby brushed aside angry tears. 'Did you change your mind?'

'No. You changed it for me,' he said, looking beseechingly at her as he wiped the tears from her face with his fingers. 'I saw you. I saw Frank and George, and Frank's family, walking down the road together. You looked such a happy family, and because of that I misunderstood the situation. Ruby, I thought you'd given up on me and started a new life with Frank. Now I know that isn't the case. But can you not see how it would have appeared to a man standing on the corner, watching from afar?'

'But why didn't you speak to me?' she sobbed.

'Because I was foolish. I was angry. Frank seemed to have everything I wanted. Besides, in my eyes, you'd had another man's child. I was working down the brickfields alongside Derek Green. He was sworn to silence about my presence in the town. As it was, he didn't want to be involved. I thought that was for the best, but now I know I was wrong. But it's too late, even with us both knowing the truth: I'll be leaving tomorrow.'

'Leaving – where are you going?'

'I've joined the army, and by tomorrow evening I'll be out of your life once and for all.'

'But, Eddie, aren't you too old now to be a soldier?'

'I lied about my age. Joining the army . . . it just seemed to be the best solution. I didn't think I had anything – or anyone – to stay for.'

Ruby knew then that if she didn't do something quickly, she'd lose Eddie forever. 'I feel as though so much has come between us. I know I still love you, although I hated the man you became by the time we moved here. You frightened me, and to be honest, back at that time I was ready to leave – that was, until I fell in love with the house and made friends here. I knew it could be a good home for George, and for us, if you were to return. Losing Mum like we did, and then you disappearing on the same night, frightened the hell out of me. But I'm proud to say I coped – I worked hard, and I coped. Frank is a dear, dear friend. He helped me, and in return I was able to help him. He knows that Pat is your child, and he understands. If I told him today that you were moving back into the house as my husband, he would still understand. He would welcome you with open arms, and I hope that you too would accept Frank as the family friend who kept me going through thick and thin. He never once stepped in and spoke to George as a father figure; he knew that was your position. He always thought of you as George's father and himself as nothing more than a friend to George, and George knows that. No one has taken your place in the household.'

Eddie didn't know what to say. From the way Ruby spoke, he could walk back in the door this very minute and be accepted. 'Too much water has gone under the bridge now. I'd hate anyone to talk about you, or Frank, come to that. I appreciate his friendship. Please pass that on to him. As for me pinching your mother's money like that; I know it was for a reason, but I can never forgive myself.' A look of shame crossed his face.

Ruby wiped her eyes and gave him a smile. 'I want you to come back with me now, Eddie. You could tell him yourself, and I'm sure everyone would understand.'

'No, I can't do that. It wouldn't be fair to Frank. The world would see this and assume the worst. We would be seen as the couple who turned out the man who loved you. Where would he go but back over the road to his mother and ridicule from his family and the nosy neighbours? Apart from that, everyone looks on Pat as being his child. I'd not do that to the man who has taken care of you all these years.'

'I see what you mean, Eddie. Frank does have rooms over the bookshop. It was always his intention to move there once they'd been cleaned up and decorated, but I invited him to stay with us as it was convenient for his family, who believed Pat was his and we were a couple. I'm not sure now how we can undo things. Until you spoke, I hadn't even given it a thought. What can we do?'

'Are you sure you want me back in your life, Ruby?' Eddie's voice was raw with emotion.

'I really do, Eddie. I know that if you'd explained all this to me when we first moved here, I might not have been sympathetic. But now – I do believe you. Even so, how can I do this to Frank? He'd be a laughing stock. And Stella would be heartbroken.'

Eddie thought for a moment before speaking. 'Do we have to tell anyone? I'm going away tomorrow, and God knows when I'll be back. Could we keep this our secret until I return? *If* I return?'

Ruby gasped. 'Please don't say that, Eddie. Not after everything that's happened. We keep hearing already that this war won't last long, so why not tell everyone now?'

'Look, love,' he said, squeezing her hand. 'I don't want you or the children hurt by nasty comments from ill-minded people. As far as others know, I'm out of your life completely. Only Derek knows that I've been around here, but he's prepared to keep quiet. We will both be off to war, so why not carry on as normal?'

Ruby hated what she had to say. 'I suppose you're right.' She took a deep breath. 'It'll be a good idea for me to go home now, before I keep begging you to stay. Will you walk me to the corner?'

'Of course I will.' Eddie took her hand and they left the cafe, walking slowly towards Alexandra Road hand in hand. 'I'd best say my goodbyes here,' he said. 'I don't want anyone to see me standing at your gate. Besides, I don't think I could bear it. But before I go, I have some-thing to give you.' He reached into his pocket, pulling out a long Manila envelope. 'There's no need to open it now. It's the deeds to the house, and they're in your name. It's what you deserve after what I've put you through. There's no need to say anything. I was owed some money for helping the police, as there was a reward offered for information about the killing of that man, and I had a bit put by. Cedric's wife and kids were glad of the money, and to be shot of the house. This is yours, with my love.' He pressed the envelope into her hands.

Ruby fell against his chest. Her heart was breaking. 'Oh,

Eddie, I don't know what to say. This is a dream come true, but in other ways it's a nightmare, knowing I won't see you for so long. You will write to me, won't you? I'll explain everything to Frank the moment he's home from the bookshop.'

Her voice broke as Eddie crushed her in his arms and kissed her until she was breathless. Holding her at arm's length, he gazed into her face. 'I want to remember you just as you are right now. I'll carry the memory with me.'

'God, I must look a right sight!'

'You'll always be beautiful to me, Ruby. Now hurry along home,' he said, giving her a final gentle kiss.

Ruby hurried along Alexandra Road, wiping her eyes with a handkerchief. She didn't see Stella standing in the bay window of number fourteen, holding Pat in her arms. Turning to look back, she waved to Eddie until he disappeared from sight.

Taking a deep breath, she let herself into the house – still unaware of the frozen look on Stella's face as her neighbour watched the door of number thirteen close behind the woman she'd thought of as a trusted daughter-in-law.

12

31st October 1917

'Stella's resting now. Wilf's with her, although he's almost as distraught. I think perhaps you should go over and sit with her, Frank. You need to be with your mum,' Ruby said gently, placing her hand on his shoulder. The news that morning of Donald Green succumbing to injuries while fighting to defend his country had shocked them all. Stella's grief was beyond anything Ruby had ever witnessed before. Her screams of distress could be heard across the road, and Ruby had rushed over fearing the worst as she spotted the telegram boy cycle off down the road.

'I'll go over now, thanks,' he said, climbing wearily from his chair. The strong tea Ruby had made for him remained cold on the table. 'It should've been me,' he muttered. 'I should have been the first of us to go. It doesn't seem right that the youngest in our family should have perished in such a way.'

Ruby wanted to agree – it was all so wrong – but she knew that Frank wasn't expecting an answer, as he was deep in his own thoughts. A day didn't seem to pass without news appearing in the newspapers of the loss of more young lives.

'She needs you, Frank, so rather than go back to the bookshop tonight I'll make the bed up in your old room. You need to be close by. Have you heard from Derek recently?'

'It's been over three months. He sent Mum a card with embroidered silk flowers on the front. She was thrilled to think she had something that had been sent from France.'

'Eddie sent me one too; they must've been together when they bought them. It didn't say where they were. Apart from some French words in the pattern it could have been anywhere. Double Dutch to me. George told me what they meant, but I'm none the wiser.'

'I do wish Eddie well,' Frank said. 'It may not seem like it at times, but I do.'

'You're a good friend, Frank. I wish I could help heal your heartache and do something for your mum. I'll bring some food over later. You never know, perhaps you can encourage her to eat a bite. She told me when she cared for me after I lost Sarah that I needed to keep my strength up. Now it's our turn to say the same to her and Wilf.'

'It's you who is the good person, Ruby. After she attacked you openly about kissing a man in the street, her anger knew no bounds.' Frank shook his head, remembering his mother's anger and bitterness. 'At least it's all right now, and she knows that we are simply good friends and that's all it's ever been.'

'I fear if she ever finds out the truth about you, it will

be too much for her, Frank. We must always keep this to ourselves,' Ruby said, looking worried.

'Thankfully she seems to accept that Stephen is simply my lodger at the bookshop,' Frank said, thinking of his dear friend who now lived with him over the bookshop in Pier Road.

'And that's the way it should always be. Keep your life as private as you can. God knows what would happen if anyone found out you were as close as you are,' Ruby insisted. 'I love you like a brother and would hate any harm to come to you.' She knew that if Frank's secret of having a relationship with another man was to become known, he could end up in prison. 'I wonder, do you think Stephen would like to come here for his dinner this evening? I'm making a pot of stew, as I expect George to arrive at any minute, and there's plenty to go around. He's going to be very upset when he hears about Donald.'

'When do you expect to meet his young lady?' Frank asked, trying to shake off the thought of his youngest brother lying dead in a foreign land. He knew that although George was almost eighteen years of age, Ruby found it hard to accept that he was old enough to be walking out with a girl.

'I'm sure it's nothing serious. He has so many friends at work and they seem to socialize in a group. I'm more concerned about his talk of joining up. So many at Vickers are doing so. I thought when he was transferred over to the Crayford factory, he would put aside those ideas about enlisting; after all, he still hasn't finished his apprenticeship. Mr Grant having put him in charge of a team ought to be enough to keep such thoughts out of his head.'

'I don't think that's going to happen. Even with so many deaths and men going missing in action, the fervour to join up and fight for the king is stronger than ever. After three years, so many people want the war over, and if that means sacrificing their sons . . .' Frank let the sentence trail off wistfully. He reached for his overcoat, which was hanging over the back of an armchair, and something fluttered to the ground.

Ruby reached out and picked it up. 'Oh God, not another one! What are those damned women playing at? Where were you given this one?' she asked, bending the white feather in two and throwing it onto the fire that was glowing in the hearth.

Frank put his hand in his pocket and pulled out three more feathers. As he passed each one to Ruby he said, 'This was from the woman serving in the greengrocer's; this from the huddle of old women standing at the corner of the high street; and this had been put in the basket of books in front of the shop. At least they'll keep the fire burning bright, although the smell will linger.' He laughed without showing any real humour.

'Please don't let it upset you, Frank. You do enough for the people of this town without volunteering to take up arms and head over the Channel to uncertain death. One loss is enough for your mum. Any more will kill her.'

'I'll never fire a gun against another man,' he said. 'I ignored my conscription notice, but it's only a matter of time before they realize and come looking for me. But I'm prepared to refuse to go.'

Ruby was shocked. She knew Frank had never liked the idea of men fighting each other, but to refuse meant he'd likely go to prison – or worse. 'Please don't say that, Frank. Don't they shoot men who refuse to fight?'

'I have no idea, but I must stick to my beliefs.'

'Perhaps it'll never happen. Why, the war may be over before too long,' she said, trying to sound positive.

Frank agreed as he pulled on his coat, although Ruby could see how troubled he was. 'If you need help with your mum, you must come and get me. Whatever time it is, I'll be over in a flash,' she said as she kissed her friend's cheek and saw him out the door.

The mention of Eddie had her wanting to read his letters once more. Reaching into the bureau by the fireplace, Ruby took out her mother's small box where she kept all her treasured memories. She first pulled out the long Manila envelope and smiled to herself. To think she owned a property, and it was this very house that she treasured so much. She liked to think that number thirteen Alexandra Road was a place where family and friends could come when they were troubled, or simply to have a cup of tea and a natter. Even her two sisters had taken to visiting more, although she had yet to explain to them what had happened to Eddie. His letters were bundled together with a piece of ribbon. She knew it was something younger girls were doing when they received letters from their beaus, and as she still loved Eddie so dearly she had a fancy to do the same. The red ribbon had been purchased from the haberdashery department of Hedley Mitchell's and she'd purchased a length of pink ribbon at the same time for Pat's fair hair, not wishing anyone to think she had a man friend. Her daughter was so like Eddie, even down to his outspoken ways when things didn't go as he wished them to. Fortunately, Pat understood how to control her temper, even at the tender age of six.

Deep in thought, she didn't hear the front door open until George appeared. She looked up with a start. 'George, is it that time already? Let me check your dinner.'

'I have a couple of friends with me, Mum. Can they come in for a cup of tea?'

'Of course, love, you never need to ask. Come along in and sit down, warm yourself up. It's a bit chilly out there.' She was rather surprised when two girls came into the room rather than his workmates, and they smiled shyly at her.

'Oh, hello,' Ruby said as she helped to take their coats. The dark-haired one thanked her. Ruby was surprised to see that the girl was heavily pregnant.

'You probably don't remember me, Mrs Caselton. I was Maureen Stokes from Manor Road. I'm Maureen Gilbert now I'm married, and I live with my mother-in-law in Crayford Road.'

Ruby thought for a moment. 'Of course – I know your mum, as well as your mother-in-law. Doesn't your husband work at Vickers with my George?'

'Yes, that's right, he did, but he's in the Rifle Brigade now. George looks after us, doesn't he, Irene?'

The other girl sat primly in the armchair that had been offered to her and nodded without saying a word. Ruby could see her eyes sweep the room, inspecting every stick of furniture as well as Ruby's knick-knacks.

'Congratulations on getting married, Maureen. George didn't tell me.'

'It was all rather quick,' Maureen giggled as she looked down to her stomach.

Ruby couldn't help smiling, She'd always liked Maureen, and only a year ago had hoped her son had feelings for the girl. Obviously that was out of the question now. Besides, her son was looking devotedly towards Irene. He seemed to be enamoured with the girl. She wondered if Frank was right and they'd been walking out for a while? 'George, why don't you help me put the kettle on; then I'll see about our dinner?' she said, wondering what her son saw in the thin, po-faced girl.

'You look smart, love,' Ruby said, admiring George in his uniform as she checked the stew bubbling away on top of the stove while George filled the kettle.

'Oh Mum, you know it's not a proper uniform. It's just what I'm given to wear while I'm teaching the Boy Scouts how to use our machine guns.'

'I think what you've been given to do by your bosses is very important. They must value you a lot to put you in charge of training the scout troops all about the guns you make and how to fire them.'

George shrugged. 'It's not really the army, though, is it?'

'Don't you start talking like that, my son. You've got an important job to do. Why, you've not even finished your apprenticeship and they've moved you over to Crayford and put you in charge of people. That counts for something. I reckon you will go places, George Caselton,' she said proudly.

George chuckled. 'But you would say that, you're my mother,' he laughed before the smile slipped from his face.

'Something bothering you, son?' Ruby asked. She was reminded that George hadn't yet heard about the death of his friend Donald.

227

'I know I've got a good job . . . and in a way, working on the Vickers machine guns and turning out as many as we are is playing a big part in the war. But I really want to join up.'

Ruby sighed as she thought of Stella not a hundred feet from where they were, distraught over the death of her youngest son. That could be her before too long, if George went off to fight for his country. She looked at her fine, upstanding son; his hair was still the same light brown colour it had been in childhood, and no amount of damping down the curls could tame them. Ruby knew she had to tread carefully, otherwise she could alienate her son: if pushed too hard, he might join up just to spite her. 'What are your plans, love?'

'I'll no doubt join the engineers, as with my experience at Vickers it would be the obvious choice. The management have indicated they can make sure I'm seconded to the right regiment.'

Ruby caught her breath. It seemed this was going to happen, regardless of what she thought about it. 'It sounds as though you've already made your mind up, love. I'd not want to stop you . . . but you know I don't want you to go. I'm like every other mother in that respect. But what about Irene? I can see you're keen on her. Have you known her long?'

George looked a little embarrassed. 'We met about a year ago. She worked with Maureen and came along with her to a dance down at Vickers – it was at the Rodney hut.'

Ruby had heard about the hut, and always thought it a strange name, considering it was more of a dance hall and meeting place. It had been donated by someone called Lady Rodney, in memory of her son. George liked to go there for the dances and educational lectures, but she'd had no idea he had his eye on a girl all this time. 'So it's serious with you and this Irene, is it?'

'I like her a lot, Mum,' he said, turning pink-cheeked.

'I can see that. But then, I thought you were soft on Maureen a while back?'

'She's just a friend, nothing more.'

Ruby thought for a while as she dropped dumplings into the stew. 'And how does Irene feel about you joining up?'

'She knows it will happen for all of us lads when we're eighteen, and I reach that age in January. I'll get called up anyway. Irene believes I'll be an officer before too long.'

Oh, does she? Ruby thought to herself. She certainly didn't like this little madam who seemed to have stolen her son's heart.

As she poured boiling water onto the tea leaves in the pot, she took a deep breath before breaking the news of Donald's death to her son. 'George, I've got some bad news. Stella received a telegram this afternoon. It's Donald . . .'

George turned pale. 'Has he been injured?' he asked hopefully.

'No, love, he was killed. We don't have any other details at the moment. I wondered if you'd pop over and have a word with Stella and Wilf. As you can imagine, they are beside themselves with grief. Frank is with them at the moment.'

George nodded, unable to speak for a moment. 'He's

the third person I've known to have been killed in this war,' he said, his voice no more than a whisper. Ruby held out her arms and enveloped her son, wishing she could hold him close and safe forever.

'You're never too old for a cuddle, George, always remember that.'

'I will, Mum, and I'm sorry . . .'

'Whatever for?' she asked, noticing that he was blinking back tears.

'Going on about joining up, with you standing there knowing about Donald.'

'There is no need to apologize. A man's got to do what a man's got to do. I won't be the first mother who's worried about a son. I feel we're going to lose many more loved ones before this is all over. You know I'm not one for religion, and never have been, but even I say my prayers before I go to sleep at night. It's only been weeks since the Luck family up the road heard about their Edward. By all accounts he's buried over in France – it's not as if they can even pay their respects.' She shook her head sorrowfully.

'Don't forget Tom Crispin two years back – and John Smart not long afterwards, drowned at sea. That's just people in this road.'

'And now we can add young Donald to the list.' Ruby's voice started to wobble as she embraced her son again. 'Just promise me this, George: you must be careful. I don't want your name added to a list of dead lads from Alexandra Road – do you hear me?'

'I hear you, Mum,' he answered, his voice as shaky as hers. 'I wouldn't dare let you down.'

'Right, let's get this tea in to the girls before they wonder what we're up to. Do you think they'll stay for dinner?'

'What have we got in the stew?' he asked, peering into the pan.

'I've made a nice mutton stew. I've only to add a few more dumplings in the pan. I suppose you'd like two – one each for the girls?'

'I don't think Irene likes stew. Besides, they're going to Maureen's. We only popped in for a cuppa before I walk them round the road. But saying that, you want me to pop over and pay my respects to the Greens, so I'll come straight back. Can you put some dinner by for me? By the way, where is our Pat?'

'She's gone to her first Brownie meeting. I know she's a bit young for it, but with the girls she plays with down the road already attending, and the Brown Owl agreeing, I decided she could join in. It won't hurt as she'll have a bit of fun for a few hours, and it will take her mind off this war. Since she saw that Zeppelin going overhead, she can't think of anything else. A couple of hours of playing and such like will cheer her up. I'll need to pick her up from the Mission hall at Northend in three quarters of an hour.'

George took the tea tray. 'Why don't I pick her up after I've dropped the girls at Maureen's? I'm halfway there anyway. It'll give you time to put your feet up for a bit – you look worn out.'

Ruby gave him another a hug. 'You're a good lad.'

'Steady on, Mother, I nearly dropped the tray,' he grinned before pecking her on the cheek and giving her a wink.

'You'll always be my baby boy,' Ruby smiled, although her heart felt heavy.

After saying goodbye to George and the girls, Ruby settled down with her knitting. Her head was full of the men who had died, as well as those she knew who were still serving overseas. She'd stopped reading the newspapers so much, and since Frank's good friend Stephen was living over the bookshop and helping out most days, she only popped round to work there part-time. Now that she didn't have to find the rent money each week, and George was giving her a little towards the housekeeping, the pressure was off her shoulders to bring in a proper wage. Frank would treat her and Pat to gifts of food, as number thirteen was still as much his home as it was Stephen's, who was a welcome guest. To the outside world, Frank still lived with them. If Frank's parents thought the set-up at the bookshop was strange, they never commented.

Placing her knitting beside her chair, she again reached for her box of memories and pulled out Eddie's last letter. He'd not mentioned anything about his situation, but instead told her of his sorrow at hearing of the death of Charlie Sears, the son of his landlady where he'd lodged in Arthur Street when working in the brickfields. Ruby had heard of the loss, and had broken the news to him in her previous letter. Eddie's reply was full of memories of the way the family had looked after him. He even mentioned his work, which interested Ruby very much. Although there were a few brickfields surrounding the town, she'd known nothing of how bricks were made. She remembered Derek Green telling her how they could only make bricks during the warmer months, and wondered what Eddie had done for the rest of the year.

Ruby smiled as she re-read his words about Derek, and how the man would lecture them in the trenches about bricks to the point Eddie thought about joining the enemy trenches just to escape. There was mention of when he would be home with Ruby and their future together, and she blushed as he mentioned being alone with her. She quickly folded the letter and replaced it in the envelope. She'd put them somewhere safe in case Pat's curious eyes came across them.

Unable to settle until she knew that her two children were back home, Ruby reached for a book. It was one that Frank had recommended to her, on which he was waiting for her opinion. Her mind wandered after she'd read the first couple of pages as she thought about German planes dropping bombs on her children while they were away from the house. She'd been astonished when she was told of the planes flying as far as London and then dropping explosives. George explained that they also dropped something called incendiaries, which caught fire and caused so much destruction and death, so when they'd first seen the Zeppelins and then later spotted an enemy plane, she'd been petrified. 'What has the world come to?' she muttered to herself. The public had been warned that if they should hear whistles, car horns and shouts from the police, they were to take cover, as it meant that a plane was in the area. At first Ruby was unsure where the family would hide if this happened, and worried about the safest place in the house. George said to go into the cupboard under the stairs – being surrounded by brickwork, it should give some protection if the house was affected by bombs dropping nearby. Ruby wasn't so sure about that, and told George in no uncertain terms that she'd rather sit in the middle of the garden – at least then she could see what was going to land on top of her, rather than hide in fear in the dark.

What had made her smile was the news that they would know it was clear to come out from hiding when they heard the Boy Scouts riding past on bicycles, blowing their whistles. As she said to Pat, what mother in their right mind would let her sons out on their bicycles at a time like that? Looking up at the clock on the mantelpiece, she noticed it was getting late. George should have collected Pat by now and been home. Perhaps she should have a look to see where they were? Pulling her coat around her shoulders, she walked out to the front gate and looked up and down Alexandra Road. Wherever had they got to? Feeling as though she was being watched, she turned to look at the bay window of next door, and there was Miss Hunter watching her. Ruby jutted her chin out in defiance and stared back at the nosy old woman. Why didn't she mind her own business?

As she stood there wondering what to do, the door opposite opened and Frank stepped out. Catching sight of Ruby, he waved. 'Is there something up?' he called out.

'George is picking Pat up from Brownies, and they should have been home by now. I'm getting worried.'

Frank hurried over the road. 'They probably stopped to chat to somebody,' he said. 'Do you want me to walk up the road and look out for them? I could go as far as Britannia Bridge and wait there.'

'There's no need, thanks all the same, Frank. You're probably right; George hasn't eaten yet, although I fed Pat before she went out. I reckon she'll be hungry again too. Why don't you come along in and warm yourself up by the fire? I'll give you a bowl of stew. I have a nice crusty loaf as well, if you'd like a bit of that to dip in the gravy.'

Frank rubbed his hands together. 'Sounds good to me. Evening, Miss Hunter, how are you?' He waved to where their neighbour was again peering round her curtain.

'My God, that woman is nosy,' Ruby all but swore. 'I don't seem to be able to do anything without her clocking what I'm up to.'

He chuckled. 'She's probably just a lonely old woman.'

'Shush, Frank. You make me sound like a moaning old witch. If you were here as much as me and had her watching your every move, you'd be moaning too,' she laughed back at him. 'Come and warm yourself up while I get your food,' she nagged gently.

Frank smiled and shook his head; Ruby could be such a worrier at times. That's why I love her so much, he thought, stopping short as he thought of the word 'love'. Yes, he did love Ruby, very much. He wanted only the best for her, just as he did for his brothers. Or should that be brother, now that Donald had died? As cut up as he was over the loss, he was more worried for his mother and father. Wilf was displaying his typical stiff upper lip, even talking about going back on the river tomorrow, but Stella sat staring into space, every now and then dissolving into sobs. This had happened several times; she would scream Donald's name while holding herself tight, her arms wrapped round her body as she rocked back and forth in her armchair. Wilf watched helplessly, while Frank hugged his mother and soothed her tears. If she was no better in the morning, he would call the doctor to see if there was something that could be done. No one should have to suffer this much grief.

His thoughts wandered to Derek. The last Frank had heard, he had been out on the Somme somewhere. Frank took comfort in the fact that he was with Eddie Caselton and their mate Ernie Minchin. They could all watch out for each other.

'That looks good,' he said, rubbing his hands together as Ruby carried in the bowl of hot stew.

'I know we should sit at the table and eat, but the fire is so nice in here, it seems more cosy on such a miserable evening. Just mind you don't spill it on my rug,' she cautioned him good-naturedly. 'Will you be going back to Stephen at the shop this evening? It's a shame you never got to go back and bring him here for his dinner.'

'I was going to, but I think instead I'll stay with Mum and Dad. They shouldn't be left alone tonight. Dad seems completely lost while Mum . . . She is falling apart,' Frank said, the words catching in his throat.

'Oh, my poor love,' Ruby said as she took the bowl of food from him and placed it on the floor by the hearth before hugging Frank close. 'This bloody, bloody war. I hate it all – I'm frightened to sleep in my bed at night and I worry for the children. Who'd have thought bombs could be carried by planes and dropped on people? Monsters, these Germans are!'

'You have to remember, we have planes dropping bombs on the enemy as well. Does that make us monsters too? There are mothers on each side of this war worrying about their sons and crying when they don't come home. War is bad for everyone, and we need to try and stop it.'

'How can we do that – how can we stop a war without fighting?' Ruby asked, confused by his words.

'By refusing to fight. I've been to a couple of meetings along with Stephen. It seems if we put our case across properly, they can't make us fight.'

Ruby didn't like what she was hearing. Although she hated the war, now that she was imagining George out there risking his life for his country, she didn't like the thought that some men wouldn't fight to keep him safe and make the same sacrifice he was prepared to make. But then again, she agreed with Frank's views. She felt so confused at times. 'Did the white feathers you've been given not prick your conscience?' she asked.

'Don't tell me you think like those women?' Frank asked with anger in his voice. 'I thought you were better than that?'

'No, you've got me wrong. I don't agree with giving white feathers to men. That's an awful thing to do. No one has the right to insist that every man signs up. All the same, Frank, don't you want to play your part in this war?'

'I do, I do. But I refuse to carry a gun or do anything to antagonize the enemy.'

Ruby looked hopeful. 'Can you do that?' she asked. 'Surely there's some way you can contribute?'

'Yes – I could ask if I can work helping the injured. I

know I don't have the skills of a doctor or nurse, but perhaps they would let me carry stretchers or read to the injured . . . hold the hands of the dying. I know I can be of help if I do that.'

Ruby thought for a moment. 'I do know that if I was injured, having someone like you hold my hand and talk to me would give me great strength. If you decide to do this, you have my blessing,' she said, kissing his cheek before picking up his bowl of food. 'Now, eat up before it gets cold. I do believe that's my children I hear coming in the front door,' she said with great relief.

Pat came rushing into the room, pulling off her scarf and gloves as she did so. 'Guess what we saw?'

Ruby bent to unbutton her coat. 'It must've been something exciting to make your cheeks glow like that. Now sit yourself down before you burst, and tell me all about it.'

Pat leapt onto the spare armchair that was set the other side of the hearth and grinned with delight. 'We saw one of those German planes. It was flying over Slades Green – but we didn't see it dropping any bombs,' she added regretfully.

George's face twitched in amusement as he joined his sister sitting on the arm of the chair. 'The despicable child was disappointed because no one was blown up. Wherever did this bloodthirsty girl come from? Only the other day she was petrified of the Hun,' he chuckled before noticing his mother's concerned face. 'It's all right. We took cover, just in case there was more than one.'

Ruby gave a deep sigh of relief. 'Thank goodness for that – perhaps we will all get a good night's sleep for once.'

'Mummy, Uncle Frank – did you know that people sleep in train stations in London? Why do they do that?'

Frank wiped a piece of bread around the bowl, collecting some gravy as he spoke. 'They go to the stations where the platforms are underground. That way, if a bomb drops, most of them will be safe.'

'It's a shame we don't have any stations like that in Erith, isn't it?' Pat replied.

'I told you, you'll be safe if you sit in the cupboard under the stairs,' George explained. 'It is the safest place in the house.'

'Unless the bomb explodes as it lands on the roof, or comes down the chimney,' she said making a bloodthirsty noise.

'Oh, you disgusting child,' George said as he started to tickle her until she cried out for Ruby to rescue her.

'Come on, you two, let me get you some food. And you can sit at the table,' she said as Pat started to whine. 'No, you're not eating in here. I can't trust you not to spill your food.' She gave Frank a little nod as she spoke, indicating that he'd spilt gravy down his tie.

'When you've had your supper, would you like to come over with me to see your Nana Stella?' he asked them both. 'She is rather upset at the moment, and seeing the two of you might just cheer her up a little.'

'That's a splendid idea,' Ruby said, 'but please, don't ask her any questions. Pat, your Nana Stella doesn't want to talk about Donald at the moment. I want you to be a good girl and just be nice. Tell her about Brownies and school.'

Pat gave Ruby a smile. 'I know she is very sad about

Donald. I am too,' she said, going quiet for a couple of seconds. 'But what happens if the planes come back while you're here on your own?'

'I'll go and hide in the cupboard under the stairs. I've put a few rugs in there, and an old pillow. There's also a couple of candles so if we have to sit in there any length of time, we will be able to read our books if we can't sleep,' Ruby added, trying to be cheerful about what was quite a horrid experience.

'But if I went over Nana Stella's, wouldn't it be better to get under her staircase instead?' Pat asked.

'Don't worry about it, Pat. I'll decide if that should happen,' Frank said, pulling one of her pigtails.

Ruby was thoughtful as she dried up the plates and cutlery after Frank had left with the children. She hoped Pat wouldn't be too inquisitive about Donald's death. Perhaps I should've kept her here instead, she thought. There again, Stella needed cheering up, and what better than her favourite little girl? The two had formed a close bond, with Stella still allowing the child to call her Nana even after it was explained to her that Pat's father was really Eddie Caselton. The relationship between Ruby and Stella was still strained; part of Stella still badly wanted Ruby and Frank to be a happily married couple, and Pat to be their offspring. She'd only ever seen Eddie as a ne'er-do-well, and couldn't believe that Ruby loved him more than her son. She also found it strange that Frank preferred to be in rooms over the bookshop with his friend Stephen, when he had a ready-made family at number thirteen. So far the couple had managed to avoid her questions. Ruby knew it was wrong to hope as much, but perhaps with Donald's death Stella would forget to ask about Frank's love life for a while.

Ruby had the feeling that Wilf understood Frank's life-style but preferred to keep quiet, or to ignore his eldest son's choice of companion. Wilf was never happier than on the Thames working as a lighterman, and would be just as happy sleeping on his boat and doing his work, although she knew that he cared deeply for Stella and his children.

She wondered about retiring to bed – but then, she'd need to be up for when the children returned. Pat still slept on a small bed in Ruby's large bedroom. George had the larger of the spare rooms, with the smaller back bedroom being made up for when Frank stayed or, come to that, one of George's friends.

To keep herself busy, she boiled a kettle of water and pulled out four stone bottles from under the sink, filling them carefully with the water and screwing the stoppers tightly to avoid leaks. She made two trips upstairs putting them under the bed covers so they'd all be cosy and warm whatever time they got to bed. Settling back down with her knitting, she tried to relax. She was making a cardigan for Pat, which made a welcome change from the balaclava helmets she'd been donating for men fighting at the front. Again, her mind wandered back to what she could do to help the war effort. A few knitted items did not seem enough. She'd been going to ask Stella what she thought, but doubted the woman was now in the right frame of mind. How could she ask about helping with a war that had killed her youngest son? Next time Ruby went to the church hall to join the knitting circle, she'd ask the advice of the women she'd got to know there. Yes, she thought to herself, that's a very good idea.

Her eyelids closed and her head started to drop as the knitting slipped from her fingers before she suddenly became alert to sounds outside in the street. Whistles were being blown frantically, while the horns of several cars were sounding long and often. That means something, she thought to herself as she tried to clear her foggy brain. Then it hit her – that's the signal there are planes in the sky. She could be in danger. Her first thoughts were for her children and she rushed to the front door, swinging it wide open just as a policeman passed her gate on his bicycle. He stopped suddenly, pulled the whistle from his mouth and shouted at her to take cover.

'But my children are over the road. I need to get them,' she cried.

'Not now you don't, love. Your neighbours will be taking care of them and you need to do the same for yourself.' As he spoke, there was a large explosion and the ground beneath Ruby's feet shook. She screamed as slates from the roof clattered around her. The policeman jumped from his bike, which crashed to the pavement, and dived at her, pushing her back in through the front door. 'Where is the best place for you to take shelter?' he asked as he helped her to her feet and pushed the door shut behind them.

'The cupboard under the stairs,' she said, pointing with a shaking hand.

'Then let's go there now. I hope your husband won't mind,' he joked as he followed her into the small space.

'Perhaps we should be circumspect and leave the door slightly ajar,' Ruby chuckled, trying to hide her fear. 'Under the circumstances I'm sure my husband will understand. He's probably taking cover himself right now,' she added.

'Is he at work?' the officer asked.

'No, he's over on the Somme somewhere. I think that's where he is – he's fighting for our country,' she said proudly.

'Then I think he'll understand,' the policeman agreed.

Ruby lost track of how long they sat there talking. She'd lit one of the candles to give them a little light, and it had burnt down quite a way. She learnt that he had a son who was younger than her George, and the boy was hoping to join the police force himself when he was old enough.

Ruby wondered if George knew the lad. 'Are there any other policemen in your family?'

'Yes, my father – so if our Mike joins up, that will be three generations,' he added proudly.

Ruby told him about George and his apprenticeship at Vickers, along with her worries that he would soon be joining the army.

'With your boy's skills, he will be much in demand over there. I doubt he will be fighting like most of the lads. He'll be needed to keep the guns working.'

Ruby was comforted by his words. 'My good friend lost his brother; we only heard the news today. His mother is beside herself with grief. Is it wrong of me to think that could be me? I don't want it to happen to my son.'

The policeman patted her hand. 'Every mother in the land is thinking the same. My wife is overjoyed that Mike is too young at the moment to be conscripted. Then in the next breath she's telling me she feels guilty for her thoughts. I can't say I blame her; I feel the same. We live in a very strange world at the moment. Hark, listen: that sounds like the Boy Scouts with their rattles and bugles. It must be the all-clear,' he said as he helped Ruby to her feet and they both brushed themselves down. 'Perhaps we should go outside and see the damage?'

Out in the street, Ruby couldn't believe her eyes. The long road of bay-fronted houses was a mess. Gates were hanging off, windows were missing their glass. One house had lost its roof completely, while others, like hers, had only lost a few slates. The road seemed to be shrouded in dust and smoke, and she wrinkled her nose at the smell of burning. Looking around in disbelief, she heard the shouts of residents as they emerged from their homes. Further up on their side of the road was a gap where once there had been a family home. Ruby put her hand to her mouth to stop herself screaming in shock as the policeman took her by the elbow and guided her to the small wall between her house and next door. 'I need to go and help,' he said. 'Will you be all right?'

'Yes, yes, I'll be fine. You must go and do your job. Thank you for looking after me, Sergeant . . . ?'

'Jackson – my name is Bob Jackson,' he said as he gave her a nod and went to retrieve his bicycle from where it still lay on the pavement, luckily undamaged.

Ruby hurried across the road to number fourteen and was pleased to see that everyone was fine. The shock of the raid had brought Stella to her senses and she was busy making hot drinks for everybody. 'I've never been so pleased that I've still got my coal-fire stove,' she remarked. 'With all this damage, they've turned the gas off.'

Ruby smiled. With all that had happened out in the street, she was relieved that Stella seemed more like her old self. Frank and Wilf looked out the front door. 'We need to go and give a hand,' Wilf said. 'Will you be all right here with Ruby?'

'You go,' Stella said. 'There are lots of people that will need help, I would think, going by all the noise we've heard this evening.'

Ruby helped Stella make a tray of tea using all the cups she had in her cupboard. 'People will be glad of something hot as they help with the clearing up,' Stella said.

'I'll go and get my cups as well. Then there should be enough to go around. Would you like to come and help me, Pat?' Ruby asked.

'You stay here; I'll help your mum,' Stella told her. 'We can carry more between us,' she added as they headed back across the road. Stella stopped for a moment to look up at the destruction and tutted in sympathy. 'We definitely need more cups,' she said as they walked up the path to Ruby's house. 'Goodness, next door's windows are a mess. Almost every pane has been broken.'

'Oh, I do hope Miss Hunter is all right. I know she is the most irritable person on earth, but I'd hate to think she'd been injured. Do you think it will be all right for us to look through the window?'

'Well, we're not going to know otherwise, are we?' Stella said, and rather than go back round through the gate, she lifted her skirt and climbed over the low wall. As Ruby followed suit she heard Stella gasp in horror. 'Oh, my

245

Lord, she's been hurt. Quick, call my Frank – he knows a bit of first aid and might be able to help.' She started to pull shards of glass from the window frame to clear a way to get through to Miss Hunter.

Ruby rushed off to find Frank and was dismayed to see two bodies laid out on the pavement further up the road, covered with ripped curtains that must have been pulled from the bomb-damaged house. She told Frank what had happened and he hurried back with her, beckoning to a couple of men nearby to follow, calling out that someone had been injured as they all approached number fifteen. Frank shouted to his mother to step back out and away from the window, and with the aid of the other men, they broke the front door down. Ruby and Stella followed Frank into Miss Hunter's front room.

Frank bent down and felt for a pulse. 'She is still alive, but going by the blood and the way she's lying, she's been injured badly. Can you get a cup of water, Ruby? And Mum, you pull those cushions off the settee so we can make her more comfortable.'

A couple of the other men went out to flag down an ambulance as Ruby returned with the water, passing it to Frank. He propped up Miss Hunter's head. 'Here, take a sip and you may feel better.'

As the water touched her lips, the woman's eyes shot open. As she looked around her she recognized Ruby and then looked at Frank, pulling away as she did so. 'Get your hands off me,' she muttered, her lips covered in dust from where the lath and plaster had fallen from the ceiling. 'I don't want the likes of you touching me. I'm a God-fearing woman, and men that share beds with other men will burn in hell for eternity. I've seen the pair of you coming and going from that bookshop. You should think about closing your curtains of an evening,' she spat out, before collapsing back against a chair.

Stella looked at her son and frowned, then turned to see Ruby's shocked face. 'I can't believe she knew,' Ruby blurted out before stopping dead, realizing that Stella would have heard her perfectly.

Stella glared at Ruby and then turned to her son. 'It all makes sense now,' she said harshly as she got to her feet and pushed past Ruby to get out of the house.

Ruby started to follow, but Frank called her back. 'Leave it for now – we have much more important things to deal with. Nothing that's said now will alter what my mother thinks of me.'

13

Christmas Day 1917

Ruby looked at the table. She had done her best to make their Christmas Day meal festive. In years past, there had been more people sitting down to dinner. Sadly, this year there was only Frank representing the Green family, and even though he'd brought Stephen along at her insistence, it still felt like a very small group. George had asked if he could bring Irene, and although Ruby had taken a dislike to the posh young lady, she had agreed. The last thing she wanted to do was alienate her son. She'd also tried to make peace with Stella, but when her friend had crossed the road rather than speak to her, Ruby had decided to let things rest. The last thing she wanted was to be snapped at in the street and for nosy neighbours to make more of their falling out than they already had.

Smoothing out the white tablecloth, she stepped back and smiled. Her sisters had both promised to visit later in the afternoon for tea – at least that was something to look forward to. Never before had she entertained her own family to a special meal. Perhaps it was because both their husbands had joined the army, although Fanny liked to remind Ruby that they were both officers.

Pat was in the front room, playing with the beautiful doll that had been her gift from Frank. With its pretty china face and soft body, dressed in the most delicate lace gown, Ruby knew it would have been hard to come by and probably quite expensive. When she scolded Frank for spending too much, he shrugged off her comments by saying he had picked it up in a house sale.

Frank had gone back to the bookshop to check everything was fine, and would return with Stephen in time for their meal. Frank's friend, as he liked to call him, was as quiet as Frank, and both would have their nose in a book when Ruby visited, making the bookshop the perfect peaceful haven for browsers. Whatever their relationship when the front door of the shop was locked up at night, it did not bother Ruby. Live and let live was her philosophy of life. Only if her loved ones were ill-treated would she ever get involved in someone else's business. Apart from a few white feathers handed to both men, which did upset her, the men's life was peaceful.

George had gone to collect Irene, who lived in one of the posher houses at the top end of the Avenue. Ruby didn't know much about Irene's family and she didn't like to pry in case George thought she was interfering. Perhaps one day he would tell her; there again, she hoped that the couple would drift apart, as she didn't feel Irene was the right person for her George – far too prim and proper. Now, if it had been Maureen it would've been a different kettle of fish, as the girl was likeable and bubbly. Of course, she was taken – not only that, but she'd recently given birth to a beautiful baby boy. Young Alan was the opposite of his mother, being fair-haired, although they shared the same laughing eyes. Ruby thought it would be lovely to one day be a grandmother, but she shrugged off her fancies, laughing at herself as she heard a knock at the front door. There were plenty of years before a new baby was likely to join the family.

Wondering if Frank had forgotten his key, she opened the door to find a stranger on her front step. 'Can I help you?' she asked, wondering if the man had knocked at the wrong door.

'I'm sorry to bother you on such an important day in the Lord's calendar. I have some news to impart about your dear neighbour, Miss Hunter. I'm Reverend Gilroy, from Queen Street Church.'

Ruby frowned. Miss Hunter had been in hospital ever since her injury on the night of the bombing raid. 'I don't really know her that well,' she said, wondering if perhaps he wanted her to do something for the old lady. She did feel a little guilty at not having visited her in the cottage hospital with some flowers, but there again, the woman had made her life hell. Ruby feared a visit could easily turn into a nasty scene. She could well imagine the old woman throwing the flowers at her and making spiteful comments as she fled from the ward; she shuddered at the very thought of it.

The man coughed, and Ruby snapped out of her thoughts. 'I'm sorry – what is it I can do for you?'

'I'm afraid Miss Hunter has passed away,' he said, looking even more sombre, if that were possible.

'Oh dear, I'm so very sorry,' she replied, wondering

whether she should invite him in. 'Does she have family? I can't say I've ever seen anyone visit – not that I'm one to pry, you understand,' she added, thinking of all the times the woman had peeped from behind her curtains whenever Ruby or the children left the house. She was still smarting from the comments that had caused the rift between her and Stella.

'There is a distant cousin, I believe,' the man said thoughtfully. 'I just wanted to inform her neighbours.'

'That's very kind of you. I would like to pay my respects. Would you be able to let us know when the funeral is arranged? And I've been so rude, forgive me. Can I offer you a cup of tea?'

'No, thank you – I'm just going to give the news to the people at number seventeen, and then I'll be away to my own dinner. My wife will be expecting me.'

Ruby thanked him and wished him as good a Christmas as they could have in these times of war, then closed the door and went back to the kitchen, peeping into the oven to see if the goose was ready. She wondered who her new neighbours would be. For a fleeting moment she thought she'd better tell Stella about Miss Hunter's passing – but then she remembered that Stella wanted nothing to do with her, which made her very sad.

'Who was that at the door, Mum?' Pat asked, coming out to join her, still hugging her new dolly.

Ruby stroked her hair. 'It was a man to tell us that the lady next door has gone to heaven.'

'Was it the bomb?' Pat asked with sudden interest.

'No, my love; she was just a very old lady, and poorly,' Ruby said. There was no need for Pat to know that Miss

Hunter's death was a result of the bombing. The child still had a morbid interest in bombs.

'So, she will be in heaven with Donald?' Pat asked.

Ruby smiled at the thought, remembering the time Donald had been chased up and down the street by Miss Hunter after a ball he'd been kicking about had bounced off her window. It had taken Wilf to come out of his front door in his slippers, shirt undone and braces hanging around his waist, to stop the woman in her tracks. Miss Hunter had been even more horrified by Wilf's attire than by the ball incident, and had rushed into her house shouting loudly about the terrible family at number fourteen. 'Why don't you put Dolly to sleep in the armchair and help me place the knives and forks on the table? Everyone will be here soon, and it will be lovely if it's all ready for them.'

Pat set to, helping her mother and chattering nineteen to the dozen at the same time. They'd just finished when George let himself in the door, ushering Irene in front of him. 'Hello, Mum, is anyone else here yet?'

'I am,' Pat said. 'Do you want to see my new dolly?'

Irene ignored Pat and stood still as George slipped her coat from her shoulders.

'That's a very smart coat,' Ruby said, admiring the green woollen fabric and fur collar.

Irene smiled politely. 'It was a gift from my parents.'

'A very generous gift,' she said. 'Would you like a drink while we wait for Frank and Stephen? I have a rather nice port wine that Frank put by for today. We are having goose,' she added, thinking that at least that ought to be something Irene would approve of.

Irene rejected the wine and then informed Ruby, 'I have a very sensitive stomach at the moment. I'll say no thank you to the goose. A little soup might be better for me,' she suggested.

'I'll take Irene into the front room and let her rest in an armchair for a while,' George said, looking rather pale himself. 'I'll come back in to help you after,' he went on, as Ruby gave him a puzzled look. She wasn't about to cook a small bowl of soup for her guest. The girl would have to eat what was offered to her, or go without.

With Stephen and Frank suddenly appearing with arms full of gifts, Irene's indisposition was soon forgotten. Stephen handed Pat a large item covered in brown paper. He helped her put it on the floor before the child dived in, ripping the paper away. 'Oh look, it's a pram for my dolly,' she exclaimed, excitedly hugging Stephen's legs before he leant down to accept a kiss on his cheek.

'Here's the other part of your present,' Frank said, giving the child a soft parcel which turned out to be bedding for the pram.

'You spoil the child, the pair of you. You already gave her that fine dolly! That would have been enough,' Ruby said. They were as good as uncles any day.

George joined them, and was thrilled with his gift of a pipe and a pouch of tobacco from Frank. His initials had been carved into the soft leather.

He gave his mother a shy look, but Ruby nodded. 'You're old enough now to smoke a pipe, and that's a fine specimen,' she said as her son unwrapped the tobacco ready to feed the pipe. 'Perhaps not now, though, George. I'm about to dish up our dinner,' she added.

'Before you do,' Frank said, 'you have to sit down and open your own gifts.'

'Oh, you shouldn't have,' Ruby said. 'Why did you bother with me? Christmas is all about the children.'

The men ignored her as they handed her a parcel each. Stephen's was a delicate silk scarf. She ran her fingers through it and smiled. 'I shall keep it for best and remember you every time I wear it. Thank you, Stephen.'

'Don't save it for best, Mrs Caselton, wear it every day. We never know what tomorrow will bring.'

Ruby held the scarf to her cheek: its softness and gentleness reminded her of Stephen. 'I'll do that – yes, I'll certainly do that. Thank you. But please, Stephen, do I have to keep reminding you to call me Ruby?'

Stephen gave her a shy smile and promised that he would.

Frank's gift was a larger package and felt quite heavy. 'I hope you've not been spending your money on me too,' she scolded, thinking she sounded just like her mother. Eagerly pulling off the paper, she gasped in delight.

'It's not new,' Frank said quickly, knowing how thrifty Ruby tried to be. 'I spotted it months ago at a sale. I just knew you would love it.'

Ruby ran her fingers over the carved wooden box. The use of different colours of wood made a pattern so intricate that all she could do was stroke its shiny surface and sigh. 'I've never seen anything like it,' she said.

'It's called marquetry: all the patterns are made from small slivers of wood.'

She smiled as she traced the pattern of birds that seem to fly across the surface of the box.

'Open it up,' Frank urged her.

Ruby turned the small brass key and slowly lifted the lid. As she did so, a tinkling tune started to play. The box was lined with red velvet.

'The tune is called the "Waltz of the Flowers",' Frank said, as Ruby leant closer to listen to the wonderful melody. 'I thought the box would be somewhere you could store your memories. I know how you love to keep bits and pieces.'

Ruby sighed again with delight as they listened to the tune until it slowed and came to a halt. Frank showed her where there was a small handle underneath, to rewind it. 'It's such a beautiful tune,' she said, her eyes dancing in delight.

'The composer is called Tchaikovsky,' Frank said. 'When you next come to the shop, I'll take you upstairs and you can listen to the full recording on my gramophone.'

'There is more than this part?' Ruby asked. 'How wonderful.' She wound it up and they listened one more time, while Pat danced around the room like a ballerina. 'Now, you are all to go into the front room and join Irene. My children can help me clear up this mess and sort out the dinner.'

George followed his mum into the kitchen, while Pat continued to play with her new pram.

'So, what have you got to tell me?' Ruby said, looking her son straight in the eye.

George was now inches taller than her and a fine, strapping man. Even so, he cowered under her gaze.

'I take it Irene is in the family way?' she prompted.

'How can you tell? I mean . . . we were going to say

255

something later, after dinner, when Frank and Stephen had gone home . . .'

Ruby could only shake her head. 'Oh, George! Whatever have you done?'

As George looked at his mother, Ruby was reminded of the little boy who always ran to her when he had a problem.

'I don't know what to do, Mum,' he cried.

Ruby pulled him into her arms just as she had when he was a youngster. 'It's a bit late now, lad. You've got to do the honourable thing. What do her parents say about this?'

'Irene's father wants to arrange a wedding as soon as possible. He said the neighbours and his friends would only be told we were getting married quickly because I'm about to join the army.'

'But . . . but you're not, are you?'

Again, George couldn't meet his mother's eyes and looked away towards the window over the sink, even though there wasn't much to look at. 'Well, it's like this,' he said, coughing nervously to clear his throat. 'As I'm eighteen in a few weeks, I'd be conscripted anyway, so I've been to the office and enquired . . .'

'You bloody, bloody, fool,' Ruby said angrily. 'You had a bright future and are in a job that meant you might not have been called up due to your war work. Mrs Grant found you the best apprenticeship any young man could dream of, and you are thought of so highly at Vickers – and now you're walking away from it all, leaving a wife expecting a baby at home, while you run off to play soldiers? What is to become of you, George?' A single tear dropped onto her cheek.

George reached out and wiped the tear away. 'I do know I've made a mess, Mum, but I'm a man now and I'm going to make a go of things. I'm very fond of Irene, and she is fond of me. I didn't want to tell you without knowing that my future plans were secure. I've spoken to Mr Grant at work, and he told me that any time I came back there would be a job for me. The thing is, I want to go away knowing that Irene can turn to you if she has any problems. You might think she's a bit snooty, but when you get to know her, I hope you will love her as much as I do.'

'Oh, George, how could I not love anybody who loves you? Do you happen to know where you're going to live once you're married? I could always move Pat back in with me and let you have two rooms upstairs, if you wish.'

George looked a little embarrassed. 'The thing is, Mum, Irene's mother wants us to live with her . . .'

'Oh, I see. It's like that, is it?' Ruby said, knowing Irene's family had a much larger house and were a better class of people. 'It looks to me as though you're moving up in the world.'

'Not if I can help it,' George said. 'My feet are firmly stuck in Alexandra Road. It's good enough for me and always will be. Irene's dad is a good sort – he just wants to make sure his daughter does all right for herself. He is interested in me and my job, and treats me like a son rather than somebody who fathered his grandchild out of wedlock. We had a bit of a discussion the other day. He told me I had to speak to you as soon as possible.'

Ruby considered this. 'He does sound like a decent sort,' she acknowledged. 'What did he have to say, apart from you speaking to me?'

'Well, he reckons Irene's a bit on the spoilt side . . . and now she's going to be a wife and mother, she needs to stand on her own two feet. I'm not sure Irene's mother agrees with that, but she wasn't there at the time, so she didn't have a say. He reckons we should set up home on our own before too long, as it will give Irene something to focus on while I'm away. He says it will be the making of her.'

Ruby chuckled. 'I'm looking forward to meeting him. What does Irene have to say about all of this?'

'I think my dad is right,' Irene said as she joined them, slipping her arm through George's. 'I hope you're not too upset, Mrs Caselton?'

'How can I be upset with you? Why, I was not much older than George when I married my Eddie. By then I had a nipper on the way as well. It was your nan who wasn't happy. She was none too pleased, I can tell you.' Ruby chuckled again. 'I'm not going to interfere with your plans. The last thing you want is a nagging mother-in-law,' she said, giving Irene a gentle smile. 'However, if you want my advice and my help any time, I'm here, so just remember that.'

'Thank you, Mum,' George said, kissing her on the cheek.

Irene did the same. 'Thank you for not being angry with us,' she said. 'There is one thing I do want to ask you.'

'Fire away,' Ruby said as she opened the door of the oven again, worrying about the goose being too dry.

'I wondered whether you might know of somewhere we could rent? My dad is giving us a generous allowance for our wedding present. I'd like to live nearby, if you don't mind? I know my parents expect us to stay with them for a while, but I want my own home before the baby comes along.'

'Mind? I can't think of anything better. Are you looking for rooms or a house?'

'I'd adore a little house, even though we would have to rent. Would your landlord have any properties on his books?'

Ruby laughed kindly. 'I don't have a landlord, love; I own every stick and brick of this house,' she beamed proudly. 'However, I know of a house that has just fallen empty. Leave it with me for a couple of days and I'll make some enquiries.'

'That will be great, Mum, thank you,' George said, looking mightily relieved. 'Is it far from here?'

Ruby glanced towards the wall that divided her home from number fifteen next door. 'Not too far at all,' she replied with a gentle smile.

There was silence around the dinner table apart from Pat chattering on about her presents. In some ways, Ruby was glad the child was unaware of what was going on with her close family and friends. Even Frank and Stephen were not their usual joyous selves. Trying to break the icy atmosphere, she turned to George and Irene. 'Darlings, why don't you share your happy news with everybody?'

George glanced to Irene, who nodded her approval. 'I've requested Irene's hand in marriage, and she has accepted. We plan to marry before I join the army in January,' he said, looking to the two older men for approval.

Ruby looked to Frank to say something supportive, but her nudge was not required. 'I say, that's wonderful news,' he exclaimed, leaping to his feet to kiss Irene's cheek and shake George's hand enthusiastically. 'What do you say to this, Stephen?' he asked his friend, who was already joining in with his own congratulations.

'Jolly good show,' Stephen said. He was the perfect foil for Frank, usually being the quieter one of the couple. Ruby smiled to herself. That was the first time she'd actually thought of them as a couple, and indeed they were. She'd never felt there was anything wrong in this, but was certain a rocky road lay ahead for her two friends. 'You must tell us what kind of wedding you plan to have, Irene. Will it be a grand affair?'

Irene looked into her lap, but retained her usual air of aloofness. It was very seldom that Ruby was able to get behind her attitude. 'It will be a simple wedding, under the circumstances,' she said quietly.

Frank raised his eyebrows at Ruby, who gave a small nod back. Her friends had surmised the situation at once, realizing the need for haste. 'I suppose with you going off at any time to serve our country, it is best to have the wedding as soon as possible,' he said, doing his utmost to help preserve the illusion of everything being well in order.

Once the small group had finished eating, Frank cleared his throat. 'I too have some news,' he said, as Stephen nodded for him to continue speaking. 'I brought these round with me today so we could have another ceremonial burning.' He reached into the pocket of his jacket and pulled out a handful of white feathers.

George looked angry. 'Who is doing this to you? It's disgusting,' he spat out.

'Reading the newspapers, you would think brave women walked up to us and handed them over, but I've found that not always to be the case. I fear Erith is full of cowards,' he said sadly. 'To begin with, I never spoke when the odd one was handed to me. It is not in me to be rude to a woman. However, I now turn my back on them and ignore their unkind words. I find enough left around the bookshop to stuff a pillowcase.'

'But is it not our duty to encourage men to join the army?' Irene piped up. 'My mother says we women need to urge men to fight for our country.'

George shifted uncomfortably in his seat and waited for his mother to say something. Stephen looked wide-eyed at Irene's comment. 'I don't think you quite understand the implication of what is happening here,' he said, looking none too pleased.

Irene became quite animated as she explained how her mother's friends saw it as their duty to encourage all men to join the army. 'Mummy says there is no excuse for men not to fight.'

'May I ask what your mother thinks about people who have principles and don't believe that war is the answer?' Stephen asked, his face turning rather pink.

'Leave it,' Frank said quietly.

'No, I'm sorry, I won't leave it,' Stephen said. 'I applaud any man who has strong principles and believes that war is not the answer to the problems in our world at the moment.'

'But Mummy says . . .'

'Please, Irene . . .' George said as he started to fiddle with his pipe and tobacco. Ruby could see her son was finding it hard to support his fiancée's views as well as those of his dear friends. Frank shrugged his shoulders at Ruby in despair.

'Irene, dear, is your mother involved in handing out these white feathers?'

Irene beamed, oblivious to the tension around the table. 'Yes, she chairs several committees where, as well as doing other good works, they seek out men who have yet to fight for their country.'

Ruby couldn't believe what she was hearing, but tried to stay calm. After all, this girl was carrying her unborn grandchild. 'Does your mother work? I understand that many women are now taking on the jobs that men have relinquished so they can go to serve their country? Why, I've seen women working on the trams. Is this something your mother would do?'

Irene looked shocked. 'No, a woman should not do a man's job. It is most unseemly.'

'That's rather unpatriotic, wouldn't you think?' Stephen spat back.

'I intend to do some war work,' Ruby announced. The conversation around the dinner table had helped her make up her mind. For some time now she had thought she could do more, as she was certain her knitting did not contribute much at all. However, she was still not sure what work she could do to contribute to bringing the war to an end.

Frank grinned. 'It seems to be a day for announcements. Mine is that after all this time, and searching my conscience, I too am going to take the king's shilling.'

Ruby felt her heart plummet. 'But you're the most peaceful man I know; you always said you couldn't bear arms. What made you change your mind?' she asked.

'Well, it's not these.' He pointed at the pile of bent feathers. 'Shall we put them on your fire, or perhaps Irene would like to return them to her mother? To answer your question, Ruby, I intend to join the Royal Army Medical Corps to help people. I know I only have basic first-aid knowledge, but if I claim to be a conscientious objector and get thrown into prison I won't be helping anyone, least of all myself. I can help treat the injured – both friend and foe,' he said, throwing the last sentence in Irene's direction. She had the good grace to look embarrassed, but said nothing.

'I wish I could go with you, but there's no way they'll let me go with my health the way it is,' Stephen said. 'It'll be so hard being here alone knowing what you're facing – but I'll be so proud of you.' He reached out and took Frank's hand.

This really did shock Irene. 'Perhaps it's time we left,' she said to George as she stood up. 'Thank you for the delicious meal, Mrs Caselton, and for your offer of help in finding us somewhere to live.'

'Please, you must call me Ruby. Mrs Caselton seems so formal,' Ruby said, trying to lighten the atmosphere a little. She was sure Irene couldn't be as snooty as she made out. There must be some shade of decency in the girl, otherwise her son would not have fallen in love with her. She hung on to that hope as she helped with their coats and waved goodbye to George and his fiancée at the front door.

Now she'd made the announcement of doing war work, she really must put her mind to it.

Over the road at number fourteen, Stella sat alone. Wilf, not able to face spending the day in a house that had once been so full of laughter, had returned to the river. There was work to be done even on Christmas Day, and he felt needed. At the moment he didn't feel as though his wife needed him at all.

Gazing from her window, Stella watched as Ruby's guests arrived. She recalled Christmases past when her own door had been open to neighbours, just as Ruby's was now. When her Donald was alive, and with his two older brothers bringing friends home, Christmas was always the best time of the year. Now, with Donald gone and Derek serving his country, her Frank preferred the company of a married woman: Ruby Caselton.

How had someone she'd helped on her very first day in Alexandra Road – at the lowest point in the other woman's life – ended up taking her family away? Even Wilf preferred not to be at home and spent all his time on the river. Turning away from the window, she thought long and hard before taking a sheet of writing paper from the sideboard drawer and placing it on the table. Picking up Donald's fountain pen, she grasped it tightly and started to write.

My dearest Derek,

It breaks my heart to inform you that we lost our Donald recently. I was told he was brave until the end, when he succumbed to his injuries. I have no idea how I am to go on. Frank seems to be a stranger to me and prefers the company of Ruby Caselton. As I write this letter, it is Christmas Day, and I've seen strange men entering her home. If the rumours are true, she is carrying a child, but goodness knows who is the father.

I only have you now, Derek. Please stay safe for me and give my regards to Eddie if you see him. My prayers fly through the miles, and I hope you can hear them. Until we meet again,

Your dearest mother

She folded the paper and placed it inside an envelope, using the address details she had been given some time before. Taking the envelope to her bag, which sat near the window, she tucked it away securely, not wishing Wilf to find it. As she straightened up she noticed Frank and his friend leaving number thirteen. Ruby kissed and hugged both of the men and waved as they walked down the road. It was fortuitous Derek had mentioned Eddie Caselton was serving with him. How would Eddie react after he heard her news? No one could tell, but he was bound to be jealous – and Ruby would suffer for it. Stella had no qualms about lying to her son: hadn't Ruby done just that, pretending young Pat was her own granddaughter when in fact she had been fathered by Eddie? The same man who was supposed to have been such a bad husband and run away years before, no less.

Stella nodded to herself with satisfaction and snapped the clasp of the handbag closed, muttering, 'I'll have the last laugh, Ruby Caselton.'

Ruby enjoyed her sisters' visit, as they passed a pleasant couple of hours chatting of nothing special while enjoying watching young Pat play with her toys. Ruby had confided in them about her son's impending marriage and her sisters had been sympathetic in the situation, insisting it was the war that was to blame for the loose morals of the young people of today. Ruby bit her tongue and promised they would receive an invitation to the wedding, begging them to keep the secret of the baby to themselves. She wasn't sure how Irene or her parents would react if they knew Ruby had been talking to others about it. But somehow it seemed the news of the baby had united the three women, with Fanny and Janie teasing their younger sister about being a grandmother and insisting they would help with knitting the layette after inspecting Ruby's handiwork with her knitting needles.

After clearing away the tea things when her sisters had left, Ruby helped her tired daughter to bed and tucked her in alongside her dolly. By the time George arrived home, he found his mother pleasantly tired, sitting by the hearth in darkness apart from the glow of the fire.

'I thought you'd have gone up ages ago,' he said as he knelt by her chair.

Ruby stroked his hair. 'Where have the years gone?' she asked him. 'It doesn't seem five minutes since you helped me move into this house as a little boy of five.'

George laid his head against her shoulder.

'It doesn't to me either. I remember everything about that day: being so frightened when you collapsed in the street, and then being taken into the house by Nanny and not knowing what had happened to you. Nobody would explain to me, and it was days later that I was allowed to see you, and you looked so ill. I remember asking about the baby because you'd told me about how I was going to have a baby brother or sister – and there was nothing. When I asked, people cried. Nan even slapped me for asking. She told me that little boys should be seen and not heard. All I wanted to do was see the baby. This is what I fear most about Irene expecting our child. She is so young. What if our baby dies?'

In the light from the flickering fire, Ruby could see the fear on his face. 'You can't think like that, George. You've got to be the strong one for Irene. She is a healthy young woman and she will be the perfect mother; you have nothing to fear, believe me.'

'But what if I'm away when the baby comes? I doubt her mother will be of much use. Will you promise me you'll be there with her, please?'

'I promise. Don't you fret, I'll be by her side and I'll remember it all. I will write to you and tell you about your beautiful baby when it's born. I suppose you're hoping for a strapping young boy?' she said, trying to lighten the air of gloom.

'Not necessarily. Mum, I've discussed what happened when you lost Sarah, and Irene agrees with me that if we are to have a little girl we will call her Sarah, just as I promised you when we went to visit her grave on the day we met Mrs Grant.'

Ruby couldn't find the words to thank him. To think he'd remembered that day from when he was a little boy. Deep, shuddering sobs came from within her and she found herself crying, not only for her lost daughter but for Derek, for all that had happened with her and Eddie, for Frank and Stephen and their dangerous future together, and also for her dear son, who might perish on the battlefields of France. When her tears subsided and she wiped her eyes, she said, 'Now you are a man, George, there are things I need to tell you about your father – why he left us, and why I still love him to this day.'

George listened carefully as the words poured from Ruby's lips. 'To think I never told a living soul apart from Frank, even down to the one night that Eddie came back and then disappeared again. So, you see, whatever anyone says, Pat is your sister.'

George took his mother in his arms and held her tight until he could feel that she'd settled and was calm within herself. 'Mum, I've always trusted you. I've looked up to you: the way you've coped, the way you've made a home for me and Pat – and I've seen that others respect you. When Dad returns from the war I shall welcome him with open arms, if that's what you want. Let's put all of this behind us and start again. 1918 is going to be a good year for our family, I can feel it in my bones. Besides, you're going to be a grandmother,' he chuckled.

'Don't you start,' Ruby smiled as she wiped her face with her handkerchief. 'I had your two aunts pulling my leg about that this afternoon. I've got my own back, though: I reminded them that they'll be great-aunties. I also showed them my terrible knitting skills, so they are already planning to kit your baby out in the finest garments. She'll be a lucky young lady.'

'Or young man,' George smiled.

'Oh no, I really think we're about to meet our Sarah,' Ruby said contentedly.

14

January 1918

Ruby would have liked to be able to say she'd enjoyed her son's wedding, but it would have been a lie. Irene's father was delightful; however, her mother was a different matter. Mrs Desmond was a snob, there was no other word for it. She did her best to outshine Ruby, and without really saying a word she made it clear that she was from a different class to Ruby and her son.

Ruby was happy to see that Mr Desmond welcomed George with open arms. He was a jovial chap, and the few words he had with Ruby before the wedding reassured her that he would look out for her son and would make a good father-in-law to him. Of course, he also made it clear he was not impressed with the situation, but as he said, there was no point in crying over spilt milk. They had to make the best of the situation. George was already in uniform and would be joining his regiment within two weeks. To see him standing waiting for his bride to walk down the aisle was a sight Ruby would never forget. It reminded her of seeing her Eddie standing there on the day she was married, although her own wedding had been nothing like Irene's. Mrs Desmond made sure her daughter had only the best of everything, and Ruby had to admit Irene looked a sight for sore eyes, dressed from head to foot in lace and wearing a silver tiara handed down from Mrs Desmond's grandmother.

Pat made the perfect bridesmaid and did everything as Irene instructed, which was a relief to Ruby. Afterwards, at the Desmond's home over wafer-thin sandwiches and glasses of sherry, Ruby mingled with the guests, making polite conversation. Already she felt a blister on her left foot, but she pinned a smile to her face and soldiered on. Granted her two sisters were there, but apart from that she had no other family to support her. She had spotted Stella and Wilf sitting at the back of the church and had been pleased that they'd been invited. However, as everyone had left the church to stand outside in the winter sun, she had seen them walk away, knowing the rift between them had not yet healed. She decided it would be a good idea to pop over to their house later on with a slice of wedding cake, to thank them for attending. If she took Pat with her, it would break the ice. She missed Stella and the easy way they'd once had of talking with each other; but grief did strange things to people's lives, she thought.

Towards the end of the reception, as Mr Desmond called the couple over, Ruby joined him. This was the time to give the young couple their wedding gift; it was to be a joint present, and Ruby had never felt so excited. She wanted to see the look on her son's face when he was told. With just a few words, Mr Desmond handed an envelope to Irene.

'I know your plan was to stay here while you looked for a home for you and George, but we – that is, your mother, myself and Mrs Caselton – have a surprise for you.' He faltered, not knowing what to say next, so Ruby stepped in.

'You mentioned to me at Christmas how you'd like to live near the town, and I said that I would be nearby while George was away. This house became available, and between us it has been purchased and put into your name.' She didn't add that her contribution had only been one-tenth of the house's value; it was only thanks to the generosity of the Desmonds that the purchase was possible.

Irene opened the envelope and pulled out a legal document. 'Oh, my goodness!' she shrieked. 'George, look. I can't believe it – thank you all,' she said, throwing herself into her father's arms before hugging Ruby, then giving her mother a polite kiss on the cheek.

George had been looking at the document and was lost for words. 'It's the deeds to number fifteen Alexandra Road. We'll be living next door to you, Mum. I can't tell you what this means to me. Thank you, sir,' he said, shaking Mr Desmond's hand and doing as Irene had done and kissing Mrs Desmond's cheek. He then hugged his mother and swung her round in a circle, much to Mrs Desmond's surprise.

'I take it you're happy,' Ruby chuckled. 'However, please don't think I'm going to be an interfering mother-in-law, Irene. I don't even want to hold a spare key. Number fifteen is yours and yours alone.'

'Oh, please, Mrs Ca . . . I mean Ruby, you must have a spare key. I insist. If there's any time you have no one to care for Pat, she is as welcome in my home as she is in yours. George, I can't wait to look at the house. I shall have such fun making it a home, my love.'

Mr Desmond said, 'I shall give you a banker's draft so that you can furnish the house whatever way you wish.'

'Oh goodness, that will be wonderful,' Irene beamed as she linked arms with George. 'I want to make it the perfect home for you to return to, and for our baby to be brought up in.'

Ruby smiled at George. No doubt he was thinking, as she was, about the few modest sticks of furniture they'd had when they moved into number thirteen. She just hoped the young couple would love living in their new home as much as she had loved living in the town these past thirteen years.

Ruby took Pat's hand as they crossed the road; she'd put a few tasty tidbits on a plate along with two slices of the wedding cake, courtesy of Irene's parents. She hoped Stella seeing Pat in her pretty lace dress would soften her heart a little. The life seemed to have been sucked out of Stella since the news of Donald's death. Ruby so wanted them to be friends again, and life to be as it used to. She missed their shopping trips into town, with cups of tea and a good natter in the cafe. In some ways, Ruby had found life without Stella a lonely existence.

Hopefully, with Irene moving in next door and George off to his regiment, her life might change a little, even if Irene wasn't the kind of person Ruby usually mixed with. The girl had surprised her in some ways – deep down, there was a likeable side to her. She just needed to push it to the surface more. Approaching Stella's house, Ruby's thoughts turned to Maureen Gilbert, who she hoped would be a regular visitor to Irene. Ruby would then get to have lots of cuddles with her delightful toddler, Alan.

Ruby noticed the curtains move as they opened the gate. Ah, she thought, at least someone is home and can see we are about to knock on the door. She smiled at Pat as she handed the little girl the plate of food. Her daughter had so much wanted to hand over the gift herself.

It was Wilf who opened the door, a glum look on his face. 'I'm sorry, love; if it's Stella you wanted to see, she's having a lie down at the moment. The news about Derek was just too much for her. I'm not feeling that great myself, so I'm sorry if I don't ask you both in. We've only just heard,' he said, shaking his head in sorrow.

Ruby didn't understand what he meant. Pat, oblivious to what was being said, held out the plate of food. 'I've come to show you my dress. I was a bridesmaid for George, and he sent some wedding cake for you,' she beamed up at the man she thought of as a grandfather.

'You look as pretty as a picture, and Stella will be sad to have missed seeing you,' he said as he took the plate.

'I can come back and show her another day,' she smiled. 'Irene said I can keep the dress.'

Ruby stroked her daughter's head. 'I tell you what, why don't you take my key and go back over home and start to draw a picture of the wedding? You can give it to Stella when she feels better,' she said, and watched as her delighted daughter skipped back across the road. 'Wilf, this must have been sudden. I spotted you both sitting at the back of the church earlier.'

Wilf nodded his head. 'We did want to see your George get married, but under the circumstances and the way Stella feels about things, she didn't feel up to socializing. The letter was lying on the doormat when we got home.'

'Letter? Would the army not have sent a telegram?'

'They only do that when the person has died. Our Derek has sustained terrible injuries, and he's not expected to survive. He was the only one of the lads in his trench not to be killed outright.'

Ruby felt an icy fear grip her heart. She reached out to steady herself against the wall of the house. She knew that Eddie and Derek had been sticking together like glue; Eddie always mentioned Derek, and a chap called Ernie Minchin they both knew from working in the brickfields not a mile down the road from where she stood at that moment. 'Was there any word of Eddie?' she asked.

'Eddie? You ask about Eddie?' Stella screamed as she pushed Wilf to one side, doing her utmost to get to Ruby. Her hair was dishevelled and her face streaked with tears. In her hands she gripped a letter screwed into a ball that she waved at Ruby. 'You make a song and dance of it with my son, and you still want to know about your husband? I've never known such a selfish cow. For your information, your Eddie died thinking you were carrying on with anyone who would look twice at you. I made sure of that,' she spat. 'Not content with ruining your own marriage, now you've talked my Frank into joining up. Isn't it bad enough that I've lost two sons without you sending the third to his death?'

Wilf took Stella's arm and guided her back inside before going to close the door. He gave Ruby a vacant look, more concerned about his wife than Ruby's protestations.

'But it's not what it seems . . . we haven't . . . I don't understand . . .' she cried, unable to make sense of Stella's words, or make herself understood.

'You should take yourself back home. If Pat wants to come over to see us, she's more than welcome, but it's best you stay away. Stella doesn't even want to see Derek. She can't bear to think of him with terrible injuries, and wants to remember him as he was before the war. I can't leave her to go and see him, so in a way I feel very much as she does at the moment. You may not be totally to blame, but it would be best for you to stay away.'

Ruby refused to be beaten when she'd done nothing wrong. Even though in her head the words 'your Eddie died' kept screaming out, she refused to accept them. Surely she would feel it in her heart if he was gone? Wouldn't someone write to her – unless Eddie had forgotten to make her his next of kin? She took a deep breath and tried to think clearly. Nothing should change until she knew more about her husband.

She knew Derek should not be alone, and out of respect for Frank, who was now serving with the Ambulance Corps, she couldn't let the lad die without anyone there. Not only that, but he might also know something about Eddie – and she needed to find out how her husband had died. 'Where have they taken Derek?' she demanded.

'He's been taken to some place called Queen's Hospital in Sidcup; it's where they take soldiers who . . . who . . .'

Tears fell from Wilf's eyes as he trailed off and turned away, closing the door in her face.

Back indoors, Ruby checked to make sure Pat was all right and sat down at the kitchen table. Resting her head in her hands, she forced herself to think carefully about what had happened.

She desperately needed to talk things through with someone. Her first choice would have been George, but it was unfair to do such a thing on the day of his wedding – besides, he was going away to the country with his bride for a long weekend before returning home, and then he would be going to join his regiment. And anyway, it had been so long since George had seen his father that Ruby couldn't bring herself to tell him at that moment, especially as there was no proof his dad had died. She didn't feel she could confide in her sisters, as they just wouldn't have understood; besides, it would have meant explaining about Frank and his relationship with Stephen, and it wasn't right to do so. There was a time when Stella would have been the first person she spoke to when she had a worry . . .

'Everything is such a mess,' she said out loud.

Pat slipped her hand into her mother's. 'I haven't made a mess, I've been very tidy,' she said, 'and look, I've taken off my bridesmaid's dress, so it doesn't get spoilt.'

Ruby hugged her close. 'I wasn't talking about you, my darling. You've been such a good girl today. How about we go and visit Stephen at the shop? You need to take a look at George's baskets. We've not been near the shop for a few weeks now.'

Pat considered the suggestion. 'You do know that

George gave me the baskets, don't you? If any books have been sold, then the money is mine,' she beamed.

'Then we must certainly go to the bookshop, but first you need to put some clothes on,' Ruby laughed, causing her daughter to chuckle. 'It's rather too chilly to go out in your underclothes.'

With luck, it would be quiet in the bookshop and Ruby would be able to pour out her heart to Stephen while Pat kept herself busy sorting out the unsellable books. Even if it was raining, the baskets would be just inside the door and away from where Ruby could talk in private.

It was late afternoon as they set off through the town towards Pier Road. Already streetlamps were starting to be lit and there was a smell of smoke coming from the chimneys of the houses. Ruby usually liked this time of day, when thoughts were of heading home, closing the door on the world and settling down with family for the evening. Instead, her thoughts now were on her troubles and whether Stephen would be able to advise her.

There was only one customer when they entered the shop; Ruby recognized her as a regular. She helped parcel up the latest purchases while Stephen took the money. After passing the time of day and chatting about George's wedding, the lady bid her farewell.

'I can tell this is not a social visit. You know we are never busy at this time of day, so you've not come to help me out,' Stephen said, looking at her pale face. 'Here, sit down. I'll just turn the sign on the shop to closed, and you can tell me what's troubling you.'

She watched as he put the key in the lock of the door

and reversed the sign to show they were closed. Although she'd only known Stephen for a couple of years, she knew whatever she said would not be passed on. Stephen's family came from the West Country and, apart from Frank and a small group of their friends, Ruby was the closest family he had who knew of his relationship with Frank.

'Now,' he said, taking the other seat by the counter, 'tell me why the mother of the groom has such a glum face.'

Ruby shook her head despondently. 'I really don't know where to start. I assume Frank has explained to you about my Eddie and our situation since we moved to this area?'

'Yes, I do know much of what has happened. We've never gossiped about your life, but it has come up in general conversation. You are like a sister to Frank. He once told me that if he ever thought of marrying, he would marry someone just like you, rather than some fussy flibbertigibbet who only thought about herself and the latest fashions.'

'I'll take that as a compliment,' Ruby said, recognizing the words as exactly like something Frank would say. 'I miss him so much already.'

'As do I. He charged me with several duties that he wished me to carry out while he was gone; one of these was to take good care of you, and as I take my duties seriously, I insist that you tell me everything that's bothering you. I'll do my best to help.'

Ruby poured her heart out to Stephen, ending with Stella telling her that Eddie was dead.

Stephen exhaled slowly, scratching his head as he did so. 'That is certainly a big problem. Most importantly, I'm

279

sorry to hear about your husband. If it's true, I'm saddened for your loss and that I'll never meet him.'

Stephen's words had the effect of releasing the flood-gates, with Ruby sobbing until there were no tears left to shed. Stephen fussed around her, fetching a dry hand-kerchief and a cup of cold water to sip. She refused the brandy he placed in front of her.

'I'm sorry,' she gulped, trying to pull herself together. I had no one I could speak to about this and you are like a brother to me . . . I'll be fine now – I have to be,' she said, trying to straighten herself up and deciding to try a sip of the brandy. Grimacing, she handed it back. 'How can people drink this?' she spluttered. 'Please go on with what you were saying. I'll be all right now.'

Stephen nodded, and after Ruby urged him to continue, he started to speak slowly. 'Now, the way I see it, Stella is very fragile at the moment – I can't even imagine what she's going through, with one son dead, another at death's door and a third heading off into hell carrying only a stretcher. As much as you want to talk to her, I feel it's best you keep away. By all means let Pat go over there, but make sure the child knows that Stella is poorly and to keep the visit short. She's a bright kid – she will under-stand. It does worry me that Derek could pass away without seeing a friendly face. He is in a hospital in Sidcup, you say?'

'Yes, but I have no idea where it is. All Wilf told me was Queen's Hospital in Sidcup.'

Stephen rose and pulled out a large book from one of the shelves. 'There are some maps in here. You do know Sidcup's not far away, don't you?'

Ruby shook her head. 'It could be Timbuctoo for all I know. I have no idea.'

He flicked through the pages. 'Ah, here we are,' he said, beckoning her over. 'Here we are in Erith, and over here is Sidcup.' He pointed with a pencil. 'It would be possible to travel over there to visit the patient and return in one day.'

'It doesn't look that far away when you look at it like that. But how would I get there?'

'Now there lies the problem. If you leave it with me, I'll ask around and find out more for you. Would that help?'

'That would be wonderful. If I can visit Derek, it might give him a boost to know that someone cares. I could also go back to Stella and tell her how her son is – that is, if I'm not too late . . . And Derek may have news of my Eddie, and that would be a bonus. I can but hope,' she said, as Stephen smiled at her outpouring of thoughts.

'There is something else I want to speak to you about,' Stephen said. 'I feel you have too much time on your hands now that you don't put in so many hours at the shop. We aren't very busy these days, so it's not as if I can ask you to come more often. But you do need to fill your time, Ruby, otherwise you will grieve for Eddie and it won't be good for you, especially when we don't know for sure if he has perished on the battlefield. Had you thought any more about war work? I know if it wasn't for my own health problem, I'd have joined up in a shot, although I'd have elected, like Frank, not to be combative.'

'I've thought so much about it, but I'm none the wiser. Seeing so many women take on men's jobs, I feel I should play my part. But what can I do? Do you know of anything?'

'It just so happens that a customer mentioned his sister is working in a munitions factory. It seems she enjoys the work and has made many friends, even though she's never done manual work before. He is due to come into the shop next week to collect a book I've sourced for him. I could ask him if his sister would meet you and tell you more about the job. What do you think?'

'I've read about the munitions workers in the newspaper – they seem to be a brave group of women, and I'd like to give it a go. Once I know more about it, that is. Thank you, Stephen. It sounds interesting.'

'Why don't I call round to see you in a couple of days? By then I should have found out details of how we can get you to Sidcup, and hopefully I'll have news from my customer.'

Ruby quickly agreed, feeling much calmer. She kissed his cheek, collected her daughter and left for home.

Stephen watched Ruby and Pat as they walked down the street. Had he done right – not only by helping her work out how to see Derek, but by advising she work in such a dangerous place?

He reached to the inside pocket of his jacket and pulled out a folded sheet of paper. Inscribed upon it was a short list of wishes. Looking past his instructions of what to do if Frank should not return from the front, he looked at the short note that concerned Ruby. Stephen already knew that the shop should go to him, but there was a note added that said a certain percentage, if the shop was ever sold, was to go to Ruby, with Frank's love. He was also expected to keep the basket of books and continue to call it 'George's baskets', with any proceeds being passed to young Pat. What seemed to concern Frank most was Ruby's well-being, and that was why Frank had sat down with Stephen and explained to him about his friend's life since she came to Erith. He wanted Stephen to always look out for Ruby, to keep her occupied in the likelihood that her life should take a downward turn. He particularly wanted Stephen to find her some useful work that would keep her mind active and help her to feel as though she was contributing to society.

Stephen picked up a pencil and went to place a tick next to the words, but then he held back. The job was not yet completed. Instead he replaced the list in his pocket, picked up his sheet of notepaper and quickly wrote a letter to the customer whose sister might be able to advise and help Ruby take the next step in her life. Once he had done that, he folded it and placed it into an envelope. Taking a postage stamp from the desk drawer, he checked the time on the clock that hung on the bookshop wall. He knew he had five minutes before the last post went, so he pulled the shop door to and ran across the road, posted his letter and returned to the shop. There was half an hour left before he needed to close up for the day; time enough to work out directions for Ruby to make her way to the Queen's Hospital. With luck, what she found there would give her some kind of closure.

Ruby smiled shyly as she walked into the tearooms. She was more a cafe type of person than one for eating dainty sandwiches and sipping tea in quaint teashops.

'Over here, love,' a woman called. 'That's if your name is Ruby?'

'It is,' Ruby smiled as she joined the women. 'Which one of you is Cissie?'

'That's me,' a rosy-cheeked, friendly-looking girl said as she pulled out a seat next to her. 'Park yourself down there. The tea's still hot,' she added, passing the pot to Ruby. 'We don't come here often, but it's Doreen's birthday treat, and seeing as it's Saturday we thought we'd celebrate in style, so to speak.'

'Happy birthday!' Ruby smiled as she poured milk into her cup. 'It's awfully good of you all to let me interrupt your celebrations like this.'

'We don't mind,' the other girl at the table said. 'I'm Jean, by the way. Do you come from around here?'

Ruby nodded. 'Yes, I live in Alexandra Road.'

'Blimey, just down from us,' Jean said. 'Doreen and me live in Manor Road. Not in the same house, though,' she laughed. 'I have a husband in the army, and Doreen here lives with her mum and dad.'

'Cissie lives in one of the big houses up South Road,' Doreen pointed out. 'She's a bit posher than us.' She hooted with laughter.

'Don't take no notice of them. Here, have a bun,' Cissie said, sliding a plate across the table.

Ruby accepted gratefully. 'Thanks. I was that busy, I've not had anything to eat since breakfast time. I've been helping my daughter-in-law move in to the house next door to me, and I forgot the time.'

In truth she'd been too nervous to eat anything. Meeting three strangers to chat about the W. V. Gilbert munitions factory that would hopefully help the war effort had put her nerves on edge. Was she biting off more than she could chew?

'Blimey, you don't look old enough to have a grown-up family,' Jean said. 'I've got two lads in the army,' she added proudly.

'My son, George, has just joined up. He got married before he left for the front. I also have a little girl who is coming up for seven. What about you two?'

'Just one girl. I lost my husband last year at Ypres,' Doreen said.

'Oh, I'm so sorry,' Ruby said. 'I believe my husband died recently, too.' It was an awkward situation to explain, but she felt that since she could be working closely with these women, she ought to be open about her life.

Cissie wrinkled her nose as she absorbed Ruby's words. 'You believe?'

'It's complicated,' was all Ruby could think to say. 'I hope he's safe, but until I find out I can't really say, as I have no idea.'

'Then you could be told wrong,' Jean said. 'There was a girl working in the next hut to us who received a telegram saying her husband was brown bread. Ten months later she had the fright of her life when he walked in the front door, large as life.'

'Gosh – what did she say? Was she shocked?'

'I think he was more shocked, as she'd moved in another chap and was up the duff,' Jean hooted.

Ruby joined in the laughter. These women seemed such fun. She did hope she could work with them. 'What about you, Cissie? Do you have children?'

Doreen nudged Ruby's arm. 'She's saving herself for the right man,' she grinned.

'Far too busy dreaming about her handsome army officer,' Jean added.

'Shut up, the pair of you!' Cissie blushed. 'We've only passed the time of day, that's all.'

'What work have you been doing up to now?' Jean asked Ruby.

'I've mainly been working in my friend's bookshop in Pier Road, but business isn't as brisk as it used to be, so I've cut my hours right back. I could have looked for similar work, but I feel as though I should be doing something towards helping the war end. Doing my bit, if you know what I mean?'

Cissie nodded her head enthusiastically. 'That's exactly how I felt. I've been down there two years now and I really enjoy the job.'

'You can tell by the colour of the face,' Doreen hooted. 'Me and Jean are just doing it for the money; the pay is good and we get well fed. The hours aren't too bad, either.'

As Doreen spoke, Ruby looked more closely at the three girls' faces. 'Crikey,' she said without thinking, 'now that you mention it, your skin is quite yellow. Is that why they call you canaries?'

'She's a fast one,' Doreen nudged Jean. 'Just take a look at her hair,' she added, lifting up Jean's smart hat and showing a bright ginger band of hair at the front of her head.

Cissie tutted. 'If you covered your hair like you were told, it wouldn't turn that awful colour.'

'I think it looks quite nice,' Ruby said, not wishing to be rude. 'Tell me, do they supply overalls?'

'They do, and we are covered almost from head to toe to protect us from the explosives,' Cissie tried to explain as the other two girls chatted over her.

'It's to save us from being killed by the poison. I take it you don't expect to have any more babies?' Doreen asked with a glint in her eye.

'Well, I hope not,' Ruby said. 'I'm getting a bit long in the tooth for that kind of thing. Why do you ask?'

'They say that we swallow some of the explosives as we work, and it messes up our insides,' explained Doreen, who seemed to relish telling such tales.

'The bosses give us milk to drink. It's supposed to help,' Cissie said, seeing the alarm in Ruby's face.

Jean patted Ruby's arm. 'Don't worry about it. They also say if we didn't chat so much while we worked and kept our mouths shut, it would be safer. I hope we're not putting you off?' she said with a grin.

'Oh no, I really want to do the job if I can. I just thought if I could talk to somebody who works at the munitions factory, I could get an idea of whether I'd be any good doing the work. And then I'd be more prepared and could decide if it was for me or not.'

Cissie went on to explain more about their daily job and what to expect. 'There is a special train that goes from Dartford station down to the works, which are by the banks of the Thames. Out on the marshes, past Slades Green.'

Ruby frowned. 'You mean I've got to catch a train to Dartford as well as the special train, when I could almost walk down to the riverbank from where I live?'

The girls chuckled. 'No, we either walk or cycle. Going

home, we can hitch a lift with one of the army lorries, although the drivers are getting crafty and will expect us to slip them tuppence. They don't earn as much as us, the poor lads,' Doreen explained.

'May I ask what the money is like? I hadn't given a thought about the wages.'

'We get thirty shillings a week,' Cissie said, 'and five bob extra for working with dangerous materials. It's much better than what the girls who work up at the Arsenal get.'

Jean interrupted. 'Don't forget we get another five bob if we fill sixty shells a day. Once you get the hang of the job, it's easy,' she said, looking at Ruby's shocked face. 'What we tend to do is help the new girls, and those who aren't as nifty with their fingers, so everyone benefits. We just don't let the bosses know, or there'd be hell to pay.'

'That seems very kind of you,' Ruby said. 'I take it everyone is in good spirits there?'

'It's a lovely place to work,' Cissie assured her. 'Why don't you apply? You can walk down with us. I'll show you the ropes and we'll make sure to ask for you to be in our shed. There are lots of girls work there from round here, even some up your road.'

Ruby nodded her head as she absorbed all the information. 'I want to join you. I only really thought of working to help the war effort, but if I can earn some money and enjoy myself at the same time, all the better. I'll go home and write a letter asking for an interview. There's time to do that and catch the last post. But first, let me treat you all to some fresh tea and cake.'

15

'If you follow that lane, Miss, you will see the hospital,' the carter said as Ruby climbed down from beside him. Delving into her purse, she tried to offer him a few coins for his trouble, but he pushed her hand away. 'Get off with you – I was coming this way, and it's an honour to help a young lady meet her beau. Have you been before?'

'No, I haven't, that's why I was so grateful you allowed me to travel with you. It has been quite a journey for me,' she said, although she thought she would never be able to sit down properly again. The board they sat on had bounced up and down as the horse and cart travelled over every rut in the road. As much as she would have liked to stretch all of her limbs to ease her aches and pains, she didn't like to in case he thought she was being ungrateful. 'It's not my beau, though. I'm coming to see our family friend – and I'm not quite sure what to expect,' she admitted.

'All I can say is, the people in this town have opened their hearts to the lads that were damaged in the war. You're bound to hear some lovely stories about the fund-raising. Why, there's even a little teashop for them – well, that's for the ones who want to walk to the high street. I do hope your friend is on the mend soon. There is no better place in the country than Queen's Hospital. I've heard that Mr Gillies can perform magic on damaged faces. Now, I'm going to be back here in two hours' time, and I'll wait a while – that's if you want a lift back?'

Ruby thanked him. 'That would be marvellous, thank you so much. I'll make sure I'm here dead on three o'clock.'

'Don't worry if you're a bit late. I always have a break, a bit of bread and cheese on the way back. Take your time, love, and don't forget to prepare yourself for what you're going to see. Just remember that under all those bandages and scars there is someone's son or husband looking back at you – so you just keep a smile on that pretty face of yours.'

'I certainly will. Thank you again,' she said, as he made a clicking noise between his teeth and the two horses began to move away.

Ruby had been pleasantly surprised when Stephen came knocking on her door two days after she'd had tea with the girls from the munitions works.

'Can you possibly be ready to visit the Queen's Hospital tomorrow?' he had asked, looking quite excited. 'I bumped into a carter I know who makes the journey to Sidcup once a week. I explained the circumstances and he was more than pleased to take you with him on his next delivery. It may be a bit of a rough journey but it would save you so much time, especially as you don't know the way.'

'Why, that's marvellous. I can't thank you enough. Come along in – I've been baking and can offer you a slice of cake with a cuppa.'

'Have you ever heard me say no?' he said as he followed her inside. 'It's fair nippy out there. I wouldn't be surprised if we get a bit of snow before too long. You'd best wrap yourself up warm tomorrow. Wear your warm coat and your woolliest stockings,' he grinned. 'Is young Pat home from school yet?'

'She shouldn't be too long. Do you know she doesn't like me picking her up any more? She comes home with the other girls. She's quite grown up and independent these days, and she's got a tongue on her that reminds me of my mother.' Ruby smiled fondly, gazing at a picture of her mum, who was grimly looking down on them from a small frame hanging on the wall.

Stephen laughed. 'Sometimes the apple doesn't fall far from the tree. I've often thought your Pat was an old soul in a young body.'

'God forbid,' Ruby said as she fetched the tea tray from the kitchen. 'The kettle won't take long to boil. Sit yourself down – or would you rather sit in the front room? I've not lit the fire in there, but it won't take long to catch.'

'Don't stand on ceremony for me,' he said as he settled down at the table and reached into his pocket. 'Before I forget, there are a few shillings here for Pat. Someone cleared me out of books from George's baskets. I need to restock before too long. I think it was one of those teachers from the school. It's good to know they were made good use of.'

'Oh, that will please her; she's on about saving up to

buy a calf. Have you ever heard anything so bonkers? She reckons she's going to marry a farmer when she's old enough, so she may as well start collecting animals now. Goodness knows where she thinks she's going to stick this calf when it grows up. I just hope she gets bored with the idea and decides to spend her money on a puppy instead.'

'She's a one,' he chuckled. 'Have you heard from George?'

A fleeting shadow passed over Ruby's face. 'Not yet. He could only have got there in the last few days – wherever "there" is. Irene came in to tell me she'd received a postcard, and to say there'd be a letter on its way very soon. I do hope he's all right. We're hearing such things at the moment.'

'He's a bright lad and will do his best to keep out of trouble. He can run fast as well,' Stephen grinned, trying to keep her spirits up. 'I do have a letter from Frank,' he added, pulling an envelope from his pocket. 'Here, read it.'

'I don't want to read your private correspondence,' she scolded him. 'There might be private things in there.'

'As if I'd show you if there was. Here – take a look,' he said, holding out the single sheet of paper.

Ruby scanned the familiar handwriting. 'Oh, he's made some friends, that's good. I worry about him so much. I really don't think Frank's cut out for war.' She folded the letter and handed it back.

'Me neither; you know I have dreams about him getting caught by the enemy and tortured for secrets.'

'You've been reading too many adventure books,' Ruby smiled. 'That's the kettle boiling. Let me go and fill up the pot.'

'Have you heard anything back from the munitions works yet?' he called out.

'I have!' she called back from the kitchen. 'I can't believe they got back to me so quickly. I'm to go there the day after tomorrow and meet a manager who will interview me to see if I'm suitable. I'm more than a little bit nervous. So, what with having to go to Sidcup tomorrow, which should be another nervous day for me, I'm beginning to think I might never eat again. I'm not sure I can keep anything down, such are the butterflies in my stomach.'

'So you don't want me to cut a slice of this delicious-looking cake for you?'

'Perhaps just a small slice,' she chuckled as she walked back in the room. 'I did wonder about taking some over to Stella and Wilf and telling them where I'm going. What do you think?'

Stephen looked serious as he gave her question some thought. 'To be honest, I don't feel you should. It's not as if you've made any headway with them since the day of the wedding, have you?'

'No, I haven't, although I've tried several times. I spotted them as I walked home from the shops the other day and waved. They both looked the other way. I do miss their friendship, but I can understand how they feel; I'd hate to be in Stella's shoes at the moment. But if I can talk to Derek, who knows? He may write to his mother, and that would persuade her. Even though he's injured badly, there might be a way to persuade her to go and see him?'

'Don't count your chickens, Ruby. You know they said that Derek is badly injured. I just hope he's still there for you to see. Don't go making up any happy-ever-after stories, will you? Just go and see what you can do. The carter said he'd be outside the bookshop just after seven in the morning; I'll parcel up some books for you to take. If Derek's not interested, they may be of interest to the other lads there.'

'That's very good of you, Stephen. I'll make sure to pop in after and let you know how he is. If he is indeed still alive,' Ruby said, hoping that would be the case.

If Ruby had expected to see a hospital full of sickly men, she was in for a surprise. The beautiful grounds were full of men she would have described as 'walking wounded'. Some had nurses assisting them, some were in bath chairs, but generally there was an air of, if not happiness, then contentment. In the main she saw heavily bandaged soldiers, and some who must have been in the hospital longer as they were devoid of bandages but still had red raw scars that were a reminder of their suffering. Yes, some of the men were terribly disfigured, but no one seemed to stare at them, so she too did her best to keep a calm exterior and a smile on her face. She nodded to say good day to everyone she passed on the long walk to the building up ahead. Regardless of their injuries, some of them were quite cheeky, calling out compliments to her and being scolded by the nurses and helpers, but it was all good-natured.

Entering the building by the main entrance, she went up to the enquiry desk to explain who she was and why she was there. She hoped she'd be allowed to see Derek, even though she wasn't family. Knowing how strict most hospitals were, she feared she might have made the journey for nothing.

'Corporal Green hasn't seen any visitors so far. He's been rather down, I'm afraid, as his injuries are severe. We have written to his family, but there's been no reply.'

'His parents aren't very well at the moment, as not long before they heard about Derek, they were notified that they'd lost their younger son. His mother couldn't cope with the news of Derek as well. She's not been taking it well at all,' Ruby tried to explain, although she wasn't sure whether it was right for her to speak of Stella that way. 'I'm a good family friend and live straight across the road. My husband, Eddie Caselton, is . . . was a comrade of Derek's. There's been no word of my husband,' she added, fighting hard to keep her composure.

The kindly almoner left her alone for a few minutes while she went to find out whether Derek was ready for a visitor.

Ruby waited nervously. It was a hopeful sign that the lady almoner hadn't said Derek was too poorly to receive visitors – or indeed that he had passed away from his injuries. She chewed her lip. Somewhere close by she could hear music, possibly a gramophone record. It was a cheerful song, and male voices were joining in. How strange, she thought, I've never heard that in a hospital before – but then, I've really only visited the cottage hospital.

She sat down on a wooden bench, which reminded her of the journey over on the cart, so she stood up again and stretched, wincing as she did so. It would be a hard journey home, but worthwhile if she could get news of Derek and maybe even her Eddie.

The almoner returned and gave Ruby a gentle smile. 'Derek is sitting in the rose garden with his nurse. His doctor wishes you to know that he may not be his old self, as he is prone to bouts of depression and his language can be quite volatile. Would you like to wait and speak to the doctor first?'

'No, I'd rather go and see Derek. If there's a problem, I promise I'll leave him be. I really just need to see that he is well.'

The woman looked sad. 'I'm afraid that many of the young men here will never be well again. For some, it is hard to accept their injuries. We like to encourage them to lead normal lives in between the many operations they need to have. This is a pioneering hospital: we are trying everything to bring back some sense of normality to these brave young men for whom life will never be the same again.'

Ruby was beginning to understand how special this hospital was. 'I promise I'll do my best not to upset him. Could you point the way to the rose garden, please?'

Trying hard to remember the directions, she left by the front door and followed a footpath around the grounds until she spotted a rose arbour. At this time of year there weren't any roses blooming, but it was still a pretty garden. Up ahead, she could see a soldier sitting on a bench wearing an army greatcoat, his head swathed in white bandages. By his side sat a pretty nurse, holding his hand. Ruby approached slowly, wondering what to say now the time had come to talk to Derek. She was lost for words.

'Can I help you?' the nurse asked.

Ruby saw that she was no more than a girl – about the

same age as Irene. 'I was directed this way hoping to see Derek Green,' she said.

The soldier's head turned sideways towards her. 'Ruby – is that you?' he whispered, his voice frail. This was not the loud, boisterous lad she had known before the war.

Ruby sat on the bench at the other side of Derek. 'Yes . . . yes, it's me, Derek. I've come to see you.'

'I would've preferred you stayed away. You haven't brought my mother with you, have you?'

'No, I've come alone. I dearly wanted to know how you were; I didn't tell your mum I was coming. I hope you don't mind?'

Ruby could see the nurse was following her every word. 'I'm a neighbour,' she tried to explain, 'and his family are good friends. My husband, Eddie, joined up at the same time as Derek and their friend Ernie Minchin.'

Derek's head bowed as if it were weighed down with many problems. 'Please . . . please don't mention their names,' he cried out.

Derek's bandages covered most of his head apart from one eye, which stared out blankly. Ruby noticed that as she moved to sit down he'd followed her movement as she spoke, but the eye didn't focus. She looked to the nurse, who simply nodded as if to confirm her thoughts. Derek had lost his sight.

'I don't want Mum and Dad to see me like this. It's better they don't come; in fact, I don't think I want to see them again. So much has changed for me, it's best I don't return to Erith. I'd rather stay here, where I have friends who understand,' he said, reaching out for the nurse's hand and gripping it tightly. Ruby smiled. There was obviously more between the couple than just a nurse looking after her patient.

'May I ask what your injuries are? I promise not to tell your mum.'

'It was a bullet from the gun of a sniper. I was told I am lucky to be alive, but I'm not so sure. I've had many operations on my face; I'll never look the same again. Mr Gillies did his best for me, and for that I'm truly grateful, but the war has changed me; what I've seen, what I've heard.' There was bitterness in his voice. 'I can't think further than being here, but hopefully with Susannah by my side, I might just be able to face the future. Even though I'll never see it.'

Ruby reached out to take his hand, and it was then she noticed that beneath the bandages, he clearly had several fingers missing. 'My dear, dear friend,' she said. 'You'll always be the same person to me.'

The nurse, Susannah, had tears in her eyes at Ruby's kind words as they sat in silence for several minutes.

'Tell me how George is,' Derek asked, breaking the silence.

'Would you believe he's married,' Ruby chuckled, 'and he will be a father later in the year?'

The news had Derek laughing for the first time since she'd arrived. 'Why, he's still a boy. Have I been here in this hospital for so long that I've forgotten how many years have passed, and George Caselton has grown into a man?'

Ruby joined in with his laughter. 'No, my son is still a baby – he will be a baby to me even when he's an old man. He married only weeks ago and joined his regiment days later,' she said, fighting against the ache in her voice.

Derek reached across to take her hand. He grasped it tightly. 'When you write to him, please give him my best wishes; he's a good lad. I wish him well.'

'I do have an address for him,' Ruby said, 'If you'd like to write . . . ?'

'I can help with that,' Susannah said.

'I'd like that very much, thank you,' he said.

'Did you know that Frank has also joined the army? He is in the ambulance brigade; Stephen heard from him recently.'

'Stephen?'

Ruby could have kicked herself. 'His friend Stephen is running the bookshop now. I still help out a little bit, but I'm hoping to be doing some war work myself before too long.'

'So you've given up on the knitting?' he chuckled.

'Please, Derek, you know I'm not very good with my hands. I'm going to work at the munitions factory down the marshes.'

'Good grief,' Derek said. 'You can't knit a balaclava – how the hell are you going to stuff bombs without dropping them? You'll blow the town to kingdom come.'

Ruby and Susannah joined in with his laughter.

'You've been a real tonic for me, Ruby. Will you come again, if you can manage it once you start your job? I just ask that you don't bring my parents. I couldn't bear for them to see me like this.'

'Are you sure you don't want to see them? Just tell me if you change your mind. But I promise I'll come again in a few weeks, if I may. Can I ask you one thing, Derek? Do you have any news of my Eddie?'

Derek pulled away from her as if he'd been scalded by hot water. 'I'm sorry . . . I can't . . . I can't think of what happened . . .'

'Oh Derek, I'm sorry, I shouldn't have asked,' she said, seeing the sudden change. His body had become rigid and although bandaged, his face turned away from her as if he were lost in his thoughts.

'I think it is best if I leave you to rest now. Take care, my dear,' she said.

'I'll walk you to the front drive,' Susannah said. 'It's a bit of a maze round here and you may get lost. I'll be back shortly, Derek.' He didn't seem to hear her, and the two women walked slowly away.

'I hope it wasn't too much of a shock,' Susannah said to Ruby. 'He's a dear man, and he's been through a lot.'

'Will he leave the hospital soon?'

'No, that's not possible. He will have rehabilitation, and we will make sure that he has a good life. I care for him deeply, Mrs Caselton; if there should be any change, I will write to let you know.'

They stopped while the nurse took a small notebook from her pocket and Ruby wrote down her address, as well as one where they could write to George.

Then she placed her hand on the younger woman's arm. 'Please, call me Ruby – and do please keep in touch with me. I didn't like to say, but Derek's younger brother was killed recently. That's why his mother is not herself. The news of Derek on top of that was just too much for her.'

'I've seen it happen before,' Susannah said sympathetically. 'Now, can I get you a drink or something to eat before you start your journey home? We have a very nice cafe here for the visitors.'

'That would be nice,' Ruby said, 'but you must get back to Derek. I had hoped he would have news of my Eddie. I'm sorry that I asked.'

'I'm afraid Derek only has nightmares about his time in the trenches. Have you not received notification of your husband?'

'No, nothing at all. I've been told that sometimes it can take a while for news to come through. I'll hang on to the hope that he will come home to me one day.'

'That's all you can do for now – but don't forget to make enquiries. You never know . . .'

Ruby kissed the woman's cheek and thanked her for all she'd done for Derek.

Making her way to the cafe, she sat drinking her tea thoughtfully, feeling more herself and grateful that at least Derek had been saved. After handing the books over to the almoner, she took a slow walk back down the lane and sat on a low wall, waiting for the carter to appear. The day had turned even colder. As she pulled her collar up around her and crossed her arms across her body to try to keep warm, snowflakes started to fall.

She thought back to when she had first met the Green family: a contented husband and wife with three healthy and happy sons. Tears dripped onto her cheeks as she thought of the family torn apart by tragedy. When would this war be over?

3rd September 1918

'What are you up to tonight?' Cissie asked, linking arms with Ruby as they hurried along Manor Road. It had been a warm day, and both women felt exhausted after their hard day's work.

'I just want to kick my shoes off and have a rest,' Ruby said. 'I'd like to drag the tin bath in and have a soak as well, but I don't know if I've got the energy. Mind you, the first thing I'm going to do when I get indoors is put the kettle on to make myself a cup of tea and read Frank's letter. It came through the letter box just before I left this morning, and I didn't have time to open it before I had to leave. Pat wouldn't get out of her bed, and it made me late.'

'You should've brought it with you and read it while we was eating our lunch,' Cissie said.

'No, I like to sit and read things like that privately,' Ruby replied. As much as she enjoyed her new friend's company, she knew there were things she wanted to keep to herself.

'Are you sweet on him?' Cissie asked. 'I know you talk about him a lot, but you never mention your old man.'

Ruby gave a tired laugh. Each time she spoke of Frank, she felt as though she had to be careful what she said. What would people say if they knew the truth about him? 'It's not like that, Cissie. We are just very good friends.'

'Is this Frank married?'

'No. He used to be my lodger. Now he serves in the Ambulance Corps.'

Cissie cocked her head to one side. 'Did he sell up the bookshop?'

'No, his friend Stephen runs it now and still lives there above the shop.' Ruby could have bitten her tongue. She knew she'd said too much, the way Cissie gave her an old-fashioned look.

'Oh, it's like that, is it?' she said, raising her eyebrows. 'Fancy you mixing with the likes of them.'

Ruby stopped on the spot and turned on her friend. She's got to know Cissie quite well, even covering for her a few times when she was late for work; and once, when she had wanted to keep a secret about going out with her army officer friend, Ruby had pretended she'd gone to the picture house with her. She later found out that the officer, although very nice, was a married man. Since then, she'd always said she was busy if Cissie wanted her to cover for her. 'Now look here, Cissie,' she said, putting her hands on her hips, 'I don't know what you're getting at, but Frank is a nice bloke. He's been a good friend to me over the years, and a good friend to my children, and he wouldn't hurt a fly. I happened to know him because his mother lives over the road from me. So stick that in your pipe and smoke it,' she finished, starting to flounce ahead.

'Oh I didn't mean anything by it, Ruby. You know what I'm like, always making a joke about things.'

Ruby slowed down. She didn't have the energy to fall out with anyone. The day had dragged on so, and she had to remind herself she wouldn't have met her daily target when she first started at the munitions factory if the girls hadn't stepped in to help her. She'd just felt so sluggish as for the past few nights she'd sat with Irene in her house next door. The girl was missing George terribly and now, in the late stages of pregnancy, she did nothing but whine and cry. Ruby had suggested Irene might like to move back in with her mother until after the birth, but Irene refused point-blank, stating that her mother fussed too much and would pack her off to one of those maternity homes. She wanted to be in her and George's house when her baby came along, and she wanted Ruby to help her rather than her mother. Above all else, she wanted George home with her. As much as Ruby kept telling her she had to get up early for work and needed her sleep, Irene just didn't understand. It meant late nights for Ruby, so she wasn't quite herself when she did get down the munitions works for half past seven the next morning.

Tonight, although she felt guilty thinking about it, she knew she would creep in quietly in the hope Irene might not hear she was home. The day before, she'd gone in through the back gate to avoid being spotted. All she wanted was some time to herself – why, she had hardly sat and spoken to Pat for days now. At least the girl was able to go over and sit with her nanny Stella, as she still called her, until Ruby got home from work.

Stella had never really been the same since hearing of Donald's death. Wilf had tried to talk to her about Derek, but still she would scream and shout, stating that he was dead to her – she simply couldn't cope with the thought of her beautiful son being damaged. Occasionally Ruby tried her best to talk to Stella, but she was always ignored or sent packing. She did know that Frank would write to his mum; but, as he explained in his letters to Ruby, he kept it brief, as he just didn't know what to say to her any more.

Ruby decided to try again and take Frank's letter over to show Stella – after she'd read it herself, of course, in case there was any mention of Stephen. She prayed that one day Stella would be able to return to the person she'd known when Ruby first moved to Alexandra Road all those years ago. As friendly as she was with the girls from work, Ruby longed to be close to Stella once more.

'I'll say goodbye here,' Cissie said. 'I want to pop into the town. I'll knock for you tomorrow on the way to work?' She leant in and kissed Ruby's cheek.

'See you later,' Ruby called as she turned and walked up Alexandra Road and approached her gate.

'Ruby!' Wilf shouted from his open front door. He looked so upset that Ruby froze for a moment.

'What is it, Wilf?' she asked, hurrying over the road. 'What's wrong?'

'It's Stella. She's ever so poorly. She's burning up, and I don't know what to do.'

Wilf had continued to care for Stella since Donald's death, although things had changed to the point that he was no longer the proud man who worked on the Thames. It was as if he'd shrunk up inside, becoming older than his years.

Ruby hurried past him, pulling off her coat as she did so. The Greens' house was stiflingly hot.

'I lit a fire because she said she was cold – but look at her. I've never seen anyone sweat so much, and she is delirious.'

Ruby went over to the sofa where Stella lay. She looked

as though she was asleep, but as Ruby approached her she could see her eyes were fluttering and she was mumbling all the time. She seemed quite distressed.

'Can you get me a bowl of water and a cloth please, Wilf,' she said, kneeling down next to the sofa and loosening Stella's clothing, which was damp with perspiration. 'It's all right, Stella, I'm here. I'll help you. I can see you don't feel well.'

Stella stirred and focused on Ruby. 'Where is my Donald?' she muttered as she grabbed Ruby's hand. 'Get my Donald for me, please.'

Wilf returned with a bowl of water. As Ruby sponged Stella's face, she asked him how long she had been like this.

'A couple of days now. I thought she'd get better.'

'I wish I'd known. I'd not have sent Pat over to bother you.' Ruby couldn't help wondering if whatever was wrong with Stella could have been passed on to her daughter.

'She's been in bed the last couple of days, and Pat played down here quietly. You know she's no trouble, but today Stella decided she wanted to come downstairs. She took a turn for the worse, so I settled her on the sofa and had your Pat go over and sit with Irene. Do you think it's the Spanish flu?'

This had not occurred to Ruby. Dear God, she thought, please don't let it be the Spanish influenza. She'd heard of so many people in the town going down with it. There'd been quite a few deaths as well. The girls down the munitions reckoned the soldiers were bringing it back from the trenches, but Ruby thought it was all hearsay. All she knew was, it was a nasty illness and there'd been so much about it in the newspapers that she'd stopped reading them. If it wasn't the war, it was the flu. At work her colleagues spoke of nothing else, and then the shopkeepers would go on and on. Like so many people, she was worn down by four years of reading about the horrors of war and knowing so many people who'd lost loved ones. The war didn't seem to discriminate, as there were huge losses on all sides – and now the Spanish flu was doing the same. It was about time they all had some good news in their lives.

'I don't know, Wilf, but I think you should go and get the doctor. I'll make her as comfortable as I can while you're gone.'

'I thought only younger people got it, so perhaps it's not Spanish flu,' he said hopefully.

'Whatever it is, Stella is poorly. Please can you hurry and get the doctor?' she urged him.

Wilf did as he was told and Ruby set to work making Stella more comfortable. She hurried upstairs to the woman's bedroom and found a long cotton nightgown. Being careful, she cooled her down with the water Wilf had brought in and dried her before putting her in her nightwear, then plumped up the cushions around her head.

'There you are, that's much better, isn't it, Stella?' she said with a smile. 'Wilf will be back shortly with your doctor. You'll soon be as right as rain.' She thought she knew why her neighbour had taken so poorly. She was just skin and bone – there was hardly anything of her.

Thinking back, there had been an occasion recently when Ruby had seen her walking through the town and Stella hadn't even seemed to recognize Ruby. A group of soldiers had passed nearby, and she'd heard Stella call out: 'Donald, is that you?' before going into a cafe and sitting down.

Ruby, afraid of being rebuked again, had seen that there was another of their neighbours in there talking to Stella, so she had gone on her way; but what she had witnessed worried her. The light inside her friend had been gradually dimming, and Ruby felt she should do something. But what?

She sat on the floor close to Stella's head and chatted away, hoping that Stella would hear her and be comforted by her voice. She talked about Frank, mentioning that there had been a letter and that she would bring it over later to share his words. She spoke of George and how he hoped to be home soon before the birth of his baby. At the mention of the word 'baby', Stella opened her eyes and looked straight at Ruby. 'Your baby died,' she said, before drifting off into a restless sleep.

Although shocked, Ruby continued to talk, as she felt it was important for Stella to know that somebody was there. Would it hurt now to mention Derek, she thought? Taking a deep breath, she chatted about Stella's middle son and how she'd gone to see him several times at the hospital. She told Stella about Susannah, and how good she was for her son. She told her that he had regained the sight in one eye, although his face was badly scarred. She added that the last time she'd gone to visit, Susannah had shown her an engagement ring. Derek planned that when he left the hospital for good, they would rent a little cottage where he would tend his garden and work with a fellow injured soldier, starting their own carpentry business. Susannah was good for him, she kept telling Stella.

'I think when you're better, you should go and see him. You'd be so proud of your son,' she pleaded. Running out of words at last, she fell silent.

After a moment, Stella's eyes slowly opened. She looked at Ruby directly, seeming to see her clearly for the first time since she had arrived. Ruby waited anxiously; Stella looked as if she might be about to speak.

'I'm sorry,' Stella whispered finally, and with one struggling breath, she passed away.

Ruby softly cried for the friend that she'd loved; she cried for Wilf, who would be lost without his wife; and she cried for Frank and Derek.

'It's all over now,' she said, as she closed Stella's eyes and kissed her forehead.

Only minutes later, Wilf rushed into the house, the doctor following at his heels. He took one look at his wife's peaceful face and fell to his knees, imploring her to wake up.

The doctor checked Stella before turning to Wilf, helping him into a chair. 'I'm sorry, Mr Green – you were right. Your wife must have contracted the Spanish influenza; at least she's at peace now. Would you like me to get word to Mr Hind, the undertaker?'

Wilf nodded. 'Please . . . if you could tell them I want only the best for her,' he said before going to his wife's side, lifting her in his arms and hugging her close as he sobbed.

The doctor asked Ruby if she would be all right. Ruby nodded her head.

'I'll stay here with Wilf for a while,' she promised as she saw the doctor out.

For an hour, she sat with Wilf. She tried to give him a drink, and offered to make him something to eat. But Wilf refused, all the time still holding on to his wife's body.

After a time, the undertaker arrived. While he was still encouraging Wilf to let them take Stella away, there was a tap at the door. Ruby opened it to see two older men, who introduced themselves as Wilf's brothers.

'The doctor got in touch with us, as we work near the surgery,' the elder one explained as she let them in. They both looked distressed at the sight of their brother. 'We will take care of him now, my dear – you don't need to witness this.'

Ruby told them where she lived, then left the house. Walking slowly across the road, deep in thought, she saw the door of number fifteen open and Pat come rushing out, her face ghostly pale.

'Mum, come quick! Irene's very poorly. She said to tell you the baby is coming. Where have you been? I've been waiting for you for ages!'

16

Could this day get any worse? Ruby thought. Hopefully Irene was worrying over nothing. They'd had more than one false alarm before, with the girl thinking she was about to give birth.

'Where is she?' she asked Pat, following her into Irene's house.

'She's in the front room,' Pat replied, looking tearful. 'I don't want to go back in there . . . Can . . . can I go home?'

'Yes, of course you can, lovey,' Ruby said, giving her a quick kiss on the forehead. 'But can you do something for me? It's very urgent.'

'Of course I can, Mummy.'

'Would you go into the front room and pull the curtains closed, then go upstairs to my bedroom and do the same? I'll explain to you later why I want this done. Then I want you to stay indoors,' Ruby asked, knowing that she ought to do something to pay her respects to Stella.

'Can I go over to Stella and tell her that the baby might be on its way?'

'No,' Ruby said sharply. 'It's best you don't. I'll explain shortly, but I'd prefer you stay here for now.'

'Is Stella still poorly?'

'Yes, my love, she is,' Ruby said, doing her utmost to smile and act naturally for the sake of her daughter.

Irene cried out for help. 'I'm here!' Ruby called back. Kissing Pat one more time, she ushered her into number thirteen and closed the door behind her.

'I'm here, there's no need to worry now,' she said, taking a deep breath as she stepped into the room. 'Oh my goodness, you have been busy,' she grinned.

'I've made a mess of my tablecloth,' Irene smiled from where she lay on the floor. 'I had Pat grab it for me and then sent her outside.'

'Now, why didn't you get her to call somebody?' Ruby asked as she bent down next to the girl and looked at the small baby swaddled in the tablecloth.

'Meet your first granddaughter,' Irene smiled weakly.

'It's a girl? How splendid,' Ruby said as the baby started to cry, and Ruby felt close to tears. 'She's got a good pair of lungs on her, I'll give her that. If only George and your parents had been here,' she added, looking sad.

'It would've been rather crowded, don't you think?' Irene grinned. 'And I'm not sure this kind of thing is my mother's cup of tea. Speaking of which, I'm parched and rather stiff down here. I feel as though I've been lying on the floor for an age, when it's probably less than an hour.'

Ruby stood up. 'Right, let's get organized. I'm going to pop up the road and fetch Mrs Leighton – she always does the bits and bobs for the ladies in the street when they're giving birth. She knows everything there is to know. Can you stay there another ten minutes, until I bring her back? Then I'll get that cup of tea for you. George will be delighted. He used to tell me when he was a little boy that one day, he'd have a daughter,' she said, looking down at the prettiest baby she'd ever seen. 'She's adorable – but then, I am a little biased.'

'Don't forget that we're going to call her Sarah,' Irene smiled. 'She looks like a Sarah, doesn't she?'

Ruby thought her heart would burst with joy as she gazed at the child before hurrying out the front door just as the undertaker was taking Stella away from number fourteen. As one soul leaves this life another arrives, she thought to herself.

Stella's funeral was a sombre affair with few attending. Ruby had expected to see many more people there; she'd always had the impression Stella was much loved. She supposed the war had done much to distance friends who had lost sons, and Stella had rather distanced herself from other locals; her grief had made her bitter towards anyone who had something to celebrate.

Ruby left the pretty graveyard that surrounded St Paulinus church. She was at least pleased her friend had been laid to rest in such a peaceful place. Apart from herself, Stephen, and Wilf's brothers, there had only been a few neighbours in attendance. Both she and Stephen had decided to walk back to Erith.

'Ruby!' a female voice called out, and she turned to glance back. 'Surely it couldn't be . . . ?' she whispered, looking at Stephen in surprise.

'What's wrong?' he asked.

'I thought I heard a voice I recognized call out to me.'

'Ruby!'

'I heard it that time,' Stephen said. 'Look, back there – by the front of the church. It's a woman waving to you.'

'Oh my goodness,' Ruby said. 'I wrote a letter – but I wasn't sure if they would come.'

'Who?' Stephen asked as he followed Ruby, who by now was almost running towards the person who'd called out her name.

'Susannah! Thank goodness you managed to get here,' she said as she hugged the younger, taller woman, who looked demure in a sombre black dress and hat.

'I – that is, we – wanted to come to pay our respects. For Derek, it was to say his goodbyes and to make his peace with his father. For me, it was to try to forge links with my new family. I'm so sorry that I never got to meet Derek's mother.'

'You'd not have known the woman we all loved and respected if you had seen her before she passed away. Stella had not been herself in recent years,' Ruby consoled her. She turned to Stephen, who had just caught up with her. 'I'd like you to meet Susannah. She is the fiancée of Derek Green, Frank's brother.'

As Stephen reached out to shake Susannah's right hand, she held up her left one to show a shiny new gold wedding band. 'I am Mrs Green now. I'd like you to meet my husband,' she said, turning to where Derek was leaning against a wall, partially hidden by a tree.

He stepped forward as Ruby squealed with delight and rushed over to give him a gentle hug. 'I won't break,' he said as he hugged her back and swung her round. 'How do you do?' he said to Stephen, as he set Ruby back on her feet and straightened himself up.

'I'm very pleased to meet you,' Stephen said, returning his handshake. 'I hear you've had a rough time of it? Thank goodness you were able to be cared for at the Queen's Hospital. I've read many great things about them.'

'For me they were a lifesaver. There are many men who were more badly injured than I was. I'll wear my scars for the rest of my life, and of course I have lost three fingers. My eyesight is affected, with partial sight in just the one eye – but I'll get by. I have no choice,' he said, giving a gentle laugh. 'My wife won't allow me to wallow in self-pity. Ruby witnessed my mood change when she first visited. I've never apologized. I'm sorry.'

'You have nothing to apologize for. I'm just relieved we didn't lose you,' Ruby said, marvelling at the change in him. 'Have you been to pay your respects?' she asked as she looked towards where two men had started to fill in Stella's grave. 'The mourners have left, so you won't meet anyone if you don't wish to. The path is a little uneven; will you take my arm, so I don't stumble?'

Derek roared with laughter. 'Ruby Caselton, I can see right through you, but I'll play along. Here take my arm,' he said, continuing to chuckle as they strolled through the churchyard to Stella's grave.

'This is a beautiful setting,' Susannah said as she looked out to the fields beyond the church, which sat on higher ground. 'What is that building?'

'I have no idea. I'm not a local,' Ruby said.

'That will be the manor house,' Derek informed them.

315

Ruby was amazed. 'Has your eyesight improved that much?' she gasped.

'I wish it had – but no, the truth is, I often came here with Mum and Dad. My grandparents are buried here. Dad told us boys about the history of the owner, Sir Cloudesley Shovell, and his exploits at sea over two hundred years ago. As a young lad, it caught my imagination. Part of me now wishes I'd followed Dad and worked on the river.'

'Have you seen your dad?' Ruby asked as they reached the grave.

'We arrived late, as I got us lost,' Susannah explained. 'I was concentrating on my driving and not the route. We slipped into the back of the church just as the service had started.'

'You drove a motor car?' Ruby asked in surprise. She didn't know a man who drove a vehicle, let alone a woman. Frank had toyed with the idea at one time, thinking that it might help his business, but he hadn't gone further than talking about the idea. 'Oh my,' she added, imagining trying to manoeuvre a motorcar, let alone steer it in the right direction.

'Susannah's father works in the industry and says his daughters should be able to do the same as his two sons. It is lucky that she can, as I'm not much good with this hand,' Derek said, holding up his arm. 'Then there's the matter of seeing where I'm heading. Not having decent eyesight could be a problem,' he grinned.

Ruby marvelled at the way Derek had bounced back from his injuries. Only the love of a good woman could have created the miracle now standing in front of her.

*

They stood in respectful silence around the grave, paying their last respects. The gravediggers walked away, giving the family time alone to grieve.

Derek looked up from his thoughts and prayers. 'She was a good mother, wasn't she?'

'I know she was a good friend to me,' Ruby said, trying to dismiss all the hateful things Stella had said or done in the last couple of years.

'I wish I'd got to know her, or even met her,' Susannah said, dabbing her eyes with a delicate lace handkerchief.

Stephen nodded as they spoke. 'I've only ever heard good things about Stella,' he said, trying to avoid Ruby's eyes as they both knew that wasn't quite the truth.

As they walked away after thanking the gravediggers, Ruby asked Susannah when they had to head for home. 'If you have time, would you like to come back to the house and I can give you some tea?' Ruby had baked a cake and made sandwiches, imagining that she might have some guests. Stephen was also going back to the house because he wanted to meet baby Sarah.

Susannah looked towards Derek. 'How do you feel about going back to Alexandra Road? I know I'd love to see the baby. Perhaps it would be good practice in holding a newborn?' She noticed the grin spreading across Ruby's face, and smiled in return. 'Yes, you are the first people I've mentioned it to. We've not even told my parents yet.'

Ruby kissed Susannah's cheek. 'I'm so pleased for you; why, it's like a new beginning!' Ruby could see that this must be the reason Derek was so upbeat and positive about the future.

'I think I'm ready to go back home,' he said. 'We need

317

our child to have roots and family – and how can we teach a child that, when I have let go of my own?'

'Does that mean you'll see Wilf? I'm sure he'll be thrilled with the news. He has so little left now,' Ruby said.

'I'm ready; that's if we get back in one piece, as I insist you travel with us, and Susannah's driving leaves a lot to be desired – being such a weak example of the female race.'

Susannah playfully slapped him on the arm. 'I'll have you know that in my time I've been a suffragette. I am one of these new women they talk about,' she grinned, and winked at Ruby. 'Don't take any notice of my husband. He can be insufferable at times.'

'Do we have any choice not to be?' Ruby laughed. 'I quite enjoy working for a living. If and when this war finishes, I shall continue with my own job.'

Stephen chuckled as he helped the ladies into the vehicle. 'I hope you do, Ruby: your yellow face so becomes you.' Ruby ignored his joke. She was used to it, and was proud of the yellow tinge her complexion had acquired. It showed everyone that she worked in munitions and was playing her part in the war effort.

She was impressed with Susannah's driving. She'd hardly ever been in a motor vehicle before, so it was a thrill not only to be transported at such speed, but to see a woman operating a vehicle with such prowess. The two women sat in the front of the vehicle and ignored the playful jibes from the men, who joked about hiring a man with a red flag to walk in front.

Back at number thirteen, Susannah helped Ruby lay

out the tea things while Stephen went next door to assist Irene in bringing the baby in to visit.

Pat, who had already run out of Irene's house when she saw the motor vehicle pull up, was sitting with Derek, updating him on what she'd done since he went to war. He took it in good spirits, asking the little girl questions and admiring her dolly and pram.

Ruby beckoned to Susannah to get a little closer to her so Derek could not hear them talking in the kitchen. 'Do you think I should go over the road and bring Wilf back here for tea?'

'That's an admirable idea. Why don't I come with you? If you introduce me to Wilf in his house, at least he won't be able to easily refuse the invitation.'

'Why, Mrs Green, you seem to be a very cunning woman,' Ruby joked.

'Living with Derek, I have become adept at cajoling and being cunning enough to bring the best out of my husband,' she smiled. 'He still has moments of depression. I fear it is something we will live with for the rest of his life, but in between these times he is the most loving husband. I thank my lucky stars that I was the nurse assigned to care for him. I'd heard of romances between nurses and soldiers when I first volunteered to work at the hospital, never dreaming that it would happen to me. I'm truly blessed.'

After settling her guests with their tea and giving Susannah enough time to fuss over baby Sarah, the two women made their excuses and crossed the road to see Wilf. When he opened the door to them, he greeted Ruby with a gentle smile and looked quizzically at the stranger.

'Please come in,' he said. 'You must excuse me; I've just undone my tie. I know Stella would have told me off, but it's quite warm, and I'm ready to sit down and have a rest. It's been such a tiring day. Are you going to introduce me to your friend?' he said, offering them a seat.

'Wilf, I think you ought to sit down for a moment. This may be rather a shock. My friend is married to someone you know.'

'Really?' Wilf said, with a little frown.

'Yes – please meet Mrs Susannah Green.'

Wilf looked puzzled. 'Green, you say? Are you married to one of my nephews?'

Susannah went over to Wilf and took his hand. 'My husband is Derek Green. I am your daughter-in-law.'

Wilf looked at her for a moment, absorbing the news. 'If only Stella could have been here to meet you,' he said. 'I wish now that I'd told her to forget the daft ideas in her head. Whatever injuries Derek had, he was still ours. I fear the loss of Donald changed her in so many ways.'

It was all Ruby could do not to burst out crying at Wilf's words. 'She wasn't herself at that time, we've got to remember that. For me, Stella will always be the person who saved my life and kept me sane after I lost my baby. I'll tell you all about it some time,' she said, in response to Susannah's puzzled glance. 'For now, I reckon Wilf should see his son, don't you?'

'I do. Why don't you come over to Ruby's house? She has laid on a lovely afternoon tea as a kind of wake. I've just met Irene and baby Sarah, as well as Stephen, who I believe is looking after your Frank's bookshop? We do have another surprise; but I want to be with Derek when we give you the news. Please do say you'll come?'

Wilf nodded in agreement and reached for his tie. 'Let me just make myself presentable,' he said.

'There is no need for that. We're not standing on ceremony in my house,' Ruby said. 'I like my guests to be comfortable.'

'You're a good woman, Ruby Caselton. I've got a lot to thank you for. I've been a foolish old man keeping away from everybody since I lost my darling wife. Why, my brothers even laid on tea for the mourners, but I couldn't face it. I came straight home. They may be family, but they're not my close family. I just wanted to be home here with my memories . . . but I'll gladly come over to your house, Ruby, because you are more family to me than some who share the same surname. Besides, I've got to make up for lost time. I have bridges to build with Derek.'

When Wilf walked into Ruby's house and saw his son, he did not flinch. Instead he grabbed the lad in a bear hug, which Derek reciprocated. Stephen gave up his chair so that the father could sit next to his son.

'How have you been, son?' Wilf asked as he looked at Derek's scarred face.

'I've been better, Dad, but then I've been worse as well. My eyesight is not so good any more, but I'm here and I'm alive. I heard about our Donald. I just pray that Frank gets through this war and comes home safe and sound.'

The look between the younger adults present showed that all of them understood the relationship shared by Frank and Stephen.

Wilf reached out and took Stephen's hand. 'As a friend

of our Frank's, you are part of our family,' he said, 'and we owe it to Stella to stick together.'

Ruby put her arm around the shoulders of Pat and Irene. It was a touching moment to see the Green family reunited.

Susannah cleared her throat. 'We have some more news, Wilf. Perhaps you'd like to tell him, Derek?'

'Dad, you're going to have your first grandchild arrive in the spring.'

'Let's hope the baby arrives into a world free of war,' Wilf said. 'That would truly be something to celebrate. However, I'll say now: never will a child be more loved than one that's welcomed into this family. We owe it to your mother.'

The afternoon was spent catching up on news of what had happened while the family members had been apart. Eventually Irene made her goodbyes to take her daughter home to be fed, while Ruby went to the kitchen to do the washing-up, refusing offers of help from her guests. She'd almost finished when she heard a chair scrape on the floor. Turning, she saw Derek making his way towards her and marvelled at how well he managed now his sight was limited. 'Do you need a hand, Derek?'

'No, I'm fine, thanks. I wanted to have a word with you, alone.'

'Then sit yourself down and I'll join you,' she said, folding the tea towel and leaving it on the wooden draining board before moving into the living room to join him. She'd never been so grateful as she was then to have a separate front room and living room, because at times there was a need for privacy. 'What was it you wanted to tell me?'

'It's about Eddie. I know it's been some time since I was injured, and I wondered if you'd heard anything about him?'

Ruby felt her heart flutter as she placed her hand to her breast. 'Not a word. I try not to think of him these days. From what I've read, there are many men who perished whose remains were never found. It must have been terrible over there, Derek; I can't begin to understand what you've been through.'

Derek nodded thoughtfully. 'Don't think for one moment that we were all in the trenches fighting all the time. There was other work to be done, and we were also able to come away from the front on leave occasionally. Most of that time I spent with your Eddie, as well as Ernie Minchin. How life has changed . . .' Derek stopped speaking to think. 'My last memory is of when I was injured by a bombshell. If Eddie was injured, I don't recall, as I was near to death. But during my pain and all the activity around me, I felt he was there, as someone was talking to me and trying to keep me conscious. I swear, when I look back, I feel it was Eddie – so he couldn't have been killed, could he?'

'But then where is he now?' Ruby asked. 'I would have thought that by now, if he had been killed – even if he'd been blown to smithereens – somebody in authority would have written to let me know. Therefore, my heart is telling me that somewhere my Eddie is alive. The problem is, I don't know who to ask for information.'

'That is something I might be able to help you with. I'll write some letters and see what comes of it.'

Ruby thanked him. 'It would be a great help if you

could, even if it's bad news. I'll have some closure, at least. In a way, I've already moved on with my life. So much has changed – but I do still love my husband. I need to know what happened to him.'

'Ruby, I hope you don't mind me asking . . .' Derek looked uncomfortable as he tried to find the right words. 'It's like this. Mum wrote to me often, and when she did, she told me things about you and what you were doing. She implied that you weren't faithful to Eddie.'

Ruby shook her head. 'I've never been unfaithful to my husband. I'm surprised Stella thought I had. I will say, in my defence, that she did act rather strangely towards me at times. You see, when Frank lived here as my lodger – when I was expecting Pat – he thought it best that we let the world see us as a couple. Frank was worried about my reputation, what with Eddie not being seen for some years, and then me expecting a child. Pat is Eddie's,' she added hastily. 'He came back for just the one night and . . .' She coloured up as she stumbled over her words.

'There's no need to explain to me,' Derek smiled.

'I want to. You seem to understand the friendship between Frank and Stephen. In a way, our deceit was convenient for me and for Frank. We both appeared to be respectable to anyone who watched us, which was important at the time. When Eddie returned before he headed off to the front, I explained everything to him, and as far as I knew our marriage was back on an even keel. We corresponded while he was away, and I thought all was well.'

Derek looked a little sheepish.

'Is there something you've not told me?' she asked, as warning bells started to ring.

'I showed Eddie some of the letters where Mum mentioned you . . .'

Ruby was shocked. 'Oh no! Why did you do that?'

'You've got to remember that we are – were – comrades. When men are thrown together like that, fighting and putting up with all sorts, we tend to bond. Eddie could be bloody irritating at times, brave but bolshie; and one day, when he kept saying how wonderful you were while I was tired and hungry, I pulled Mum's letters out of my pocket and threw them at him.'

'What did he say?'

'Nothing. Only minutes after that, I was injured and didn't see him again.'

Ruby put her head in her hands and sighed. Knowing how hot-headed Eddie could be, he could have done something really daft and, rather than write to ask her about Stella's letters, simply vanished. It was then that Stella's dying words came back to her . . .

'I'm sorry, Ruby.'

'That's what your mum said just before she died . . . She was sorry.'

'I'll do all I can to find him for you.'

Ruby hoped that Derek would be true to his word. She just wanted her husband back home with her, safe and sound. Or, if the worst was true, she wanted to able to mourn him properly.

17

11th November 1919

'Have you ever been to London before, Mum?' Pat asked. She hung on to Ruby's arm as they were jostled by the crowd. 'Everyone seems so sad.'

Ruby looked through the crowd and could just see the outline of Buckingham Palace. 'Yes, love, I came up to London when George was young. The late king had died, and we came to pay our respects. That day, we went to a place called Westminster in another part of London, and it took hours just to get to where the king's body lay in state. That was even more sad than today, but we wouldn't have missed it for the world.'

Ruby was thoughtful as she remembered the day. George would have been ten years of age. Stella had been alive, as had Donald, and all the men had been young, fit and happy without any thought of war hanging over their heads. She remembered Eddie had been missing that day, as he had so many others, and the sadness and fear that came to haunt her so often returned with a vengeance – but then she thought of their few stolen hours together later that night. 'God, Eddie, how I miss you,' she whispered to herself.

She looked around her at the men in uniform. So many still looked weary, but many wore their injuries with pride. There were as many men and women in uniform as there were in civilian clothes. Had it really only been a year since the guns stopped firing and Great Britain was declared the winner of the war?

She'd been at work that day, when word filtered through that the war was finally over. The women had laid down their tools, somewhat confused.

'I suppose that means we're out of work?' Cissie had said as the foreman came over.

'Keep working, girls, no one's told us to stop. If you want to take home a pay packet at the end of the week, it's best you do your quota. There'll be other wars that need bombs,' he'd said, smiling towards Ruby, who had been listening nearby.

And continue working they had. All Ruby knew was that she turned up at half past seven in the morning and stuffed explosives into bombs; where the bombs would end up being used, she wasn't sure, but it wasn't hers to question. So she donned overalls that covered her body, observed the rules of no hair clips or anything metallic that would cause a spark; and she worked hard, knowing the money she took home gave her and Pat a good life. She pondered at times how many men, or even women and children, had died because of her helping to make bombs. She mentioned it once to her friends and they laughed, so she kept it to herself. That is, until one day when she was taking a breather outside the house where they worked and a young foreman stopped to chat. She asked him the same question, and instead of shrugging it off, he told her there would always be a war somewhere.

'However, I've been informed that production is about to change. We are going to be extracting powder from the Verey Light cartridges, so at least you'll still have a job.'

'I've prayed for this day,' she said. 'I've been worried of late about making bombs, now I have a young grand-child.'

'Think of something happier,' he said. 'You're a good worker, Caselton; don't let your thoughts hold you back. I reckon if the war had continued, you'd have been made a supervisor on the lines. Perhaps one day you'd have been fighting me for my job,' he'd laughed before walking away.

Back at Buckingham Palace, being pushed about by the crowds, Ruby suggested to Pat that they move on a little. 'Don't forget, George said he would meet us,' she reminded her. 'Irene is leaving baby Sarah with her mother. He said to meet us by the gates of the Palace. I don't know what we were thinking of, coming here today to see the parade amidst these crowds. Why did we not realize there would be so many people? I doubt we will spot them,' she tutted.

'We will,' Pat said. 'We've just got to look for a hat covered in silk roses. I helped Irene stitch them onto her best black hat. It was George's idea, as he knew how Irene wanders off to look in shop windows and he was worried he'd lose her.'

'Why ever did he think of roses when everyone is talking of poppies?'

'She had them in a vase in her front room, so thought

they'd do. I do think poppies would have looked prettier,' Pat said, considering her mum's words. 'Why do people think so much of poppies?'

'They are seen as a symbol of the war, which is now called the War to End All Wars,' Ruby explained. 'The poppies grew on the battlefields after the guns stopped.' Thinking of this turned her mind once more to her friends and what the war had done to them.

Frank was back home, his face haunted by what he'd seen. He'd told her that there was a time when for weeks on end they had never removed their boots or even slept, as the guns pounded relentlessly while they tended to the injured and dying. He'd remained at the field hospital, where he had done every job imaginable. Ruby had wanted to know more about what that was like, but Frank refused to go into detail, saying that it would only haunt her dreams.

'A lady should never see what I have seen. If anything, it has reinforced my belief that war is terrible and no side ever really wins; so what is the point in fighting?' He would argue long into the night whenever the two friends got together.

Frank had given Ruby a copy of a poem and told her to read it often, and understand the words, and to make sure that Pat too understood the futility of war. The poem was 'In Flanders Fields' by John Alexander McRae, a poet who had served in the war. Ruby wasn't one for poetry, only ever having read nursery rhymes to the children when they were younger, but this poem resonated greatly with what she'd read, and the little she had been told of the war was brought home to her by its simple lines. She had copied the words out for Pat to keep and understand and not forget.

As she stood there now, just by the crowds, she murmured the words. *'In Flanders fields the poppies blow . . .'*

Was Eddie one of the fatalities of war? Did he have poppies marking the spot where he'd perished?

Derek had been as good as his word and written numerous letters to those in authority, but their replies had failed to explain what had happened to Eddie or where he might be. Ruby needed to know, so that she could move on with her life. It was as if she was in perpetual mourning. Several times, one of the younger foremen at work had invited Ruby to go to the picture house with him or even just take a walk, and she'd had to explain that until she knew what had happened to her husband she would have to refuse – even though, as she admitted to herself, she found him very handsome.

'Well, I'll be blowed,' Ruby said, as Pat started to jump up and down with excitement as she spotted Irene and her hat. 'I shall have to borrow that hat for next time we go shopping in Woolwich market and you wander off.'

'Mother, don't you dare,' Pat scolded before pushing through the crowd and leaping onto her big brother. 'We found you,' she exclaimed as she beckoned to Ruby to hurry up and join them.

'That is certainly a startling hat, Irene,' Ruby said, admiring Irene's handiwork.

'It's suited the purpose of standing out in the crowd, and at least you found me,' Irene said. 'You must help me remove the roses now, though. My mother would be rather upset to find I'd used them to adorn a hat, rather than letting them sit in the crystal vase she also purchased.'

Ruby looked at George. 'You seem rather miserable, my dear – is this upsetting you?'

'No, Mum. I feel, one year on from the end of the war, it is rather uplifting. The two minutes' silence will give me much to think about,' he answered.

All the same, Ruby thought, there was more on his mind than he was saying. She knew her son well.

'Mum has a picnic,' Pat exclaimed. 'When can we eat it?' she asked.

'After we've observed the two minutes' silence and watched the march past. We can walk to find somewhere to sit and eat our food. It looks like there's a pretty park over there.' She nodded to where they could see the top of trees.

'As long as everybody else doesn't have the same idea,' Irene pointed out. 'It is rather chilly to be eating a picnic.'

'Are the king and queen going to come out on the balcony?' Pat asked. 'I don't think I'll be able to see them.'

'Don't worry, squirt, I'll lift you up on my shoulders,' George told her. 'Perhaps you ought to remove your hat as well, my dear?' he said to his wife. 'I fear the people behind will not be able to see a thing.'

'I'm beginning to think it wasn't such a good idea after all,' Irene said.

Ruby linked arms with her daughter-in-law. 'Come on, let's see if we can find a better place to view the balcony. I don't know about you, but I can't believe a year has gone by since the war ended.'

'And our little Sarah is fourteen months old and such

a sweetheart. With the war over and a bright future ahead of us, I have such plans for my child's life.'

Ruby sniffed. She hoped Sarah would not grow up to become one of those snooty women who Irene and her mother mixed with. Although Irene was nice enough, she could turn on her poshness at the drop of a hat.

When the cannon in a nearby park fired to mark the start of the two minutes' silence, Ruby found that standing there, head bowed, was rather upsetting. It made her think of young Donald – such a waste of life – and of dear Stella, who would no doubt have been here today if not for the war dragging her down, and then the terrible Spanish flu. Her mind wandered to Derek and how he'd coped with his terrible injuries with the help of his devoted Susannah. They doted over their son, who had been named Donald in memory of the much-missed youngest Green brother. Wilf had become a permanent fixture at Derek's home, helping his son with his carpentry business and enjoying the happy family atmosphere. So much so that he'd recently announced he was signing over his tugboat to his brothers and selling his home in Alexandra Road. Ruby knew it was for the best, but even so she felt sad whenever she walked out of her front door and saw the board on the wall declaring the house was for sale.

As the cannon fired a second time to mark the end of the two minutes, Ruby's thoughts turned to Eddie. Her heart ached just thinking about him. Their last meeting before he went off to war was etched on her heart, and all she dreamt of was him returning to her. Had he perished, or was he still alive? If indeed he had died, then he deserved to have his name recorded as such. Then at least she could continue with her life, even if it was a hollow shell of what it had been when Eddie loved her. She knew she needed to move on now, and perhaps marry again – if any man would take her, with her yellow-tinted face from working at the Gilbert munition works.

George slipped his arm around her shoulder as Pat skipped ahead with Irene. 'A penny for them, Mum? You were miles away.'

'I was thinking about your dad. Do you know it's been five years since I last saw him? We corresponded while he was in the army, and then it just stopped. I really would like to know what happened to him, even if it was something bad.'

'What do you mean by bad?'

Ruby thought for a moment. 'I don't mean him being dead, because I now believe that if he really were dead, I'd have been informed. Derek wrote a few letters last year looking for information, and nothing came of it. It's as if Eddie has vanished off the face of the earth.'

George shook his head in disbelief. 'Honestly, Mum. I know he's my dad, but I could swing for him. He's led you a merry dance all these years, and you deserve better. I couldn't believe it when you told me about him and all that Cedric business.'

'We've got to find him first, before you can even think about fisticuffs.'

'I wonder. Is there anyone who knew him – anyone you could ask who might have heard from him since 1914? Perhaps once you've checked with everyone, you can go to the police and have him declared dead?'

'I still love him, George. Call me daft, but I do. You've

got a point there, though. I'll have to sit down and make a list. I'll ask the Green lads to help out as well. You never know; we might just come across something that'll lead us to him,' she smiled.

George grinned back, although personally he believed that his dad didn't want to be found. However, he loved his mum far too much to argue.

18

~

24th December 1921

Ruby couldn't have been more surprised if Father Christmas had jumped out in front of her and said 'boo'.

It was Christmas Eve 1921, and nearly the end of the working day. All the girls in the munitions factory were excitedly talking about heading into town to pick up the last of their shopping, then going home to their families to enjoy Christmas. Along with Jean and Doreen, Ruby was going to meet Cissie, who had given up working down at Gilbert's after having her baby son, Cyril. The girls liked to keep in touch, and all had little parcels wrapped up for the new baby.

Ruby had been summoned to the manager's office, and she feared it was to be given her cards. After all, she was one of the older women working in the sheds, and the company had recently taken on many younger women. There'd been a new influx of work the week before, and she knew there would be more coming after Christmas. The move over to breaking open Verey Light cartridges and extracting the powder within had been different to filling shells and cartridges, but it was still a job. After the war ended all shells were decommissioned, and this gave welcome work to the women who had been in munitions. There was plenty for everyone to do and Ruby was glad of that, because despite her searching high and low, she had found no trace of her husband in the last few years. Even though she now owned her home, she still needed to be able to support herself and Pat.

What pleased her most about the change in her work was that the yellow tint to her skin had gradually faded away. During the war, she and her friends had quite enjoyed people looking at them when they went out together – they were nicknamed the Canary Girls, and Ruby saw it as a mark of their contribution to the war effort. She was proud when people looked her way. All the time they worked with the explosive materials, their skin remained tinted yellow.

Oh well, if she was going to get the sack, she'd just have to think about doing something else for a living. Perhaps George could put a word in for her. It was easy enough to get to Crayford and the Vickers factory from her house.

Thinking of George, her heart ached to see him. Only weeks before, he and Irene had sold up and moved their family to Devon. Irene was full of it, and had found a beautiful house close to the sea. When at such a tender age George had been offered promotion to management, Irene had jumped at the chance of moving up in the world, but Ruby had wept when she heard the news. She doted on little Sarah now she was walking and starting to chatter; she completely melted her grandmother's heart. George had promised that they would come often to visit; after all, he needed to visit the Crayford works to be able to continue his job as a designer in the engineering section of the company. He'd said he would bring Sarah with him, although Irene had mentioned that she was sure she would be very busy creating a home and hoped that Ruby would visit them instead. Ruby was disappointed with Irene: the girl was becoming more like her mother every day. But she had always said she wouldn't interfere, and so she didn't. George seemed happy enough.

Tapping on the office door and entering when told to do so, she was surprised to see not only the manager but also the owner of the filling factory, as it was known.

'Sit down, Mrs Caselton,' the manager said, picking up a folder with her name on the front. 'I see you've been with us for quite a while now.' He tapped his fingers on the desk, looking at the paperwork before passing it to the owner.

Ruby waited for the owner of the factory to say something, but he simply looked at the couple of sheets of paper and nodded back to the manager. Ruby wasn't sure he ever spoke; in the times he'd come to inspect the factory she had only ever seen him walking round, deep in thought.

Here it comes, she thought, sacked on Christmas Eve because I'm older than the new workers. But I won't let them see me upset. I'll take it on the chin. She waited, looking steadily at the men.

'Mrs Caselton, you may have noticed that there have been some changes in the factory since you joined us.'

'Yes, sir,' was all she said.

'With the war being over, we no longer make munitions for the forces . . .'

Does he think I'm blind, she thought to herself? We've not made a bomb in a while now. Come on, get to the point . . .

'These days our work is breaking down the ammunition, sending the shells for scrap and the contents for other uses,' he rambled on.

Ruby could have screamed. She wished he'd carry on saying what he'd really got to say. Rumour was rife amongst the workers that the explosives went off to other factories. Old man Gilbert wouldn't stay poor, she thought to herself. 'Yes, sir,' she repeated.

'We'll have another intake of young staff after Christmas. It means setting up another section, and we need another foreman. I'd like to offer you the position, Mrs Caselton.'

Ruby was flabbergasted: a promotion, and more money! And there she was thinking she's got the sack. 'That's very generous of you, sir, thank you.'

'There will be a small increase to your pay packet because of the responsibilities involved. As you have much to learn, I intend to place another foreman with you until you've learnt the ropes. Do you know Herbie Wilcox?'

'Only in passing, sir. We've not spoken much,' she said. Herbie was a quiet man. She knew he was a widower and a few years younger than herself. He didn't mix with most of the staff – but then, why would he want to mix with a group of cackling females?

The manager passed a sheet of paper over the desk to Ruby. 'This will be your new contract,' he said, as she quickly read the words on the page and blinked at the amount of money she would be paid each week.

'Thank you, sir,' was all she could say as she signed at

the bottom of the contract, politely wished both men a merry Christmas, and left the office. As she walked across the yard to the shed where she was working, she smiled to herself. Life was certainly looking good. The girls would be pleased for her, although she was grateful she wouldn't be supervising her own mates; that would have been hard. After all, Doreen and Jean had started at Gilbert's long before she had. With a spring in her step, she walked across the yard to the shed, and as she opened the door she bumped into Herbie Wilcox.

'Hello, Ruby – I was hoping to catch you. I take it you've just come back from the manager's office?' he said politely. Herbie was of slimmer build than Eddie and had darker hair and green eyes. He was well spoken, and she liked his manners.

'Yes, I'm rather pleased to be given the opportunity. I will enjoy the work,' she smiled as he shook her hand.

'I look forward to working with you,' he said as he went on his way.

As she got back to her worktable, Doreen and Jean grinned at her. 'It's not what you think,' she said, smiling back at them. 'I've got a lot to tell you once we leave work.'

At Cissie's house, she told them about her promotion. 'I did think that one of you two would have been offered the job first, though,' she was quick to say.

'Blow me, I don't want to be in charge of a load of kids,' Doreen said. 'I'm thinking of giving up working at the factory. I'm going to work at the Co-op, it's closer to home. I'm fed up working in draughty old sheds. The excitement is gone now the war is over. Chances are they picked you because you're older than everybody else,' she added, making Ruby feel ancient.

'I'm not that old,' she laughed. 'Why, I'm only forty-one.'

'That's older than all of us,' Cissie laughed as she rocked her son in her arms.

Promising to treat her friends to tea in the New Year to celebrate her promotion, Ruby wished them all a merry Christmas and headed down from South Road back to the town, where she picked up a few extra bits and pieces for Christmas Day. She stopped by the bookshop to see Frank and Stephen. The shop looked beautiful, decorated with ivy and a few sprigs of holly; it felt warm and welcoming.

'Stop and have a cup of tea,' Stephen said. 'I'll just serve this customer, then I'll be with you. Frank wants a word with you – feel free to pop upstairs and see him.'

Ruby very rarely went upstairs to the men's private quarters, so as she climbed the steep staircase, she called out ahead of her to let Frank know she was coming.

'Coo-ee, Frank – Stephen told me you wanted me?' she said as she found herself in a cosy living room with large windows that overlooked Pier Road. 'You've got this looking awfully nice,' she said. 'Do I smell fresh paint?'

'Yes, we've decorated the whole flat now. You know how long I've been waiting to do this, ever since I moved in,' he laughed. 'I got sick of Stephen nagging. What do you think?'

'It's very attractive,' she said, looking at the old paintings on the walls and the leather settee and chairs set around a large fireplace. 'You've made it so cosy and welcoming.'

'Most of the bits and pieces I've picked up from house sales when we are buying books there. It looks expensive and only costs a few pounds.'

'I'll have to get you to look out for some of these bits for me,' she said, 'especially as I've been promoted now and got a bit more money to spend. I'm going to be a foreman in the New Year.'

Frank was pleased for her. 'You've worked hard down there, Ruby. You deserve the promotion – well done.'

'So what was it you wanted to see me about?' she asked.

Frank went to a side table and picked up a letter. 'I've heard from our Derek. Did you know there is another child on the way?'

'I did – Susannah wrote to me. I'm thrilled for them. Your dad seems to be settling in as well. The last time I visited, Wilf looked ten years younger. It must be all that fresh air and Susannah's cooking.'

Frank nodded in agreement. 'I'm pleased for Dad. I don't know what he would have been like living on his own at number fourteen into his old age. I know you'd have been over the road to help him, but you know what I mean.'

'I do, although it would have been nice to have his company now that George and Irene have moved away.'

'Don't be too sad,' Frank said. 'Your George is going to go far in the business world, but he will never forget his roots.'

'So was that what you wanted to talk to me about? Could you not have saved it until Christmas Day?'

'No, there's something else. I thought it best to tell you without Pat around your feet. She picks up on anything that's being discussed.'

Ruby chuckled in agreement as she sat down in one of the armchairs. 'Come on, then, tell me. What is it?'

'I don't want you getting excited, but Derek's found out something about Eddie. He wanted me to speak to you first, so that I could break it to you face to face.'

Ruby felt lightheaded and breathless as she gripped the arm of the chair. Taking a deep breath, she blurted out, 'Come on, I can take it, whether it's good or bad news.'

Frank sat down opposite her. 'He's not dead, Ruby. He is very much alive.'

Ruby felt anger wash over her suddenly. 'You mean all these years he's been alive, and he's never bothered getting in touch with me? I'm not sure I want to see him now,' she spat out, her happiness at her new job and Christmas forgotten.

'It's not like that,' Frank said. 'Eddie did sustain injuries at the same time that Derek was hurt, but for some reason, he was given the name of another soldier. I don't know the ins and outs of it,' he said, as Ruby opened her mouth to fire questions at him.

'But where has he been all this time?'

Frank looked her straight in the eye. 'Eddie's in prison.'

Ruby sat rigid-backed, a handbag resting on her knees. Never in a million years would she have thought she'd find herself sitting in the waiting room of a prison. When Frank had told her of Eddie's situation, she hadn't believed it. How could he be fighting in France one minute, and then back to England and in prison, without us knowing anything about it? she'd asked Frank.

'He's been locked up for over three years now, and has another three years to go.'

'Oh my goodness, whatever has he done? This sounds serious, even for Eddie. He's never had a squeaky-clean life, but to go to prison for six years? Why, and how come he never let me know he was there? It's so cruel of him. I want to see him, Frank. I need to get to the bottom of this.'

'I wish I hadn't told you,' Frank had said. 'He's going to spoil your Christmas.'

Ruby had sighed. 'Don't think I wouldn't know you had a secret. You've never been able to keep a secret, I'd see through you in minutes. Tell me all you know.'

It had taken Frank three weeks to obtain a visiting order for Ruby to see Eddie. He'd taken the day off from the bookshop and driven her to Wandsworth Prison himself. This was not something Ruby should have to face on her own. Granted he couldn't go inside with her, but he could wait in his motor car. He had a book with him, so he was comfortable for as long as it took, although his eyes kept straying to the high walls of the prison and the locked door.

When Ruby was called through to the room where she could meet Eddie, she gasped in shock. He seemed so downhearted, and had aged terribly.

'What have you done, Eddie?' she snapped. 'And what have you done to my family? I bet you don't even know you are a grandfather, and you wouldn't recognize our Pat if you walked past her in the street – you are like a stranger to us. I don't even know why I've come to see you.'

'I know everything about your life, Ruby. I know where you work, I know that George has moved away with his wife and child, and I know our Pat is thriving. The only thing I've not been able to do is hold you in my arms and kiss you,' he said, searching her face desperately for a sign of forgiveness.

Ruby was aware there was a prison warden standing in the corner of the room. He could hear everything that was said. 'Please don't,' she whispered. 'Don't talk about us like this. Why didn't you get in touch with me, Eddie? That's all I want to know. I thought you'd died when Derek was so badly injured. I was confused when no one could tell me anything about you. You could at least give me the answers to what I've been wondering all these years?'

Eddie continued to look at the face of the woman he'd loved for so long and couldn't bear to disappoint. He spotted a couple of silver hairs and minute lines around her eyes, but deep down, she was still the feisty young woman he'd married. 'I'm no good for you, Ruby. You're better off without me.'

'Just tell me what happened,' she pleaded.

'I was injured at the same time as Derek. I thought he'd died. To look at him lying there, his body twisted, his face covered in blood . . . I thought he was a goner. Ernie Minchin lay lifeless nearby; all my mates were wiped out in one blow. I was concussed, in a lot of pain, with injuries to my shoulder and leg. Like a coward, I got up and I ran. There was heavy gunfire and so much commotion. If I'd run in the other direction, I'd have been taken out by snipers. I ran blindly until I fell into a trench and lay there for a while, close to a couple of lads. They could see how bad I was. You've got no idea what it was like there, Ruby, with the persistent bombing, not much to eat. I was going out of my mind with fear.'

'But Eddie, so many men were in the same boat as you. They haven't ended up in prison. So what did you do to get here?'

'It was wet. It was cold. The two lads in the trench took my jacket off me, wrapped up my wound and gave me a cleaner trench coat that had belonged to one of their comrades. I worked my way blindly through the trenches before collapsing. When I came to, I was being carried back to a medical unit behind the lines. They quizzed me to find out who I was, but I was completely out of my mind. They searched my pockets and found the paperwork of a Corporal Daniel Gordon. After a few days, as my memory came back to me, I could see this was a way out. It could give me a fresh start – away from you, and your lies.'

Ruby was astonished. 'What are you talking about – lies? What has this got to do with me?' she asked. And then the penny dropped. 'It was those letters Stella sent to Derek, wasn't it?'

Eddie gave her a hard stare and shrugged his shoulders.

'If only you'd written to me to ask. Stella wasn't the woman you remember. After Donald was killed, and she found out Pat was your daughter and not Frank's, she turned very bitter towards me. It was only when I saw Derek and we gradually pieced together what happened that we realized, as awful as it sounds, Stella had been deliberately causing trouble between me and you. Do you know that when she heard Derek had been injured, around about the same time that Donald was killed, she turned on me and said Derek had let her know that you'd been killed? When I didn't receive notification from the army of your death, I hung on to the hope that it was a big mistake and you were alive, and that one day you'd find me and come back. Eddie – I never for one moment expected you to turn up in prison. And how do you know so much about my life? Has someone been watching me? Why didn't they make themselves known?'

'It was the daughter of the person I used to lodge with when I worked in the brickfields. She used to work down the munitions factory, and spotted you. She told her mum and dad. I'd corresponded with them for quite a while, wanting to know what was going on in the old town, and they promised not to let you know where I was.'

Ruby shook her head. 'What a bloody mess,' she said. 'I should turn my back on you and walk away once and for all.'

'But you won't, will you?' he pleaded, knowing that now he'd seen her he couldn't let her walk out of his life. 'Because you love me.'

Ruby trembled. Being this close to Eddie, she could feel the magnetism between them. 'You've pushed my love too far at times.'

Eddie said, 'You know me and my temper. When I'd been brought back to Blighty and discharged because of my injuries – they were nothing serious,' he added, noticing her startled look, 'I moved back over Erith way. I got a job down the brickyard during the summer, and even took up with my old lodgings for a while.'

'You mean you were less than a mile away, all the time I was worrying?'

'Like before, I couldn't keep away from you, but I was too much of a coward to make my presence known.'

'So how the hell did you end up in here?' she asked, her head still full of questions.

'I got into a fight, and the other bloke almost died. It wasn't my fault – he had started laying into somebody I worked with.'

'But it's never your fault, is it, Eddie? There's always excuses. Well, I've had enough of it. I don't want to live wondering what's going to happen to you, and if there will be trouble again. I've got a lovely life now. I've got a job, I'm a grandmother, our Pat is a beautiful girl . . . I don't need you in my life, Eddie. You broke my heart far too often, and now it's me that's going to say goodbye. I'll always love you, Eddie, but I can't live this way any longer.' Ruby stood up and walked from the room as he called out to her.

If she'd looked back, she would have seen the tears in her husband's eyes and his arms reaching out to her beseechingly, and she would have changed her mind. Instead, she walked away from Eddie Caselton for the last time.

19

18th February 1924

'It's not fair, it's really not fair. George has one, and he talks about it all the time,' Pat pouted.

'Come on, Pat, you know that's not true. George mentioned his wireless set once in his letter, and when he last brought Sarah to visit I never heard the word mentioned once. It's probably a fancy of Irene's – you know what she's like when she gets something like that into her head. Why don't you use your gramophone player Frank and Stephen bought for you for Christmas? Not many girls of your age have one. You should be grateful.'

'If my dad lived here, he would buy me one,' Pat said, giving her mum a sharp look.

Ruby rolled her eyes; this was Pat's stock answer. Anytime she didn't get her own way, she mentioned Eddie. Not that the girl had ever met him.

'I'll be glad when you're old enough to start work. You'll be thirteen next week and it's time you acted your age. This time next year you'll be looking for employment.'

Pat thought for a moment. 'If I put more hours in at

the bookshop, do you think the new owner would pay me more money? That way I could save up for my own wireless.'

'Don't pester the poor man. He pays you more than the going rate for helping out when you aren't at school because Frank asked him to keep you on. Now come along, what are you doing? I'm going to be late for work if you stand about here pestering me. Are you walking down the road with me or not, and what are you going to do after school?'

'I might take a walk down the farm to see if they need a hand with anything.'

Ruby shook her head. Pat had been obsessed with farming ever since she'd saved up to buy a calf as a little girl. Thankfully, by the time she had enough money she'd changed her mind. 'Can you be back in time for your tea? I thought we might go down the picture house tonight. There's a film I'd like to see.'

Pat grinned. 'Can we go and see *The Monkey's Paw*? Daphne at school said it was great fun.'

'I'm not paying good money to be frightened out of my skin,' Ruby tutted. 'We're going to see *Bonnie Prince Charlie*. That handsome Ivor Novello is in it,' she said, giving an exaggerated sigh just to embarrass her daughter.

'Oh, Mum, why can't you act your age?'

Ruby chuckled. 'Are you coming or not? Only I don't want to be late. It doesn't set a good example to the workers.'

'I'm not ready. I'll see you tonight for tea. Please do think about *The Monkey's Paw* – you can always put your hands in front of your face at the really scary parts.'

Ruby looked at herself in the large mirror hanging over the mantelpiece. Her hat was straight and her hair tidy. 'Remember to close the door properly when you go out. Last time you left it open and next door's cat got in.'

Pat gave an exaggerated sigh. 'Oh, Mum, just go, or you'll be in trouble with your boss. He may be sweet on you, but he won't like you being late,' she smirked.

Ruby gave her daughter a quick kiss on the cheek, ignoring the comment about Herbie Wilcox, who was now her manager. 'God help any man who marries you,' she muttered before she headed off.

Pat hurried upstairs and looked out of the front bedroom window to watch her mother walk to the end of the road and turn right to head down Manor Road towards the marshes and the munitions factory. 'Good, she's gone. I thought she'd never go,' she muttered aloud.

Hurrying back downstairs, she opened the front door and rushed out to the gate. Waving to a figure standing at the top end of the road, she left the door ajar and went back inside to put the kettle on the hob.

'Anyone home?' a deep voice called.

'Come in, Daddy, you don't have to wait on the door-step,' she grinned as Eddie Caselton walked into number thirteen.

Ruby stepped out at a brisk pace. She hoped Herbie had waited for her. It had become the norm for him to wait in his motor car further down Manor Road so they could chat on the way to work. She'd promised to give him her answer today, and whatever she decided would cause ripples in her life and possibly alienate loved ones.

Up ahead, she spotted him leaning against the car, smoking a cigarette. She waved and walked faster as he stubbed it out, walking a few steps to meet her. 'I'm so sorry. I hope you haven't been waiting long?' she said as he pulled her close and kissed her cheek.

'It felt like a lifetime,' he smiled, opening the door for her.

Ruby enjoyed the attention of this handsome man. It had been so long since she'd received attention from the one man who meant something to her – Eddie. 'Pat was dragging her heels as usual,' she sighed as the car headed out of Erith towards Dartford. Although the marshes were close to Erith, there was not a road passable by car.

'I take it you've not told her about us yet?'

'Not in so many words, but she knows you take me to work in your car. She's no idiot, Herbie.'

'Then tell her I love you and want us to live together, and that you will seek a divorce from Eddie.'

'Give me more time,' she whispered. 'Aren't you happy the way things are?'

Herbie swore as a child stepped into the road, causing him to swerve. 'No, it's not enough for me. I've told my boys I have a lady friend, and they want to meet you. I know people are gossiping about us at work. I just want to make an honest woman of you, and for us to live together as man and wife. I'm not one for skulking about and snatching a few stolen hours here and there. I know we agreed you would make your decision by this evening when we meet – but surely you know by now?'

Ruby felt her stomach flip with anxiety. She'd forgotten about meeting Herbie later. Did this mean she didn't care for him? 'I'm sorry, but I'm taking Pat to the picture house this evening. She's been more than difficult lately, and I really need to keep her happy if I'm to drop a bombshell about us.'

Herbie shook his head in desperation. 'I do wonder sometimes if you really love me, or if I'm just a convenient person to have around?'

Ruby was taken aback by his outburst. 'I'm sorry you feel that way. I truly have affection for you . . .'

'But you still carry a torch for Eddie?' he interrupted.

She was annoyed at the interruption. 'I was about to say that I have enjoyed our courtship, but that we are not love's young dream. We both have children to consider – and I believe we both hold a torch for our past loves,' she added, knowing Herbie still had fond thoughts for his deceased wife.

He gave a sarcastic laugh. 'My dear, the difference is that you are carrying a torch for someone who is still alive.'

Ruby was thoughtful as they travelled in silence. Herbie had hit the nail on the head. She did still love Eddie, and in the years since she'd seen him, he'd never been far from her thoughts. However, she enjoyed Herbie's company. Even if their relationship didn't have the passion of her first love, she found the comfort and the companionship she had with him consoled her now that she'd lost Eddie.

They'd fallen into a pattern over several years of travelling together for work and the occasional trip, but she had no wish to introduce her daughter to a man friend if the romance did not work out. If Pat, who seemed old for her years, suspected anything, she'd never said. There was the occasional jibe about Herbie being her boyfriend, but it was more a childish joke then anything concrete. Pat knew only that Ruby's boss would drop her home after work on the odd occasion she worked late. That was, until two days ago, when Ruby had told Pat over their evening meal that Herbie was a little more than just her boss and wanted them to become a couple.

Pat had been outraged. 'But you are still married to my dad,' she threw back at Ruby. 'He has no right to want to go courting with you.'

'I'm only married in name, love. Me and your dad have not even spoken for over three years.' She didn't tell Pat that Eddie had written to say he was coming out of prison and wanted to see her. She'd torn up the letter and thrown it onto the fire. Even then, there were times in the months that followed when she'd wondered if she had done the right thing. A small part of her longed for the Eddie she knew.

Pat had said little more, although Ruby was aware the child was not happy. Ruby knew that Herbie was almost at the end of his tether and wanted an answer. For some unknown reason, she'd told him she would give him an answer by the eighteenth of February. It had seemed far enough away to give her time to think about the future, as she knew she couldn't string him along much longer.

Trying to imagine life without Herbie, she knew it would feel empty, what with so many of her friends having moved away. Doreen and Jean no longer worked at Gilbert's; Cissie had given birth to two more children in quick succession, and now that her life was full with her new husband and babies, she and Ruby no longer had much in common. This saddened Ruby, but she accepted it; with the passing of the war, so many people's lives had moved on.

Just before Christmas, Frank and Stephen had sat her down and explained with much kindness that they had decided to move to the coast. They'd insisted she must visit them often in their new home in Eastbourne, where they had purchased another bookshop. As Frank had said, they would have a fresh start, away from gossips and people who knew their business – and the sea would be within walking distance. He never spoke of what he'd seen while away at war, but now his face was lined and his hair prematurely grey. He and Stephen needed to feel as though they were set up and ready for their old age. Ruby was heartbroken, but couldn't tell them so; instead, she had joked that as she wasn't much younger than Frank, old age seemed a rather feeble excuse. It was then that Stephen had ex-plained he was ill, and the sea air had been prescribed by his doctor for the chest problems that had haunted him all his life.

In some ways, Ruby felt as though she'd been aban-doned; apart from Pat, everyone she knew had moved away from Erith. No wonder, then, that she clung to Herbie even though she wasn't necessarily ready to make a commitment. She was loath to lose his friendship.

As the motor car pulled into the grounds of the factory, Ruby took a deep breath. It was only fair to tell Herbie of her decision. As she opened her mouth to speak, a man came running from the office block, waving his arms for Herbie's attention.

'I wanted to say . . .' Ruby began.

'What's wrong, Dick?' Herbie asked as he rolled down the window, ignoring Ruby's words.

'Sorry, boss, we've got a problem with the clocking-in machine. I wanted to catch you before you went off on your inspection of the sheds.'

Herbie got out of the vehicle and, with a quick backward wave to Ruby, started to walk away.

'Herbie, I want to tell you . . .' Ruby faltered, not sure if she should continue talking to his back.

'I'll see you when I reach your shed,' he called back.

'I was going to say yes . . .' she all but whispered as she watched him walk away. Ruby turned and went to shed number six to start her work.

'So, how's my girl?' Eddie asked as he took a gulp of the hot tea she'd placed in front of him.

Pat beamed at her dad. This was the third time she'd seen him since he'd left prison. 'I'm worried. That's why I sent you the postcard,' she said, offering him a biscuit. 'I made these myself.'

Eddie shook his head and smiled. It surprised him how old Pat seemed. She was so like her mum, and at only twelve years of age she spoke like an adult. 'Your postcard said you're worried that your mum has a man friend?'

Pat leant her elbows on the table and cupped her chin

in her hands. 'If we don't stop this, I have a feeling she will marry him, and then you'll never be able to move back home and be a proper dad to me. We have to do something now,' she said in earnest. 'Don't you want to be a part of this family again?' she asked crossly as he laughed at her words.

'My love, I've tried to be a part of this family over so many years – but between me and your mum, we keep messing up. Since I've been out of prison and in a proper job, I've written and begged her to meet me. But she ignored my letters,' he said. He didn't mention that Ruby had replied just the once to say she still loved him and always would, but feared he would never change his ways and so would not read any more of his letters.

'She throws them onto the fire. That's how I found your address, when one hadn't burnt through properly.'

'I'm pleased you did. At least we can keep in touch. But you shouldn't be playing with fire.'

Pat rolled her eyes. 'I don't believe you understand how serious this is, Dad.'

But I do, Eddie thought to himself as he humoured his daughter. If what Pat said was true – and he had no doubt she was telling the truth – then he was about to lose Ruby forever. Since he'd last written to his wife, he'd secured a good job as a milkman and had moved into lodgings, the very same ones where he'd stayed before he'd joined up. All he needed was for Ruby to understand that he meant what he'd promised.

'I'll need to get back to work soon, love. I've parked the milk cart up at the top of the road and I don't want my horse breaking loose and talking off with the milk, as my customers won't be at all pleased,' he grinned. Seeing her glum face, he added, 'I do appreciate how worried you are, love, and I intend to do something about it very soon.' His thoughts turned to the money he'd put aside; that surely would show Ruby he'd changed his ways. 'Now, why don't you show me what you've been up to at school? This time next year you'll be thinking about leaving and finding yourself some work. Will you go down the munitions factory to work with your mum, or would you like me to find you work at the dairy?'

Pat scoffed at his words. 'I'm going to work on the farm over Slades Green way, where I help out now. You'll not catch me working down at Gilbert's – especially not if *he's* my boss,' she pouted.

'By "he" I suppose you mean your mum's boyfriend?' Eddie laughed.

'Why are you laughing? Don't you realize he could take Mum away from you forever?'

'My darling daughter, your mum has not been mine for many years. I'm not sure she will ever speak to me again, let alone continue to be my wife. Perhaps you need to understand that adults can grow apart?'

Much as Eddie hoped his words wouldn't come true, he felt he ought to prepare Pat for the possibility. She might not get her own way and see her parents together – ever. Seeing her eyes start to water and a sob escape before she started to cry inconsolably, he hurried to her side and pulled her to him, rocking her back and forth. 'Come on, now, there's no need for this. I'll do my best to make your mum see sense.'

As her tears slowly subsided, a shout could be heard

from outside, followed by screams. They both rushed to the door – and before Eddie could ask what was happening, a grumbling explosion could be heard from the direction of the river.

Ruby had gone to shed number six to check the girls under her supervision had set to with their work. A happy group, they seemed to enjoy the job of prising open the Verey Light cartridges and emptying out the explosive powder, placing the casing and the powder into the right receptacles. Ruby thought it was monotonous work, but so had her job been when she'd worked for hours stuffing explosive into the bombs that were sent to the front during the war. She wandered back and forth along the long wooden building, answering queries and checking stock numbers from her clipboard. Hearing chattering and laughter from the next shed over, she put down her clipboard and headed to hut number five.

'It's Lil's birthday,' one of the girls said as Ruby entered the shed.

Ruby smiled. 'Keep the noise down, girls,' she warned them, nodding to a supervisor to follow her outside.

'The girls were still working,' she explained before Ruby could speak. 'It's just a bit of high spirits.'

'I have nothing against high spirits as long as safety is observed. I'd hate anything to happen to the girls if their minds were taken off their work. Here,' Ruby said as she took her purse from her pocket and handed over some coins. 'Treat the girls to a bun and a cup of tea on me when they stop for their break.' God knows they need a treat sometimes, she thought, knowing that some of them came from poor homes.

'Thank you, Mrs Caselton,' the supervisor said as she hurried back inside the hut.

'Ruby!' Herbie called out before she could return to her duties. She turned as he came rushing up to her, pulling her away from the door to the hut and leading her around the corner, out of sight of prying eyes. He pulled her to him and kissed her in a way he'd never done before. 'I'm sorry to have left you so abruptly earlier. I felt you had something you wanted to tell me,' he said as his eyes searched her face for an answer.

Ruby felt as if her breath had left her, such was the effect of his kiss. He'd never acted this way before. Did he feel she was about to call off their relationship? 'Why, Herbie . . .' she said, feeling flustered, and at the same time wishing they were somewhere more private and hoping he would kiss her again.

'Ruby, please tell me you will stay with me and you want to live out the rest of your life with me?' he begged, kissing her again before she could draw breath.

Ruby froze. Why was it that when Herbie's kisses swept her away on a cloud, she thought of Eddie? Her Eddie . . . Would he ever leave her dreams? Would she ever stop thinking of him, while rejecting him every time he made contact?

'What the hell?' Herbie said suddenly. His hands dropped from her shoulders and Ruby turned to follow his gaze. A plume of black smoke was billowing out from the back of shed five.

'Oh my God,' Ruby cried out as an explosion erupted

from the shed, followed by screams of panic from the girls inside.

Eddie rushed from the house, telling Pat to stay where she was. From the road, he could see clouds of smoke rising from the river. The woman who had been screaming was on her knees in the middle of the road, sobbing and wailing. 'It's Gilbert's, I know it's Gilbert's going up in smoke, and my daughter works there,' she cried out in desperation. 'Please – can you help me get to her?'

'Come with me,' Eddie called as he ran away from the smoke and up Alexandra Road towards his milk cart. Helping the woman up onto the seat next to him, he told her to hold on tight and set off as fast as his gentle, passive horse would allow. Waving to Pat to reassure her as he passed number thirteen, he carried on at a brisk pace down Manor Road towards the banks of the Thames and the dirt track leading through the marsh towards the filling factory. It stood out against the morning skyline, outlined by black smoke. He could hear a series of explosions, and what sounded like gunfire.

'That'll be the Verey Lights. They're emptying them of gunpowder,' the woman said anxiously.

As the track became rougher, and the horse had trouble pulling the milk cart over the ruts, the woman jumped down and ran on towards the buildings, calling out for her daughter. Seeing that he couldn't get much further, Eddie hitched his horse to a nearby bush and ran like the wind, praying Ruby hadn't been injured. He was one of the few people pushing his way towards the scene of the disaster, through hordes of distressed workers fleeing the explosions coming from what was left of their huts. Strange lights glowed from the black smoke as the heat caused bullets to fire out in all directions. To one side, he could see men holding up pieces of corrugated iron as shields while they edged towards what was left of one of the sheds.

'Keep back!' one of them shouted, as Eddie edged closer.

'I'm looking for Ruby Caselton,' he bellowed to no one in particular as he gazed wildly around him for help.

'I saw her outside hut six just before this started,' a young woman called out to him. 'She was with Herbie Wilcox.'

Eddie felt an anger burn inside him like he'd never felt before. Had this Herbie held Ruby back from escaping? He spotted a group of men wearing suits and carrying clipboards. Hurrying over, he snapped: 'Ruby Caselton was near hut six. Have you found her? She was with a man called Herbie Wilcox, if that helps . . .'

One of them checked his list. 'We don't have her name marked as safe, or Mr Wilcox's,' he said, showing his list to another man standing close by. 'They could have escaped, but we've yet to know,' he advised Eddie.

Eddie ran a hand through his hair in exasperation. 'Where is hut six?'

'What's left of it is down there – but be careful . . .' the man called as Eddie started to run towards it. 'The cartridges are going off all over the place . . .'

Eddie ignored the warnings and ran on; he had to find Ruby at any cost. As he passed what remained of hut five, he averted his glance – several lifeless bodies were lying where they'd been blown by the explosion. Black smoke swirled around the scene as he pulled his jacket up over his head for protection and started to shout out Ruby's name. She must be somewhere nearby, he thought as he approached the hut.

'Over here,' a muffled voice called out.

Turning the corner of the hut, he spotted a man trapped by his legs under a fallen wall. There were sheets of corrugated iron lying about that had blown from the most damaged of the huts. 'Have you seen Ruby Caselton?' he asked as he pulled the man free.

'She was here. I was talking to her,' the man said as he brushed dust from his clothes and gingerly moved his limbs.

'Are you Herbie Wilcox?' Eddie asked as he continued to look for Ruby, pulling away wood and anything that could be hiding her body. Herbie nodded, looking distracted.

'Look out over there!' came a shout from men a little distance away, who were helping the injured. 'There could be another explosion at any time.'

'Please – you've got to help me search for Ruby,' Eddie pleaded, as Herbie started to back away from the hut.

But Herbie was hurrying away. 'It's dangerous to stay here . . .' he called over his shoulder.

Eddie wanted to wring the man's neck, but instead he continued to look for Ruby, calling her name as he did so.

'Eddie . . . Eddie . . . Is that you?' a faltering voice asked, as he turned towards the worst of the damaged work huts.

He rushed over to where Ruby lay amongst a pile of rubble. Blood was dripping from the side of her head, and from a gash where the sleeve of her jacket was ripped away. Lifting her in his arms, Eddie turned and ran with her away from the sheds just as an almighty explosion decimated what was left of shed number five.

Stopping by the gate of the yard to make way for the fire vehicles, he carefully set his wife onto her feet. 'I won't let you go,' he promised as he searched her face before gently kissing her lips. 'I'll never let you go.'

Epilogue

8th May 1945

Ruby sat at her dressing table, checking that the dab of lipstick her granddaughter had insisted she needed had not smudged onto her teeth. 'Not bad for an old one, eh, Eddie?' She smiled at the silver-framed photograph beside her. It had been taken at the dairy's annual dinner and dance for retired employees, not long before Eddie had been taken ill and gently slipped away.

Running her finger over the image of his smiling face, she sighed. 'What would you make of the world today, my love? Here we are, celebrating the end of another war, and me all done up to the nines.'

She walked over to the window of her bedroom and looked out to where the residents of Alexandra Road were preparing for that afternoon's street party. Bunting had been pulled out of lofts that had been packed away since the king's coronation. All kinds of tables and chairs were being lined up and would be covered with bedsheets as tablecloths before the food for children was brought out, donated by most of the families in the road. Ruby had promised her piano to the celebrations; the men would wheel it from her front room onto the pavement later in the day. They would play tunes for children's games, and later the adults would sing around it when the barrel of beer was opened. It would be a grand day, one they'd waited a long time for.

'You'd have enjoyed this,' she said to Eddie's smiling face. 'You always did enjoy your beer. You'd have loved to bounce one of your grandchildren on your knee – why, even your two great-grandchildren,' she added, thinking of Sarah's youngsters. 'Time has certainly moved on, and I have so many memories to hang on to in my older years. I hope you're looking down on me today, my love, and giving me your blessings.'

'Talking to yourself, Mum?' George said as he entered the bedroom. 'I thought I'd come up and see if you were all right. The women are getting jittery in case you've changed your mind.' He joined her at the window.

'I was reminiscing. It seems to be the day for it, with so much happening in our little road.'

'It certainly is a day for looking back as well as forward,' George agreed as he put his arms round Ruby. 'Do you remember the day we moved here – and Stella helped you when you lost the baby?'

'It's something I will never forget. The kindness of the Green family, and how those boys suffered during the Great War. It's as if it happened yesterday. Time has flown by so fast. Did I tell you I received a lovely card from Frank? He wasn't up to coming today. Oh, he gave his reasons, but I felt it would have been too hard visiting the town and digging up so many sad memories. He's never been the same since Stephen died, bless him.'

'Once this is all over, we must go down to Eastbourne and visit Uncle Frank. I have my faithful Box Brownie, so hopefully there will be some photographs to show him as well. That's if I haven't chopped everyone's heads off,' George chuckled. 'I'm sure Frank will be delighted to meet the new Mrs Bob Jackson.'

'I'm not sure how I'll get used to being called Ruby Jackson, after all these years of being Ruby Caselton,' she said. Returning to the dressing table, she picked up the photograph. 'I hope I'm not letting him down.'

'Oh, you daft woman,' her son said fondly. 'Dad would be so proud of you. In fact, I like to think he's up there now in a celestial pub in the clouds, raising a pint pot to all of us. I'm not sure my Irene would be with him, although she'd be pleased for you all the same. Marrying a retired police sergeant is something she'd be impressed with. Possibly she would raise a glass of dry sherry.'

'I am doing the right thing, aren't I?'

George sighed. Anyone who knew Ruby would say that Bob had brightened her life in recent years. He smiled at the thought of how their paths had crossed so many years before, when Bob, then a young constable, had spent hours in the cupboard under the stairs sheltering from a raid in the first war alongside Ruby. She was only dithering now because of her loyalty to his late dad, even after the merry dance he'd led her for so many years before he rescued her from the terrible disaster down at the Gilbert factory. George could have lost his mum that day. Twelve of the workers had perished – one of them from this very road. Since that day in 1924, his parents had hardly left each other's sides, making up for all the lost years until his dad passed away just before Christmas 1937.

Eddie had been as good as his word: apart from an occasional glass of bitter at family parties or down the working men's club, he'd been a reformed character. George knew that his parents had had a good life together, even if it had taken them twenty years to settle into it. Now his mum had met Bob – and he and his son Mike had slotted into the fold of the Caselton family and friends so well.

'Yes, Mum. You are doing the right thing in marrying Bob, and you know it. So come on – let's put your hat straight, and then we can get on with the party afterwards. It's not just your wedding we are celebrating, but the end of the war as well. I'll see you downstairs,' he said, kissing her cheek.

Left alone, Ruby stared at the little photograph, then lifted it to her lips and kissed the glass. 'There will always be a place for you in my heart, Eddie Caselton,' she murmured, before placing the photograph away in a drawer and closing it slowly.

She drew a breath, then said to herself, 'Time to move on.' And went to join her family.

Acknowledgements

My fear when writing these acknowledgements is that I will forget someone who played a part in the creation of this book. My deepest apologies if I do. I appreciate everyone who plays a part in helping my stories leap from my mind onto the page.

My agent, Caroline Sheldon, and her lovely staff who are there at the end of the phone when I need help and advice. Caroline Hogg, my brilliant editor at Pan Macmillan, along with Samantha Fletcher, Camilla Rockwood and the editing team who work their magic on my words. I apologize again for the rubbish you have to wade through. Bethan and Meghan from ED PR for getting news of my books out to readers – you do a wonderful job, thank you. Some of you may have come across my new website and blog, and it would still be in the imagination of this dinosaur if it wasn't for the skill of author and web designer, Charlotte Duckworth. Thank you!

Writing *A Mother Forever* took me to another moment in time. Although this book is set in Erith, just like the Woolworths series, it is set in an earlier time period. It

369

was such an adventure to move back through the years to 1905, the year trams appeared in the streets and the riverside town was thriving. The streets were lined with beautiful houses and there was an abundance of shops, with Alexandra Road just a few years old. As I took those first tentative steps into this new world, I had many questions about the town that I feared getting wrong. So, who better to turn to than the team at Bexley Archives. I've lost count of the many gems I've come across while delving into the records, or attending library talks and the Bexley Book Buzz Literary Festival, or just dipping into the records. I'm fascinated by the stories of the brickfields around the town and grateful for the way staff kept alive the memories of the fallen of World War One. Will Cooban, I kept my promise and included a certain name . . .

As a child a local story from 1924 had always fascinated me, and I was keen to include it in one of my books. A terrible explosion at the W. V. Gilbert munition works, on the banks of the Thames between Erith and Slades Green, on 18th February 1924 took the lives of twelve young women and their foreman. As a child who had played on the riverbank in the 1960s it was unimaginable, but to visit Brook Street cemetery with my mum and stop to look at the memorial to the dead just inside the gates brought home to me the enormity of the tragic event. I had no idea my paternal grandmother had worked in munitions and had left the works just a year or so before to give birth to her first son, my uncle Cyril. It was never mentioned and we grandkids never asked. Now it is too late. Imagine then how thrilled I was to come across recordings, courtesy of the Imperial War Museum, of women who had worked at Gilbert's and also the Woolwich Arsenal during World War One and afterwards. These women most probably rubbed shoulders with my nan – in fact, if you spotted a character in my book named Cissie, who lived in South Road and befriended Ruby, it may just have been Nan . . .

Speaking of W. V. Gilbert, you may have spotted a very young Maureen Gilbert pop up in this book. Maureen is a much-loved character from the Woolworth series and is no relation to the munition works owner – a pure coincidence.

I'd best say thank you to my husband, Michael, and our dog, Henry, who keep me grounded and sane while I work on my novels. My husband likes to remind me that if it wasn't for him the name on the cover of my books would not be Everest!

Again, thank you all for your help.

A Letter from Elaine

~

Dear Reader,

Hello again. It doesn't feel that long since I sat down to write my last letter to you, and what a time it has been. Who would have guessed what we were facing back in the spring? I pray that you and yours are keeping well as it is all we can ask for at the moment.

Thank you to readers who searched out a copy of *Wedding Bells for Woolworths* even though the world was in lockdown and we could not venture far from home at the end of April. Our supermarkets did their best to stock the book, but I have to confess that I was worried anyone would endanger themselves by going out of their way to buy a copy. Online we discovered the joy of buying from independent bookshops. I discovered Hive.co.uk, who not only deliver books but pass a percentage to local bookshops. Isn't that nice? I'm sure like me you have used your e-reader more than usual. Did your reading material change at all? I found myself reading more crime and psychological thrillers as well as lots of new romcom authors. Pure escapism!

Working from home, I had thought life would go on as usual, but of course I was wrong. Being told to stay home can mess with our heads, and with cancelling so many author talks, workshops, book signings and events I've been climbing the walls at times. However, thank goodness for social media where we've been able to chat about every subject under the sun. Our moods must have been lifted by being able to turn on our laptops and natter with our friends. I've enjoyed watching author talks via Zoom, along with weekly chats with fellow saga authors on Messenger. July saw me reach a special anniversary when I celebrated forty years free of breast cancer. How those years have sped by, but how grateful I am that the dedication of my consultant meant I was able to live to write my books, grow old (ish), and get to know you all. I'm truly grateful as many people, my own mother included, never had that chance.

I've been posting on my blog and have set up a newsletter section for readers. Have you signed up to both? If not pop over to my website (details below) and complete the box for the newsletter, and also for blog notifications, which you will find on the blog page. I plan to have special competitions available for anyone following my newsletters.

What do we have to look forward to? Well, at the time of writing we've got Christmas – I plan to read as many Christmas books as possible to get me into the festive spirit, and as it's my birthday I may just raise a glass or two to fellow Christmas babies. Is there one in your family?

2021 will see two books from me: the first, of course,

is this one; the second is something completely different, but you will have to wait a little while longer to hear more . . .

With love,
Elaine xx

You can visit me here:
Twitter: @ElaineEverest
Facebook: Elaine Everest Author
Instagram: @elaine.everest
Website and blog: www.elaineeverest.com